AF400779

Nobody Knows
Anybody

Katarina Gomboc Čeh

Translated by Jasmin B. Frelih

First published in 2026 by Printim Editions

Printed and bound by TJ Books 2026

ISBN 979-8-9874792-3-0

Translated from Slovenian into English by Jasmin B. Frelih

First Edition

First Book

Originally published as *Nihče nikogar ne spozna* (2024) by Cankarjeva založba

85 Great Portland Street, First Floor
London, W1W 7LT
www.printimeditions.com

"So of course in the midst of everything, the state of the world being what it is, humanity on the cusp of extinction, here I am writing about sex and friendship. What else is there to live for?"

—Sally Rooney, *Beautiful world, where are you?*

When writing Maks's emails from the border, the author drew upon Ines Majcen's master's thesis, *Social Work with Refugees at the Borders* (2016). The linguistic anthropology exam is based on Saša Babič's article, *Linguistic Anthropology and Ethnolinguistics*. The dialogue on ecofeminism relies on an interview with Ariel Salleh, published on MMC RTV Slovenija on September 18th, 2018. All material regarding Rojava and democratic confederalism is taken from the book *Revolution in Rojava: Democratic Autonomy and Women's Liberation in Syrian Kurdistan* by Michael Knapp, Anja Flach, and Ercan Ayboga, published in 2019 by the ČKZ Institute.

The novel is entirely the product of the author's imagination. The composer Ciril Šavli does not exist, 21st of May 2016 was not a rainy Saturday and the American Association for Middle East Anthropology does not organise expeditions to Oman.

I

Summer, autumn, winter 2015

1.

The ground floor of the Music Academy was empty when I entered, save for the sound of a string instrument drifting from somewhere. I thought it was a violin at first, but as I sat on one of the benches to listen, I recognized the deep tones of a viola. I pulled a water bottle from my backpack and took a sip. My cheeks were burning, the July heat had followed me from the street all the way to the entrance—the kind of heat that feels like it has swallowed everything off the paved streets: the people, and even the sounds. It was the time of day when, in a small Italian town, you would find every door barred shut. But I wasn't wandering through Europe, and neither was Agata, who was waiting for me in the classroom.

The door, bearing a worn plaque with the number one nailed to it, opened. A girl I didn't know stepped into the hallway, glanced at me for a moment, and then headed for the exit without a word. I caught only a fleeting glimpse of her expression before she turned away, and it was hard to decide what it meant; she looked neither disappointed nor satisfied.

I stood up and headed for the door. It had nearly slammed shut behind the girl with a loud bang, but I caught it just in time. Agata was standing by the upright piano, which was pushed against the wall, shuffling through sheet music. The open window looked out onto the Hercules Fountain on Upper Square. I greeted her quietly. Without turning to face me, she said indifferently, "Oh, it's you."

It seemed like she was shuffling the papers without a purpose. She wore a black dress with thin straps that ended just above her knees. Her black curls, stiff with hairspray, fell over her bare shoulders. She sat on the piano bench and swept her hair back. She struck a random chord; it sounded somewhat grim. I put my backpack on the chair by the door and stood before her.

There was a large mirror next to the piano, in which I saw a petite brunette in jeans and a white T-shirt, wearing black All-Stars. I looked like a teenager next to Agata, even though I was twenty-one.

"So, how was the exchange?" Agata fixed her grey eyes on me. Her eyebrows, plucked into thin lines, were slightly raised. The flush on her cheeks showed that she was hot, too.

"Fine." Just as she had done, I fixed my hair. I envied her those thin straps. "How was it here?"

She swiveled back to the piano and snorted. "What do you think? We slaved away the whole time. Didn't Urška tell you anything?" Without waiting for an answer, she continued, "Did you look at the sheet music?" She pierced me with her gaze again. I nodded.

"Well, then you know everything. Let's get started. I don't have all day."

Her behaviour didn't surprise me; I was used to it. I just found all this ceremony excessive. I had already been singing in Agata's choir for two years; I had passed the audition two years ago in this very room, shortly after finding out I had passed my matura exams.[1] But now she insisted that, after I had been away on exchange for three months, she couldn't just take me back into the choir. She claimed she needed to see "where I was at."

"Have you practiced?" she asked. I wasn't ready for the question.

____

1 Translator's Note: National high school graduation exams

I pressed my lips together, then shook my head.

Agata said nothing; she merely stared at the keys beneath her fingers as if waiting for them to play themselves. Her voice was strangely subdued when she finally spoke. "Well, what are you going to sing?"

I told her *Death in the Hills*. She laughed, which surprised me.

"What's funny?"

"That you chose the same piece for your audition two years ago." I hadn't expected her to remember that. I was about to say so, but she waved her hand and told me to sing.

I closed my eyes before I began, trying to remember the starting note for the first soprano melody. Although I wasn't sure if I had hit it right, I sang: "*In the summer glow on rocky cliffs, with lead in his breast a partisan lies...*" At that moment, I thought I heard a cyclist whiz past the open window, followed by the sound of two people speaking a foreign language, and I involuntarily lowered my voice: "*Done is the dream of distant future days...*" Then I opened my eyes. I saw the classroom and Agata, who sat silently by the piano, staring at the sheet music. I continued singing, eyes open, until I reached the line "*and for the last time, his eyes gaze proudly at the world.*" I worried that I had sung the final notes too softly.

A suffocating silence filled the room, broken only by a distant bang, as if heavy doors had been slammed by a draft.

"Why didn't you sing for your voice?" She raised her eyebrows high again.

"I like the first soprano better."

She frowned. "But you are a second soprano."

I nodded, then admitted very slowly, "Sometimes I wish I sang the first."

"Why?"

I shrugged. The second soprano parts often seemed boring to me, living in the shadow of the first, but I couldn't tell her that.

"The first sopranos always have the prettiest melody."

Her face gave away nothing of what she thought. She placed her hands on the keys and told me to sing whatever she played. She struck a few notes, and I sang back what I heard. First, we headed into the lower register, then into the highs.

The higher Agata went, the harder I tried to sing well, but with every higher note, my voice grew more strained. At points, I felt like it was going to break. Eventually, I could only give out a squeak.

Agata murmured, "Good," picked up a folder lying on the piano, and made a note with a red pen.

"As every year, we start the week after August twentieth. See you then."

I frowned and asked hesitantly, "And... will I still be singing second soprano...?"

She lifted her gaze from the folder but didn't look at me; instead, she stared at an indeterminate point on the wall and sighed.

"I'm sorry, but we have enough first sopranos. I need you in the second."

I swallowed hard and nodded. I grabbed my backpack from the chair, said goodbye, and walked out of the classroom. The dark voice of the viola could still be heard in the empty hallway. When I stepped onto the paved ground in front of the Academy, I took my phone out of my backpack, put my earphones in, and opened YouTube. *Summertime Sadness* severed me from the cold hallway of the stern Academy and consumed the sadness wafting up from the overheated cobblestones.

2.

We gathered on the first Tuesday after the twentieth of August, in the small hall where we had practiced from the very beginning.

"If we start in August," Agata claimed, "we have a two-week head start." She never specified ahead of whom we were supposed to be.

When I entered, the room was already filled with the hum of female voices. The singers were telling one another about their summers while arranging the uncomfortable wooden chairs stacked folded against the wall into a semicircle. Many of them hadn't seen each other since the annual concert in mid-June—a concert I had watched from the audience, having missed the previous three months of rehearsals. My chair was already set up, so I sat down and started rummaging through my backpack, just to look like I had something to do. I didn't have much to say about my summer; my father had found me an undemanding, low-paying office job at the company where he worked. The summer had slipped away in a dusty office behind drawn blinds. I dedicated my free afternoons to studying, as I still had three exams to pass, and in the evenings I was often too lazy to go anywhere. Instead, I spent hours in bed with my laptop until my eyes burned, and I saw white, flickering dots when I closed them.

Once we were seated, Agata remained standing by the piano for a few moments, rearranging a hefty sheaf of papers. Then she turned toward us; the chatter among the girls died down, leaving only the occasional hiss of a whisper. She waited a few more seconds until complete silence reigned in the hall.

"I am happy that we are together again, and I am crazy excited about the new season. I am especially thrilled that we have a few new singers joining us. Will you introduce yourselves?"

Among the first sopranos, a tiny girl with thin blonde hair stood up and offered a weak greeting. There were no new singers among the second sopranos, but there were two in the first altos. The last to go was a girl sitting at the edge of the choir, among the second altos. She seemed familiar. She said her name was Sara. Straight, bobbed hair reached her pale cheeks, and her bangs were short and blunt. Dressed in an oversized Nirvana T-shirt and drab, shapeless denim shorts, and wearing beat-up, swamp-colored All-Stars, she didn't fit in with the other singers who wore tight, colorful tops, knee-length summer dresses, and sandals with glittering straps. Even her hairstyle was different from the long hair, brown curls, braids, and ponytails around her. As she sat back down, I remembered seeing her at the Academy in July, coming out of the classroom.

"I am very happy, and *grateful*," Agata emphasized, "that Barbara has returned to us."

We greeted the rejoining singer sitting next to me with polite applause—Barbara had returned after a year of maternity leave. I waited to see if Agata would mention that I had also come back from my exchange, but her smile lingered on Barbara, then she turned back to the piano and the papers. Staring at the sheet music she had placed on the stand, she took on a completely different, cold tone: "The recordings we sent to the competition are still in the selection process, so I have no news regarding that." She paused briefly while the hall held its breath. "So, for a while, we will continue with the repertoire we started in the spring. The newcomers, along with those who were absent,"—I was flipping through my music folder as she spoke, and when she paused for a moment, I looked up and met her gaze—"will have to catch up on their own. Is there anything else, Ivana?"

She glanced at the scrawny brunette sitting hunched at the edge of the choir, at the head of the first sopranos. Ivana shook her head with pursed lips, but then turned over her shoulder to look at Urška, who was sitting behind her. Urška stood up and looked around at the choir with a wide smile. "My boyfriend *finally* got up the nerve this year and proposed." As the girls greeted the news with an excited outcry, she laughed in joy, then continued: "We can count on you, right? We want you all to sing at the wedding in May." The singers responded with a long "Yeeeees," and some even clapped.

Urška, looking like she was about to cry from emotion, sat back down with a flushed face and stared expectantly at Agata. Agata watched the singers with clasped hands, her face like stone.

"Congratulations," she finally said, louder than usual, cutting off the chatter surrounding the news. She added that Urška should email Ivana with the details, then told the young women to stand up.

The chairs in the hall creaked as thirty-three young women rose and assumed their singing posture. We did a few breathing exercises, then tuned our voices; it took only a few chords for our voices to intertwine into pure harmony. As we sang the chords, I realized how much I had missed this fusion of female voices.

Two and a half hours later, we headed to a bar not far from the rehearsal hall, as was the custom after the first rehearsal of the season. A few girls apologized and left, Barbara among them. All the newcomers tagged along, and since there were quite a few of us, we pulled several tables together. By chance, I ended up sitting next to Sara, the new second alto.

Urška and her engagement were the center of attention. The girls listened with interest to how the pivotal moment had happened. Even though I had already heard the story of the engagement, which took place in July on either Mala or Velika Mojstrovka[2] (I could never remember which), I silently listened to the tale of how Urška and Andrej had hiked into the mountains, until Sara, sitting beside me, suddenly asked, "So, how long have you been in the choir?"

It seemed she was asking because Urška's engagement didn't interest her. She took a sip of the beer the waiter had just brought her, while he placed a glass of Coca-Cola filled to the brim with ice in front of me.

"Two years. How did you find out about us?"

She told me that Ivana, Agata's right hand, was her cousin, nodding lazily toward the girl sitting next to Urška, clutching a glass of apple juice. I remembered Ivana once telling me she had a cousin who sang in a band, but I wouldn't have connected her with Sara; unlike Ivana, Sara looked independent and authentic, whereas Ivana blended unnoticed into the background wherever she went.

"She convinced me when she told me the choirmaster also teaches vocal technique to the singers," Sara explained casually. "I sing in a band, and I want to work on my voice a bit more. Plus, Ivana told me that you guys, well, that we are probably going to Tallinn."

I smiled. I liked her honesty. She made no effort to hide that she had chosen the choir for the vocal training and the trip to Tallinn.

I nodded, stirred my drink with the straw, and drank some cold Coke; the ice was slowly melting. I asked her the name of the band she sang in, and she told me: *Marija Ivanovna*. Without me asking a follow-up, she explained that it was Russian slang for marijuana. I laughed, took another sip, and asked her what she studied.

"Sociology and German. You?"

---

2 TN: Mountains in the Julian Alps, standing 2,333 and 2,366 meters tall, respectively.

When I told her I studied anthropology, she frowned as if thinking, then said she knew someone studying the same thing, a classmate from high school.

"Maks Hafner. Do you know him?"

I had been rolling a piece of ice around in my mouth like candy, and when she mentioned Maks, I bit down on it so hard my teeth hurt. I nodded and swallowed the crushed ice.

"Yeah, we've known each other since we were little. Our moms were roommates in the dorms," I explained, clearing my throat. "But he's a year ahead of me. I think he's graduating this year." I tried to sound as indifferent as possible. Sara raised her eyebrows.

"I still can't believe he made it this far," she said, taking a sip of beer.

"What do you mean?"

"Well, just the fact that he decided on anthropology was really unusual. If you know him, you know what he was like in high school." I shook my head, though I had a hunch what she was getting at. "No, don't get me wrong, Maks is great, but until his fourth year, he showed no sign of being interested in anything other than partying." She laughed. "Then, in his fourth year, he suddenly announces he's going to study anthropology. It was really weird. We all just thought he didn't know what to do and picked it at random."

I was about to tell her that Maks definitely hadn't chosen anthropology by accident when I heard my name called from the other end of the table. I turned toward a cluster of girls staring at me with glowing faces.

"I'm telling them that you're going to be my maid of honour," Urška said with a smile, clearly pleased that the conversation was still revolving around her wedding. I smiled and nodded.

"Are you friends?" I heard Sara ask on my right.

I shook my head. "Sisters."

"Oh, Ivana told me Urška has a sister who also sings in the choir. I just didn't think it was you."

The table suddenly went quiet. Agata, who was sitting not far from us, stood up, smoothed her black curls, and apologized to the singers, saying she had to leave. She left behind an empty wine glass. The singers bade her farewell in unison, and she disappeared into the night.

"Ivana keeps praising Agata," said Sara, watching her go. I barely stopped myself from rolling my eyes; Ivana worshipped Agata, and we weren't allowed to say a word against the choirmaster in her presence, or she would passionately defend her. "Based on today's practice, I can only say she seems pretty strict. I actually felt a little sorry for those two new girls in the first alto section."

I laughed and nodded, and Sara added, "I'm really interested to see how it goes. Definitely pretty different from being in a band."

"Oh, that's for sure. What kind of music do you play?"

In reply, she offered me her earphones and found a track on her phone. I heard a slow intro with bass guitar and unobtrusive drums in the background, followed by a really good, low, dark female vocal. I widened my eyes and gave a thumbs-up in approval. Sara smiled.

"I like it," I said when she stopped it after barely a minute and took the earphones back.

"Thanks. What kind of music do you listen to?"

"Ah, you're not going to like the answer," I said, glancing at the inscription on her T-shirt. She shook her head, looking slightly offended: "I know music taste is highly individual. I'm really interested."

"I like... Lana Del Rey, for example. And Lorde. And Sia," I listed a few names.

"I've heard of them, but I don't know them very well."

"With Lana Del Rey, almost everything fascinates me. She embodies," I thought for a moment, "American melancholy." I chuckled, but immediately grew serious, thinking I sounded weird. Sara raised her eyebrows inquisitively, so I added in a more serious tone, "She writes most of her own lyrics, and that's probably why her music is so original."

Sara murmured, "Interesting," and I finished my glass of Coke, which tasted bland from the melted ice. From the other end of the table, Urška signaled me, asking if we shouldn't be heading home. It seemed the conversation about the engagement had finally ended, and a somewhat weary look rested on her face, so I said goodbye to Sara and stood up. The drinks, we soon learned, had already been paid for by Agata.

3.

I saw Maks for the first time since June during the first week of September, when I was taking my final exam. I rode my bike to the college under the early September sun, and when I entered the building, I could see almost nothing at first; it was so dark compared to the sunny day outside. I headed toward the professor's office, sat on the chair by the door, and pulled the folder of notes from my backpack. Uneasily, I began to read the parts highlighted in yellow marker.

Just then, I heard two voices coming from the other end of the hallway and looked up. I recognized him immediately. I felt a dull pang in my stomach. As always, I wasn't ready to see him. Even though I knew I could run into him any time near the college, it usually happened when I least expected it. Walking beside him was a guy I knew only by sight; I didn't know his name. I lowered my gaze and stared at the individual words circled in red pen: *signification, Jakobson, langue.*

"I decided to tackle the thesis thoroughly and slowly," I heard his voice say. "So, I'm going to take the extra year." The guy beside him remained silent, so he continued: "I think I'll use the time for an extended trip, too. I'm really drawn to the Middle East. But not the mainstream countries—Jordan, Egypt, and such. I'd go to Syria, Iraq, Palestine in a heartbeat —"

He stopped there. I looked up, and our eyes met; I felt a tremor in my chest, as if a volcano that had been dormant for three months had suddenly woken up.

He raised his hand in a relaxed greeting, and I waved back awkwardly. We had last seen each other in June at Metelkova, where he was celebrating his birthday and a friend had invited me to the Young Rhymes marathon. Now, compared to then, he was tanned, and the hair on his arms, bleached gold by the sun, gleamed. He was wearing flip-flops that slapped against his heels as he walked, and a T-shirt from one of those skate shops where the prices are pretty steep. He wore a cap with a wide brim on his head.

"So, what are you up to?" He sat on the empty chair next to me.

"I have an exam. The last one. You?" Whenever I spoke to him, my voice pitched slightly higher, becoming more fragile.

"Same. Once I pass this, I'm officially in my extra year, and I can devote myself entirely to the thesis." The guy who came with him sat silently across from us and clutched his backpack. I glanced at him quickly and saw dark circles of sweat forming under the armpits of his short-sleeved shirt.

"So, you decided to take the extra year?" I asked him. We had discussed this back in June, and he hadn't been sure then. He nodded and immediately started explaining why it made the most sense, since the topic he had chosen for his thesis couldn't be written over the summer. I only half-listened, realizing that next year we might be in the same grade.

Maks repeated what he had been telling the guy, who was watching me silently: that he wanted to go to Syria, but that due to the current situation it wasn't possible, so he was thinking about another destination in the region. At this point, the guy interrupted him, saying that in his opinion, other countries in the Middle East weren't currently a smart choice for a vacation either. He said this with a smile, as if trying not to cause offense with his otherwise sensible remark, but Maks grimaced, insisting he was by no means talking about a *vacation*, but that his travel would be exclusively research oriented. As they began to debate the war situation in Syria, I seized the moment to turn another page in my lap.

"That usually doesn't help," Maks remarked, seeing me reviewing my notes, and grinned. I wanted to object, but I knew he was right, so I put them away in my backpack with a loud sigh. Just then, the professor's silhouette appeared at the end of the hall, and all three of us stared at her in silence. Walking down the corridor, she held a mug in her right hand and a bunch of keys in her left.

"Colleague, are you here for consultations?" The question was directed at the other student, who nodded. "Good. And you, Mr. Hafner, have the exam on Ethnolinguistic Research, is that correct?" she asked, turning to Maks with a smile. He nodded. "And you are here for Linguistic Anthropology." After I nodded, she added, "Let's get the exams out of the way first, and then I'll attend to you, Mr. Hozjan." She unlocked the door, turned to Maks and me, and motioned for us to enter.

Because it hadn't occurred to me that Maks and I would be taking the exam together, I remained seated for a few long, agonizing moments, watching Maks confidently stand up and follow the professor. Only then did I rise—my legs felt unusually heavy, and I felt as if I might buckle—and followed them into the stuffy office.

The professor opened the window, while Maks stood in the middle of the room. She told him to sit at the chair by the main desk, and directed me to a chair at a small table by the door. I caught his eye and gave him a weak smile. He sat at the desk and took off his cap. Only then did I notice that his usually brown, slightly curly hair was a shade lighter from the summer sun. The professor placed a sheet of paper and a pen in front of him and held out a fan of slips with exam questions. He took one, placed it on the desk before him, and picked up the pen. I tried to read from his face what he thought of the questions, but he was already leaning over the paper with pursed lips, writing.

Then the professor offered me a sheet of paper and a pen as well, and held out the fan of slips. I took one and, with my heart beating harder in my chest than usual, looked at the questions. The first one was laughably easy: the Sapir-Whorf hypothesis. The next question was more complicated: the concept of *performance* in folklore. The third one made me happy; it was a question about how gender influences language use. I grabbed the pen and started taking notes.

For a few minutes, we both scratched away at our papers. I tried to recall as much as possible from the notes I had borrowed from a colleague, since I had missed most of the lectures in the second semester while I was in Barcelona. After returning to Slovenia, I had thrown myself into studying to catch up. In June, when we met at Metelkova, Maks had been puzzled by my determination, saying he didn't understand why I wanted to finish my degree so quickly, as in his opinion, it made sense to remain a student for as long as possible. He added that I would only end up at the unemployment office sooner—a comment that would have angered me if he wasn't also studying anthropology. As it was, I just gave a bitter laugh.

When Maks put down his pen, the professor told him to answer the first question. He took a breath and, swivelling slightly on the chair, began to explain the difference between the Moscow and Lublin schools. Very soon, I sensed he had drifted into a discussion about linguistic stereotypes, but the professor just nodded contentedly, as if she hadn't noticed.

When he fell silent, she turned to me, and I began answering my question. It went well; I said everything I needed to, and she quickly returned to Maks. I studied my notes on the paper, which were much sparser for the second question, and I began to regret not studying more.

But Maks was doing worse now, too—he was fumbling for an answer, and it appeared the professor noticed his confidence was waning. She seemed to be helping him with follow-up questions, but instead of answering them, he kept listing unrelated facts. Finally, he finished, somewhat uncertainly, and the professor turned to me.

"Um... In folklore, performance is an activity where the manner in which something is expressed is primarily important. For instance, with Jakobson, when he speaks about the poetic function of speech, this refers to... to something creative." I fell silent and looked at the professor, unsure of myself. She nodded and asked me where performance is most often demonstrated.

"Hm. Mostly in music," I began unconvincingly. "In choral and folk singing. Also in theater and singing in general, and, say, in storytelling, where the... aesthetic dimension is in the foreground." I hesitated for a moment, and the professor asked what I meant by that. I replied that the aesthetic dimension is present primarily in the judgment or response of the listeners interpreting what they hear. In this way, I concluded, performance is the dimension of language that includes creativity. I stopped there, knowing I had said far too little.

The professor stared at me expectantly for a few moments—I saw that the shade of her eyes was similar to Agata's—then nodded briefly and turned back to Maks. He took a breath to answer his third question, but the first thing he said was, "My colleague failed to mention Chomsky, who is *extremely* important regarding the question of performance and competence." He said this in a learned, intellectual voice. I wanted to roll my eyes, but I only gave a tart nod, admitting I really had forgotten, though in truth Maks's words didn't surprise me at all—whenever we talked, he mentioned Chomsky frequently, always emphasizing that everyone should read him. The professor nodded and gave Maks free rein to answer in his own way, even though he strayed completely from the original question.

I stared at my notes and wished I could take the exam alone, or at least that Maks wasn't there. I would have preferred to have that guy from the hallway here in the office with me. The only thing that hadn't completely swallowed my confidence was the fact that I had worn my favorite outfit for the exam—a thin, pale violet blouse, which Urška had once said with envy suited my dark brown hair, and long olive-green trousers.

I caught myself realizing I had stopped listening to Maks and was watching his Adam's apple bob as he spoke. Then the professor turned to me.

I was lucky—we had discussed the very last question at the university where I did my exchange, so I confidently began to recount what Robin Lakoff writes about the differences between male and female speech: women use more modal adverbs, such as "perhaps," "probably," and "maybe," whereas men are more convinced and direct; women's speech is more polite, while men interrupt more often; men's speech contains more swear words, and they have a better sense of humor compared to women; female speech is characterized by hypercorrection as well as more precise language use, for example, in describing colors; men adjust their speech to social interactions where they bond more easily with other men... Women, I concluded, often use a questioning intonation in declarative sentences. At the end, I added that her claims are outdated today because the situation of men and women in the 21st century has changed. The professor nodded.

"Good. You mentioned that women use more modal adverbs and that a questioning intonation is often present in their declarative sentences. Why do you think that is?"

I thought for a moment before answering, then said quietly, "Probably because they aren't completely sure of what they are saying?"

I caught Maks's gaze; the corners of his lips turned up, and he reached up with his right hand to cover his mouth to hide the smile. I felt myself blush vividly.

A heavy silence enveloped the office, and the sound of a drill could be heard somewhere in the distance. The professor gave a short sigh and looked down at the notes she had taken during the exam.

"Good," she said again, while I held my breath. "Ms. Pavlin, this will be an eight. You may go. You, Mr. Hafner, stay here; I'll give you one more question for a nine."

I felt an ache that ran from my throat to my womb. I thanked the professor with bitterness, stood up, and headed for the door. I said goodbye so quietly it could barely be heard.

4

I stepped out into the hallway, and before the door closed behind me, I could still hear the question the professor was asking Maks. Given that I had just passed my last exam, I should have been pleased, but instead, I was overcome by disappointment at the thought of my lackluster performance.

I was about to mumble a "Bye" to the guy waiting outside the office and leave, when he asked me, "So, how did it go?"

I stopped and looked at him. His hair was cut very short, and unattractive, angular glasses without a frame rested on his nose. His forehead glistened with sweat.

"Okay, I guess. She gave me an eight."

"That's fine. Pirc doesn't give high grades," he said placidly.

I had heard this from other students, too, but it didn't console me now. My grades at college were quite varied, and I knew that I could have done better at many exams if my studies wouldn't suddenly make me interested in too many unrelated things. I hadn't prepared as well as I could have for this one, either. Or maybe, it struck me, I did know enough for a higher grade, but I just couldn't show it in front of Maks.

"What grade did you get last year?" I asked him, not knowing what else to say, but the fact that he blushed at my question spoke for itself. He smiled awkwardly.

"Linguistic Anthropology is kind of my thing," he explained, trying to seem modest. He paused for a moment, then said: "I wrote my thesis with Pirc, too." He gestured at the stack of papers he was holding in his lap. "That's why I'm here for consultations. She suggested I rework it into an academic article."

"Cool. What was the topic?"

"A linguistic analysis of the speech of Slovenian citizens in Germany," he rattled off, as if embarrassed by it. He quickly added, "It was a double-major thesis, since I study German as well."

"Then you probably know Sara," it crossed my mind.

"Sara Černe?"

I realized I didn't actually know Sara's last name. I described her in a few words, and he nodded.

"I know her, of course. Are you friends?"

"Actually, I only just met her. She joined the choir where I sing."

"You sing in a choir?"

I nodded. "Yeah, the women's choir Philomela."

"Interesting," he murmured, just as the office door opened and Maks walked out. I tried in vain to read whether he had managed to raise his grade from his face, which gave out nothing. I noticed the guy with glasses was also studying his face, before he stood up and headed for the door, then turned back to us. "Do you guys have time for a coffee? After I'm done with consultations?"

Maks's eyes met mine, and for a moment it seemed we were both waiting to see what the other would say.

He was the first to pluck up the courage. "I do. Maša?" I nodded quickly. "We'll go ahead and order, you just come find us."

The guy gave an awkward thumbs-up, then disappeared behind the office door. Maks and I walked down the hallway in silence. I wanted him to see I was angry with him, but before he could say anything, I snapped, "You could have kept your mouth shut. You didn't exactly help me with Chomsky." I shot him an angry look.

Maks sighed, and his eyes drooped slightly, as if he regretted speaking up during the exam. Nevertheless, he said, "But I just don't understand how you could skip that. I mean, Chomsky is…"

"I just didn't think of him. Don't lecture me." I didn't look at him again, staring stubbornly ahead instead.

"I wasn't lecturing you, but —"

"Maybe that's why she gave me an eight. And then you laughed at me."

Out of the corner of my eye, I sensed him staring at me in astonishment. I felt my ears were burning.

"Laughed? When did I laugh at you?"

"You know, back there. When I answered the last question. The one about women and how they speak."

Maks chuckled quietly and tried to apologize, "Well, it really was funny."

He held the door open for me so we could step out into the light, and when our eyes met, I rolled mine. He nudged me gently on the shoulder. "Hey, come on, it really was funny. Don't be mad." For the first time since we met that day, he smiled at me, and my knees turned to jelly. We walked to the bar in silence. When we sat down at a table on the small terrace, I crossed my arms over my chest.

"Don't worry about it," I heard him say. "Pirc isn't exactly a gem. She doesn't even really have a solid grasp on what she's teaching us. Compared to Istenič's, her lectures are totally average. You'll see next year; Ethnographic Research is even worse than Linguistic Anthropology."

I sighed. "Maybe. Anyway, the main thing is that it's behind me." I uncrossed my arms and settled comfortably into the chair. A wave of peace washed over me; I was free of all obligations until the beginning of October. The sun was already high in the sky, baking the white-hot asphalt, and for a long moment it was possible to forget that summer was fading. A waitress came over to us; I ordered a cappuccino, and he ordered a Coca-Cola.

"Istenič agreed with the thesis topic I proposed to him," Maks said when the waitress brought our drinks, without me asking him about it. "I'm going to research the revolution in Rojava," he said with pride, adding, "Anthropological aspects of democratic confederalism." His brown eyes shone like amber.

I hid behind my coffee cup so Maks couldn't tell that I had never heard of Rojava.

"And what is democratic confederalism?" I asked cautiously. Maks leaned closer to me clearly pleased and explained, "The political system they've implemented in Rojava, a region in Syria where the Kurds live." He took a few sips of Coke, then continued. "It's based on principles of environmentalism, feminism, democracy, and so on." He burped very slightly. "I'd like to focus primarily on the role of women, which is really essential in Rojava." He fell into thought for a moment, sliding his index finger along the rim of his glass. "If I could, I'd just go there," he murmured.

"To Rojava?" I asked, astonished, and he nodded with passion. I sighed.

"You will. Someday," I said calmly, but with a touch of sadness in my voice. Maks looked at me, grateful, but said nothing.

"What were you talking to Blaž about?" he asked me.

"Who?"

He nodded toward the college building and explained that was the name of the guy who was waiting with us in the hallway.

"He told me they are going to rework his thesis into an academic article with Pirc."

Maks raised his eyebrows, then said casually, as if trying to conceal his agitation, "He's become quite ambitious lately. Apparently, he's already thinking about a doctorate."

"Already?"

He nodded. "We were talking the other day, and I even gathered that he wants to become a professor at the department. Rumor has it Pirc already suggested he do his doctorate with her." He shook his head. "He is doing well with his studies, but for an academic career, you have to be a little more open-minded."

"What do you mean?"

He didn't answer immediately; he leaned back in his chair, searching for words. Without looking at me, he said, "Well, he's from some small town near Murska Sobota…" He stopped there and looked at me as if this should explain everything. Seeing that I wasn't convinced, he continued, "Maybe it has nothing to do with that, but sometimes he says things that are a bit narrow-minded. And he has a slightly patronizing attitude toward women."

"How does that show?"

"He often feels the need to help our female colleagues. With college stuff. Some of them do take advantage of it, but most find it annoying and don't need his help at all. For instance, he's tried to impose himself on Gaja like that several times, completely unnecessarily."

At the mention of Gaja, I felt a nasty knot in my stomach, and I asked him in a weak voice, "Did she tell you that?" Maks nodded, then chuckled and shook his head.

"And he's tried to hang out with us several times, but he just somehow doesn't fit into our group. It always came off as weird, forced."

My chuckle was forced, too. I knew Maks's friends—the ones he hung out with in college and with whom, judging by photos on

Facebook, he had spent a few days at his parents' weekend house this summer—only by sight: among them was Gaja, the daughter of a journalist at the national broadcaster; another girl whose father was a lecturer at the Department of Philosophy; and besides Maks, three guys, one of whom was the brother of a young leftist politician, while I didn't know much about the other two except that they were roommates. They were surrounded by a kind of impermeable aura, and perhaps Blaž had experienced that, too. Although not in words, they quickly let you know you weren't good enough for them—even when they looked at you, it was as if they didn't see you.

I realized I had got lost in thought and only caught half of what Maks was saying: "...helps girls out of kindness," he was frowning while stroking the short stubble on his chin with his right hand, "but he subconsciously underestimates them." It seemed he wanted to say something else, when we saw Blaž coming toward us, and Maks fell silent.

He joined us at the table and ordered coffee with milk.

"What does Pirc say?" Maks wanted to know. Blaž was modest. "Nothing special." As we waited in silence for him to say more, he added that they had gone through her comments and corrections and that he now had until the end of September to improve the article.

Maks responded with a very cold "Cool." I saw his face had darkened at Blaž's arrival, and I wondered why he had agreed to have coffee with him if he clearly didn't like the guy very much. Even when Blaž asked him how his exam went, he first just waved his hand, then said a touch snidely, "She gave me a nine, but the questions were pretty average."

So, he got a nine after all. I thought about how wonderful it would have been if I had been prepared for us taking the exam together, had mastered the material, and got a straight ten. Maks might be looking at me with eyes full of admiration now. As it was, I was just an average student with average grades in his eyes. I got lost in thought again and missed part of their conversation.

"...the most incompetent one in the department. In lectures, she just reads what she has written on the slides, which I'm not sure she even prepared herself. She lectures on useless material, and in the reports, she demands these extensive analyses that she couldn't put together on her own. The practicals are a waste of time." Maks was looking at Blaž somewhat provocatively, as if challenging him to a duel. Blaž just smiled askance and said, "I don't know, I think she presents the material very clearly and vividly. Plus, she's an excellent mentor and is always present at office hours. She takes time to talk and is willing to help." He cleared his throat and added, "I also considered writing my thesis with Istenič, but he's unreachable most of the time, and it takes him forever to reply to an email."

What Blaž said was completely true, and it seemed Maks was aware of it too, as he didn't contradict him.

In my first year of studies, I often went for coffee with colleagues from the same year after lectures, but then I stopped—I got tired of conversations about the professors and their whims. I sighed loudly, leaned on my palm in boredom, and stared at Maks in the hope that he would end the debate. But it was Blaž who changed the subject.

"Did you know she sings in the same choir as Sara Černe?" he asked Maks, nodding toward me.

"That's right, you know Sara, too," I remembered. "She told me you were classmates in high school."

Maks nodded, then asked with a frown, "Don't you sing in some Catholic choir?"

I looked at him in surprise and shook my head. "No, it's just...

a regular women's choir." He still looked at me as if he weren't entirely convinced.

"But didn't you record a CD with some Gregorian chants? The one you gave me."

I brought my right hand to my lips and bit the nail on my middle finger. The sun was beating down unusually hard for September. At the next table, a man and a woman were sitting, both smoking; cigarette smoke drifted over to us, and the smell of tobacco filled my nostrils. Despite the heat, I remembered the winter evening when I had brought Maks our CD. *Daughters of Jerusalem* was the title, and we had spent a good two months recording it. Every singer in the choir got her own CD, and I had given mine to Maks, figuring I could listen to Urška's. At the time, Maks thanked me quietly, put it in his backpack, and hadn't mentioned it again.

"Those weren't Gregorian chants, it was Palestrina. Renaissance," I explained. "And, well... most choirs perform sacral music because there's just so much of it for choirs. Even if it isn't... a church choir." Blaž nodded, agreeing.

Maks was silent at first, and I thought he wasn't going to say anything, when he said, "I listen to it in the car sometimes. You girls are very good."

He completely disarmed me. He had never once mentioned that he listened to it. Our eyes met, and at the same time, our knees bumped under the table.

"Sorry," I murmured, picked up my coffee cup, and quickly drank what was left.

"When is your next concert, so I can come and listen to you?" Blaž asked suddenly; I had almost forgotten about him. I put the cup back on the saucer.

"Hm, let me think. Every year in December, we have an Advent concert with another choir, at St. Joseph's Church in Poljane. I think that will be the first concert of the new season."

"So, you aren't a Catholic choir, but you have an Advent concert in a church?" Maks asked in a teasing tone. I sighed.

"Churches have the best acoustics. Come, why not," my words were directed at Blaž as I counted out coins for the coffee in my palm. "And bring him along, too, so he can see we're good live as well," I said, nodding at Maks without looking at him. Out of the corner of my eye, I sensed him smile.

I stood up and told them I was heading off. Neither of them offered to pay, so I left a two-euro coin on the table. I said goodbye and headed for my bike. The whole way home, I listened to Palestrina and pictured Maks driving alone along unknown, empty roads, listening to the same music I was listening to now.

5

On a Tuesday evening, during the first heavy downpour of autumn, Urška and I got in the back seats of Ivana's silver Toyota Yaris. Sara was already sitting in the passenger seat.

"Do you know what I found out at the last vocal technique?" Ivana's question was directed at Urška, and their eyes met in the rearview mirror.

"What?"

"Ciril Šavli is writing a piece. For us."

Urška grimaced but said nothing. I noticed Sara looking from one to the other, intrigued.

"Who is that?"

"A composer," I answered. "We already performed one of his pieces back when we won the competition in Ptuj."

"And he isn't good?"

Neither of them said anything; Ivana stared stubbornly at the wipers sweeping across the windshield at high speed.

"He is good," she finally admitted, "just annoying."

Urška agreed with her, and I remained silent. I looked away from Ivana's pale face and stared outside. I almost rolled my eyes. Ivana would never admit that she worshipped him during the preparations for the competition in Ptuj. She talked about him constantly, and if he came to rehearsals, she would hover around him during the break, staring at him with a gleam in her eyes, laughing loudly at his jokes as he gave us guidance. She wasn't the only one in the choir; most of the singers were enthusiastic about him—one of the best composers of the younger generation, only a few years older than us, who had received the Student Prešeren Award for his master's thesis in composition. But then rumors began to spread through the choir that he had divorced a Polish violinist just as quickly as he had married her, and that he advocated for open relationships in which both partners could have multiple partners. Ivana's semi-infatuation cooled overnight.

Personally, I preferred to avoid conversations about Ciril. He reminded me of Shia LaBeouf, and he always smelled of patchouli.

We parked not far from the hall where we practiced and ran to the entrance under umbrellas. We were already late. When we entered, the chorists were waiting on their chairs, chatting quietly with one another, while Agata sat on the piano bench, pressing completely gentle, barely audible chords on the keys. Only when we sat down did she look up, her gaze testifying that she had been waiting impatiently for our arrival. We were the only ones running late, so the whispering in the hall died away.

Agata stood up and, with deliberate movements, opened the red folder lying on the upright piano; it was the same color as the polish on her nails. She took out a single sheet of paper, folded in thirds. She stood before us, unfolded it, and stared at it for a few long moments, waiting for the hall to be filled with perfect silence.

"Dear Agata Trinko," she began to read, struggling to maintain control over her voice, which trembled with excitement, "we are delighted to inform you that the choir Philomela, under your esteemed leadership as the conductor, has been shortlisted for the International European Choir Contest!" She spoke louder toward the end, and the girls were already gasping for breath as she continued in a high-pitched voice: "This prestigious contest is scheduled to take place on the 11th of June 2016 in Tallinn, Estonia!" Enthusiasm spread through the choir like an infection; the girls whistled, clapped, and hugged one another. Barbara squeezed my hand, too, and I looked over at Urška, who was hugging Ivana over her shoulders from behind.

In my mind, I saw a stage with wooden floorboards illuminated by blinding spotlights. I saw us, the singers, standing on that stage in white blouses and black skirts sash-tied with bright red ribbons, while at the edge, Agata looked out at the full hall before her with gray, misty eyes, pointing to us with her left hand, then looking at us with a proud smile, pleased. We bow in unison while applause echoes through the hall, settling into the rhythm of synchronized clapping. An elegantly dressed man steps onto the stage carrying a huge bouquet of flowers—

"Girls!" Ivana shouted suddenly, pointing at Agata, who looked as if she wanted to say something but couldn't because of the noise. The girls fell silent; only a few continued to murmur excitedly.

Agata's smile vanished.

"I think it is crystal clear what this means," she said in a serious voice, waving the paper. "Yes, it means we are good, but it also means you really have to get to work now. If you don't do the work, both at home and here, we will make a very poor impression in Estonia, and I don't think any of us wants that."

The young women nodded solemnly one after another, and Agata smiled with satisfaction. She placed the folded paper on the piano and took another one from the red folder.

"Now for the best part," she said, staring at the sheet before her, a joyous smile still reigning on her face. "Wait until you hear what I've chosen for our competition program." Out of the corner of my eye, I saw Ivana lean forward in her chair, staring at the choirmaster with interest. Agata sat on the piano bench and cleared her throat.

"We will present four pieces at the competition," she began, once deathly silence overtook the small hall. "Of those, two must be foreign and two Slovenian. It's polite to present a piece by one of the host country composers... And it doesn't hurt to flatter them a little, too." She smirked, and some of the girls giggled. "I found us a piece by the exceptional young composer Pärt Uusberg, *Luiged läevad* is the title, I think that's how it's pronounced... It is wonderful, you'll see. A sort of poetic ballad, the voices intertwine beautifully, the first sopranos have a truly lovely melody. Well, all the voices do. You'll like it, I promise. And besides..." She looked up, and a mischievous glint flashed in her gray eyes. "Uusberg is still young, and since composers like to come and listen to performances of their work, we might even meet him." The girls laughed boisterously again, but Agata continued in a serious tone: "The next piece we will perform is *Ubi caritas* by Ēriks Ešenvalds." Some singers clapped, pleased by the choice. "Then, as I said, we have two Slovenian ones. I chose *Ave Maria* by Ambrož Čopi... In my opinion, one of the most beautiful Slovenian compositions. It has been performed by several female ensembles, but I believe it deserves our rendition, too. Actually, I'm surprised we haven't sung it yet." She stared thoughtfully at the paper before her, raised her head after a painful moment of silence, looked around the choir, and then said, "Well, the last piece will fire you up if the others haven't; it was written specifically for our choir by... Ciril Šavli!"

The outburst of joy at this was indescribable—the news of being chosen for the competition itself was nothing compared to the mention of the young composer. Agata laughed and waited for the excitement among the girls to settle.

"Aren't you interested in what he wrote for us?" she asked, and at the enthusiastic "Yes!" she laughed even louder.

"It is a musical setting of a poem by Svetlana Makarovič," she began to explain, and the singers listened attentively again.[3] "A poem that has a very folkloric character, so the piece is like that too. The text is poignant, truly... unrelenting. In fact, once we've warmed up, we'll start right in with it."

After the warm-up, which was shorter than usual this time—it seemed Agata was in a hurry to get to work on the new piece—she shoved a thick stack of sheet music into Ivana's hands, and Ivana began distributing them. I received my copy of the composition titled *The Bush*, and in the right corner of the score it read: *"Ciril Šavli for the women's choir Philomela and choirmaster Agata Trinko."*

"The piece combines elements of folk singing with completely modern moments," Agata explained as we rustled our sheaves. "The second altos have a fantastic melody; it actually holds the best line through the whole piece and drives it forward, so," she looked up and stared at the girls on her right, "I expect the altos to really master it. No, what am I saying, you all have to master it!" She laughed somewhat chillingly, then continued, "But we also have a solo, in the second soprano." She leafed through the pages. "It starts on page five. After the choir sings the first three stanzas, the solo sings the last one." She looked up and stared at Barbara. "I had you in mind, Barbara, alright?" Barbara, who was holding a tuning fork to her ear, looked up from the score and nodded with a wide smile on her face. "Excellent. I really missed your timbre. But you need a backup, I was looking for a voice, similar to yours... Maša?"

I jerked my head up from the sheet music and stared at Agata, probably a shade too incredulously. She watched me with glowing eyes, smiling, waiting for my reaction. She had never chosen me for a

---

3 TN: Svetlana Makarovič is a legendary Slovenian author whose independent stance on social issues often courts controversy.

solo, not even as a backup. *What about Klara?* it struck me. She had a beautiful solo in *Don't Plow, Don't Sow*; why hadn't she chosen her instead? But the question mark hanging on Agata's smiling face was only for show—I knew she wasn't *asking* me if I would be the backup for the solo, she was *assigning* me to it. A solo was a privilege, an honor. It was not up for discussion.

I nodded very slowly and took a pencil from the case resting in my lap. I leafed to the page where the solo began, drew a large exclamation mark next to the bar, wrote "solo" beside it, and "backup" in parentheses.

"Excellent. I will kindly tell you both: don't even think about missing practice when we are working on this piece," Agata added, then sat at the piano and struck the first chord.

"Congratulations on the solo."

Sara sat down on Barbara's empty chair next to me during the break.

"I'm only the backup," I protested, unwrapping a granola bar and taking a bite.

"True, but it's obvious it's very important to Agata."

"You're right. I see you learn fast."

In Philomela, every soloist had a backup. It was one of Agata's moves, or rather rules, that she enforced in her choir: alongside backups, there was the "iron repertoire" that we always had to know by heart; the fact that every singer possessed multiple bright red ribbons, which we had to bring to concerts in case anyone forgot theirs; and we suspected Agata had an arrangement with a few people to attend every one of our concerts. I told this to Sara, and she laughed loudly enough that a few girls loitering among the chairs turned to look at us, which filled me with satisfaction.

"What do you think of the selection of competition pieces?" I asked.

"I don't know any of them. But I did notice they were all written by men."

"I don't think there are many female composers," I remarked, and she nodded.

"But I do like the lyrics of the poem, don't you? And the author of the poem is a woman." She took my score, started leafing through it, and read aloud: "*Do not go courting to the mountains, you won't be my husband nor my brother*'... '*Nobody knows anybody anywhere in this world*'. And this: '*Only if you drew my blood would I finally know you.*' It's really good." Sara didn't look up from the sheaf of papers, her slightly narrowed eyes slid from word to word. I nodded, though I couldn't say the lyrics spoke to me.

She handed the score back and pulled a knitted pouch from her pocket, took out tobacco and rolling papers, and right there, in the middle of the small hall, began to roll a cigarette. She placed the tobacco onto the paper with great precision and care, rested the half-finished cigarette in her lap, took a filter from a plastic wrapper, placed it in the roll, and licked it precisely, like a cat licking its fur. While I watched her do this, Urška and Ivana approached us.

"Bravo," my sister murmured, nudging me slightly in the shoulder. Urška had never had a solo, and she had never been a backup. I wanted to get up, go to Agata, and tell her to choose Urška as the backup instead of me—but she sang first soprano, not second.

"What do you two think of the piece?" Ivana asked Sara and me, crossing her arms over her chest. Judging by the expression on her face, she didn't like it.

"Hard to say," I admitted. "We haven't practiced it enough."

Urška sighed nervously. "Ivana and I were talking... Isn't it a little weird that we're going to be performing a text by Svetlana Makarovič?" She glanced at Agata, who was standing by the piano, absorbed in a sheet of paper.

I knew what she was getting at, and I looked at Sara with dismay. What will she think of Urška? Will she think I was like her, too? But Sara showed no sign that Urška's words upset her; she continued to busy herself with her cigarette.

"Why should there be anything wrong with that?" I asked my sister. Ivana, still with her arms crossed, measured me with a stern gaze. Urška didn't answer immediately—she looked as if she didn't know what to say.

"I don't know, it just seems controversial to me. I mean, *she* is controversial, as a person. Didn't she publicly announce that she had an abortion and that she doesn't like children?" Urška took my score in her hands and stared at it. Her gaze expressed revulsion, but also confusion. I noticed her swallow. "I don't know if I want to sing this," she said quietly. She leafed through the music, and with every page, her eyes grew rounder. Then she looked up, and our eyes met; there was something childlike, uncertain in them.

"I understand," I said in a calm voice, "but the text is good." Out of the corner of my eye, I sensed Sara nod. "Besides, we read and listened to countless fairy tales of hers in our childhood."

Ivana snorted. "I certainly won't be reading them to my children. That woman openly hates Christians."

Urška shifted her uncertain gaze to Ivana, and at Ivana's words, it turned into an angry one. "Me neither," she said firmly.

Her sudden reaction tightened my chest. I thought of the bookshelf in our childhood room, where *Sapra the Little Mouse*, *Oka the Owl*, *Cosies on the Flying Spoon*, and Urška's favorite, *Pussypaws*, stood. Their spines were worn, and in some places, torn pages were taped back together with yellowed duct tape. On the first page of *Mišmaš Bakery*, written in blue ballpoint pen and clumsy letters, was "M A Š A."

"You don't have to connect the work with the author," I told her, ignoring Ivana, who was staring daggers at me.

"That isn't always simple," Sara suddenly spoke up. She had finished rolling the cigarette but held it in front of her eyes, inspecting it without looking at us. "I, for example, can't watch Woody Allen movies anymore because he allegedly sexually abused his stepdaughter."

"But that's much worse than what Svetlana Makarovič supposedly did," I replied, and Urška's eyes widened in indignation: "Worse than an abortion?" I sensed Sara tear her gaze away from the cigarette to look at my sister with surprise.

"Maša is right, in a way," she said then, calmly. "I just remembered, Caravaggio was a murderer. But when I look at his paintings, I don't think about that."

It seemed this didn't appease Urška. My sister sighed and returned the score to me without a word; the pages were slightly damp from her fingers.

Sara, staring thoughtfully at the door through which singers were coming and going, added, "It's true that no one is without sin, and if we went and read biographies, we'd probably find something controversial in the life of every artist, something we don't like. People probably have to decide for themselves what is acceptable to them and what isn't."

Urška said she agreed, then fell silent for a short while.

"I don't know," she said finally. "Maybe I'll just quit the choir."

This surprised Ivana the most, and she stared at her with her mouth agape. "Why would you do that?"

"Well, it's not just because of this." She nodded at the sheet music resting in my lap. "The competition is only two weeks after the wedding." She fell silent, as if that explained everything.

"But you knew the competition would be in June when you were choosing the date," Ivana reproached her. "Maybe you should have chosen a different date."

"I don't understand why it's a problem that the competition is two weeks after the wedding," I said, and Ivana looked at me with appreciation. What my sister said surprised me. Ever since she became a member of Philomela in her first year of studying Pedagogy, she had adapted her life to singing in the choir and attending vocal technique lessons; she was utterly loyal to the choir with Agata at the helm.

For her, it was a bandage that had healed the deep wound from that summer when she hadn't been accepted into the Academy of Music.

"Well," she began, bringing her left hand to her mouth and starting to bite her cuticle, "I'd really like to prepare well for the wedding. The choir takes up a huge amount of my time."

Ivana fixed a strand of dark hair that had strayed onto her face.

"But what about the time we'll devote to *your* wedding instead of the competition? Agata didn't hesitate at all when you asked her if we would sing."

Sara kept staring at the roll she held in her hands, while I looked worriedly from Ivana to Urška, who were glaring at each other until Urška looked away, her pale blue eyes dropping. She lowered her hand from her mouth. A tiny drop of blood glistened on her thumb at the edge of the nail. If we were alone with Sara, I would tell her: See, now you are witnessing what the first sopranos are like: they take singing in the choir too seriously, their zeal is often excessive. First sopranos are the ones who swallow tears after a bad concert, roll their eyes during other sections' rehearsals, sigh wearily when other singers struggle to keep up with them, and take criticism poorly.

"That's true, but... If *you* were preparing for a wedding, you'd understand," Urška looked reproachfully at Ivana, who just pursed her lips.

Sara stood up, looked at us, and asked, "Anyone joining me for a smoke?" The rain was still beating against the panes, but I stood up to go with her anyway, just as Agata appeared at the door and motioned for Sara, who was already heading for the exit, to turn around—the rehearsal was about to continue.

7

At the start of October, I was riding my bike to the faculty. When I turned from Rimska Street onto the Foerster Garden, I saw Sara approaching me along the path, which was strewn with yellow leaves. She had earphones in her ears. I stepped off my bike clumsily, took my own earphones out, and waved.

"What are you listening to?" I asked as she approached. In response, she pushed one of her earbuds into my ear. I heard a gentle guitar transition followed by a harmony of voices: "*Overhead the albatross hangs motionless upon the air*"—it had been years since I last listened to Pink Floyd.

"*Echoes!*" I shouted with enthusiasm, even though the melancholic melody caused a sharp pang beneath my sternum: it reminded me of the dark periods I went through in high school and the lonely evening walks through Ljubljana, when my parents thought I was at the Friday's parish youth group meetings. Sara smiled and took the earbud back.

"What were you listening to?" She nodded at the phone wrapped in earphone cords, which I was stuffing into my backpack.

I hesitated before answering. I had been listening to Allegri's *Miserere* performed by The Sixteen, a Renaissance masterpiece I had played every morning for the last few days as I rode to college while the October mist still swirled in Tivoli Park.

"Just some choral music," I murmured.

"Cool. Do you have time for coffee?"

Her invitation was unexpected; around the college, I was constantly running into people I knew. We would always exchange a few brief lines and promise to grab coffee together, but we never actually went—not then, and not later.

"Did you ever listen to Pink Floyd?" she asked as we headed toward the nearest café. We sat at an outdoor table so she could smoke. The weak October sun was filtering through the trees.

"I used to listen to them a lot, yeah. Actually, I had a really long phase in high school. Not exactly a happy one."

"What was going on?"

"It was the fourth year, in the autumn. My class was full of ambitious people; the girls all knew what they wanted to study and wanted to get into all the hard programs—medicine, law, psychology. And I was completely lost. I had no idea what I was even interested in."

The waiter came, and we both ordered cappuccinos. Sara placed her knitted tobacco pouch in her lap and silently began rolling a cigarette. With a nod, she signaled for me to continue.

"And then I got excited about journalism. In reality, journalism had been with me the whole time, I just hadn't realized it. I'd spent four years writing for the school paper, covering the section where students could send in critical letters about the school, and I wrote commentaries on them. Then it dawned on me that I could go study that."

"That must have been an interesting section. Why did you change your mind, then?"

I sighed. It pained me to admit: "My parents. The more enthusiastic I got, the more they opposed it."

The waiter brought our cups. I poured sugar into mine, stirred, and took a sip, while Sara was still busy with her cigarette.

"They didn't like you studying at the Faculty of Arts?" Sara was direct. I wanted to dodge the answer, even though her question hit the mark. I nodded.

"They thought I wouldn't find a job. They're both economists. They hoped I would go into economics too, and my father—I don't know why—was even rooting for chemical engineering, claiming I'd have no trouble with employment. Thinking about it now, he was probably right," I admitted bitterly. Sara gave a sour smile.

"So how did you end up in anthropology?" she asked, licking the paper of her cigarette and flicking her lighter.

"You know, Maks?"

"Hafner?" she checked, and I nodded.

"He got me interested. When I was enrolling in college, he was a freshman." The memory made me smile, more to myself than to Sara. When I was in my final year of high school, I went with one of my classmates to the information day at the Faculty of Arts. The ground floor was teeming with students handing out flyers and inviting people to their departments. Among those students in black T-shirts with the college logo, I saw a freshman wearing black All-Stars and a baseball cap. At first, I wasn't sure if it was really Maks, since it had been a few years since I'd last seen him. But his gaze betrayed that he remembered me from somewhere, and just as I concluded it was him, he walked up and asked what I was doing there and if I planned to enroll in the Faculty of Arts. I told him no, that I just came with my friend who had already vanished into the crowd of students. He pressed a flyer for Ethnology and Cultural Anthropology into my hands and invited me to his department's presentation.

"I came to the info day at the Faculty of Arts purely by chance. We met, and he told me to come to their presentation. I went, and at the end, I had to admit to him that it was pretty cool. And then he said something that stuck in my mind: that what he liked best about studying anthropology wasn't how foreign cultures become familiar, but how one's own culture becomes foreign. That sparked my interest."

My voice trembled slightly. I hoped Sara wouldn't read into what it was really about. I had come to anthropology because he was there. I had convinced myself that being an anthropologist would make me an even better journalist.

I drank some more coffee while watching Sara take a drag and blow out a cloud of smoke. She set the cigarette in the ashtray, leaned forward, and picked up her cup.

"And your parents agreed with that decision?" she asked, fixing her green eyes on me as she set the cup back on the saucer.

I burst out laughing and shook my head.

"Of course not. But they couldn't convince me otherwise anymore. I had made up my mind."

Sara chuckled.

"That reminds me of Ivana. She wanted to study classical philology, and my uncle and aunt almost lost it." I raised my eyebrows. I hadn't known that about Ivana, she was already in her master's program for biochemistry.

"Why's that?"

"Same reason as you. According to them, she wouldn't find a job."

Sara and I fell silent for a long moment as I pondered her words. Ivana was incredibly ambitious and studied diligently. Ever since I'd known her, her life seemed picture-perfect; there were no wrong decisions or slip-ups. She had everything under control. I knew she often went running in the morning, sometimes baked banana bread and blueberry muffins to bring to choir rehearsals, and that she, Urška, and some friends occasionally went to the mountains for the weekend. It didn't surprise me that Agata trusted her with demanding bureaucratic tasks related to the choir—tasks Agata claimed she couldn't handle herself. Ivana performed all of this with ease; she never forgot anything and always stuck to agreements and deadlines. Everything in her life ran smoothly. It was hard to imagine her arguing with her parents about wanting to go into classical philology. I told as much to Sara.

"Well, she didn't persist for long. Imagine this: four years of straight As, a gold award in chemistry, a golden high school graduate. And she wanted to go into Latin and Greek." She chuckled and shook her head. "I supported her, of course," she added in a calmer voice, "but Tone and Vera had the final say." She fell into thought for a moment, then added quietly after a brief pause, "Ivana doesn't exactly have it easy."

"What do you mean?"

Sara didn't look at me; instead, her gaze combed the path where students were walking past the café. She scratched her nose with the hand not holding the cigarette.

"A lot is expected of her. That's just how it is with the Božič family."

I didn't know much about Ivana's family—she was the youngest of five children and had four older brothers. The first three were already married, and the oldest, a powerful lawyer, occasionally appeared in the media as a political commentator. The fourth brother, as far as I knew, was a theology student.

"I can imagine," I murmured. Sara tore her gaze away from the path and looked at me.

"I think that's why she was quiet the whole way home after what Urška said to her at the last rehearsal. I think it hurt her a little."

It was true, a heavy silence had reigned in the car.

"What do you think hurt her?"

"What Urška said. *If you were preparing for a wedding, you'd understand,* or whatever it was. Ivana gets comments at home too, about when she's going to meet someone." In truth—though I wouldn't betray this to Sara now—Urška also sometimes fussed over why her friend didn't have a boyfriend. When she told me she and Andrej were engaged, she admitted she was worried about how Ivana would take it, fearing she might be envious. Nevertheless, she had sent her the message with the news immediately after she and Andrej came down from the mountain.

Sara continued: "Just last year at Christmas, someone teased her about it. I'm not surprised at all by what happened after New Year's."

"What happened?" My eyes widened. She sighed, emptied her coffee cup, leaned back in her chair, took a drag, and began the story.

"At first, no one noticed, but she evidently decided that this time things would be different. She connected with some girl who writes a blog. One of those extremely attractive blogs where the photos are perfect. All pastel colors. You know what I'm talking about?" I nodded, and she continued. "So, this girl posts photos of herself, her apartment, her clothes, her meals, her workouts. And she really is very attractive. I admit, when I saw the blog, even I found it quite cute, and that aesthetic isn't usually my thing. Just a pleasantly harmonious world, without any flaws." She paused, brought the cigarette to her mouth again, and inhaled. "She writes a lot about dealing with low self-esteem, accepting yourself, other people's prejudices, and also about shopping; she posts recipes and so on. Anyway, the point is that this girl also offers individual training and nutritional counseling. For a fee, of course. Ivana contacted her, and they met up." She cleared her throat and went on. "She started going to the gym with her. I noticed something was different on her Facebook. Every day she posted several motivational quotes, and shared giveaways for protein shakes and sports gear. Did you notice anything?" I had indeed noticed a change on Ivana's Facebook in the first months of the year. My news feed was constantly showing me her posts of quotes that were unusually similar to one another (*"Reach for the moon. If you miss, at least you'll be among the stars"; "It does not matter how slowly you go as long as you don't stop"; "Failure is simply the opportunity to begin again, this time more intelligently"*). They began to annoy me so much that I unfollowed her posts—I told Sara this, and she laughed.

"That's exactly what I'm talking about. She once showed me the blog and told me this girl gave her a heap of useful advice, designed a meal plan for her, advised her on which supplements to take, which protein bars to eat, which sports gear to buy, where to go to the gym, how to exercise. Ivana took it all very seriously—you know how she is. She tackled it with total devotion and started counting calories precisely, weighing herself, and so on." Sara took another drag and blew a smoke ring. She stared at it thoughtfully for a few moments, then looked at me and continued. "And then in April, she showed up at my place unannounced. She was a nervous wreck; I'd never seen her like that. At first, she beat around the bush, but eventually, she told me why she had come. She asked if I could lend her some money."

"Money? And what did you do?" Before my eyes, I saw tall, thin Ivana blushing as she asked her cousin to lend her cash. It was a very unusual scene, one I struggled to imagine.

"I lent her what I had on hand, which—believe me—wasn't exactly much." She chortled, spreading her arms and pointing at herself as if her modest appearance demonstrated her poverty. She was wearing a worn leather jacket, washed-out jeans, and the same All-Stars she had on for the first rehearsal. They were the only sneakers she wore.

"Of course, I asked her why she needed the money, and she said she had to pay someone back. Or rather—it was really hard to understand her—she was mumbling something about needing to pay someone for a favor. It was really weird. I gave her the savings I had on hand. When she took it, she immediately counted the money, and I detected panic on her face. I realized it wasn't enough; that was when it finally hit me that the situation was serious."

"How much money was it?" I asked quietly, assuming Sara wouldn't tell me out of consideration for her cousin. She really did search my face for a few long moments, as if weighing whether to tell me.

"I gave her a couple hundred euros," she finally said.

I asked if Ivana told her to whom she owed this money. Sara shook her head and said Ivana left soon after and that she wasn't worried about the money—she knew she would pay her back.

"Right around that time, something happened that derailed me so much I forgot about the whole thing. A few weeks passed, and then her mother—my aunt—came to our place. She grilled me on whether I knew anything about this girl. I said I didn't, but I also didn't dare mention the money. She told me and my mom that Ivana was getting constant phone calls. That she had stopped answering the calls and messages because they made her uncomfortable, but then this girl just showed up at their house. She knew where she lived because she'd done a wardrobe review or something like that for her a few weeks prior. In short, she came and claimed Ivana owed her because she hadn't paid for all her services. Ivana insisted she *had* paid for everything, but that she and the girl had agreed at the start on a lower price without an invoice, so it wasn't clear how much she was supposed to pay. This girl insisted she was in debt. And then, right there in front of them, she declared that she'd realized Ivana also needed psychological support because she had issues with food, and that she suspected she had anorexia. Therefore, she was providing her with holistic support, including therapy. They were having some kind of therapy sessions. It gives me the creeps just talking about it." Sara shuddered.

"Anorexia?" I was astonished.

She nodded. "But Ivana doesn't have anorexia. This girl just diagnosed her on her own. Oh, I forgot to mention—she used to have anorexia herself, and now she is sharing her story and promoting a healthy lifestyle and body positivity. Which isn't wrong, in my opinion, but you can't just start diagnosing someone and conducting therapy with them without any qualifications." She sighed deeply; a slight flush took over her face. I said I agreed and asked what happened next.

"Tone and Vera saw that Ivana was embarrassed, so they said they would pay whatever she owed. They demanded a receipt, but the girl insisted she and Ivana had agreed to work without one. In the end, they gave in and paid her out right there—I think a few hundred euros." She angrily crushed the cigarette into the ashtray. "Finally, she left, and the two of them wanted to figure out what was behind the whole thing. Ivana admitted that she had spent more money under the girl's influence than she had planned. She said the protein shakes and bars, the supplements, the sports gear—all of that cost quite a lot, and the girl insisted on specific brands. And that she had treated Ivana to a hairdresser—some senior stylist—but in exchange, Ivana had to order supplements using her referral code. To be honest, Vera couldn't even fully explain everything that had been going on." Sara's hands reached for the tobacco pouch lying on the table, then paused slightly, as if deciding whether to roll another cigarette. Finally, she withdrew them to her lap.

"They forbade her from ever contacting her again. The debts were settled, and Ivana brought me the money back some time later. By then she was back to her usual self, though it seemed like something was different. She looked... dejected." She crossed her arms and stared sadly into the void. She shook her head. "I still don't understand why she fell for it."

"Neither do I. What happened to the girl?" Sara looked up—something flashed angrily in her green eyes. The skin on her pale face turned slightly red again.

"Nothing. I went to check her blog recently, and it said that alongside training and nutritional counselling, she now offers style makeovers and something she calls 'personality consulting.'" She made air quotes with her hands. "One hour of her consulting costs fifty-five euros. She also made an Instagram, in the same colours as the blog." She grimaced, as if to indicate what she thought of that platform. "And she found some guy. He's also some type of 'coach'—I turned his whole Facebook upside down to figure out he used to be an unpopular chubby kid who turned to sports, and now he's posting motivational quotes and photos of himself in a suit or at the gym every day." I burst out laughing, but Sara's face remained stony—it looked like the whole thing genuinely angered her. Finally, she gave in and laughed along with me.

"I also found out they're both dropouts. She was studying wellness but didn't finish, and he quit economics."

I rolled my eyes. A brief silence descended on our table.

"I knew nothing about this. I'm sorry that happened to her." That was true, but I also couldn't help thinking that even Ivana's outwardly orderly life was apparently not without flaws.

"I don't think many people know. Urška probably doesn't know either, and it's better that way. It's unusual that Vera even told us about this."

"Why?"

Sara shrugged, then said hesitantly, "Our mothers are close, but they have their moments. Vera loves to create the impression that everything is perfect at home. Whenever she talks about Ivana's brothers, for instance, she always makes it sound like they're golden. But with Ivana... I don't know. Sometimes it feels like they're actually preying on her to make a mistake." Sara wasn't looking at me as she spoke; her gaze was fixed somewhere in the distance.

I watched her silently. I wanted to tell her that, based on Urška's descriptions, Ivana's family always struck me like one of those Catholic families where nothing ever goes wrong, where every child walks the straight path joyfully approved by the parents, and where no one makes radically wrong decisions. But I kept the thought to myself.

"Anyway, when Ivana brought me the money, she invited me to your concert," Sara finally spoke up. "I went. After the concert, she asked if I'd come to an audition. At first, I didn't feel like it. If I were going to decide to sing in a choir, I think I'd prefer a mixed one. But then I saw she had deleted her Facebook. As if she wanted to erase all those motivational quotes. I felt sorry for her, and I decided to go."

Sara sighed deeply and cast her eyes downward. The reasons she had listed in August for joining the choir faded.

"But I realized at the first rehearsal anyway that the choir is full of great singers. I still find it hard to believe you guys are amateurs."

She smiled at me, and I returned the smile, then remembered I had to go to a lecture soon. I told her, and she started patting her jacket pockets.

"You know what, it's on me," I said. For a moment it seemed she wanted to object, but she just thanked me. We stood up to pay at the counter, and at the last second, Sara noticed she had left the tobacco pouch lying on the table.

8

"So, you didn't know about this?"

I was in bed with my laptop, watching Urška getting ready for a new day. She had packed her bag, checked her planner, and was now standing by the wardrobe, choosing what to wear. I could never adopt this habit of preparing everything the night before, and even when I tried, it didn't last long. Because I was in a rush during most mornings, I frequently forgot things—my wallet, phone, pencil case—at home.

We were in the room we had shared ever since we moved to this apartment in Lower Šiška. I was too young at the time to remember the previous apartment, but we used to live in a one-bedroom rental in Šentvid. Our room was packed floor-to-ceiling with furniture and wardrobes full of our notebooks, books, and clothes. Some of the desk drawers were so full of junk they could barely be opened.

I had just summed up for my sister what Sara had told me about her cousin. Urška stood before the open wardrobe, staring at the hangers holding blouses, cardigans, and jackets. Her hand glided over them, then dropped. Without looking at me, she shook her head.

"I didn't know. I mean, I knew Ivana was working out. She was very happy at first—maybe even a bit too happy—and I remember telling her once that she might be overdoing it." She looked at me. "Come to think of it, I guess I was right."

She pulled a black skirt out of the closet and laid it on the bed.

"So, what do you think about it?" My hair, which I had just unwrapped from the towel, lay damp on my back, a wet patch forming on my pajama shirt.

Urška didn't answer immediately. She was eyeing a green blouse, trying to figure out if it matched the skirt on the bed. Finally, she made a face and returned the blouse to its place in the closet.

"I don't know. At one point Ivana stopped telling me about the workouts, and I just assumed she wasn't going anymore. Or that she realized it was getting on my nerves. Is this too loud?" She was holding a red turtleneck and red tights.

I grimaced. "Yeah, I'm afraid that's not the most inspired combination."

Urška sighed and rolled her eyes.

"Tomorrow after work, we're going to see the priest to talk about the wedding. I want to look nice."

In recent months, Urška had found a way to mention her wedding in every conversation. I was about to ask her if it wasn't a bit early for that, but instead I said, "What about that green dress from Zara? That one is nice, but casual enough." Urška put the red turtleneck back in the closet and took the green dress off the hanger.

"Maybe you're right." She took black tights and clean underwear from a drawer and set them on the desk. Then she turned to me: "I'm not surprised, you know. Ivana doesn't like to talk about herself and often hides things. She's like you in that regard." She winked, and I blushed bright red. I didn't want to be anything like boring, stuck-up Ivana, but I didn't know what to say to that, so I just rolled my eyes. My sister watched me with a faint smile on her face, as if trying to gauge whether I would protest. I remained silent on purpose.

"She might have told Agata, though. She often confides in her."

"Seriously?"

Urška nodded. "Agata and Ivana are pretty close and tell each other a lot. Ivana knows many things about Agata that we don't."

She took a bathrobe from the hook on the back of the door and put it on.

"Like what?"

"Hmm... Who her husband is, what he does, where they live—things like that. But Ivana only mentions it in passing. She is very secretive about other things. She's diligent about Agata's privacy."

I whistled softly, and Urška laughed.

"For example, she once mentioned that Agata and her husband only have one car and that he often needs it. So Agata frequently asks her for a ride, and Ivana drives her around."

"Interesting," I murmured. She nodded, sat on her bed, and looked at me.

"And once she told me Agata's husband is from Trieste and that he's actually the one who uses his connections to organize the yearly concert in Trieste."

"Seriously?!" We sang in Trieste every spring, and Agata always proudly emphasized that we would be performing in Trieste "because they invited us again." I reminded my sister of this, and we laughed.

"Oh, and this. Once at vocal technique, she asked Ivana to wait a bit and then drive Ciril to the airport. Someone else was supposed to take him, but they canceled, so she asked Ivana. That was in fact how she and Ciril met."

"Ciril Šavli?"

Urška nodded. "After that, she was totally crazy about him for a while."

I wanted to remind her that *both* she and Urška were crazy about him, but I bit my tongue.

"But what happened then? Why doesn't she like him anymore?" I only knew part of the truth.

"Once she was invited to dinner at Agata's. She took Ciril home afterwards, and since he was drunk, he told her that he wanted to be with Agata. To get together with her occasionally, no strings attached, and that her husband could know." Urška grimaced as if this disgusted her. "And Ivana was put off by that." She sighed softly and stared at the pattern on my bed sheet. "It's a good thing," she finally murmured. "She deserves better than that egomaniac."

I swallowed hard and nodded. "I'm going to take a shower," she said, standing up and heading for the door.

"Okay," I answered. When she opened the door, a draft blew in, and the wet spot on my pajamas made me shiver. I wrapped myself tighter in the blanket, pushed my earphones back into my ears, and pressed play. For the hundredth time, I watched Sia's music video where Maddie Ziegler in a nude leotard danced with Shia LaBeouf, whom I considered the most attractive man in the world.

9.

Mom and Dad didn't seem to mind that I hadn't joined them for Sunday mass that morning. Since I started college, I rarely went with them, even though it had been a long-standing family tradition. In high school, I sang in the parish youth choir and attended mass regularly, but when I joined Agata's singers in college, I stopped going to the youth choir rehearsals. And since Urška had started spending the weekends at her boyfriend's, I didn't feel like going with my parents at all anymore. If they ever asked if I wanted to come along, I'd say I had to study and might go to evening mass—only I never went, and they never made a fuss about it.

They left while I was still lying in bed. I listened for the front door to close behind them, then crept out of bed. I loved weekends because I had our room entirely to myself. I couldn't wait for Urška to finally move out—even now, I used her bed as a dumping ground on weekends, clearing it off only right before she came home. Since the engagement, I had been covertly encouraging my sister to move into Andrej's attic apartment before the wedding, but she insisted it meant a lot to them to wait until their wedding night. A few times, I barely bit my tongue to keep from laughing out loud: didn't she already spend her weekends at his place, in his boring attic? She was looking forward to the move, whereas I found the fact that she was moving out of Ljubljana to one of those depressing, characterless towns in the suburbs completely unsavory.

In the kitchen, I heated up some toast, spread a thin layer of Nutella on it, and made coffee in the moka pot. I turned on the TV in the living room and switched to MTV, which was playing a video by The

Weekend where he crawls out of an overturned car with a bloodied face. I turned the volume up so the bass bounced darkly off the old living room furniture. We lived in one of the tallest apartment blocks in the area, and neighbors sometimes complained about the music by knocking on the walls. Usually, I stopped on my own out of caution, lowering the volume and changing the channel. A few days ago, I had forgotten to do that, and Dad turned on the TV right at the moment two men in a Hozier video were kissing to the sound of a raspy baritone voice.

A new video started—*Royals* by Lorde. "*And I'm not proud of my address in a torn-up town, no postcode envy,*" she sang. I have listened to some songs so many times they became part of the soundtrack of my life, and this was one of them. It was about resigning yourself to mediocrity, and I could easily identify with that. Although I had lived in Ljubljana since birth—which compared to someone from, say, the Slovenian countryside might be considered an advantage—I would have gladly swapped the small, stuffy Slovenia for a larger country with metropolises full of vibrant cultural life, like Berlin, New York, or Tokyo. I wanted to be part of a culture that could boast of art and literature of global importance, not just sports achievements. Sometimes I would have even swapped my mother tongue for something more accessible and widespread. I admitted this to Maks once; he agreed, but just launched into a debate about Žižek and Laibach, and since I didn't know much about either, I quickly changed the subject.

I spent some time watching MTV videos, finished my cup of coffee and breakfast, then turned off the TV and went to take a shower. While the water ran down my body, I heard the front door unlock and made out four familiar voices in the hallway: Mom and Dad had been joined by Andrej and Urška. I had forgotten they had invited themselves over for lunch today. When their voices vanished behind the living room door, I put on my bathrobe, slipped into our room, cleared the pile of dirty clothes off Urška's bed before she could see it, and got changed.

I went into the living room. Dad and Andrej were sitting on the couch where I had been lounging just moments before. I could hear Mom and Urška in the kitchen. Dad had just turned on the TV.

My sister's fiancé and I exchanged a few pleasantries, but as usual, we didn't have much to say to each other, even though he had been part of my life as her boyfriend for a good three years. Andrej often called me an "artistic soul" in front of others, even though I didn't practice any art besides singing in a choir. It seemed to me this stemmed from his poor distinction between the humanities and the arts.

Our brief conversation was interrupted by a report on a long column of refugees gathering at the Slovenian border. Such reports on TV were unusual at this hour on Sundays, but it was not surprising, as the refugee crisis had been the constant topic on television and elsewhere for the last few weeks; even Facebook had gone crazy over the topic, and it seemed everyone had something to say about it. I sat down on the couch to hear what the report would say, and Andrej also leaned in toward the TV. The journalist was explaining the difficult conditions at the border, while the camera showed a young mother with a black headscarf covering her hair and a one-year-old child in her lap.

To my left, I heard Andrej's deep sigh.

"They keep showing only women and children," his voice drowned out the journalist's, "when in reality, it's mostly young men coming. Women and children are the minority, but journalists know what effect that has on people. They know it touches them more."

If what he said was true, the journalists were succeeding. Seeing the crying, shivering children, I was overwhelmed by a sense of helplessness, and I thought of my notes for the migration course with sadness. It felt like I should be able to offer a sensible opinion given my knowledge, but nothing convincing came to mind. Next to Andrej, what I was studying often seemed like dry, useless theory. I looked with worry at the empty coffee cup I had left on the table. The coffee had been too strong, and anxiety was setting in.

"Besides," Andrej droned on after neither Dad nor I said anything, "they keep saying they are *refugees*." He emphasized the word with an utterly annoying tone. "I don't know why they call them refugees when they are mostly *economic migrants*. If they were refugees, they wouldn't push on to Germany, they would be satisfied with the first asylum they got."

Out of the corner of my eye, I noticed Dad nod without taking his eyes off the TV and say, "I don't understand what these politicians are playing at. We don't have money to provide free school meals, but we're going to take care of such a mass of foreigners?" He stared in disbelief at his future son-in-law, who eagerly agreed. "Why don't these men stay home and defend their country? If anything, they should ensure the situation in their countries is fixed to the point where at least part of the territory is liberated or safe. Appropriate shelters for war refugees could be set up there, ensuring they are kept dry and fed, while we should send the army to close the European borders." He fell silent, but a tiny smile hung on his face, showing he was pleased with his retort.

"But," I suddenly spoke up, "migration is part of human history. Every human being has the right to move away from an area where they aren't safe. Even our ances—"

"Maša," Andrej interrupted me, looking at me with disdain, "these are *illegal* migrants. People who go on a journey without documents.

That's not what you're talking about. You couldn't go anywhere without documents either."

His voice was didactic, and for a moment made me feel like a little girl. I objected: "It's not that simple. What about the colonialists who invaded their lands and violently changed entire cultures?"

Keeping his eyes on the TV, Andrej replied, "Well, there's your answer. We don't know what intentions these people coming here have. Every tenth one could be a terrorist."

The morning coffee had been too strong, anxiety got stuck in my chest, heavy as crude oil. I wanted to tell Andrej that every tenth refugee isn't a terrorist and that it was his fear of the unknown speaking. But the words died in my throat, and I merely shifted uncomfortably on the couch.

I realized why I couldn't contradict him. I had unwittingly thought the things he said myself. I wouldn't admit this to anyone, but even now I looked suspiciously at men with darker skin or thick beards. When I was flying back from Barcelona in the spring, I found myself sitting next to a young man who looked Muslim. I became afraid when I saw he was nervous. He kept looking out the plane window, biting his lip, sweat running down his forehead. And when he pulled a phone out of his backpack, I was seized by panic—until he started playing a game. Only when we landed and he visibly sighed in relief did I realize he was just afraid of flying.

Urška appeared at the living room door, walked to the couch, and sat down between Andrej and me. She looked up at the TV.

"But what is even happening in their country that they're coming in such large numbers?" she asked quietly. I didn't know if her interest was sincere, as she mostly didn't care about world events, crises, or political discussions. Besides, she was like a sponge—whenever someone shared an opinion about the world with her, she immediately adopted it and took it as absolute truth.

I took a breath, intending to recap what Maks had explained to me a few months ago: "The war in Syria started in 2011 due to protests against the government of Bashar al-Assad—"

"That's oversimplifying," Andrej interrupted me, waving a hand at the TV. "Look at those faces! There are black people among them too, they're full of people from other countries, not just Syria." I stared at his face, not knowing what to say. He looked back at the TV. "Of course I also feel sorry for them being in such a state. But what kind of man goes and leaves his family?"

Urška gave him a blissful look and stroked his knee.

"They want to destroy Europe from within," he added for good measure.

I rolled my eyes but said nothing. I felt that whatever I said, Andrej would deny or ignore it.

10

I got up from the couch and headed into the kitchen to ask Mom if she needed help. Steam was rising from the pots on the stove, and she was leaning against the counter, typing on her phone.

"What are you doing?"

"I'm writing a message to Darja. During mass, I remembered it's her birthday today."

At the mention of Maks's mother, my stomach churned. I realized this conversation would be just as awkward as the one in the living room. As usual, when the subject turned to Darja, Mom asked me, "Do you see Maks at college at all?"

I could have told her I had seen him a few days ago. I rode my bike to college, and as I was locking it to the fence, I saw him standing in front of the entrance with a cigarette in his hand, talking to Gaja and the guy who was the younger brother of a leftist politician. I hoped they wouldn't notice me as I walked by, since I wasn't having one of my best days: the humidity had made my hair frizz so much I looked like I was wearing a sponge on my head, and the skin on my chin was a ruthless map of hormonal imbalance. They saw me when I near, and Maks said hello. I returned a lukewarm greeting and hurried through the door. If he had been alone, we might have said more; I would have asked him how he was and what he was doing there, and he would have asked me the same. But whenever I ran into him when he was with his friends, the conversation between us stalled with awkwardness and uncomfortable silences, so I preferred to avoid it.

But I didn't tell Mom about that. I told her I had last met Maks in September and that he told me he was writing his thesis with Professor Istenič.

"What does he teach again?"

"Social anthropology. He mainly deals with migration." I sat on a chair by the dining table and watched her busy herself with writing the text message. She didn't look up from her phone. She rarely asked me about my studies, and even if she did, it seemed like she was asking just for the sake of it, without being particularly interested.

"When did you and Darja last see each other?" I asked with feigned nonchalance, as if just making small talk.

Maks's mother and mine had been roommates in the student dorms. Among the messy collection of photos taken with an analog camera, which we kept in one of the living room drawers, I had found several photos of them together from their college years. In one, they are sunbathing on a beach in Umag; both have beautiful, tanned, youthful bodies, my mother is petite like me, while Darja has a slender, athletic build. In another photo, they are on a hike in the mountains, dressed in plaid shirts and wearing heavy, unattractive hiking boots, standing by a tree stump eating bread and salami with their hair tied back in ponytails, a bottle of wine between them. Then I found a few more photos of them in their dorm room with their boyfriends; in one, they are holding glasses, and my father's guitar is lying on the bed next to them. In another, they are lying on deckchairs in front of a small house somewhere in the Karst, the weekend cottage owned by Maks's father's family. Then there are some photos from when they already had children: one from a New Year's Eve celebration in Bohinj showing me, Urška, Maks's brother Mitja, and Maks, a scrawny, tiny boy, sitting at a table eating pancakes.

One of the photographs had disappeared from the collection in the drawer. It was a photo of just Maks and me, he was four and I was three, which I knew from the date printed on the back: 1997. In the photo, we are standing in an inflatable pool in front of their weekend house, both naked. My toddler butt is visible because I am turned toward Maks, who is posing for the camera, and his little willy is right in the center of the photo. When I found it, I took it to my room and hid it in the nightstand drawer where I kept the underwear that didn't fit in my wardrobe. It was shame that made me hide the photo in the drawer in which I knew Urška wouldn't rummage through: the fact that Maks and I had once stood next to each other naked and wet in an inflatable pool made me uncomfortable.

Mom didn't look at me when she said that she hadn't met up with Darja for quite a while, as she was opening the oven and examining the chicken roasting inside. I didn't prod her about what "quite a while" meant, but I imagined they had pared down their meetings to about once every two years.

The photo with naked Maks and Maša was one of the few physical photographs of our time together. Later, analog cameras were replaced by digital ones, and we stopped developing photos. Perhaps there were still some from our joint trips or gatherings on my father's computer, but I tried to look for them once and couldn't find a single one. I thought that Dad might have deleted them after our gatherings became less frequent, until they suddenly stopped altogether. Once, when I was still in elementary school, my father told my mother that the Hafners were "Reds." And it wasn't until college that Maks mentioned to me that his father had labeled us "Janšists."[4]

At Mom's instruction I silently began setting the table.

---

4 TN: Janez Janša is a prominent Slovenian right-wing politician.

11

"It seemed to me you weren't too happy about it at rehearsal."

Agata and I were in our usual spots in the classroom at the Academy: she sat at the piano looking at me, while I stood in the middle of the room.

"When?"

"When I assigned you the solo. I've been meaning to mention it for a while now." She looked away, staring at the keys beneath her fingers.

I frowned; I didn't know why she was bringing this up now. A good month had passed since the rehearsal where she chose me as the backup. But it wasn't the first time Agata had dragged something ancient out into the open.

"I'm just the backup."

She looked up from the keys and raised the two thin, dark lines of her eyebrows.

"Backup, Maša? *Backup?*" she snorted. "No one in this choir is a backup, remember that. I don't want any freeloading. If you got a solo, you got a solo."

I massaged my neck, which had been hurting all day. Agata's words confused me. We had been rehearsing Šavli's piece for a month, and Barbara was performing the solo well and convincingly. In vocal technique lessons, Agata and I had focused on individual parts of pieces that were giving us other sopranos trouble, and we hadn't even mentioned Šavli's piece. Besides, I wasn't overly fond of it. Agata claimed it had a primal energy and that she imagined us standing by a bonfire, dressed in white, holding hands and dancing in a circle. Most of the singers agreed, but I found the piece primarily very difficult: it had some very beautiful and harmonious folk chords, but they broke into sort of mournful modern dissonances and at times completely fell apart.

Agata stared at the sheaf of sheet music on the piano and didn't move her gaze, only the furrowed brows on her face testified to her displeasure. I turned my gaze to the mirror standing by the piano. The reflection I saw disappointed me: lusterless hair fell onto a face that was now, in early November, pale from the lack of sun. I sensed I would get my period in a day or two, so my cheeks were gaunt, and my chin was sown with several clearly visible red pimples, as if it were a field of ripening pumpkins. So much time had passed since morning, when I had applied the cheap foundation, that it had worn off my face, and crumbs of mascara that had fallen from my lashes had gathered under my eyes. I noticed a long hair on my black sweater. I picked it off and let it drop, watching it slowly fall to the classroom floor.

"Have you practiced it at all?"

Agata turned to me. Her face was the opposite of mine. There was no trace of dark circles or pimples, on the contrary, it was palely colored with quality foundation, the contours precisely drawn with apricot blush that left a slight sheen, so her face shone luxuriously under the chandelier. Her dark curls were pinned back with a pearl-studded clip that created an impression of timelessness. Draped over her shoulders was a shawl in Parisian blue, its quality texture showing it hadn't been cheap.

I hesitated to answer because I hadn't opened the sheet music at home once. I knew Agata expected us to practice pieces at home, and some loyal singers, my sister among them, stuck to that, while the rest of us quietly complained that we were overburdened with studies or work. I slowly shook my head.

"Let's warm up," Agata commanded and played a few exercises. Once I was warmed up, she ordered me to pick up the piece by Ciril

Šavli, which I didn't have with me. After sighing dramatically, she rummaged through the pile on the piano and handed me a sheaf of sheet music that was covered in writing. At rehearsals, she always emphasized that "diligent singers have marked-up sheet music."

I leafed to the page where the solo began, ignoring the stage fright rising within me.

"First you'll hear this," Agata said, and without noticing I was beginning to panic, she played a few chords so painfully dissonant that it felt like we were in a surrealist film. Then, with a guttural voice coming out of a folk song, she sang: "*If you get closer, I will end you*," she played the next few chords that sounded more harmonious now, "*and I will make you new,* then there's a half-rest, and then it's your turn." She played a bright chord that the singers were supposed to create with different voices, and that was my cue, but I didn't open my mouth.

"Are you going to sing or not?"

"I have no idea where to start," I answered nervously. "I can't hear the pitch I'm supposed to start on. I can't imagine it."

Agata watched me with an impassive expression, then pressed the key for the note I was supposed to sing with her index finger. Compared to the bright chord for the singers, it seemed completely disharmonious.

I started biting my lip. I asked Agata how I was even expected to find that pitch; I apologized for not having such a good ear. In a calm voice, she said: "Once you've practiced it countless times, you'll remember it. Yes, it's a difficult chord, but you'll master it with practice. You don't have to be a trained musician for that."

I massaged my aching neck again. She noticed I was having trouble standing and nodded at a chair by the wall. I went to get it, placed it by the piano, and sat down.

"Just don't panic," I heard her say. "Try again." She played a few chords, and this time I followed her finger as it pressed the right key, to begin uncertainly: "*When the thorny branches sprout,*" my voice was weak, like a lamb just born and bleating blindly, "*I press you to my heart.*" She struck a decisive chord, we were at the very climax of the piece, I should have opened up and sung as if screaming inside: "*If you wounded me to the blood,*" I should have gone into the high notes belonging to the first sopranos at this point, "*only then would I know,*" my voice suddenly cracked on the highest note, breaking, *snap,* like a rubber band stretched too far. I fell silent. I should have finished with the mournful "*who you are,*" but I didn't, and a deafening silence filled the room. From somewhere, the mournful sound of a trombone floated into the classroom.

"Why did you stop?"

Her searching gaze indicated she expected an answer. Hesitantly, I replied that it was because she seemed displeased, and indeed, I saw her frown while I sang. The expression on her face changed in an instant: she rolled her eyes, which relaxed her tense facial muscles, and a tiny smile danced on her lips.

"I really am a little, you know. Not so much because of your singing, but because you are flying blind. Because you haven't even looked at the music, and," she raised her voice when she saw I wanted to protest, "don't pretend. As if you don't have a tuning fork at home, along with a sister who *almost* got into the Academy."

The words cut into the thick atmosphere of the unventilated classroom. Her gaze was anything but predictable; her gray eyes looked at me mischievously, as if they wanted to mock me. She turned back to the piano and pressed a random key with one finger.

"That's why I'm not happy. I constantly invest in you, devote myself to you, work on you, help you, while you girls give nothing back. You act like this is all one big party. But it isn't."

My shoulders slumped. I felt a leaden exhaustion in my body after the long day, and I wanted to go home.

"I sacrifice an enormous amount of my time and energy for this choir," she wouldn't let up, "but I do it only because I'm aware of the incredible potential you have. You know what gets on my nerves the most in this country?"

She looked at me with incisive eyes full of angry vitality. I shook my head.

"Wasted potential. There are so many talented people in Slovenia, and no one notices. Remember when we won in Ptuj? Did anyone write anything about us? Only *Our Choirs* published the news and a short interview with me. Did the national broadcaster ever give us a sniff? Never. You can be a genius, but they won't notice you if you aren't involved in the right things. Just look at Ciril, for example"—she nodded her head toward the sheet music on the stand—"a top-class composer without competition, yet no one gives a damn about him. Or about my husband," she added more quietly, and it seemed to me that her cheeks reddened under the carefully applied foundation.

I gave a short nod, as she cleared her throat and, without looking at me, said, "That's why I'm unhappy. Yes, you are the backup, but I need a determined girl for this piece. Show a little more confidence. It's clear to me you aren't a trained singer, but if you love singing and music, you can sing this. Besides," she looked at me sternly, "I've meant to tell you this several times. If *you* enrolled in solo singing, you would be accepted."

I raised my eyebrows. I wouldn't have thought that about myself. But the look on Agata's face showed otherwise: her eyes had become so soft they looked like two buttons. Then she turned away from me and stared out the window overlooking Upper Square.

"Every voice in the choir is important because it has its own line, which is always *equally* important." She emphasized the word *equally* with a cold sharpness and looked at me. "Does the first soprano often have the leading melody? Yes, it does. But without the other three, it's pathetic. It's nothing. Just a line. The other three voices give it juice. Look at Urška, for example. She's a good first soprano."

The mention of my sister came out of nowhere, but a trace of apology could be detected in her voice, as if she had said something inappropriate earlier with her words about the Academy.

"But you are a good second soprano. A very good second soprano, Maša." I noticed how much warmer her eyes looked because of the Parisian blue shawl. "To me, the second soprano is the most fundamental female voice, without which there is no choir. It is the most capable and adaptable voice. Don't you agree?" I noticed she was smiling faintly. I nodded. Then she grew serious: "I don't know if I can rely on Barbara. She has a one-year-old at home. How do I know she'll stick with it? You *must*, you *must* learn this solo. This piece"—she pointed a finger at Šavli's composition—"is an excellent score, do you understand? We can't mess it up." By the end, her voice was no longer as gentle and encouraging as before. It had taken on her strictness again. When I nodded, she sat back down on the chair and placed her hands on the keys.

"Let's sing it again," she commanded.

She played the dissonance of chords once more. With a gentle, clear hum, she enacted the voices that should be heard on those notes: it sounded utterly uncoordinated, somewhat restless, yet still completely melodious and painfully beautiful. She's right, it struck me, when she performs the piece, it's a first-class score, an exceptional work. Her fingers played the final chord, which, in contrast to the previous ones, was clean, harmonious, and simple. In the middle of this bright chord, I entered: "*When the thorny branches sprout, I press you to my heart*," I sang, and this time my voice was stronger, even though I still couldn't fully utilize it, "*if you wounded me to the blood, only then would I know*"—it sounded good, but I stopped before singing "*who you are*" because I was distracted by a knock on the door. Ivana entered the classroom, smiling cautiously, then she hunched over as if to emphasize that she didn't want to disturb us, walked to the coat rack, and began taking off her coat. I sent her an angry look, but she didn't see it. Her arrival upset me, as we had all agreed to wait outside during a vocal technique. A second ago, I had sensed Agata was pleased with my singing, but this evaporated with Ivana's arrival.

I turned to Agata, who was examining me with a long, expressionless gaze. Her fingers paused on the piano keyboard. Then she gently placed her palms on her thighs, looked straight ahead, and said, "That was much better. Think about what the lyrics mean at home, because I want you to perform it like you understand them. We're done for today."

I went to the coat rack, put on my coat, and shouldered my backpack. I routinely checked my phone: no calls, no messages. I put my earphones in and stowed my phone in my pocket. As I headed to the door and said goodbye, I looked back at them: Ivana was already standing in the same spot I had been, her posture upright, sheet music in hand, reminiscent of armed and ready soldiers guarding besieged tourist attractions. Agata didn't look at me when I said goodbye, she waved a hand in farewell and said, "See you." Only then did I notice that Ivana had curled her dark hair, which now resembled Agata's.

"Bye," I said again and pressed the worn handle.

"Bye," they replied in unison.

12

I was sitting at my desk reading an article for a seminar, Lévi-Strauss's *"The Elementary Structures of Kinship,"* and I was only on the third page when my phone beeped. On the screen, it read:

Maks Hafner

Up for a walk?

Maks and I had exchanged phone numbers when we met at the university information day, after several years of no contact. A few days later, he sent me a message asking if I wanted to meet up. I thought we would sit in a bar somewhere, but we just wandered the streets around my apartment block. We did that again when I became a student two years ago, and since then, we had met for walks here and there, every few weeks or months, depending on the season. We never went out for drinks, we just stuck to the streets near my building, meeting in the evenings, at dusk, walking along familiar paths, never running into anyone we knew. It seemed to me that Maks's friends didn't know we hung out on occasion. I couldn't explain why he met with me, as he never invited me to hang out with his friends and never introduced me to anyone as his friend. Apparently, I wasn't cool enough for that, and although it ate away at me, I did nothing about it.

I looked out the window facing the empty street; a cone of orange light was forming around the streetlamp, illuminating the thick November mist. It was a little past seven in the evening.

I am. At my block in 20 mins?

That was how long he needed to bike from Bežigrad to our building. He replied with a short *ok*, and I got up to get ready. While applying mascara, I wondered when we had last gone for a walk. It had been the end of May, not long after I returned from my exchange. Then we accidentally ran into each other at Metelkova in June, and after that, not again until that exam in September.

I told Mom and Dad, who were watching TV in the living room, that I was going for a walk. I didn't tell them I sometimes met up with Maks, as I didn't know what they would think of it and didn't want to upset them; they only knew I occasionally saw him in college.

When I walked out of the building, Maks was already locking his bike to the rack. He was wearing a black knit beanie and an army-green bomber jacket. When he saw me, he waved, and I returned the greeting.

"Where are we going?"

"How about toward ŽAK?" I nodded, and we set off into the not-too-cold November evening. As we found ourselves among the old villas, we were embraced by the amber silence of the Šiška streets.

"I was just reading about a Slovenian journalist who went to Turkey, illegally crossed the border into Syria, and is now in Kobani, living with the Kurds striving for a sovereign Kurdistan," Maks immediately started on his favourite topic. "That's super interesting to me. I'd go in a heartbeat too, but," his voice faltered slightly, "the conditions are unstable there right now." He looked up at me somewhat unsure, as if to check whether I had registered his lack of courage. I had, but I pretended I hadn't; I nodded and said I agreed. He looked away and added: "Still, I wish this situation with the refugee crisis wouldn't just pass me by."

"What do you mean?"

With a grimace, he admitted, "I feel useless. I was thinking of organizing a series of discussion evenings in college, in our department, about the Syrian war or the refugee crisis, or preparing something about Rojava, given that it's my topic."

"That's a great idea," I said. "What's stopping you?"

Maks dramatically kicked a piece of plastic lying on the sidewalk to the middle of the empty road. He chased after it and kicked it again, sending it onto the sidewalk across the street, then returned to me and we walked on. I felt a slight revulsion toward him; he suddenly appeared childish. Without answering, he asked, "Yeah? Would you be interested?"

"Totally. You know I don't know much about these things, and I really should learn a little more."

"I'll send you an interview with David Graeber, an anthropologist and activist who published an important article on this topic in *The Guardian* last October."

"Okay." Every so often, Maks would send me something that spoke to him. Usually, these were articles about the Middle East, but also unrelated things, something by Said, Chomsky, Foucault, Benjamin, Varoufakis. Although I could barely wrap my head around their texts, either because I didn't understand them or because they bored me, I always read them thoroughly.

We could already see the distant lights of the stadium shining at the end of the street when Maks said, "Anyway, we were talking about this with Gaja. We were thinking of organizing a series of live discussions together, with invited guests. Maybe a symposium. I mentioned something to Istenič the other day, and he thought it was a good idea."

"Is she interested in this stuff too?" I asked feebly. I was surprised that he didn't answer at once; instead, he made a sort of diffident sound and then admitted that actually, she wasn't really, and that they had discussed it more by chance.

For a few painfully long moments, we walked on in silence. I was disappointed that Maks hadn't asked me to help him, but was forging plans with that vain girl who had her family's privileges to thank for seventy percent of her success and beautiful appearance. I imagined her mother taking her to protocol events, the theater, and concerts from a young age, dressing her in beautiful clothes. While I was growing up, we didn't get newspapers at home, politics was something for adults, and we didn't attend cultural events with my family; school was responsible for my entire cultural education. Maks and I had discussed the Middle East many times, but I often remained silent, not knowing what to say, afraid of embarrassing myself, so I just listened. Gaja, although I didn't know her, seemed different: confidence, including the intellectual kind, surrounded her like a halo.

"But why would you organize it with her then?" I asked him, full of bitterness.

He thought for a moment, then explained, "I asked her if she would moderate. She already has some experience with hosting, she knows how to act in front of an audience, her mom is a journalist." He threw that last part out casually, needlessly. All of us who knew Gaja knew whose daughter she was. "It would look more professional than if I did it. And she's cute."

Although my knees went weak, I snorted loudly and rolled my eyes.

"I can't believe you said something so stupid," I said, angry. "You'd let her lead the discussion because she's cute and because her last name's recognisable?" I looked at him with indignation, and he gave an obnoxious laugh and shrugged, as if to say, what's wrong with that?

"While we're at it, your last name isn't negligible either." Maks's face darkened, and I was about to say I was just joking when a train sped past us at high speed. We were walking near the tracks. When the street fell silent again, his face was still serious, and I decided it was best to change the subject.

"You know what I noticed?"

We crossed the tracks. Ahead of us, the outlines of the illuminated, empty stadium were emerging from the mist.

"What?"

"Whenever we talk about global topics, you share theories, list facts, and quote great thinkers." He nodded, as if to say, of course, what else? "When we talk about the Middle East, you always start explaining things like the Arab Spring, the Islamic State, Gaddafi, jihadism... things like... the revolution in Rojava, Kurdistan, Israel, Palestine... America, Russia." We looked at each other and laughed at the endless list of typical Maks topics. He nodded and said: "Logical. And?"

"And now about the refugee crisis... You immediately drag politics and religion into it, you theorize, talk about leaders, conflicts, revolutions."

I paused to gather my thoughts and sighed. I had indeed thought about this before, but inside my head, such thinking was safe. Now it seemed it might sound stupid. He opened the stadium gate, and we stepped onto the field.

"It's the male view of the world, do you understand?" I knew I was walking a fine line. I was afraid my point would become shallow by introducing gender.

"No, actually, I don't understand."

I let out a barely audible breath and said, "Look at this situation, for example. When a crisis happens, men always... *manage* facts, theories, and ideologies. You, for example, although it might not be such a bad idea," I wanted to soften my words, "want to organize a series of discussion evenings or, you know, a symposium."

We walked along the red running track.

"And what's wrong with that?" he asked, somewhat irritated.

"There's absolutely nothing wrong with it, but... You just think that your knowledge of a situation that's happening, I don't know, three thousand kilometers away, in a world you don't even know or understand, that this will solve something, change something." I noticed his eyebrows draw together under the glow of the stadium floodlights, but he said nothing.

"And because of that... And also because of a conversation I was part of the other day with my father and Andrej, which was diametrically opposed to what you're saying but still somehow similar... because of that conversation, it hit me that men," I continued, uncomfortably aware that the very noun for the crucial thought I wanted to develop sounded questionable, "think problems are solved with ideas." It wasn't what I wanted to say, so I hurriedly continued. "Or rather, you think the problem lies in ideology. That difficult situations are solved on a macro level, that for them to be solved, one must change the world, society, the worldview. That it's the politicians who are holding all the strings. It feels like you keep forgetting about the real people involved. About the lives, human lives, of these people who have someone waiting and fearing for them somewhere. People who have left their loved ones, lost them in conflicts, and, for example, women, enormous numbers of women, who don't necessarily even want to live in Europe, just, you know... in a better world." Maks nodded briefly, but seeing him still stubbornly pressing his lips together, I added, "Sometimes it seems to me that men think more... globally. But not everything is global. Most of the time, things unfold on a private, intimate level."

"What do you mean, global?"

I sighed and thought for a moment.

"Well... It seems to me that you keep relying on knowledge, history, and facts, while ignoring people's actual stories and feelings. You solve problems in a way that makes them unmanageable. In fact, you don't even solve them, just complicate them further."

"But the problems are in fact unmanageable."

"Sure, but when something like the refugee crisis happens, you immediately start discussing who is to blame and why, you talk about nations, states, and territories, about money and weapons. You bring in politics, religion, wars, and leaders. I'm not saying it isn't all connected, but you don't talk about the actual victims. You don't say 'women and children,' but 'civilians.' When you see a city that was destroyed, you don't think about people losing their homes, you opine on who did it and what should be done with them."

I saw Maks bite his lip. I feverishly thought about how to untangle myself from what I was saying.

"What I wanted to say is," I took a breath and stopped in my tracks, "that your symposium idea doesn't seem bad to me, but at the moment, I don't think it's necessarily the right decision."

Maks also stopped, and looked me straight in the eye; he was only a few centimetres taller than me.

"And what, in your opinion, is the right decision?"

I shifted nervously, and looked up at the umber sky above us. In the countryside, stars might be visible now, whereas in Ljubljana in November, there was only the persistent fog, illuminated here at the stadium by floodlights.

"I don't know, I was thinking... Now that you're on your extra year and have no lectures," I lowered my gaze and looked at him, "you could go to the border."

His eyes widened, and he whistled softly. "As a volunteer?"

I nodded. Now he too stared at the sky, and I watched his Adam's apple pause.

"I thought that—"

"That's not a bad idea," he interrupted without looking at me. "That's not a bad idea at all." He lowered his gaze, and our eyes met for a long, blissful moment. Just then, his phone beeped. He took it out of his pocket, and I glanced at the screen, where a green box with the name *Gaja Meden* appeared. Before he put it back without replying to the message, I caught the words on the screen: *What about tomorrow?*

"What does Gaja want?" I asked with feigned indifference, and he waved his hand, then pulled out a pack of cigarettes from the other pocket. He always said he smoked rarely, only with friends, on Friday nights, at parties, and when he was nervous. He also claimed he wanted to quit. He cupped his hand over the cigarette to light it. He blew out the first puff of smoke with a glass-eyed look into empty space, furrowing his brow.

"I can't say I completely agree with what you said earlier." He tapped the ash off the cigarette, dropped it to the ground, and crushed it with his sneaker. I stared at it in astonishment, as I had never seen someone discard a freshly lit cigarette so quickly.

"But I will definitely," he signaled toward the stadium gate to indicate he wanted to head back home, "think about your suggestion."

13.

It was mid-November when I walked through Foerster Garden and heard someone calling my name. The Ljubljana fog had cleared for a few days, so it was bright, even warm, and students were lounging at tables in front of the cafés. In the pale sunshine, I saw Sara and that other guy from the Linguistic Anthropology exam. It took me a few moments to remember his name—Blaž. Sara was waving and calling out to me. I walked over, and she asked if I wanted to join them. Scattered on the table in front of them were sheets covered in writing and a spiral-bound notebook.

"What are you two up to?"

"Reviewing for a midterm. We're taking it this afternoon," Sara answered, beginning to clear the notes from the table, "but I can't memorize anything new anyway, so sit down."

I sat down. When the waiter came, I ordered a cappuccino, and Sara placed her knitted pouch on the table and started rolling a cigarette.

"I was just telling Blaž about the choir when you showed up in the park," she said, filling the rolling paper with tobacco. "He said he can't imagine me singing in a choir at all. In his opinion, I'm not... What did you say? *Polished enough.*" She smirked. Blaž also smiled and nodded, then took off his unattractive glasses and went at them with a blue cloth.

"What did you mean by that?" I asked him, and he shrugged, without looking up from his glasses. Then he said, "I just feel like choir singing is..."

"I know what you're going to say. You think it's boring."

He looked at me with indignation and shook his head. Before he put his glasses back on, I noticed he looked quite handsome without them.

"Not at all. That's not what I wanted to say, just that choir singing feels unusual in Sara's case because she sings in a band and doesn't seem like the type of person who would stand on stage in a concert dress and sing," he rattled off apologetically. "Come on, am I wrong?" he added a little louder, spreading his arms in defense, and the two of us laughed and nodded.

Silence fell over the table, and the smile on my face faded. The adjective Blaž had supposedly used was swirling around in my head: polished. To sing in a choir, a women's choir, you must be *polished*. Cultured. It struck me that Blaž had only tried to dress up what he really wanted to say: that, in his opinion, Sara didn't belong in a choir because she wasn't *well-behaved* enough. She wasn't obedient enough. Compliant. She didn't know how to submit. She wasn't humble enough, docile enough. Discomfort must have shown on my face because Sara asked me if everything was okay.

"I was reminded of something," I said coolly, without showing how I really felt, taking a sip of the coffee the waiter had brought me and setting the cup back on the saucer. Sara watched me expectantly as she lit her cigarette.

I leaned back in my chair and began to recount: "My sister said something like that to me when I started high school. She was in her fourth year then and sang in the girls' choir."

"She told you choir singing was boring?" Sara asked in surprise. I shook my head.

"Not that. What Blaž said. About being polished."

In September of my first year of high school, I told them, we were allowed to attend rehearsals of all three school choirs, mixed, boys', and girls'. You could get into a choir only if you passed an audition.

"Urška, my sister, who sang in the girls' choir, insisted I come to their rehearsal. I only went because she pestered me so much. I absolutely didn't want to sing in the girls' choir."

They asked why not, and I replied that it seemed boring to me.

"Wherever they performed, they were the best, but the choir had a reputation for being full of goody-two-shoes. They preferred to take the straight-A students because they knew such girls were willing to work. I was annoyed by that. I didn't want to be like my sister and her friends; I felt like I didn't belong among them." Sara and Blaž nodded with understanding, and I drank a little more coffee.

"I wanted to sing in the mixed choir. I heard they had a lot of fun—that they partied, went out, stayed up late. There were even rumors that their conductor was much more lenient than the girls' choir conductor and allowed the boys and girls to sleep together on tours. Which turned out to be untrue," I added quickly when Blaž chuckled.

"And what happened then?" Sara blew out a cloud of blue-grey smoke.

"I went to their rehearsal," I continued the story. "Urška was so excited. The visitors, even some curious boys, sat in the back, behind the singers. I was watching the girls, and they really got on my nerves, they were so calm, waiting for the conductor on their chairs. The rehearsal was the polar opposite of the mixed choir's rehearsal—they were focused, in tune from the outset. The mixed choir wasn't bad either, but they were constantly fooling around."

Blaž and Sara listened to me completely still, as if they had taken on the character of the chorists from my story. Sara put her cigarette in the ashtray. Their empty coffee cups glowed in the morning sun.

"They warmed up, spending an eternity setting up chords to sound perfect. Then they picked up the sheet music. They were preparing for an important competition abroad. Anyway, they began to sing, I still remember the song. Arvo Pärt, *Zwei Beter*. A brilliant piece. I'll send it to you," I nodded to Sara. "So, they began, but not from the beginning. Apparently, they were having severe trouble with one of the harder parts, I still remember which, because I later learned it from my sister's sheet music."

I cleared my throat, thought a little, and then, in a subdued, slow voice, sang from memory the part of the piece that had captivated me at the rehearsal. As I sang, I was overcome by the feeling that everything around me had gone quiet, that the students at the neighboring tables had fallen silent, that even the gentle breeze in the treetops had paused, and the leaves had stopped rustling. I realized the students at the next table were casting glances my way; I fell silent and felt blood rush to my cheeks.

Sara picked up her cigarette from the ashtray and took a drag, while Blaž looked at me with slight admiration.

"Anyway," I continued in a serious tone, "I realized how good they were. I went to their audition and hoped to be accepted." They waited for the epilogue in silence. I picked up my cup and emptied it in sips, Sara asked impatiently: "And?"

"They didn't accept me. I got into the mixed choir. I went there for two months, then I quit. I didn't like it." I put the cup on the table and leaned back in my chair. Blaž pursed his lips in sympathy, and Sara sighed.

"What I wanted to say is... Even though I didn't tell her I was disappointed, Urška told me she didn't think they'd take me anyway. 'You just don't seem like the right person for our choir,' she said. I asked her what she meant by that, and she said she thought I was too wild." I laughed, then grew serious when I saw Sara raising her eyebrows. "They won that competition abroad. They were very good and worked hard."

"Were you disappointed for long?" Sara wanted to know, bringing what was left of her cigarette to her mouth. Compared to Maks, who was wasteful with his smokes, she was very frugal.

I thought about it, then shook my head.

"No. I was just asking myself if I would be a different person if I sang with them. I went to one of their concerts, and afterward people were saying how good, beautiful, refined, gentle they were. I heard people say: 'How good these *girlies* are.' They weren't little girls anymore, but the image clung to them, of a sort of pristineness, innocence." I felt like I was talking too much, the caffeine had loosened my tongue. "Well, after I became friends with some of them, I realized that not everyone in the choir was like that. It was true mostly of the first sopranos." I laughed at this, but to myself; as if I had told a joke that only I understood, while they remained silent.

"It's strange that you weren't accepted," Blaž spoke up, "because your voice is really beautiful."

"Thanks, although... It doesn't mean I didn't sing well enough. It just means they didn't need my vocal colour in that lineup," I explained. He nodded, then pulled up the sleeve of his grey cardigan, looked at his wristwatch, and frowned.

"It's getting late," he announced, "my lecture starts in a few minutes." He stood up and said he hoped we wouldn't mind him leaving just like that, and when we shook our heads, he pulled a five-euro bill from his wallet, solemnly declared "Allow me," and placed it on the table. Neither of us resisted, and we exchanged a glance revealing we were on the verge of laughter.

"Oh, I totally forgot," he said, having already shouldered his backpack. "Are you coming today?" The question was directed at me. I didn't know what he was referring to, so I asked him in surprise:

"Where?"

"To the anthropologists' freshman party."

I said that I had seen it was today, but that we had choir practice in the evening. Sara snorted and said: "Rehearsal ends at half past nine. You can be at the party in thirty minutes. Surely you won't miss it because of rehearsal. Don't be a goody-two-shoes," she added, blushing at her awkward joke.

"Where is it?"

"We're meeting in front of the college at ten and going to Etaža together."

I sighed. The freshman party in my first year was a boring affair. I kept waiting for Maks to show up, but he didn't. I went home before midnight.

"Do I need a ticket?"

Blaž reached into his backpack and pulled out a stack of tickets wrapped in a rubber band. He unwrapped it, tore off a ticket, and held it out to me. I asked him how much it cost. He waved his hand and said not to tell anyone, winked at me, then placed the ticket on the table. I thanked him, even though I wasn't sure if I would go. He said goodbye to us one more time, turned around, and headed down the path toward the college.

14

"He's so kind," I said after Blaž had left our table. I waited for Sara to say something, but she just smiled and gave a curt nod. She crushed her cigarette butt in the ashtray and began rolling another one. For a few moments, we sat in silence.

"Maks once told me Blaž is a sexist," I blurted out, worried the silence between us would last too long. Only after it was said did I realize I wasn't sure if Maks had really said that about Blaž, and at the same time, it struck me that whatever Maks had said, it would have been wiser to keep it from Sara. Indeed, she pursed her lips in disapproval.

"I wouldn't say he's a sexist," she finally said, somewhat agitated, striking her lighter and taking a drag. "Knowing Maks, he's quick to say things about others. In my opinion, you can't just label someone a sexist because of a couple of weird statements."

"What kind of statements?"

She told me Blaž had once claimed that a certain professor in our department got the job because she slept with her mentor.

"It was said more in jest, but it still seemed like he believed what he was saying. I also got the feeling he isn't aware of the weight of his words. The other day he was telling me about a colleague of his, also an anthropologist, who wants to do her PhD at some American university, but she's worried because they don't have a class on statistics in anthropology at the Faculty of Arts, and she would need it there. And to that, he said that he doesn't know how she'll cope with it because she's *too blonde* to grasp statistics."

I gasped to show my horror, but at the same time, I was slightly pleased. I knew that this was about Gaja, since Maks had once mentioned she intended to continue her studies in America, and in truth, I agreed with Blaž that she wasn't smart enough for it. But I would tell him that Gaja's parents were too important to let her intellectual mediocrity stop her from succeeding.

Sara, not noticing my pretense, continued: "And a few days ago, when the subject turned to the referendum on the Family Law,"[5]—I nervously cleared my throat, as I was sick of talking about the topic that had recently overshadowed even the refugee crisis—"he also confided that he personally thinks it's wiser to preserve the family with a father and a mother, and that while he doesn't oppose same-sex marriage, he finds gender theory problematic. If you ask me," she added, disregarding my unease, "it's actually brave to admit that."

"Why?"

She didn't look at me, she was dreamily watching the people walking past us, and after a short pause, she said, "Because he isn't the only one who thinks that way, he is just one of the few who dares to say it out loud."

I thought she would say more, but she didn't. She shifted her gaze and met mine; her green eyes flashed spryly, and she smiled. I had already noticed that she was very beautiful when she smiled: she had a row of straight white teeth, and her lips were the color of ripe cherries. The light lashes framing her always slightly and lazily half-closed eyes were very long and would probably look stunning applied with mascara. But she didn't use makeup.

Her smile wasn't the mocking kind, it didn't seem to want to challenge or upset me. On the contrary—during breaks at rehearsals, when we talked, I had often seen her smile like this: she usually did

---

5 TN: A contentious public vote on the legalisation of same-sex marriage in Slovenia, taking place on December 20th, 2015.

it when she got lost in thought or had said something that might be uncomfortable for the listener. It seemed as if she was using it to connect with the person she was speaking to, as she otherwise always seemed somewhat detached.

"I learned this from my mother," she said. Her bangs had been a bit too long lately and kept getting in her eyes, and she first swept them off her face, then began to recount.

"My mom is a translator. From Polish and Russian. I don't know if she was ever really an ordinary person, but before she and my father split up, she lived a pretty normal life, I think. She had me at thirty-one; she had been married to Bine for two years by then. She worked at the journal *Dnevnik*, proofreading, because she couldn't find something more suitable with her education. Then, in a single year when she was thirty-seven, two things happened: she and Bine split up, and she lost her job."

I had gotten used to this about her too: she didn't waste words, but when she wanted to tell you something, she took all the time in the world.

"It wasn't an easy time for us. After Bine left—he went to Africa to shoot a documentary—we sold our apartment and moved into a smaller one. Mom looked for work everywhere, before they finally offered her something. She got a commission from a Christian publishing house to translate a long essay from Russian by Semyon Frank. *The Meaning of Life*. You know it?"

I shook my head, blushing. Whenever someone asked me if I knew a work I was hearing about for the first time, I was embarrassed. I thought Sara would say something about the author and his book, but she went on: "I was little, but I remember that period vividly. Coming home from school, she would be sitting at the computer, staring at those mysterious little letters on the screen, devotedly working on them. She got so into it that she sometimes forgot to ask me about my homework. She often sent me to her sister's, so I just had dinner there and played with Ivana until late, until my aunt's husband drove me home, where I found her still behind the computer dealing with that text. I think the translation needed to be done quickly, and although the book is short, that period felt as long as eternity."

She brought the cigarette to her mouth, lit it, took a drag, and then somewhat inconsiderately blew smoke toward me, as if she had forgotten I was there. Her face disappeared in the haze for a moment, and I coughed. She apologized and continued: "The publishing house was very satisfied with the translation, and she soon got a contract for a new one. To this day, she has translated several prominent Russian theologians and philosophers. Berdyaev, Solovyov, Shestov, and the like. She got so into it that the publisher let her decide which Russian philosophy and theology book to publish next. While they weren't on board with her every proposal, she devoted her days to these texts: if she wasn't translating them, she was reading them or searching for new ones."

I tried to read the emotions flooding Sara as she recalled these memories. I looked for a trace of pain because her mother, with whom she was left alone, had neglected her for some Russian religious texts, but Sara's pale face showed none of it, it glowed as she told the story.

"The texts changed Mom. She played Orthodox chants while she was cooking. She read the Bible every evening. She got rid of all of Bine's books and stopped watching TV, even movies. She changed inwardly too, she was calmer, she didn't get angry at me anymore, and she did most things alone. She cut off contact with a longtime friend. Her friend had a daughter my age and we used to hang out, but after that, we never saw each other again."

My ears turned hot, but she kept talking. She said that she got along well with her mom, that they never had problems, and that although she was steeped in spirituality, she didn't force it on Sara. During the May Day holidays, when Sara was already in high school, she left her with her aunt and went on a pilgrimage to Ukraine, where she met a man her age. When she returned from the pilgrimage, she hung an icon she had bought at a monastery above her bed. That summer, Bine—I knew by now that he was Sara's father—stopped by for a visit. After years of living in Africa, he was moving to Berlin and had come for his things.

"I remember he saw that icon and started teasing her. 'Do you seriously believe in these fairy tales? I thought you were smarter than that.' She didn't show that he had hurt her, but then, before he left, he said, 'Good thing I didn't want to get married in church, otherwise you'd have nothing but problems before God now.' The door closed behind him, and she broke down. She started crying, and I hugged her and told her to forget what he said, that he was a jerk and so on. Mom hadn't said anything bad about him to me in all those years. And then she said something that really made me think. 'You know, Sara, your father never wanted to understand that our hearts weren't alike. My heart is distinctly theistic, no matter how he tried to force his convictions on me.'"

She fell silent. She hadn't brought the cigarette to her mouth for some time, as if she had forgotten about it. I thought she had finished the story when she suddenly asked me: "Remember when you told me the other day that your parents opposed your choice of study?" I nodded.

"My mom wasn't thrilled about my decision to study sociology either, but she said she trusted me. She said she thought I would realize on my own that we are ruled by an intellectual single-mindedness, imposing certain views and personas which are supposedly best suited to interpret Western society. And in a way, she was right. That's why I said that about Blaž earlier. I don't think it's right that Maks labeled him a sexist."

The cigarette between her fingers went out. She placed the butt on the little pile of ash in the ashtray and stared at it.

"But your mom probably never said anything like what Blaž said about anyone," I frowned. Sara, still staring at the cigarette butt, nodded.

"That's true. But what I wanted to say is that sometimes people say and do things because it's built into their nature. That doesn't mean they're bad or deserve to be portrayed as such. Maybe they just don't know any other way. Blaž isn't from the same environment as Maks, and he might not even be aware that some things coming out of his mouth sound problematic. Maks could understand that. But he just lacks the insight."

Concerning this point, I could have told Sara I agreed. Maks viewed everything through the prism of narrow intellectualism, into which he often couldn't incorporate what Sara was telling me about—the stories of individuals. He could list anecdotes from books, but he couldn't truly see a person. He lacked that ability. But I stayed quiet—I didn't want to continue talking about Maks. I thought of something else: "What about that man your mom met on the pilgrimage? Are they still together?"

Sara smiled mysteriously and took a few long moments before answering.

"They are in a sort of platonic relationship. They went on two more pilgrimages together: to Częstochowa and to Israel. They still meet up, but I've never seen them... doing anything. I mean, physically, of course."

I frowned and said that maybe they were just friends. But Sara shook her head resolutely: "No. They love each other. I'm certain."

"How do you know?"

She looked at me, and I could see she was biting the inside of her lip. Then she asked me, laughing: "So you think it's necessary for two people to sleep together for a romantic relationship?"

No one had ever asked me a question like that, and it didn't seem possible to answer "no," but Sara asked it with such confidence that I just stared at her in astonishment. She smiled at me, the same way as before. Although I had known her for a good two months now, I still couldn't quite read her. We often talked during breaks at rehearsals when she would come sit next to me on her own accord. I often chose my words carefully, trying not to say anything thoughtless, and fearing she would shut me down to show me I had no business discussing things I didn't know enough about. But her retorts were often unexpected. She resisted any simplifications and hasty conclusions. And although she was always telling stories that supported her claims, she revealed surprisingly little about herself.

I felt slightly cold. The sun that had been shining on our table disappeared behind the clouds. I picked up the ticket Blaž had left for me from the table.

Sara asked, "Will you go?"

I shrugged. I asked her if she thought we could buy tickets at the venue. She said that would almost certainly be possible, but that I already had one anyway.

"I'll go if you go with me," I winked at her. Sara laughed and fell silent for a moment, then said, "If you really want me to come, I'll go."

15

After the choir rehearsal, we walked towards the college. The further we moved away from the hall, the more cheerful we became, and the heaviness of the conversation we'd had over coffee evaporated. It was a cold evening, and I was shivering in my trench coat, but the excitement was keeping me warm. When we arrived at the building, small groups of students were already loitering in front of the entrance, sending forth loud and disorderly chatter, like we were approaching a beehive. The air was murky with cigarette smoke, and a broken bottle lay on the asphalt between the groups, with red wine spilled all around it. In one of the groups, I saw Blaž holding an empty plastic cup. Gaja was standing next to him, pouring drinks.

We approached them, avoiding the red stain on the ground, and I tugged on Blaž's sleeve. When he turned to me, he smiled, then looked at Sara with surprise. She told him I wouldn't have come without her, so he took off his backpack and started rummaging through it to sell her a ticket.

"What will you have?" Gaja asked, with a bottle of vodka in her left hand and orange juice in her right. I was stunned by how much she resembled Taylor Swift: wheat-colored hair fell softly down her back, framing a cute face, and her blue eyes were heavily made up, just like the singer's. Everything about me, from my straight chestnut hair to the trench coat I had bought at Bershka the previous autumn, felt ugly and cheap. What disheartened me most was Gaja's lovely black Tommy Hilfiger bag slung over her shoulder, while I had a backpack with my sheet music folder inside stuck on mine. I was unsettled by Gaja's resemblance to the famous singer. Because Taylor Swift was so popular, I honestly wanted to like her too. I acknowledged her undeniable talent and brilliant career, but her music made me feel nothing: I couldn't identify with the lyrics, and the melodies didn't move me.

Gaja set the drinks down on the low wall by the college entrance, pulled two plastic cups from a wrapper, and held them out to us.

"Vodka? Jäger?" she asked somewhat impatiently, as I couldn't decide. Sara picked Coke with Jäger, and I said I'd have the same. Gaja turned toward a cluster of older students and called Maks. He extricated himself from the group, holding a bottle of Jäger in one hand and a Coke in the other. When he saw us, his lips formed a surprised o.

"What are you doing here? Did you come with Maša?" He awkwardly extended his arms toward Sara, who returned a clumsy hug; he couldn't really embrace her with his hands full. Watching their unwieldy hug, I realized I hadn't asked Sara if she and Maks had been good friends in high school or if they still hung out. He had never mentioned her to me, and earlier over coffee, she had spoken about him with considerable sharpness in her voice. Gaja, meanwhile, had already disappeared among the students.

Sara confirmed she was with me and that we were coming from the rehearsal—he said I had already told him that we sang in the choir together, then tepidly added he thought that was great.

"Sara was always up to something I would never guess was her thing," he remarked with a smile meant for me, then looked at his former classmate, who smiled with restraint. I didn't know what to say, and neither did they.

"So, you two are colleagues?" Sara finally asked and took a sip of the Jäger-Cola Maks had poured for her. We looked at each other and nodded. Did Sara mean "friends"? Or just students studying at the same department? Gaja called Maks from the other end of the venue, and her voice cut through the thick tension swirling among the three of us. He nodded at us then vanished into the crowd.

"How do you know each other again?" Sara asked me as I tilted my glass. Swallowing, I grimaced: the mixture Maks had prepared was quite strong and definitely contained more Jäger than Coke. Her eyes were examining me inquisitively, and I didn't know why.

"Our moms were roommates in the student dorms during college... And good friends."

"Are they not anymore?"

I hesitated: "Um... They see each other occasionally. More rarely than they used to. But we used to be quite close." I took another sip and added: "When I was little, we spent a lot of time at their weekend house in the Karst."

"Oh my god, I was there once! It's so beautiful there," Sara shouted so loudly I felt like telling her to keep it down so Maks, who was lingering nearby, wouldn't hear us. Instead, I quietly asked her when, and to my relief she regained her composure: "We celebrated Maks's eighteenth birthday there. He invited, I don't know, a third of the entire grade. But it wasn't fun," she added quickly when she saw my feigned enthusiasm. "His brother and his buddies did something... Hm, something stupid. Or rather, I don't know if the others even noticed that Maks wasn't okay with it... You probably haven't heard anything about it, did you?"

"About what?" I blinked at her. Sara gnawed on the rim of her plastic cup for a few moments before answering.

"It was stupid. They hired a stripper for his present." I gave a weak laugh, but I read from the serious expression on her face that it wasn't funny. I asked her what happened, and drank some more.

"He was drunk and probably high, but... He was sitting on a chair in the middle of the living room, a huge crowd from our school was thronging around, everyone was watching, loud music was playing in the background, and she was writhing all over him. She was Slovakian or something. Well, and you know what Maks is like, right? You know... He's a bit on the scrawny side." I nodded. I caught him out of the corner of my eye, standing with a small group of first-year students, pouring them drinks and chatting; he was the same height as most of the girls in the group, with two even taller than him.

"The whole thing looked kind of grotesque. Besides... I don't know how to explain it to you. I'm not saying Maks is like a saint or anything. But he wasn't okay with it, it was written all over his face. He was sitting there completely motionless, numb, and when she stopped jiggling with her tits, he got up and disappeared for a while. His brother and his buddies were dying of laughter. Then they teased him all night that he was gay." Sara grimaced, and I emptied my cup. The scene with eighteen-year-old Maks danced before my eyes. I saw him sitting on a chair in that house, the interior of which I faintly remembered, while a sexy stripper wriggled in his lap and shoved her swollen breasts into his teenage face. Gaja drifted by, and I asked her to pour me some vodka with Red Bull. Sara was watching me, probably waiting for me to say something, but when I kept quiet, she said: "I got worried you'd be upset because you weren't invited back then, but as you can see, you didn't miss much."

My mouth was full of drink, so I just waved my hand. Then I swallowed and told her that we hadn't been hanging out anymore by then anyway. She raised her eyebrows, and I explained that when I was twelve, our families had drifted apart.

"Drifted apart? In what way?"

I sighed wistfully, then told her that the opinions of our parents had started to diverge.

"Toward the end, very few gatherings passed without tension. It was mostly our fathers who couldn't get along. They'd have a few drinks, they'd start with the politics, and at some point it just blew up. Basically..." The expression on Sara's face was saying she didn't fully understand, so I was direct: "Maks's parents are staunch leftists. And mine just aren't."

That was a white lie. If I were to be completely truthful, I wouldn't have said "my parents aren't staunch leftists," but would have told her they were staunchly right wing.

Sara nodded with understanding: "When they were young, those differences probably weren't so apparent, but then became more so."

I nodded and took another sip, and she smiled mysteriously. I lifted my free hand, poked her in the shoulder, and asked her what she was smiling at. My hand fell heavily to my side.

"Nothing, just... Before, it felt like I sensed something between you two. Some tension. At first, I thought you liked each other, but now that you've told me the background, I understand."

A wave of heat washed over me, and it seemed the world around me was becoming slightly blurred. I couldn't remember when I had last eaten.

"Oh no, we're just friends," I said, feigning I was at ease, and took another sip without looking at her. "Sometimes we even meet up. But purely as friends. I mean, there was never anything..." The words died in my throat, and I stared at the bubbles in my cup. I took another sip and couldn't stop myself: "Except once, when I was at the exchange, he sent me... Wait. I'll show you." I reached into the pocket of my trench coat, in which I was shivering just a moment ago, but now I felt a pleasant warmth flooding my body. I reached into the wrong pocket, which was empty, so I switched the cup to the other hand and pulled out my phone, which was stone cold. I opened the Facebook Messenger app and, with the letters dancing in front of my eyes, searched for Maks's name. What I was looking for was at the very bottom of the messages, as we almost never wrote to each other on Facebook.

"He sent me this on my birthday." I showed Sara the sticker that I had racked my brains over for weeks afterward. It was actually ugly: one of those crude big-headed wrestlers, only this one was blowing a kiss with his hand, with little hearts floating in the air. Sara's green eyes stared at the screen, then at me, and it was clear she didn't know what to say to this nonsense. I became embarrassed and put the phone back in my pocket, while she bit her lip.

"Hard to say anything about that," she was finally sincere, and I gave a weak smile. Luckily, a second-year student stood at the top of the stairs just then and shouted that we were moving to Etaža, so we joined the others and went towards the club.

Once we got there, outside the entrance, Sara struck up a conversation with a student I didn't know, and I heard her say she was named after Sarajevo, where her parents had met. We were interrupted by Blaž, who appeared beside me with his hands full. He poured vodka and orange juice into my empty cup, then set the bottles on the ground and looked at me.

"I was in a hurry earlier when we had coffee," he began, taking off his glasses again and wiping them with a cloth, "but I'm glad you convinced Sara to come." He planted the glasses back on his nose, and in an instant, turned unattractive again. His hair was cut short, and perhaps he would look better with just a slightly more modern haircut and a different frame. Also, in different clothes. He was wearing a generic blue puffer jacket and repulsive corduroy trousers. I noticed that the layer of blue paint had chipped off the metal buttons on his jacket. Behind him, I spotted Maks's dark green bomber jacket, for which—I had looked it up in an online store—he had shelled out over two hundred euros.

"What voice do you sing in the choir?" he then surprised me by asking. He added that they were learning about female voices in the ethno-music practicum just last week. I told him I sang second soprano.

"Except in church," I said. "I used to sing in the parish youth choir, and there they let me sing first soprano." I emptied my cup; I preferred vodka with orange juice to vodka with Red Bull. Blaž just nodded, and I continued: "First soprano is my favorite voice. My sister, for instance, sings first soprano. And I always find what they sing, their melody, basically, the most beautiful. But I simply can't sing that high and... And Agata placed me in the second sopranos. It's fine, she says it's an extremely important voice. But the first soprano is... It has this... Feminine character, you know?" I stopped, realizing I was babbling. I felt my cheeks burn from the heat and the alcohol. I caught Maks's gaze; he was standing in one of the small groups looking toward Blaž and me. When our eyes met, he looked away without giving any indication that he had seen me. I looked back at Blaž and sensed him observing me closely.

"Who is Agata?"

Her image appeared before my eyes. I got the feeling that a random woman dressed in a black coat, walking past the bar just then, resembled her.

"Our conductor," I said. "She is... probably the greatest musician I know. Her and Lana Del Rey."

It was as if the words I had spoken caught up with me a moment later, and I laughed out loud, and Blaž, surprisingly, laughed with me.

I apologized and said I had to go to the restroom. I shoved my empty cup into his hands and headed into the club.

Walking through the venue blasting loud music, it felt like the world around me was becoming softer and the people milling around slightly blurred. I was filled with a pleasant feeling of lightness. I pushed past the figures to the restroom door, which closed behind me with a loud crack, muffling the sounds from the club. I shut myself in one of the stalls, sat on the toilet, and sensed the world spinning slightly around me.

Then I heard the door open, and the space filled with female voices. It sounded as if they were talking over one another, something I was used to, listening to this weaving of voices constantly at choir practice. Then the conversation died down, and a loud sigh was heard, followed by words cutting into the light beaming from the flickering bulbs: "How can you and Maks hook up so casually? I couldn't handle it."

I hunkered down in the stall, where the light had now gone out because I hadn't moved in a while. My heart beat painfully. I heard another voice reply and recognized Gaja: "It's not casual. We agreed it would be like this for a while because, well, after that thing with Vid, I'm not ready for anything serious, and he also says this suits him perfectly at the moment. But I can't say it's just sex, without any feelings. You know that once it's over, you can't just..."

Her voice was drowned out by water from the tap, but I could hear the girls laugh at what Gaja said, sounding like neighing mares. The doors of the adjacent stalls opened and closed. Without thinking, I got up, dressed, opened the door, and washed my hands in the sink. One of the girls flushed, and I left the restroom briskly.

I was hit by the stale smell of a student party: bodies reeking of cigarettes and alcohol loitered on the dance floor under the intrusive flashing of lights. Behind the bar, waiters served without pause. A bad remix of Bieber's *Sorry* was playing in the background, and I found Justin's saccharine voice utterly repulsive. I wished I could retreat somewhere alone, to play Allegri's *Miserere* performed by The Sixteen and daydream that I was singing the highest soprano. I had imagined this scene so many times with my earphones in as I raced toward the college on my bike in the morning: a performance in a dark Gothic cathedral, the kind you couldn't find in Slovenia, the smell of incense and wax, and me in an elegant floor-length black dress effortlessly singing the first soprano, the most beautiful part, which I knew by heart but could never actually sing with my average voice the way the soprano does: *Amplius lava me ab iniquitate mea: et a peccato meo munda me*, wash me completely of my guilt and cleanse me of my sin. Despite my drunkenness, I clearly heard the right tones in my head and remembered the lyrics, even while my brain was buzzing with questions. Is it because I am so average, incompetent, and ugly that Maks preferred Gaja, and chose her, not me, for casual sex? Does he find me too different? Does he think I'm pious? Does he find me ridiculous because I sing in a choir, because I know parts of songs in Latin by heart? What does he even think about me? Does he see me only as a boring girl from a Christian family?

I leaned against the bar and looked adrift at the students in the room. Agata had once told us to be proud that we persist with *true* music in a shallow world. Now I needed that music and the harmony and peace we achieved by truly mastering a composition. Yet it seemed that I didn't belong in this stuffy space where I was now stuck in bewilderment precisely because of this desire. What would happen if someone turned off the remix and played *Miserere*? How would the drunk students, crowding restlessly around the room, react?

"What are we having?" Blaž flopped onto the stool next to me and signaled the waiter. Even though I felt slightly sick, I wanted to drink something strong. I reached for my coat to take the ticket that counted as a drink coupon from my wallet. Blaž placed his hand on my hands holding the wallet and patronizingly shook his head. The drink was on him. Moments later, two small glasses with a caramel-colored liquid were placed before us. We clinked glasses, and I let the bitters slide down my throat. It was very soothing, and the thoughts gnawing at me began to sink into a drunken fog. I suggested another round.

The conversation was very fragmented, and I noticed his eyes were cloudy behind his glasses. I asked him about the article he was writing with Professor Pirc. He started talking about the difficulty of writing a scientific article, but I only half-listened because most of his words disappeared in the surrounding noise. Every so often, he leaned toward my ear while talking, and I felt his warm breath on my cheek. My answers were disjointed, I didn't even know what we were talking about, but he went on as if he didn't notice; he kept grinding on passionately, something about Pirc and his thesis. I began to lose my sense of time, and it felt like we had been talking for an eternity while the waiter served us drinks. At one point, I completely missed what Blaž was saying because I saw Gaja heading toward the exit, her head glowing from the lights shining on the dance floor. Unbidden, I saw her having sex with Maks in my mind—I no longer saw the flickering mass of bodies and Blaž's cloudy eyes, but a scene where Gaja's blonde hair fell elegantly down her bare back, with Max's hand grabbing her hair, his biceps tensing. A terrible pain struck deep in my chest, and I thought bloody tears would burst from my eyes. I might have collapsed right there if Sara hadn't appeared before me. I heard her say she had been looking for me, and before I could respond, she was already ordering blueberry schnapps for the three of us.

"Are you okay?" she asked me while Blaž twirled the shot glass of schnapps in his hand and stared at it. I nodded. I motioned toward Gaja, who had just returned to the club.

"See that girl? Isn't she beautiful?" Sara nodded. I asked her if she often found other women beautiful, and she said she generally found women more beautiful than men.

"Would you be with her?" Sara examined Gaja more closely, who sat at one of the tables where Maks's group was sitting. Dreamily, she said: "Maybe I would. It's not out of the question that I'll ever be with a woman, and if I am, I want her to be very beautiful, so it's an aesthetic experience too. Why do you ask?"

I was watching the table where Gaja sat. All five of Maks's friends were there, only he was missing. The boys were talking avidly about something, and the other girl next to Gaja was looking at her phone.

Very quietly, so Blaž, who was absently observing the scene, wouldn't hear, I told Sara about the conversation I overheard in the restroom. She frowned and said, "You don't think they're going to be doing that forever, right? Wait a few weeks, maybe months, and they'll get bored."

I raised my eyebrows and asked her how could she be so sure. She sighed.

"They'll get bored," she said decisively. "Even if they turned into a couple, I highly doubt they'd stay together. Cut the crap, Maša. Besides, would you like to sleep with him?"

I didn't understand how Sara could be so certain that this thing between Maks and Gaja wouldn't last, but I was grateful to some unknown guy who drifted by and got into a conversation with Blaž so he couldn't hear us. Sara's green eyes observed me calmly, telling me that I didn't need to lie. I stayed silent. She saw that I didn't intend to answer and said: "Anyway, you're very pretty too, even prettier than Gaja. You have a nice natural color"—she took a lock of my dark brown hair—"and your eyes are exactly the color of your hair. Plus, you constantly give the impression like you're pondering and analyzing something. That makes you more interesting than Gaja, and if Maks doesn't see that, he's just blind."

It struck me that Sara must be quite drunk too. And yet I couldn't entirely contradict her: it was clear to me I wasn't ugly, and looking at myself in the mirror on good days, I saw a cute girl with gentle features, it was only when I stepped onto the street that the attractiveness somehow evaporated due to cheap clothes and poor-quality makeup.

But Sara's words filled me with confidence, and I smiled at her. On the other side of the club, at one of the tables, I saw Maks talking to Professor Istenič. Unlike most students who swayed in groups on the dance floor, talked over one another, and went out to smoke, Maks looked surprisingly sober. There was a glass of beer filled to the brim in front of him, and it seemed he hadn't touched it yet. He was explaining something to the professor, fervently waving his hands. I drank the blueberry schnapps in one gulp and set the shot glass down in front of me with a bang. I moved from the bar and headed across the dance floor towards them. As soberly as possible, I sat at their table, and Maks and the professor merely glanced at me. They were engrossed in conversation, and I caught the words: *Rojava, revolution, women*.

"It's interesting," Maks said with a loud voice, ignoring my arrival, "that the Kurdish women's movement considers the capitalist patriarchal system a rape culture. Although they see the Islamic State as an extreme form of violence against women, they believe this is essentially happening all over the world, even in those parts that consider themselves progressive." The professor nodded silently while looking at the contents of the glass before him.

"Thus, the revolution in Rojava, which focuses on the woman and her well-being, is essentially the complete antithesis of the Islamic State," Maks added, then took a tiny sip of beer. Istenič agreed with him, looked at me, and asked: "Colleague, are you also interested in the Middle East?" It seemed to me he just wanted to be polite. I wavered, replying that it was certainly an interesting topic, but that I didn't like addressing Islam. As soon as I said it, I regretted it, but it seemed I no longer had control over my words. Seeing their surprised looks, I added: "I know the revolution in Rojava focuses on women, but it's still easier to discuss it if you're male. You don't feel so exposed. Your judgments are always made from a safer standpoint."

Given my level of intoxication, this was a fairly intelligible statement. But Maks shook his head: "I don't agree. I think as a man I find it even harder to discuss this because I can always slip up and come off as patronizing. If anyone has the full right to discuss this, it's you women."

I shrugged, unconvinced.

"The right to discuss, sure, but believe me, if you were a woman, you wouldn't even want to think about how somewhere they are raping and murdering women and considering it *halal* just because those women didn't submit to their ideology. You'd be so disgusted you'd prefer to live without this awareness. As a woman, you just never feel safe. You said it yourself; violence against women, misogyny, and patriarchy are the modus operandi of the entire planet. But just because you're explaining this while drinking beer doesn't mean you're actually aware of it."

The words came out quite harsh, and even I was surprised by them. They must have stemmed from some unexplained anger toward him. Maks was staring at me as Sara appeared beside us and handed me a glass with yellowish liquid and ice.

"For you. From Blaž."

I raised my eyebrows and took a sip. The cold drink was pleasant, the combination of vodka and orange juice caressed my tongue and thoughts. The professor said he hadn't met Sara in the department before, and she began to explain what she was studying. My eyes followed Maks's gaze, which stared blankly at the other side of the club, where Gaja sat on a barstool talking to a waiter. As before at the bar, I felt a sharp pang beneath my sternum, but I did have to admit to myself that Maks's gaze expressed anything but admiration. It looked somewhat indifferent.

"I'm going for a smoke," he suddenly announced, stood up abruptly, and started putting on his jacket. Sara said she would go with him and asked if I wanted to join them. I emptied my glass and was about to follow them when I realized the amount of alcohol had exceeded the capacity of my stomach. I merely shook my head, headed toward the restroom with pursed lips and brisk steps, locked myself in a stall, and threw up everything I had drunk.

16.

The rest of the night remained full of gaps and blurred in my memory. Coming back from the restroom, I ran into Blaž at the bar again, and I told him I wasn't going to drink anymore. Exhausted from the booze and vomiting, I just sat there with him and we talked for a while, though later, only isolated fragments of our discussion came to mind. Maks appeared next to us, and something was said about the Christmas concert taking place in December, and in my woozy state, I tried to recall its exact date. I retreated to the restroom again, stood by the sink, and splashed water on my face, which looked grayish-green in the mirror, with dark patches of mascara forming under my eyes. When I came back, Sara asked me how I was feeling, and when I told her "so-so," she told Maks standing next to her that she would call me a taxi. I observed them from a horizontal perspective, resting my head on the counter. When she asked if I wanted her to come in the taxi with me, I raised my head, causing the room to spin, and begged her not to send me home. They stared at me in surprise. I said I didn't want to go home in this state, and Maks whispered something to Sara. She bit her lip and then nodded. I was watching them, and then my eyes closed. I kept them shut for a while until Sara nudged me and helped me up. We left the club, and Maks and I got into a taxi waiting nearby. I closed my eyes and didn't open them again until we stepped out in front of a row house I hadn't visited in years. As we walked up the path to the front door, the cold night air cleared my thoughts, and I realized where I was.

The Hafner house was just as I remembered it, except they had renovated the living room and the kitchen, where Maks poured me a glass of water. We tiptoed up the stairs to the upper floor so as not to wake Darja and Martin, though it crossed my mind that they must be used to such pairs of footsteps in the middle of the night. In the bathroom, I washed my face with one of Darja's makeup removal gels and applied a scented cream from a brand I recognized but could not afford in my wildest dreams. My tired skin turned silky. In one of the cabinets, following Maks's instructions, I found a still-packaged toothbrush and brushed my teeth, then sniffed the shower gels and deodorants belonging to the men in the house, trying to determine if any of the scents reminded me of Maks.

He was waiting for me in his room, which was quite different from how I remembered it from childhood. It was very minimalist, with sparse furniture and a queen-sized bed. Why, it struck me, do boys always have queen-sized beds, while girls mostly sleep in singles until we move out? Urška and I, and all my female friends, slept on narrow beds, while most of my male friends and classmates had larger ones.

A closed silver MacBook lay on the desk under the window, and a TV hung on the wall opposite the bed, like in a hotel room. On the gray bedding, which I had seen in an IKEA catalogue, a clean black T-shirt lay waiting for me. Maks didn't look at me while I changed, he sat on the edge of the bed, completely engrossed in his phone. I put on the fresh shirt, which smelled of fabric softener and featured a logo with a crossed-out cross and the words "Bad Religion."

I climbed into the bed, which smelled the same as the shirt. The room was still spinning a bit, and I felt like I couldn't quite keep up with what was happening. I wished Maks goodnight, and he reached for the nightstand and turned off the lamp, but the room wasn't plunged into total darkness, as the street behind the uncovered window was lit by streetlamps casting a muffled yellowish glow into the room.

Then he stood up and took off his shirt, revealing his silhouette, a scrawny but firm torso and two tiny, hard nipples. He put on a T-shirt, unbuttoned his pants, took them off, and draped them over the back of the chair, then lay down next to me in his boxers and flipped on the side, showing me his back.

"Goodnight," I heard him say, and that was all. The next moment, I was asleep.

I was woken by movement coming from Maks's side. He was half-sitting on the bed, holding a controller, his gaze fixed on the video game on the TV. I had imagined waking up next to him before. I had imagined us in an Airbnb in San Francisco or Tokyo, or on an expedition in West Africa behind a mosquito net, not with a headache and a sour taste in my mouth. Without saying anything, I sat up and reached for my phone on the shelf above the bed. Sara had texted me to let her know how I was when I came to, and Mom had written *ok*. I didn't know what this *ok* referred to until I found my own sent message: *Sleeping over at a friend's*. That was all. It was Wednesday, nine-thirty, I had slept through the Introduction to Mythology lecture.

"Good morning," Maks said without taking his eyes off the screen, where he was steering his character running down an empty white corridor. "Sleep well?"

I replied that I had, then lay back down. I stared at the ceiling and began piecing together the fragments of the previous evening. Although I hadn't done anything I should regret, I was filled with the nasty anxiety that always seized me when I drank too much. I thanked Maks for bringing me over and asked him how much I owed him for the taxi. Without looking at me, he smiled and said there was no need to pay him back. I was ready for him to tease me over what happened, since he had never seen me drunk before, but he was quiet.

"Do you remember anything from yesterday?" he asked, pursing his lips as his character in the video game shot at an opponent. He was smashing the controller, and the action on the screen looked quite violent. I said I remembered some things, and he remarked: "You really hit it off with Blaž." He finally looked at me, grinning as if he liked the idea. I swallowed saliva that tasted sour despite having brushed my teeth before bed. His words made me worry. Had Blaž and I really gotten close? Did Maks now think I liked Blaž?

I said we were just talking and that he bought me a couple of drinks.

"I didn't even use my coupon," I chuckled.

Maks laughed too, and I tried to recall the conversations with Blaž. Especially the one after I returned from the restroom after vomiting, which was completely chaotic.

"At one point he said something funny," I remembered. "I think we were talking about the refugee crisis or something... And he started one of his sentences with: 'I'm not a racist, but...'"

Maks and I both laughed loudly, and he shook his head.

"I *love* it when people say that," he said, again striving to kill an opponent in the video game.

"Right? Me too. I'm not a sexist, but..."

"I don't hate blacks, but..."

"I have nothing against gays, but..."

"I'm not a homophobe, but..."

"I don't mind immigrants, but..."

"I'm not an antisemite, but..."

"This might sound chauvinistic, but..."

Maks had to press pause because we were laughing so hard he couldn't shoot anymore. Finally, we couldn't think of any more examples, and an empty silence filled the room. It was rarely this quiet in our apartment in the middle of Šiška.

"Hey. What's going on between you and Gaja?" I asked him suddenly, not knowing where I got the courage. The atmosphere in Maks's room was friendly, and I wanted to take advantage of it. He had already pressed play. The silence was replaced by artificial sounds from the video game.

"Is there anything going on between us?" he asked quietly.

"I don't know. Yesterday, when I was in the restroom, I heard her and a couple of friends talking, and she said you sleep together." I watched him stubbornly, and I could have sworn I detected a slight blush on his cheek.

"Oh, that," he nodded, as if I had asked him if he ever borrowed notes from her. I realized that since last night I had hoped Gaja was talking about some other Maks or that my dizzy head had mixed something up. I felt like a block of granite was stuck in my chest. I wanted to turn it all into a joke, and faking indifference, I asked him if they did it on this bed too. First, he laughed, then he grew serious and said coldly: "Yup." It crossed my mind that perhaps I had spent the night on a bed together with a hair from Gaja's head.

I remembered him telling me on our last walk that they were planning a symposium or a round table together. Were they making those plans after sex? Did they lie naked next to each other on his bed, light a cigarette, open the window to let the smell of bodies escape the room, and think about how they, as promising intellectuals, would respond to the refugee crisis? I hated that thought.

"But you aren't a couple?"

It seemed it would have been easier for him to answer a question about whether they preferred doing it in missionary or with her on top or him taking her from behind. Maks's fingers were white from pressing the controller, his eyes were stubbornly fixed on the screen. It occurred to me that he didn't turn off the video game because he did not want to look at me when talking about this.

"We don't really talk about it. It just happened by chance after a night like you had yesterday, and then it turned into a habit, which apparently works out okay for both of us."

If I had been tormented by jealousy at the thought of them a minute ago, I was now in the grips of an emotion that most closely resembled pity. The story of Gaja and Maks was painfully stereotypical, as if it were an average Hollywood movie with a completely predictable plot.

"Isn't that a bit cliché?" I offered a bitter commentary on what had been swirling in my mind since yesterday. He asked me what I meant. "The whole thing... Friends who sleep together. I mean, it's your business, of course, but I sometimes wonder how quickly we internalize patterns—"

"Well, I know why it happened, and I don't need to explain it to you," he interrupted me somewhat roughly, and I went quiet. I saw displeasure on his face; his forehead was furrowed from frowning. Then he switched off the console and turned off the TV, leaving us sitting in silence.

"You want to eat something?" he asked me in a softer voice.

"I do, but if it's possible, I'd like to shower first."

"Go ahead. Clean towels are in the cabinet under the sink. I'll go down and make us toast. You'll have coffee, right?" he asked me while pulling on the jeans he had snatched from the back of the chair. I nodded, and he left the room with brisk steps.

When the door closed behind him, I listened to his footsteps receding down the stairs, and didn't move until I was sure he was on the ground floor.

Maks's room was ascetic, as if he only slept there. There were some books on the desk. I recognized Said's *Orientalism* and Gellner's *Anthropology and Politics*. In the middle of the desk, next to the MacBook, lay a copy of the weekly *Mladina* and one of the monthly *Global*. A nightstand stood by the bed. I couldn't resist my curiosity and opened the top drawer. In it was a tube of Bepanthen, Nivea wet wipes, and Durex condoms. I imagined Maks, right before he and Gaja continued what they were doing on this bed, leaning toward the nightstand, taking a condom from it, opening it, and putting it on. The image almost made me forget to breathe, so I hurriedly closed the top drawer and opened the bottom one. In it lay a book bound in blue denim, with embroidered yellow letters spelling *Holy Bible*. I chuckled. Maks loved to trash the American way of life, claiming Americans were naive and artificial, but nothing seemed more American to me than a copy of the Bible in a nightstand drawer. I took it in my hands. It was hard to imagine what Maks was doing with this book; ever since I had known him, he was a staunch atheist and constantly criticized the church and Christianity in general. I opened it, and the inscription on the first page surprised me, it read "To Mitja for Holy Confirmation." So, the book belonged to his older brother, and I would have never guessed that he had gone to confirmation. I was convinced Maks hadn't.

I was about to put the Bible back in the drawer when I noticed a white envelope lying at the bottom. I picked it up and pulled out a thin collection of photos taken with an analog camera. In the first photo were the four of them—Martin, Darja, Mitja, and Maks—sitting by a table looking at a cake with eight candles and the inscription "Happy Birthday, Maks." Looking at the cake with the unnatural-looking blue icing that made me think of the blue sky ice cream flavor, I remembered its sugary taste, and with it, Maks's eighth birthday. I examined their faces: Maks's mother had always been a beauty, with thin blonde hair and clear facial features, and his father always had a fresh, well-rested, vigorous appearance, as if life didn't wear him out. Maks's brother Mitja was also already quite a cute teenager in the photo. It had always been my contention that it was easy for people with no money problems to look great.

In the next photo, the two- or three-year-old Maks was sitting in the lap of an elderly grey-haired lady, probably his grandmother. This photo was followed by one from kindergarten, in which he was dressed in an Indian costume, and I smiled, remembering he had recently told me how racist the masquerades we wore in the nineties were, when our parents dressed us up as "Indians, Gypsies, and Moors." I studied the photo in detail, then put it behind the others, and felt an instantaneous dull pain throughout my body. I was holding a duplicate of the photo that was also hidden in my nightstand drawer. The one from 1997, in which the two of us are naked in the little pool. I stared at it for a few long seconds, wondering what this photo was doing among the chosen four photos in this mysterious envelope. With trembling hands, I put it back in with the others, returned the envelope to its place, placed the Bible on top, and closed the drawer.

I arrived on the ground floor showered and changed into yesterday's clothes, which stank of cigarettes and alcohol. In the bathroom, I found some of Darja's makeup in a drawer, so I applied mascara and eyeliner. Maks had just placed two cups under an elegant black-and-silver coffee machine and pressed a button so that coffee began to trickle out and the velvety scent of morning filled the room. He asked me if he should froth my milk, and I said yes. The kitchen led into the living room, and I headed for the bookshelves.

I examined the shelves with classics, books from a collection by the newspaper *Delo*, mixed with poetry collections and books on mountaineering and alpinism. It would be hard to say what type of reader these books belonged to. Darja was an internist by profession, and Martin was employed at the Geographical Institute. Maks had told me his father couldn't stand being in one place for even five minutes at a time, that he constantly had to be venturing somewhere, hiking, cycling, that he got all jittery after an hour spent at home. Whenever I suggested to Maks that we take a walk along the Trail of Remembrance and Comradeship, he always said we might run into his dad, who had already cycled, run, and walked the trail at least fifty times.

Behind my back, Maks placed two plates of toast on the coffee table and went back to the kitchen for the cups of coffee. I picked up a random alpinism book with the inscription "*To Darja in memory of our feats. Darko and Sanja, Ljubljana, Oct 25, 2013.*" I returned it to the shelf and ran my finger along the titles. That was when I saw it: a hefty book titled *The Image of the Woman in the Slovenian Folk Song*. By Florijan Hafner.

"Look what I found," I waved the book at him as he set the cups on the table and sat on the couch. He gave a weary smile. I sat down next to him with the book, opened it, and leafed through.

"Have you ever read it?"

He shook his head. The book was from 1984, the edges of the pages were already slightly yellowed. There was a photograph of a man about forty years old on the cover, and I could recognize Maks's features on his face.

"You look like him."

Maks didn't react. He avoided conversations about his grandfather, a former professor at the Department of Ethnology and Cultural

Anthropology, and his grandmother Angela Potrč Hafner, who worked at the Institute for the Protection of Cultural Heritage. He didn't like it when someone said he was following in their footsteps, and preferred not to be associated with them in college. But I felt like this didn't always hold. Sometimes, perhaps unconsciously, he emphasized very clearly in front of professors that his last name was Hafner.

I put the book on the table and bit into the toast. To change the subject, Maks said that we had agreed yesterday at the party that he would come to our Christmas concert with Blaž. I vaguely remembered this, but if I had been in my right mind, I would have tried to dissuade them. I was afraid Maks would actually come, and we would then embarrass ourselves with something, giving him cause to look down on me. It was a routine concert we performed every December with another choir in St. Joseph's Church in Poljane, where we sang a few Christmas songs. But the boys insisted they wanted to come, and Sara egged them on.

"Sara told me about a piece you girls sing. Something by Svetlana Makarovič. She said you have a solo." I rolled my eyes and objected that I didn't have a solo, but was just a backup.

"Besides, I don't like the piece very much. It's heavy." I took a sip of coffee, which tasted like it came from a café. "Why do you even want to come anyway?" I finally asked him, trying to sound as casual as possible.

Maks thought for a few moments, then said with a laugh: "So Blaž won't go alone. Yesterday, he kept telling me I should come. I don't know about his intentions, but I think he likes you."

"I don't think so," I said frostily, "but you should come, why not?" I hoped to conclude the conversation.

"What makes you want to sing in a choir so much?" he asked me after a few moments of silence. He had never asked me this before, he knew I always liked to sing. I swallowed a piece of toast and replied: "I won't say it's always enjoyable. Singing demands a lot of energy, and our choirmaster is really the type who expects devotion and effort. But the feeling when a piece falls into place is truly fantastic. At first, the score is always a huge undertaking that looks insurmountable, especially if the piece is difficult. But once you master it and start working on dynamics... You hear things in music that others don't."

Maks murmured "interesting," then ate his toast in a few bites. He put the empty plate on the table and picked up his coffee. I had also finished my toast. I got up from the couch and went to the kitchen to wash my hands. When I returned, Maks was lying on the couch with his legs outstretched, a coffee cup resting in his lap, his gaze fixed on the blank TV. He was wearing white socks. For a brief moment, I could imagine what our life together would look like.

He gestured at the book I had put on the table earlier and said in a grim tone: "Darja and Martin keep pestering me that I have to make an effort to stay in college." He always called his parents by their names. "In their opinion, there's nothing I could with anthropology outside the university. I can't tell you how much that bothers me. You'd expect them to understand that studying is more than just a job and making money."

"And what do you tell them?"

"Nothing, for now, I just ignore it. I'd like to do some fieldwork before settling down. I've arranged to join the volunteers at the border at the end of November."

I received the news with enthusiasm, although I also felt slightly envious. I was tempted to abandon my life in Ljubljana and join him at the border. But I couldn't imagine what Agata would do if I took another long break from singing, as I had done in the spring when

I went on exchange. No, I couldn't do that to her, she might even kick me out.

Maks smiled modestly, but it was clear from his smile that my enthusiasm flattered him.

"I'll let you know how it goes," he added. Then he paused a little again before saying, "You were quite direct yesterday. In front of Istenič."

"Forget about that, I was drunk. I was talking nonsense," I waved my hand.

He shook his head: "You weren't. You did well."

I blinked at him, looking for traces of pretense on his face. But his face explained nothing. I thought he might say something more, when we heard the front door unlock. I turned pale and looked nervously toward the hallway. Maks's brother walked in.

I had last seen Mitja ten years ago, except on Facebook, where I checked his profile. He was a little taller than Maks and had longer hair than him. I recognized the girl standing behind him from his profile picture. I knew from Maks that she was Mitja's long-time girlfriend.

"Hi," he greeted us casually, and we greeted him back.

They walked past us, and Mitja just nodded at me, said "Mitja," pointed to his girlfriend and said "Lara," while I mumbled "Maša." I turned to Maks, thinking he would say something, but he observed the scene with pursed lips. Mitja and his girlfriend headed toward the stairs, while my heart was pounding. Just before they reached the stairs, Mitja spun around and asked Maks: "Is the PlayStation still in your room?"

Maks nodded, and they went up. I sighed deeply—I had been holding my breath all this time. It became clear to me: Mitja had no clue who I was, and Maks made no effort to explain.

17.

Every year at the end of November, the choir members held a draw in which each singer picked a fellow singer to surprise with something during the festive month of December. The idea was Ivana's, but while she had proposed that we exchange gifts, Agata said that we should do something more original. She came up with the idea that we must invite the girl somewhere—for instance, to tea, the movies, or for a walk. She explained that this would strengthen the bonds between us, creating trust that was also essential on stage. It was pointless to explain to her that in December, we had little time for such things.

At the last rehearsal in November, during the break, Ivana appeared before me and held out a velvet pouch containing our names. I reached in and pulled out a folded slip of paper that read "Agata."

Urška advised me that Agata would appreciate it most if I didn't complicate the surprise and, above all, didn't delay it. So, at vocal technique during the first week of December, I suggested we go to the Tea House for breakfast the next morning, and she accepted the invitation gracefully.

As I waited for her at one of the tables in the tea shop, the minutes dragged, and I nervously scrolled down my phone screen without knowing what I was looking at. We rarely socialized, and although we addressed each other informally and she was only about a decade older, she maintained an authority that made it hard for us to talk to her about mundane things.

The bell at the door jingled, and I waved to her as she walked in. She climbed the stairs to the table where I was waiting and sat down.

She wore a camel-colored coat, a plaid scarf, and elegant leather gloves, and she placed a lovely leather handbag on the chair between us. I had always admired Agata's refined style of dress, but I couldn't imagine myself in such clothes. I preferred wearing jeans, hoodies, and All-Stars. I sometimes felt strange in the trench coat I wore to the freshman party, but Mom had convinced me to buy it, saying it was a must have.

"It's wonderful that you proposed breakfast. My mornings are usually slow, and sometimes it feels like they just slip away. Musicians are more alive in the afternoons and evenings," she said with a smile as she looked over the menu. "So, I think it's great that we will make the most of the morning. Who got you at the draw?"

I told her it was Klara and that we had gone to the movies a few days ago. Agata was pleased and asked me if I didn't think the idea was excellent. I agreed. The waiter arrived and we placed our orders.

"I've wanted to speak with you about something for a while, but it's never the right time," she began when the waiter set a tray of black tea before us. "We always have too much work to do at vocal technique. Anyway, I know you won't be singing at Urška's wedding, but you can still help us shape the repertoire and give us some tips. Urška said she was leaving the selection of songs to Ivana and me, and we wanted to prepare something special. We'll start rehearsals right after the revue, three months should be more than enough. You'll be joining us, right?"

I hoped she wouldn't read the surprise on my face. Apparently, she expected me to attend extra rehearsals to listen to them practice, even though I wouldn't be singing. I hesitated with my answer, then said frankly: "I don't know. I have a lot of work, studies, and I have to find myself a student job to have enough money for Estonia. I'll think about it." She didn't look at me, she was pressing on the strainer with the soggy tea leaves in the teapot with her spoon. I noticed a slight flush on her cheeks.

"I understand," she said coldly.

"But I will definitely help with the selection. Urška always liked Makor's arrangement of *Bride, Make Your Farewells*. You could sing that at the wedding." Her face lit up, and she said it was a great idea.

"And what are your feelings about your future brother-in-law?" The waiter brought us the food. I picked up the cutlery and began cutting my fried egg.

"He's not exactly my favourite person in the world, if you know what I mean. It's not that he is bad, but he has his quirks."

Agata nodded while carrying a forkful of avocado to her mouth. Then she asked me what I didn't like about him. I poured some black tea into my cup and added milk.

"I don't know, some of his comments really get on my nerves. For instance, he often behaves very patronizingly toward my studies, which I'm practically allergic to. He always presents it as a joke, but in reality, it isn't. You know. The statements about how we're not actually doing anything at the Faculty of Arts."

She sighed with sympathy but said nothing. It crossed my mind that she might be thinking the same.

"Luckily, you aren't the one marrying him," she remarked tartly and smiled.

"That's true, but he will be my sister's husband." It seemed to me that maybe I sounded too harsh, as if there were something wrong with Andrej. I hurriedly added that he was otherwise a perfectly fine person and that Urška was truly happy with him.

"No, I understand what you mean," Agata said and gently wiped her lips with a napkin, leaving a barely noticeable lipstick mark.

"I have a sister too, you know? Younger." I nodded, though I didn't know where I had learned this, and she continued: "The relationship between sisters is very complicated. I read somewhere that it's the longest relationship of our lives. My sister and I were very close in childhood and then as teenagers. We were basically best friends, well, in a sisterly way. But then, when I went to study in Ljubljana and she stayed in Zagorje, all that changed." She elegantly grasped her cup, leaned back in her chair, and took a few slow sips.

"Now we rarely see each other, only when I go home, which is very occasionally, as you can imagine." She put the cup back on the saucer and picked up her cutlery again. "And even when I do, it's only a brief visit. She has three children, she's always busy, and she has a terrible job. A practical nurse in the health center Hrastnik. An extremely exhausting job." She shuddered. "I'm not saying a musician's profession is easier, but... It's just different," she added ineptly, without looking at me.

I nodded and said I understood and agreed, and after a short pause, she said, "Urška is getting married now and will most likely have children soon... You probably aren't even thinking about that yet." I shook my head rapidly and was about to say that I considered marriage just a piece of paper when she continued: "That's good, because it isn't easy if your younger sister has children before you, you know?" She looked at me with a piercing gaze, and I noticed silvery eyeshadow glistening on her eyelids.

I didn't know what to say, so I just murmured quietly that I could imagine. Mercifully, she continued on her own: "You always think of her as a little girl, as an inexperienced child who doesn't know a thing about life. And then this child suddenly announces she's pregnant. And then again. And again. Each of her pregnancies was like a knife in the back, although," she paused with her cutlery over her plate, "I love my nephews very much, of course. But every time she gave birth, it made me the one who still didn't have children of her own." She cleared her throat, then looked at me and said, "I mean, I know you girls sometimes wonder why I don't have children yet. Right?"

I hadn't burdened myself with why Agata didn't have children, but I heard Urška and Ivana talking about it, often genuinely perplexed, listing possible reasons why. I nodded quickly. It seemed to me she had been curious about this for a long time but had nobody to ask.

"Do Urška and Ivana puzzle over this often?" Frightened, as if sitting on the witness stand, I nodded again. She sighed, then said it didn't surprise her. That it was simply expected of a married woman her age to be a mother. And that she could understand that. That they weren't the only ones burdening themselves with it.

"My family does too. To say nothing about Gregor's family, though no one addresses it directly. In their eyes, I'm the one with issues." She fell silent and took a long sip of tea.

I didn't fully understand what issues she had in mind, and I used the moment of her silence to say what seemed most appropriate: "You two still have time." I lifted my gaze from the teacup and met her grey eyes, hoping I hadn't said anything wrong.

Agata gave an ambivalent shrug.

"Time. Yes and no. The female body is complex. I've had my share of problems already. First there were the terribly painful periods. Then I gained weight because of the pill, my head hurt, and... And I did not feel good at all. And when I stopped taking them, I've had hair loss, and it took almost a year for my period to become regular. And now I need to have a laparoscopy because they suspect I have endometriosis. Compared to me, my sister is bursting with health.

I always thought pregnancies exhausted a woman, but now it seems to me it's just the opposite."

I said that her sister must surely be tired too. She conceded she spoke too rashly and that her sister had indeed gained quite a bit of weight over the last decade. Finished with her meal, she put her cutlery on the plate and leaned back.

"I don't even know if I really want children. I can understand why my sister went for it. She doesn't have anything else. I have music," she said firmly, then added in a calmer voice, "or rather, of course I do want them, just not so much, if you understand. My happiness simply doesn't depend on it. But the problem is that people find that very hard to accept."

I understood her very well and I nodded. She reached into the handbag on the chair, pulled out her phone and looked at the screen, then dropped the phone back into the bag and sighed.

"Actually, I've recently been enthralled by something entirely new." She smiled in a mysterious way. "I can trust you, right? You won't spread it around?" I shook my head, and she straightened up in her chair and solemnly declared, "I've started composing." Her lips widened into a broad smile, and she looked several years younger, with a lively sparkle in her eyes. I responded with a muffled "wow," and Agata's reaction told me this meant a lot to her. I asked how this had come about.

"I was first tempted after I started collaborating with Ciril. When we worked on the score, I would suggest something to him, and it would turn out really well. He kept telling me that I had a feel for it." Her voice faltered, then she turned modest, "I know this might not seem like a big deal to you. But it's not such a small thing. You know, in the music profession, it isn't easy to succeed if you're a woman.

If you pay attention, there are still far fewer female composers and conductors than male composers and conductors."

I emphasized that I didn't find it a small thing at all.

"With a person like you, there is no doubt in my mind that the results will be exceptional," I added with conviction, and she glowed with pride. I wanted to say more about how I admired her, but the compliments got stuck in my throat. Instead, I asked her what she was working on. For a moment I thought I had asked the wrong question, as she hesitated to answer. But then she said, "It's a setting of an excerpt from the Gospel of Luke. The part where Jesus visits the sisters, Martha and Mary."

She looked at me searchingly, trying to determine if I knew what she was talking about. I said I only partially remembered the passage. She quickly summarized: Martha prepares the service, while Mary listens to Jesus. When Martha finally takes offense and asks Jesus if he doesn't care that her sister left her to serve alone, Jesus tells her that Martha is concerned by things of no importance.

"Interesting choice," I murmured, not knowing what else to say.

Agata gave me a patronizing smile.

"You must find it unusual. Most of the time, composers adapt poetry, or a psalm, if they want a sacral text. But why wouldn't I set an excerpt?" It sounded like a rhetorical question, and I said I agreed.

"But why that specific excerpt?" I asked her. She fell into thought, then answered, "I like it. Not because I'm incredibly religious... But that part at the end, *'you are worried and upset about many things, but few things are needed–or indeed only one'*... That always makes me think." She stared at a point behind my back. "Once you hear the piece, you'll see how I did it. It's for a women's choir, anyway."

"I can't wait for you to show it to us," I smiled at her. Then I took my phone from my coat pocket and looked at the time. "I'll have to get going. I have a lecture." Agata nodded and signaled the waiter. She stood up and began putting on her coat while I paid the bill. When we stepped out of the café onto the cold street, she turned to me and said: "Thank you for the pleasant company, Maša. I'm so glad you thought of this. Oh, and listen. I wanted to tell you this earlier, when we were talking about my sister." She didn't look me in the eye but let her gaze slide over the faces of passersby hurrying along the street. Then she faced me: "Make the most of the time you still have with Urška, before the wedding. She'll move out, get pregnant... And she won't be the same person anymore. You will never have a sister in that sense of the word again." I thought she would say more, but she reached out with her gloved hand and embraced me around the shoulders. I returned an awkward hug.

"Thank you," she added with a smile, turned, and disappeared among the people rushing through the streets of Old Ljubljana.

18.

In the second week of December, in the middle of choir practice, while Agata was occupied with the other altos, I reached into my pocket and checked my phone, even though this wasn't allowed during rehearsals. I expected the screen to be empty as usual, but I saw an email notification.

> Maks Hafner, Dec 8, 2015, 19:12
> Field Report
>
> Hey, how is it going? I hope you're doing well. Last week I started work at the border in Dobova...

Agata's rules were clear: we weren't allowed to use phones during rehearsals, but had to listen closely and participate, even if she was dealing with a different voice section. We didn't break unwritten rules, and even an urgent call wasn't a good enough reason to leave the hall. If anyone dared to do so, she was met with Agata's contemptuous gaze.

I anxiously put the phone back in my pocket and looked at the sheet music. Just minutes ago, I had been completely immersed in Eriks Ešenvalds' *Ubi Caritas*, but now I couldn't concentrate. I was bursting with curiosity about what Maks had written. Agata wanted us to sing together. I gathered myself and sang along with the others: "*Timeamus et amemus Deum vivum...*"

"No, no, no, no!" Agata shouted, silencing us with a hand gesture. "Second altos, where are you?! This is your most important part!" She stared furiously at the girls on her right, who looked silently at their sheet music. "And the way you are singing this?" She looked at the whole choir and mocked us with a deadpan voice, reading lazily: "*Timeamus et amemus deum vivum…* We fear and love the *living* God! Living! You must sing this with passion, with life! People need to grasp it: this God you are singing about is alive! If you keep singing it like that, no one will take you seriously." She took a breath and continued in a fierce tone: "What did we say about singing sacral texts? How do we sing them?" She raised her two thin eyebrows and stared at the singers. A moment of silence followed.

"As if we were believers," Sara spoke up from the second altos.

"As if you were believers!" Agata repeated loudly. "It doesn't matter if you are or aren't! You can be atheists, Muslims, Buddhists, whatever you want, but when we sing sacral texts, I want you to sing… To sing like nuns! Do you understand?!" Laughter spread through the choir, and the corners of Agata's lips turned up slightly too, but then she turned serious again: "That is the point of sacral music. When you are in the hall, before an audience of different people—who differ in, I don't know, in nationality, religion, language, skin color, whatever… People need to *feel* like they can connect on a spiritual level, even through their difference." Her gray eyes glistened under the bright hall lights. "Do you understand?!" she cried out once more.

When we declared that we understood, she told us to start from the top and struck the first chord. We did better this time, for a long moment performing as a single body. Agata, contented, called a break, and as the girls began flocking toward the door, I took the phone from my pocket and opened Maks's email.

Maks Hafner, Dec 8, 2015, 19:12

Field Report

Hey, how is it going? I hope you're doing well. Last week I started work at the border in Dobova. Basically, I don't even know where to start, but since this was your suggestion, I'd like to describe to you what things look like here.

Well, it's not a walk in the park, which you can probably imagine. But I had no idea it was this bad. What shocked me the most was that volunteers don't have any physical contact with the refugees. There must always be a fence between us. I kind of got used to it, but it still reminds me of a concentration camp. The refugee center in Dobova is meant to be used only for registration and entry, but the refugees of course have to sleep here too, because there's no other way, when they're kept waiting for hours. They arrive from Croatia freezing, thirsty, they need the restrooms and many need medical care. At times, I can barely believe this is really happening. You know how people say the media only shows children, when there really aren't that many? Well, I can tell you firsthand that there are huge numbers of children here. When I came—

"Oh, what's this novel?" Sara sat on the empty chair to my right. She didn't want to look over my shoulder at the phone, but it was obvious she was very interested.

"From Maks. He's volunteering at the border in Dobova."

She nodded with approval, then said she would leave me alone and go for a smoke. I smiled at her, grateful, and read on.

... when I came, the worst thing was their pestering questions. To be honest—they got on my nerves. The constant questions in their clumsy English: *Do you know where we are going? Can you tell us?* And I could only shake my head, saying I had no clue, because I really didn't. I even considered just going home because I was immediately exhausted and my will was drained. I was asking myself what was even the point of me being here. But then I met another volunteer from Austria, and when I saw his work attitude, I jumped into it too. Tonight, I have an evening to myself. I know my writing is disjointed and—

I looked up from the phone as Ivana sat on the same chair where Sara had been earlier.

"Sorry to disturb you, but I'm collecting money for a Christmas present for Agata. We're giving her perfume, I already bought it."

"Which one did you choose?" Ivana showed me a photo of the women's perfume Noir by Tom Ford on her phone. I whistled, delighted but also surprised.

"Good choice," I said, and Ivana smiled mysteriously, then said that the contribution was five euros.

"We're going to give it to her next week, after the concert," she told me while I went through my wallet for a fiver.

"Isn't that a little early?" I frowned. "We've always given her the gift at the last rehearsal before Christmas." I took a crumpled banknote from my wallet and held it out to her.

She shook her head, took the banknote, and told me that after the concert we wouldn't have any more rehearsals until the new year. I only half-listened to her, my eyes were already scanning Maks's email.

"How come?" I asked her absent-mindedly.

"Agata told me she has a procedure in the days following the concert, so she'll be taking sick leave," she shared with a touch of pride.

"Oh, that's probably the laparoscopy," I said after a brief delay, while swiping with my finger to the end of Maks's email without really reading it. I looked up and saw Ivana watching me with a curious gaze. She asked me what that was and how I knew about it.

"It's an examination where they check for endometriosis. The other day she told me they suspect she has it, then I googled it."

Ivana didn't say anything at first, she just bit her lip. Apparently, it made her envious that I knew something she didn't about Agata.

"I think she has some trouble conceiving," I lowered my voice, engaged now, "at least that's what she said. That she has a heap of health issues, and they suspect endometriosis and that she can't get pregnant," came rushing out of me. Ivana watched me, unmoving. I squinted toward Agata, who was shifting sheet music by the piano and looked oblivious of her surroundings.

"Is that so," Ivana said icily. I nodded, and she stood up and said she had to collect money from the other singers too. Finally, I could return to Maks's email.

... disjointed and incoherent, but that's also how I feel. And the policemen are not taken care of at all. The work they do is mentally and physically exhausting, but they get no rest or psychological support. Everybody paints a picture (in the media as well) that we're on opposing sides, but it isn't so black and white. And about the smart phones, I know every second comment on RTV SLO is on this topic, about what kind of phones refugees have, but what use is a smart phone if its only purpose is to connect you with your family, and with those who might be waiting for you at your destination? Once you are here, you really see that things are different. The most I can do at this moment is to show these people that in Europe, we aren't all—

"Maša, put the phone away," Agata's strained voice broke through and I looked up. She was staring at me, not with anger, but rather disappointment. I hadn't perceived the silence that had descended on the hall, nor the girls sitting calmly on their chairs, looking at Agata ready to sing. I was entirely there, in the world Maks was painting for me, my breathing was shallow as I experienced the conditions in which he worked. Now, however, I felt like a scolded child. Without a word, I put the phone away, straightened up in my chair, and arranged my sheet music.

"Let's go from the top," said Agata, already looking at the piano keys. The singers, focused on the music, followed her hand. Their mouths opened and they began: *"Do not go courting to the mountains,"* while I was still holding the score for *Ubi Caritas* in my hands. I discreetly replaced Ešenvalds' *Ubi Caritas* with Šavli's score from my folder.

I read the rest of Maks's email in Ivana's car.

... that in Europe, we aren't all a priori evil and exclusionary toward them. I was chatting with a guy today, he was a little older than me. From Iran. Through the fence, of course. His English was flawless. We talked about random things, about how he's sorry they were leaving so much trash behind, that he would help us clean and tidy it all up. Then he told me he studied anthropology in Tehran. That he was an activist and that's why they exiled him. His destination is Berlin, where he hopes to get asylum. He has a fiancée back home, he showed me her photo on his phone, she was covered with a black scarf and had a stunning face. He was overjoyed that I knew 'A Separation' and 'Persepolis'. He had never heard of Ljubljana before. These people don't even know where they are. They can't tell up from down.

I can't believe I wrote so much, because I'm bone-tired. We spend up to 14 hours out there during the day.

Well, enjoy.

Best, Maks

19

I double-checked to make sure I had everything I needed for the concert: the long, high-waisted black skirt, tailored to fit, hanging on the rack in a black garment bag, the white blouse, freshly washed and ironed, and the bright red sash we tied around our waists. I had already put on my nude bra and pantyhose. I tossed a spare pack of pantyhose in my backpack. Even though I already put my makeup on, I checked to see if I had my makeup kit. I wore the black high-heeled suede shoes I had bought for prom, and now used as concert shoes.

I was more nervous than I had been in a long time. I never took the Christmas concert too seriously, since we usually performed things we had already mastered, but this year we were going to sing Ambrož Čopi's *Ave Maria*, one of our pieces for the competition. The thought that Maks might come made my stomach churn; I hadn't mentioned the concert in the email I sent him. I had replied to him a few days ago with a not-too-long letter telling him about my days and what we did in college, and that I thought what he was doing at the border was cool. He hadn't answered me yet.

When Ivana's car turned into the parking lot behind the church, the other singers, equipped with backpacks, garment bags, hangers, and shoeboxes, were already milling about among the cars. I scrambled out and headed toward the side door to the rectory. The night was cold but clear: the stars were visible, though very faintly due to the city lights.

We crowded into the room unlocked for us by a short Jesuit. Agata walked to the out-of-tune upright piano in the corner and roughly pushed on the keys to silence us. The buzzing didn't die down, so she shouted and clapped her hands. We fell silent, and she gave us instructions: warm up, change, go into the church, sit in the back, wait for the men's choir to finish, then it's our turn.

We spread out across the room and began a long and torturous warm-up. The old classroom echoed, we could barely hear each other, and our voices were brittle. As always, things were the worst right before the concert. Agata repeated the repertoire order, then told us to change.

I took a chair next to Sara and took off my pants. I threw my jeans over the back of the chair and took off my sweater and T-shirt. In the middle of the cold classroom, like many other singers, I stood in nothing but pantyhose and a bra.

"Sara, is that the only bra you have with you?"

Agata was standing not far from us, looking indignantly at Sara. Sara was sitting on the chair in her underwear, a snow-white bra and black panties, and pulling on her pantyhose. She stared at the choirmaster in surprise. The singers around us fell silent, observing the tense scene. Sara nodded.

"You should be wearing a *nude* bra under a white blouse."

Sara frowned, and the pale complexion of her face started taking on color until her cheeks looked like a nearly ripe peach.

"I didn't know," she finally said with a cold tone. "I thought a white bra was appropriate for a white blouse."

"Of course it isn't. Under a white blouse, one wears a nude bra. You really should have known that. But it is what it is now. At least you're in the second row."

She turned and marched away. Sara stared at me with raised eyebrows: "What is wrong with that woman?"

I quietly explained to her that Agata is extremely difficult before concerts. Our appearance on stage meant a lot to her, which included our underwear.

"I bought a white bra just for this," Sara said furiously while fastening the buttons on her blouse. "I only wear black ones. What a hard-ass." She mimicked Agata with a distorted voice: "*You really should have known that.* Cow."

I decided to ignore her because I didn't want to fuel Agata's bad mood in any way. The classroom soon filled with the scent of hairspray and the sound of deodorants spritzing through the air. I was putting on my skirt when I heard her again: "Oh, fuck." Her pantyhose had suddenly ripped at the big toe and unraveled. I told her not to panic and rummaged through my backpack for the spare.

"Experience," I said when she gaped at the fresh pack.

I put on my blouse, buttoned it, and checked my make up in a compact mirror. I added a touch of blush to my cheeks with my fingers and tidied my eyebrows with a small brush. I looked at Sara again, when she whispered: "This is horrible."

The skirt she had received from a former singer, not tailored to her measurements like mine, really didn't suit her. I assured her she looked just fine, as there was no more time for the truth.

I put on my high heels and straightened my skirt so it fell softly to the floor, completely covering my shoes.

"Now you're a true Agata's soldier," Sara quipped while putting on black ballet flats. Although Agata demanded heels, Sara refused to wear them. I just frowned and said nothing.

Agata called us to gather by the exit of the classroom. When we crowded by the door, she said she knew she wouldn't be able to catch us all in one place after the concert, so she wanted to wish us Merry Christmas and a Happy New Year now, before we see each other again at rehearsals in January. Ivana seized the moment to hand her the gift bag, which Agata took with feigned surprise. When she reached into it and pulled out the neat black box with gold lettering, the surprise on her face turned genuine.

"Oh, girls. How thoughtful of you. Thank you." She looked at the box in her hands, and because I was close, I noticed her swallow somewhat nervously. With black folders under our arms, we began leaving the classroom one by one, and because some singers kept whispering in the cold hallway before the church entrance, Agata strictly ordered us to be quiet.

It was cold in the church. A few people were already sitting in the pews, only the first two rows were empty. There was a nativity scene under the altar, and the sound of water burbling in a little stream could be heard. I wished I could go closer and look at the figurines. This imitation of the world of Bethlehem, so different from the real one, reminded me of childhood. From where I stood, I could only see the figures of Joseph and Mary, staring with stony faces into the empty cradle between them.

We sat in the back rows while the church filled up. The men's choir took to the stage and began with their first piece. Their voices were good, but they sang out of tune and disjointedly, as if they couldn't hear each other.

As I watched them standing next to one another in their black shirts, I wondered if things were any different in a men's choir. Do they also talk about girls as much as we do about boys? They probably don't flock to the restroom in groups of three, nibble on granola bars, show each other photos of their nephews, talk about wedding dresses, or lend each other pantyhose, brushes, and bobby pins. They probably don't compliment each other on their looks, nor worry so much about their own appearance. Or do they? Do they notice if one of them has gained weight, gone to the hairdresser, came wearing new clothes?

They also don't bring gifts to their choirmaster, perfumes and gift certificates for massages. Their preparation for a concert is shorter and less complicated and the attire they wear on stage doesn't have so many rules and laws. Their rehearsals are more relaxed, they don't strive for perfection. After rehearsal, they go for a beer and list facts to prove who knows more about a chosen topic. And the topic is rarely their intimate relationships. They don't even necessarily know who is in a relationship with whom. We knew so many unimportant details about one another: who is in a relationship, who is engaged, married, what her partner's name is, and what's his job.

Applause roused me from my thoughts, indicating it was our turn. When I stepped onto the stage and stood next to Barbara, I was blinded by lights and I couldn't distinguish the faces in the church. Even if Maks came, I wouldn't be able to see him. I opened the folder and heard the reference tone, for which Agata didn't need a tuning fork, as she had absolute pitch.

I wasn't allowed to take my eyes off her trembling hands swaying through the air, but I nonetheless had to glance at the score a few times. On my left, I heard Barbara's velvety voice, and on the right, Klara's sharp soprano. From the right, the high voices of the sopranos advanced my way, softly filling the church, while the dark underlay of the second altos came from the left, supporting us gently but firmly. Compared to the male voices from before, this was pure perfection. Agata once told us that female voices are incomparably more in tune with each other than male ones and that it's the timbre that gives them character, and the timbre of our choir was truly beautiful. Her hands dropped after the first piece, and a grateful smile danced on her face.

Unfortunately, it soon vanished: during the last piece, Čopi's *Ave Maria*, we sang much more insecurely and even wrong at times, as the first sopranos kept going flat, we second sopranos sang too quietly, the first altos trailed behind us, and the singers in the second alto tried in vain to catch the harmony with the flat first soprano. Agata's face grew dark, despite the applause we garnered.

"You were good," Dad said to Urška and me after the concert, when we found ourselves by the laden tables.

"Like every year," Mom added proudly, while Andrej, who had helped himself to a cookie, nodded with enthusiasm. Urška grimaced, displeased, and said that *Ave Maria* didn't go as planned, as we second sopranos had sung too quietly, and I hissed at her that they were the ones who kept going flat, and we argued for a few moments until Mom shouted in surprise: "Oh, look, it's Maks!"

Maks appeared beside us. I had never seen him so elegantly dressed: he was wearing a gray coat, and a dark blue shirt with tiny white dots underneath. I sensed the noble scent of men's cologne, but I also noticed that his face looked more haggard than I'd ever seen it.

Mom welcomed him into our circle with exuberance, nearly hugging him. I looked for a trace of pretense on her face, but it seemed she was genuinely happy to see him. A memory flashed through my mind of how once, when Maks and I were little, the three of us went to the Kodeljevo swimming pool together and she looked after him as if he were her son. Now she started asking him how he was and what he was doing, without mentioning his parents or brother once. Maks was quick to answer, but despite his politeness, he looked somewhat tense. I should have prevented him from coming to the concert. My father's face was stiffening unpleasantly while Maks explained to Mom about his studies and his thesis.

I decided it was smartest to get us away, and I used the moment when Mom said something to Urška to ask him if he wanted tea. We went towards the short Jesuit, who was pouring tea into plastic cups. I felt feverish as I thanked him for coming and I thrust the cup of tea into his hands so forcefully that it splashed over the rim and burned his palm.

"Sorry," I muttered. "How did you find the concert?"

"Okay, you sang well. But I liked one song by the men's choir best." He pulled a folded and slightly crumpled program from his coat pocket and studied it: "*Bogorodice djevo*," he read and looked at me timidly.

"Rachmaninoff, yes."

"That was really great. We went once," he was excited to tell, "to Moscow. All four of us. For a whole week. One day we went to a smaller town near Moscow with a large monastery. A men's choir sang in one of the churches. It was really something special."

"I didn't know you guys had been to Russia."

"That was... in high school." He looked away. He doubtless wanted to say it was after our families had drifted apart. I drank some tea, which burned my tongue lightly, and he asked me: "Did you know they aren't allowed to use instruments in the Orthodox church? That they only allow singing?"

The adrenaline from the performance had worn off and my body was flooding with fatigue, so I wasn't in the mood for a serious debate. I was glancing at the corner where there was Blaž and Sara. Blaž must have come with Maks and he was just shaking hands with Ivana. I answered him distractedly: "Yeah, I've heard that. Well, in Islam, music is forbidden altogether."

"That's not true at all," Maks was indignant, but his voice soon mellowed, keeping a didactic tone: "It's much more complicated than that. It does say that in some Sunni books, but not all Muslims follow it. I understand that you know little of Islam. That's just a consequence of our catastrophic school system, which is explicitly Eurocentric."

I blushed at being wrong and showed I was convinced by nodding. He went on: "You know what I was thinking. I know you said at the freshman party that the Middle East and Islam don't interest you that much, but... Honestly, I feel that without a good knowledge of the history of the Middle East, we can't truly understand either Europe or the world."

I said I completely agreed, as anything else I might have said would surely come out wrong. He offered me some firm advice: "Read Gellner." I rolled my eyes. Maks knew how much that got on my nerves. I had already reproached him once that I hate it when he tells me who to read. He laughed at my reaction and without heeding it, kept at it: "No, even better, read Kamrava. I'm currently reading his *Beyond the Arab Spring*. When you read that, you gain a better understanding of the complexity of the modern Middle East."

I just sighed in response. There were times when I wanted to ask him: Maks, are you pretending when you say you've read all this, when you're just reading the shortened summaries from the internet? I was about to say he was naive if he thought I had time to read monographs in English alongside my studies, fieldwork and choir rehearsals, vocal technique, and my share of responsibilities for our household. But my Mom approached us and said they had decided we are going to go see the Christmas lights and drink some mulled wine at the market square. Would Maks perhaps like to join us?

Standing by the table with the gas heater, clinging to a cup of mulled wine, I feverishly wondered how it had come to pass that after our Christmas concert, five days before the referendum on the Family

Law—which was causing an electric atmosphere, even without it being discussed—I, my family, Andrej, and Maks were standing at a table at the Ljubljana market square, looking at the city's Christmas decor and trying to hold a conversation.

At first, the four of them chattered about their own things, and Maks and I mostly kept silent until Father spoke up with a question aimed at Maks: "So what kind of plans does a young man like you who studies anthropology have?"

I hid behind the paper cup. I thought Mom and Dad had already grown tired of arguing with me about the hopeless future that would surely follow from my decision to study anthropology, but now they had someone before them who had done the same stupid thing as I had. I noticed Maks swallowed hard, thinking of what to say, when my mother, who had the annoying habit of answering for others—which Urška had inherited from her—spoke up in his place:

"Well, Maks is a Hafner... He'll find his way, I'm sure." I understood what she meant to say: Maks, as the heir to the anthropological Hafner dynasty, would be taken care of. Maks, whose face was ashen gray, gave a tart smile, and Mom kept talking: "Ivana introduced me to two of her friends... her cousin and her colleague. He studies anthropology too, but together with German. He said anthropology is more for the soul."

I hoped my eyes would meet Maks's, so he could read "sorry" in them, but he kept looking away, as if he didn't see me.

"Society is changing," he suddenly began, and his tone was suspiciously similar to Istenič's. "At least as far as employability is concerned. In my opinion, in the not-so-distant future, most mechanical and physical jobs will be replaced by machines, and people, thanks to education, will reach a level where they will no longer be willing to serve the system by wasting time in tiring jobs, but will strive for intellectual and creative work that will no longer be dictated by the labor market." He paused for a moment, and it seemed the table was holding its breath.

"It is however true," he continued with perfect composure, "*it is a fact*, that for life in such a future, we would urgently need to introduce a universal basic income. This seems to me the most necessary solution to keep man from becoming even more dehumanized in the era of late capitalism."

Hearing Maks speak, I wished we were somewhere alone and that he would explore my body with the fingers now clutching the paper cup. To hide the effect his words had on me, I lowered my gaze, and he cleared his throat and added proudly: "But otherwise, my current plans are mostly revolving around my fieldwork at the border, dealing with the refugees and migrants. Just yesterday, I returned from the border in Dobova, where I did voluntary work for the last four weeks. I'm also interested in the Middle East, where I'd like to go on a research expedition." He took a sip of mulled wine.

Father and Mother were nodding, lost for words, but Andrej piped up: "The other day I read somewhere"—it was pretty obvious he was talking about a comment on the national broadcaster's website—"that the volunteers at the border are there just to cause confusion. Someone wrote that civil defense, meaning *professionals*, keep trying to establish order, but then the volunteers come and start handing out sandwiches, the people start crowding and total chaos ensues. Also, is it true that most of those sandwiches end up in the trash because there's pork in them?"

I looked into the empty cup before me and remembered how pleasant it had been to wash down the news that Maks was fucking Gaja with a large amount of alcohol.

But Maks confirmed it: "The blame for the chaos lies primarily with the government, which is terribly organized and whose entire response to the refugee crisis has been generally very poor." My father nodded solemnly, and Mom said with a smile on her face: "It's nice that you help at the border. I see you've grown into a serious and smart boy." He gave a weak smile, and my father, also softening his tone, remarked: "And nice of you to come to our girls' concert"—to my horror, he even squeezed his shoulder—"to church," he concluded with a smile. I remembered hearing Maks's father say to mine long ago that he would never cross the threshold of a church again, and my father was apparently delighted by the fact that the youngest Hafner, whom he otherwise considered a leftist activist, did not stick to his father's resolution.

With a stony expression on his face, Maks said that he was glad to have come, then said that he must be going now, and he left without saying goodbye to me. As I watched him walk away into the crowd in his elegant gray coat, I was overcome by sadness. It was clear that our friendship was over. Maks had now seen up close how trying my folks were, and he wouldn't want to have anything to do with me anymore. Besides, he had heard us sing and said almost nothing about it. The sadness was displaced by the feeling that I had irreparably embarrassed myself before him with my choir singing, my appearance, my family, and my thoughtless statements.

When we were cramming into the back seats of our car afterward, Mom remarked that she didn't know Maks and I were friends.

"Oh, but I knew," Urška chirped, "they even meet up every now and then. Isn't that right, Maša?"

20

In the days following the concert, my father kept pestering me with intrusive questions to get me to tell him what I would vote for in the referendum and he didn't stop until I said I would vote against. His thoughts on the matter haunted me until Sunday, when I went to the polling station at my former elementary school and cast a blank ballot. When the TV announced the results of the referendum that evening, and my parents welcomed them by gushing there was still some common sense among Slovenians, I knew that one of those void ballots was mine. Going to bed, I felt guilty before all the women in history who had struggled for their right to vote, but I couldn't even imagine the reaction of my parents if I had voted in favor.

The days after the referendum were full of errands and shopping that severely harmed my wallet, and the time between Christmas and New Year's evaporated amidst visits and binge-watching TV shows. Urška spent the Christmas holidays at Andrej's, and I frequently caught myself overcome by melancholy because of it. Every year during the Christmas holidays, we used to binge-watch *Harry Potter* and *The Lord of the Rings*, and we always did a wardrobe purge, advising each other on which pieces to keep for the New Year. Sometimes we went to the movies or took our parents' car and went swimming at the Snovik Spa. But this year, in the long, lonely hours, I often bitterly thought of Agata's words. To occupy myself with something, I tackled my wardrobe alone and filled a large bag with clothes I would no longer wear, and just before the New Year, I went to the hairdresser, where I had my chestnut hair cut into a long bob and, under the influence of Anastasia from *Fifty Shades of Grey*—which I watched instead of the fantasy franchises—got long bangs that suited me better than I expected.

The day before New Year's Eve, Sara called and asked if I wanted to join her with some friends to celebrate New Year's at Blaž's place in Murska Sobota. He supposedly had the whole house to himself and had invited some people from college, telling Sara to ask me to come too. The invitation came as a surprise, but since I didn't want to spend the evening celebrating with my parents, I said I'd go. They picked me up in front of my building around five the next day, and we set off for Prekmurje.

Besides Sara and me, there were three guys in the car; another car full of girls drove behind us, and a few more were supposed to arrive from Maribor and Ptuj. I was really enjoying the male company, their immature humor and fierce debates—probably because the movie I had seen had lit quite a fire within me, though I wouldn't dare admit it to anyone—and the hours in the car went by quickly. When we drove past the exit for Zagorje ob Savi on the highway, I remembered Agata's words about how rarely she went home. When we left Maribor behind, I realized I had perhaps been to Prekmurje only once or twice in my life, and at the sight of large single-family houses adorned with Christmas lights lining the road, I was gripped by an unexplained melancholy that the jokes of the guys in the front seats couldn't dispel. I wondered if Maks would be at the party too, but since I was surrounded by students of German, this was doubtful.

The New Year's celebration was to take place at Blaž's house, in a village settlement a stone's throw from Murska Sobota. It was a typical single-family home built in the eighties. Despite the relatively modern furniture, the spirit of socialism wafted through the living spaces due to the dark hardwood floors, and the living room smelled of cigarettes, as if the smoke was absorbed in the leather sofa set and heavy curtains.

Blaž's home was the opposite of Maks's, where elegant cleanliness reigned. Here, the rooms were full of clutter: an unsightly ashtray, some kind of souvenir from Poreč, lay on the coffee table, dusty figurines from travels and picture frames gathered on the shelves, mountains of newspapers, magazines, and advertising flyers were piled up by the TV, a cup full of ballpoint pens stood by the telephone, the slips of paper next to it scribbled with numbers. There were no books, only a short row of cookbooks.

An artificial Christmas tree stood next to the television set, glowing with colorful lights. It lacked a nativity scene, and since I didn't see a cross anywhere in the house, I came to the conclusion that Blaž's resistance to the Family Law amendment didn't stem from a religious upbringing.

The house filled up with lightning speed. There were also some of Blaž's former classmates from high school among the guests, and I quickly counted over twenty of us. Maks, as I had expected, was nowhere in sight. Blaž's female colleagues began preparing snacks, someone turned on music, and one of Blaž's high school friends turned out to be a master of mixing cocktails. The party was coming along nicely, glasses were emptied, snacks were running out, and people were constantly going out to the terrace to smoke, although judging by the smell inside, I wouldn't think that was necessary.

I stuck to Sara all evening, and when she got entangled in conversation with one of the guys, Blaž appeared beside me.

"Nice that you came." Like at the freshman party, he had to speak quite loudly on account of the noise. He checked what I was drinking, and when I showed him the glass of white wine in my hand, I told him

I intended to drink less than at the freshman party, as I had overdone it then. I meant it, but I was also on my third glass of wine already, beginning to feel slightly tipsy. Blaž smiled and said, "I invited a few other anthropologists, but only you came. Maks and the others of course couldn't make it, they already had other plans."

"What kind?"

"As far as I know, he, Gaja, and the others went to celebrate New Year's in Belgrade."

My stomach twisted with jealousy, and the party I found myself at suddenly seemed futile. I looked at the faces of the people around us. Blaž wasn't popular enough for exciting people to come celebrate New Year's at his place, and I had the bitter thought that I always end up among boring people.

I emptied the glass in my hands.

"How is your article coming along?" I asked him to stop thinking about Maks and his friends. Blaž's face lit up.

"We submitted it. Now we're waiting for the review."

"Will you continue to work together?"

Blaž shook his head and said he intended to devote himself to his studies, as the teaching track he had enrolled in for German was taking up a lot of his time.

"You want to teach?" I asked him. He didn't seem like a person who would fare well in a classroom, and it didn't surprise me when he grimaced and shook his head, then explained that he would have more opportunities for employment as a teacher, and he could still learn translation later. I nodded and said I understood.

Sara and the guy she was talking to stood up, and she asked me if I wanted to join them for a smoke. I shook my head, poured some wine from the bottle on the table into my empty glass, and took a few sips.

"Can I show you something?" Blaž asked me tentatively after a moment's silence. I felt like talking to him, but it was too noisy around us. I nodded, put the glass on the table, and followed him out of the room. We climbed the stairs to the upper floor, and I took my time as I was slightly dizzy, but leaving the room full of people also felt very good. He opened one of the doors in the hallway and showed me his room. It was larger than Maks's, but much less tidy and also very dark; the bed (queen-sized like Maks's) was still unmade, and the heap on it looked ominous in the shadows. I stood in the middle of the room, and he opened the door to the balcony and motioned for me to come out.

I was engulfed by the cold December night's chill, kept at bay by all the alcohol I drank. In the distance, I heard the barking of dogs and the popping of firecrackers. We were surrounded by houses like Blaž's, and long, desolate fields covered with a thin layer of frost stretched all around the village. The sky was clear.

I saw what Blaž wanted to show me. There was a telescope on the balcony, and he asked me if I wanted to look through it. I did and, following his instructions, admired the stars and a good half of the moon for a few minutes; he told me the moon had been full a few days ago.

"It's very beautiful," I said when I moved away and smiled. "The visibility is much better than in Ljubljana. There isn't as much light pollution here."

"That's true, but that's more or less the only advantage of living in Prekmurje," he chuckled. I rolled my eyes: "Oh, come on. It seems perfectly nice and interesting."

I said this to console him; in truth, due to the pitch darkness, I didn't see much except for a few houses. In front of the house opposite us, in the glow of Christmas lights, there was a plastic Santa climbing the fence. I thought this was the most tasteless Christmas decoration imaginable, but I didn't mention it to Blaž.

"Yeah, well, I don't know, life in these parts is pretty monotonous," he said with a stutter. "Sometimes I almost find it hard to return home on the weekend, because I know absolutely nothing has changed here in the meantime; there's no news besides who died, who got cancer, who drank themselves to death." He laughed awkwardly at his own words, and I joined in, even though I didn't find what he said funny.

"You're not thinking of coming back after your studies?"

He looked at me as if I had said something strange, and shook his head. He said he would go to Austria or Germany.

"What am I supposed to do here with my profession? I don't want to teach, and I wouldn't get a job in a school anyway. Well, I'm not saying there's nothing, maybe I could find something, in some museum, some project. But first I'll try abroad."

"What would you do in Austria?"

The question must have made him uncomfortable, as his face darkened. He said: "Anything. Since I speak German, I could get a job in a company."

"So, not something related to anthropology?"

He shook his head firmly and said he doubted anthropology would be of any use.

"Wages are so much higher in Austria that it makes sense to work there and live in Slovenia."

The way he said this, his lack of conviction, made me think that he was just repeating what he had picked up somewhere. That he was repeating what he heard from his parents or his surroundings, where many young people probably practiced such a lifestyle.

"I used to want to work with the Roma," he finally said so quietly I could barely hear him.

"How come?"

"Oh, that's a long story. I don't think you'd be interested." I perceived his mysterious smile in the dusk.

"Now I'm even more interested," I confessed.

He was eager to tell me: "In elementary school, I had Roma classmates, and I had an unpleasant experience once. *A Gypsy girl*"—the term was inappropriate and he corrected himself immediately—"*a Roma girl* pushed me into a radiator in fourth grade. I still have the scar." He leaned in to show me something on the edge of his forehead. I strained my eyes and noticed a ribbed scar in the glow of the streetlamp. When I raised my eyebrows in astonishment, he quickly explained it wasn't anything serious. "But they reacted quite negatively to it at home, and since it wasn't an isolated event, my parents complained and got support from other parents. The girl ended up being transferred to a special school." He swallowed and continued seriously: "I saw her again when I was in the fourth year of high school, on a night out with my classmates. She was working behind the bar, heavily pregnant. After that, I started asking myself who the Roma are and how they live. Preparing for the matura exam, I told my geography professor I was interested, and he gave me the book *Bury Me Standing* by Isabel Fonseca. Know it?" I shook my head, and he waved his hand and briefly explained that the book is about life among the Roma. "I liked it, and the professor told me it was an anthropological work, so I decided to go study anthropology too." He smiled, then added: "Back then I idealized it all a little; now, after three years of study, it's clear to me that anthropology isn't quite what I imagined."

"I think we all idealized it a little. The reality is different."

He nodded. "Yeah, average lectures, cramming from course readers, no lively discussions in seminars, a lot of people studying without knowing why... Well, you don't seem like that to me."

"You neither," I blurted out and felt a restlessness in my chest. The story about the Roma girl made him seem more interesting to me. "Maks told me back in September that you have a chance to stay in college," I remembered. "Couldn't you become a young researcher with Pirc?"

Loud shouts, laughter, and music were coming from the houses and the lower floor. In the faint glow of the Christmas lights attached to the balcony railing, I saw Blaž's gaze, combing the empty street, drop.

"I asked her about that," he said more quietly than before, "because she said I could write my doctorate with her. But she told me she couldn't promise me a job because the department doesn't have the money. Honestly, that made me a little angry," he said and looked at me. "I can't be a doctoral student without getting paid for it. I can barely afford life in Ljubljana as it is."

"I understand," I said with compassion. His distress was clear to me, and I was grateful that I could study in the place where I lived.

"But I would be interested in that," he added modestly, "but I could only go for it if I had a salary while working on the doctorate. You get it."

I nodded; at his admission and upon hearing sincerity in his voice that I couldn't hear before, I felt sympathy for him, and I had the thought that Blaž is much taller than Maks and his shoulders were much broader.

"Hey, why did that Roma girl push you into the radiator?"

His face made an unpleasant grimace at the memory. He hesitated before answering.

"We didn't like each other."

"What do you mean?"

I detected a tiny sigh. "You know what kids are like."

"Meaning?"

He smiled and nodded, as if relieved. It looked like he wouldn't share the true reason for the girl's violence with me. For a few long moments, we silently observed the road leading through the village. A car drove by. I always wondered who were the people who drove on New Year's Eve.

"Are you cold?" he asked me. It really was cold, and my hands were clasped tightly around my chest. I nodded and was about to suggest we go inside when we heard noise coming from the lower floor. The distinct sound of the countdown to the New Year.

"Oh, shit, I didn't even know it was that time already," Blaž said and took a step closer to me. From the lower floor, the countdown was approaching zero.

"Well, Happy New Year," I heard him say. Then he leaned toward me and pressed his lips to mine. Before I realized it, his tongue was in my mouth, moist as a slug, spreading a sour taste of red wine. I didn't pull away; the amount of alcohol I consumed made me follow the events with a delay, and though I didn't actively participate in the kiss, I hung on his face with open mouth. Fireworks flashed across the sky, and it was very noisy. Blaž hugged me and I felt his warm palms on my back; he covered me with his body, and I was flooded by a pleasant warmth. His hand had slid toward my buttocks as he gently pushed me toward the door to his room.

"Let's go inside," he mumbled while not yet completely unglued from my face. I took a step back into the room. I was experiencing two such contradictory feelings it made me afraid. Next to Blaž's body and his hands, I felt arousal, which I blamed on the unfulfilled lust caused by that slimy erotic romance. Since I didn't have complete control of my movements, I surrendered to the kiss, and our tongues finally intertwined. I felt like I could barely breathe, and an excitement was awakening in my body, only slightly permeated by revulsion.

We stood in the middle of his room kissing and slowly moving toward his bed. Blaž's hands were squeezing my ass when I hit the bed from behind and flounced down, tearing away from him for a moment. He immediately sat next to me, kissed me again, and went under my sweater with his hand. His palm was perplexed as it sought the edge of my shirt, before it began moving aside the layers of clothing: under the sweater, I was wearing a long-sleeved shirt and an undershirt.

I remembered the coat Maks had worn at our concert, and how fresh his cologne smelled, and his gray bedding that smelled of fabric softener, and the memory was displaced by the thought of Blaž's unmade bed, the stuffy house steeped in the smell of cigarettes, and the village street on which it stood.

I tore myself forcefully from his embrace and got up.

"Sorry," I mumbled, avoiding his eyes, and the next moment I was teetering down the stairs leading to the lower floor.

II.
Winter, spring, summer 2016

1.

The New Year's Eve party did not end well. When I got downstairs, it took me a long time to find Sara, who, it turned out, was getting high with two guys. One of them was supposed to drive us home the next day, but he looked so drunk that I doubted he would sober up by the morning. I avoided Blaž and spent the rest of the night talking to a group of girls. I caught him looking my way several times, and he even approached me once or twice, awkwardly trying to start a conversation, but I managed to slip away. Finally, I asked the girls who were heading home to Maribor around 3:00 AM to take me along as a fifth passenger, thinking it would be easier to catch a ride to Ljubljana from there. While I was freezing at the empty bus station, I used a ride-sharing application to find a woman leaving Maribor for Ljubljana at 5:30 AM. She turned out to be a young nurse working at the clinical center.

When I got into the car, I took out my phone and typed a message that had been rattling around in my head all night, sending it to Maks: *Happy New Year. I hope my parents didn't piss you off too much and that we'll see each other sometime in the new year. Best, Maša.* As soon as I hit "Send," I regretted it, but before I had time to wallow in the feeling, he replied: *Haha, no worries. Same to you, see ya.*

I stared at those few words that had flown back to me with such speed, trying to decipher them. Apparently, he was still awake wherever he was, even though it was half past five in the morning. In my mind's eye, I pictured a scene where the two of them, he and Gaja, lay naked in a modern hotel room in downtown Belgrade, covered by a thin white sheet. She was sleeping, exhausted from a good party and the quick, passionate sex that followed, while he sat propped up, scrolling through his phone—why he was still awake, my imagination couldn't explain. "Haha, no worries" probably referred to my parents, but it felt somewhat vague. At the same time, the "see ya" gently reassured me, so I put my phone back into my backpack and closed my eyes. I dozed off and slept all the way to Šiška.

For the rest of the holidays, I tried to think about New Year's Eve as little as possible. Besides, just a few hours after getting home, I started sneezing and coughing. By evening, my temperature had risen to 38 degrees, and I spent the first days of January in bed, surrounded by cups of tea, painkillers, and tissues. I had to cancel my vocal technique lesson and let Ivana know I wouldn't come to the rehearsal, as I had lost my voice.

On the evening before the second practice of January, I received a text message. Neither Agata nor Ivana ever sent texts, they always wrote emails. The message was brief: *Please ensure EVERYONE is at practice tomorrow. Best, Agata.*

When we piled noisily into the small hall, many of us fell silent at the sight of Agata, who sat on the piano bench staring blankly ahead, her face even more stony than usual. Even Ivana, who normally sat silently in her chair right before practice, was now typing intently on her phone. The singers took their seats, busying themselves with sheet music and water bottles.

Once all the chairs in the hall were filled, the whispering died down, and silence settled over the room. Agata cleared her throat and adjusted the black knit shawl covering her hunched shoulders. She was dressed entirely in black from head to toe, as was customary.

Her face looked terribly exhausted.

"I thought we would start fresh with the new year."

Her voice was strange, ragged. She wasn't looking at us, but staring at the keys in front of her. Some of the singers raised their heads, daring to look at her contorted face.

"But then your messages started coming in." She recited mockingly, "'I won't be at vocal technique.' 'I won't be at practice.' Ivana received about five messages like that." It was so quiet in the small hall that you could hear the crackling of the old, worn parquet floor.

"There were too few of you at rehearsal last week," she continued, her voice rising, "for us to discuss the Christmas concert. Which was *awful*." The words sliced through the thick air, overheated by the radiators and our breathing. I glanced around at the girls: a great many of them were examining their fingernails, while others studied the stucco on the ceiling.

"Half a year, girls. Half a year before the competition. By now you should have mastered the basics of *Ave Maria* so we could start working on dynamics and expression, but what I heard at the concert clearly showed you don't know it. That you aren't learning, you aren't practicing, you aren't trying hard enough."

Barbara, to my left, shifted nervously in her chair. I caught Urška's eye. Her eyes were sadly downcast, and seeing her so dejected made my heart squeeze. I knew her; I knew how deeply Agata's criticism hurt her.

Compared to earlier, when she had been as white as a sheet, Agata's cheeks were now burning red. She adjusted her black shawl restlessly and took a breath.

"Because of all this, I asked myself"—the tension in the hall felt like a layer of thick gray fog—"what are we even doing together? Why are we trying? I constantly invest in you. And you give nothing back.

Do I even mean anything to you?"

Ivana sniffled. It looked as if she might burst into tears at any moment.

"So, I came to the conclusion," she continued sharply, ignoring Ivana, while the singers anxiously held their breath, "that perhaps it's time we part ways. That we each go our own route."

The atmosphere in the room was thick with suffocating unease. Outside the windows, the dense Ljubljana fog crept like a ghost, clinging damply to the glass.

"I can no longer be your choirmaster."

Agata's gray eyes glinted in the dim glow of the ceiling lights. Fingerprints shone on the sheet music folders, from the sweaty palms gripping them.

Just then, Urška spoke up: "Are we really just going to quit? Right before Tallinn?"

The girls looked at her with gratitude. Her voice was warm and alive when everything else felt cold and dead. Urška's face flushed red as she glared defiantly at Agata. Agata sighed heavily, and behind Urška's back, Ivana buried her face in her hands.

"It's not that I want this," Agata replied, "but I simply don't get what I expect from you."

I glanced over at Sara. She had drawn her eyebrows together as if angry, staring resentfully at the floor in front of her. Since New Year's Eve, apart from a message asking where I was, the two of us hadn't been in touch. I had replied that I wasn't feeling well and had gone home early, and then gotten sick. That way, I avoided explaining why I had vanished from the party in the middle of the night.

Suddenly, Barbara chimed in: "What does this mean now? I think everyone would like to know if we should just get up and leave, or..."

Agata stared at her.

"I don't know," she said abruptly, in a completely different, much softer voice. Her gray eyes darted from one singer to the next. "Tell me how *you* feel," she added firmly.

"Confused," Urška shot back quickly, and a faint laugh rippled through the girls. "To me, it's... like breaking up with a boyfriend." She pulled a face, as if the mere thought of it terrified her. "When you're waiting for one of you to say something, and you want him to stay, but you don't know if there's any point."

Many of the girls nodded. Agata smiled faintly.

"And what would you tell him in that situation?" she asked her in a combative tone.

Urška replied that it would depend on her expectations; if she wanted to stay with him, she'd want to hear his side. Then they could look for a solution.

"You know... A relationship takes work," she said, looking patronizingly around at the girls, and many murmured in agreement.

Agata shifted on the piano bench and sighed. Despite this, her posture didn't slouch; she still took care to sit perfectly straight.

"I agree with Urška," she said slowly, without looking at my sister. "Of course, many things could be resolved if your attitude toward the choir were different."

My mouth was completely dry, and the heat radiating from the radiators was making me uncomfortably hot. I gazed longingly at the water bottles many of the singers had; this time, I had forgotten mine.

"I expect you to *belong* to the choir. If you can't, I'd rather see you leave. The choir isn't..." –she paused, as if searching for a fitting comparison—"...a *lacemaking club*, where it doesn't matter whether you show up or not."

A weak chuckle spread through the choir, though it couldn't fully mend the tense atmosphere. Agata ignored it and continued passionately: "We are all building this choir together. If one person slacks off, the whole choir slacks off."

Ivana spoke up, her voice fragile: "Agata… I think everyone here would like to give more of themselves." Her lip trembled as she spoke. I wasn't sure all the singers would agree with her. But no one contradicted her. She and Agata observed each other in silence for a few moments. Then Ivana contritely lowered her gaze.

"Would you really?"

Quite a few girls in the choir confirmed that they would. When I saw Urška nodding vigorously, I gave a weak nod myself.

"Depends on what you have in mind," said Barbara. She looked firmly at Agata, who returned an astonished stare.

The choirmaster stayed silent for a long moment, then said elatedly: "The competition *really* means a lot to me. I know it means a lot to you, too. We haven't competed abroad together yet, and we are the only Slovenian choir to qualify for this competition. And we have never had a score like *The Bush* before. This is an exceptional opportunity."

Her grey eyes shimmered softly, she looked at us very tenderly and spoke slowly, as if weighing every word.

"But if we want… If we want to achieve something at this competition, you have to invest more. I'm sorry to say it, but I'm afraid that what you've put in so far hasn't been enough. I was thinking…" She hesitated, as if unsure whether to proceed, and then added: "I was thinking how different it would be if we met twice a week instead of once."

A tiny rustle echoed through the hall, as the girls began to shift restlessly in their seats. Agata ignored it and continued with more confidence: "Twice a week. You'd only come one extra time a week, but you'd be putting in a hundred percent more. Do you know what a hundred percent more means in music? The result is a hundred percent better choir."

None of the girls spoke up for a long time. Agata waited patiently for one of us to say something. The silence was making me nervous, so I asked: "And that's on top of vocal technique?"

Agata's brow furrowed as she looked at me. She said grimly: "Of course, on top of vocal technique. Without it, there is nothing."

I swallowed hard, my mind racing feverishly. Every singer had to attend vocal technique once a week, even though Agata had repeatedly said the effect would only truly show if we went twice—but not even she could make that happen.

"That really is a lot," Barbara said weakly. I looked over at her. Her cheeks were burning red, and she stared uncertainly straight ahead. Then she looked at Agata and said: "I'll have to think about whether I can manage that. I really love singing in the choir, but Maj isn't even two yet, and..."

Agata nodded so fiercely and rapidly that it looked unnatural, and the voice died in Barbara's throat. Even though Agata claimed she understood, it was clear that the bond between them had definitively severed. Their relationship had been deteriorating ever since Barbara announced her pregnancy.

"Perhaps," she said, scanning the singers' faces, "this is an opportunity to rebuild ourselves. Those of you who... *understand* that you cannot give the choir what is expected, should reconsider your priorities. Those of you ready to move forward with me... You stay. But I understand," her voice faltered slightly, "that not all of you can handle this. I will understand that. There will be no hard feelings if... If anyone decides she no longer wishes to participate."

The ensuing silence could have rivaled that of a graveyard in the dead of night. It was suddenly shattered by Agata's laugh.

"Girls, why are you so quiet? If anyone else has something to say, do it now."

Sara spoke up. Her voice was very cold: "When would this extra practice be?" She stared at the choirmaster as if making sure it was really her.

Agata pivoted on the piano bench toward a stack of papers resting on the piano. She picked up the top sheet and, without really looking at it, recited mechanically: "The hall is still available on Sundays and Thursdays. From half past seven to ten."

She peeked out from behind the paper at the singers; some were already bending down to their bags, pulling out planners, while others reached for their phones. Some of us just sat there, uncertain. Klara, on my right, sighed.

"Thursdays are for partying," she muttered under her breath, yet loudly enough to be heard by a fair number of girls, who let out muffled laughs. Nevertheless, knowing them as I did, Klara's words must have stung them, just as they stung me: rarely did any of us actually go out.

"And Sunday evening is for family," my sister spoke up, agitated, shooting Klara a disdainful look. I was tempted to roll my eyes, knowing exactly what "an evening for family" meant to Urška. She and Andrej went to evening mass at the Franciscan church and then to marriage prep, where they sat around with other equally boring couples discussing the trials awaiting them in matrimony, before even getting married.

But most of the singers agreed. Ana raised her hand—even though we never raised hands—and waited for Agata to cue her to speak. "I often stay home on Sunday evenings and don't come back to Ljubljana until Monday," she said in a squeaky voice. Several choir members nodded. Agata swept her gaze across the choir.

"Thursday evening, then?"

She wanted us to answer with a loud yes. A few singers hesitated, staring blankly at the worn parquet. I wasn't entirely sure either: having practice twice a week plus vocal technique was no small commitment. Out of the corner of my eye, I saw Sara, a sullen expression on her face, jotting something down in her planner. When I shifted my gaze, I met Agata's eyes. She stared at me until I nodded, then I leaned over my backpack, my face flushed, to grab my phone.

Agata's face was much brighter than at the start of practice; satisfaction glinted in her eyes. She stood up decisively from the piano bench, pausing for a slightly uncertain moment before saying: "Good, starting next week, we begin anew. There won't be practice this Thursday since I need to book the space a week in advance, but starting next week, yes. And... We won't sing today. Go home. We start on Tuesday with our *new* lineup."

She flashed us a warm, almost maternal smile, then snatched up the stack of papers on the piano and shoved them loudly into her bag. I noticed her hands were trembling. Hastily, she stepped over to the coat rack, slipped on her black coat, and carelessly pulled her fur hat onto her head. Without so much as a glance in our direction, she stormed out of the hall, and right before the door slammed shut behind her, we heard her call out: "Goodbye."

Some of the singers were already packing up their things and putting on their coats, so her exit wasn't as conspicuous as it otherwise might have been. I caught Sara's eye. She stood up from her chair, put on her winter jacket, and stationed herself by the door as if waiting for me.

When I walked over to her, she asked: "Do you think this would ever happen in a men's choir?" In response, I could only shake my head.

2.

Maks's text message took me by surprise. I only noticed it after I got out of bed and went to the bathroom to change my blood-soaked pad. I had taken my phone with me to browse the internet, and saw that he had sent me a message twenty minutes earlier. I took no time to think and immediately replied that I would go for a walk, even though I lacked the strength to wander around in the cold. I had been having severe cramps all day. He replied that we could meet in half an hour in front of my apartment block. I quickly showered, changed into jeans and a hoodie, and applied my makeup. Even though losing blood made my face look pale, I was pleased to see that my new hairstyle suited me very well. I put on my winter coat, pulled on a beanie, took it off the very next moment, and went down to wait for him in front of the building.

I stood in the cold, the pad in my underwear soaking up the warm blood and tiny cramps blossoming in my lower abdomen. I suppressed them with a painkiller a few hours ago. As I was mentally calculating how many hours had passed since I took it, I spotted the headlight of Maks's bicycle at the end of our street, and within moments, he was beside me. He was wearing a ski jacket and a knitted beanie on his head. His face was flushed red from the cold, but I knew that didn't bother him. On the contrary: Maks adored the cold. Winter was his favorite season, and he always said he loved it best when the sky was crystal clear and the temperature dropped below zero.

I preferred the warmer months. I especially loved spring, particularly its arrival, because my birthday fell around that time.

I also liked the April rain, but May was my absolute favorite, as the days grew noticeably longer, the evening sky over Ljubljana turned a Parisian blue, the birds chirped wistfully in the trees around our apartment building, and the sound of a basketball bouncing on the nearby court drifted through our windows.

Maks and I would go on our walks together in every season. He never mentioned having this habit with anyone else, though I sometimes saw him around college, sitting in cafes where he drank coffee or beer with his friends. But the two of us preferred to wander aimlessly through all the various neighborhoods of Šiška. Lights burned in the windows of countless apartments, and silhouettes would occasionally appear in them. In the spring, the two of us would venture down the streets stretching between Litostroj and Plečnik's church, lined with old villas where magnolias bloomed out front in April. I once showed Maks which villa I would most like to live in: it had a charming little turret with a pointed roof. He conceded it was beautiful, but was quite indifferent to the idea of living there, probably because he already lived in a house; the four of us, unlike the Hafners, had been squeezing into sixty square meters for nearly twenty years.

We set off down the street into the unknown, as usual, except that after only a few steps, I felt a sharp cramp in my lower abdomen. Through gritted teeth, I asked Maks—who hadn't made a single mention of our get-together over mulled wine—to tell me in person what it had been like at the border. He had just begun to tell me when the pain flared up in my stomach again, making me gasp and squeeze my eyes shut. I instinctively wrapped my arms around my stomach and stopped.

"Is everything okay?"

I nodded and motioned for him to continue. Maks raised his eyebrows but said nothing, and we walked on.

"What was I saying… Oh, right, well, it was truly incredible to see the people going through this situation up close, to hear their stories. I'm not saying they're super open, just the opposite, they are quite distrustful and reserved, but —"

A pain sliced through my abdomen so violently that I squatted down and hugged my knees. I felt utterly stupid, but the pain sent white spots dancing before my eyes.

"What's going on?"

"I'm sorry, I should have told you we couldn't meet up." I slouched on the curb, pulled my knees to my chest, and buried my face in my hands. I hesitated for a long moment before telling him that it was the first day of my period and that the pill I had taken a few hours ago had clearly worn off.

For a few moments, all I could hear was my own deep breaths as I continued to cover my face with my hands. They were freezing—I didn't like wearing gloves. I moved them from my face and gazed up at Maks, who was watching me in silence. Then he asked if I had a pill on me, and when I shook my head, he looked around. That was actually kind of funny; we were standing in the middle of a completely empty street, Christmas lights twinkling in the windows around us, but other than that, there was absolutely nothing anywhere—no pharmacy, no shop, no people.

"I'm going to have to go home," I groaned in mild panic as the next severe cramp announced its arrival. I felt something soft and warm sliding into my underwear. I was terrified the cramps would become too severe, as had happened to me before when I didn't have a pill on hand and ended up bedridden for hours. Once, the pain was so bad I had even thrown up.

"Yeah, of course. Come on, get up, you can't just sit there," Maks said, offering me his hand. Our hands clasped, and his felt so warm against mine. He noticed it too. After I stood up and he let go, he said: "Your hands are freezing."

I nodded, and we slowly made our way back towards my apartment building.

"Sorry, I really thought I was feeling better."

"No worries."

"Do you want to come up? I'm home alone."

I didn't even know where that came from. I had been alone all day, Mom and Dad had gone to visit Grandma for the weekend, and Urška was at Andrej's. An empty apartment awaited me upstairs, and the thought flashed through my mind that he could keep me company.

Maks didn't waver. He took the keys from my hands, unlocked the door, and held it open for me. I stepped into the lobby, and the musty scent of the apartment block washed over me: a blend of odors wafting from the apartments—food and detergents—mixed with the faint, distant stench of the cold, damp basement. But inside the building, in stark contrast to the street, it was pleasantly warm.

We stepped up to the elevator, I pressed the button, and the shifting of mechanical levers echoed from afar. We waited in silence, the hallway light timed out, leaving us standing in the dark. I took deep breaths as my abdomen twisted in pain. When we got into the smelly, graffiti-covered elevator, Maks said that our building was a fine example of socialist residential architecture in Ljubljana. He said he had read somewhere that it was the first implementation of prefabricated heavy concrete systems and that its construction was modeled after the apartment blocks in Belgrade. I only half-listened, nodding at him with a grimace.

We walked out of the elevator into the dim hallway, and the thought of our cramped apartment with its nineties furniture made me anxious. Compared to their minimalist row house, our apartment was lined with floor-to-ceiling closets stuffed to the brim. The closets should have been sorted through ages ago, with at least half of what was inside thrown out. I unlocked the door, and we went in.

The apartment was dark, only the Christmas tree and the nativity scene beneath it cast a faint glow from the living room. I no longer bothered worrying about what Maks would think of our apartment (especially once he saw how little it had changed in the years since he was last here), because my body was coated in warmth, and I felt a profound relief at being home. Maks took off his shoes and his winter coat, he wore a dark blue sweater with a white Levi's logo underneath. I rummaged through the drawer and handed him a pair of slippers, then I took my own shoes and coat off and slipped into the fluffy white reindeer slippers with a red bauble for a nose that Urška had given me for Christmas.

I went into the room I shared with my sister, and Maks followed. I hadn't planned on him coming over, so when we walked in, the room was in a frightful state: the bed was unmade and indented from me lounging on it all day, and the sweatpants I had taken off before leaving the house were lying right there. A large red stain bloomed on them. I made my way to the bed and folded them, but Maks, who stood in the middle of the room, could not have missed seeing the blood. I told him to sit on Urška's bed, but since it was cluttered with my things, I changed my mind and told him to sit on the chair, motioning toward the one at Urška's desk—my own chair held a backpack full of books and study notes, with a few more scattered across my desk. But he interrupted me:

"No, wait, Maša. Just calm down a little."

His words took me by surprise and I froze over the bed I was making, staring at him.

"First, take your clothes off. You can't stay in those," he said, nodding at my jeans. I could hardly believe my ears. He had said "take your clothes off" in my fantasies before, but certainly not in this context. Ignoring my astonished look, he simply opened the wardrobe next to my bed, which was stuffed with clothes, and surveyed the messy contents inside.

"You need something more comfortable. Those are bloody," he said, glancing at the sweatpants I had frantically folded moments before to hide the stain. "But you have other ones, right? Or pajamas?"

For Christmas, Mom had given me a pajama set featuring plaid red-and-blue bottoms and a white top with Mickey and Minnie Mouse. It had been sitting untouched on top of my pajama pile ever since. I was afraid of staining it with blood, but it was the nicest and newest item in my closet, so I pulled it from the pile. Maks said, "I'm going to make you some tea. I'll find my way around," he stopped me when I moved to follow him.

There was still some water left in the glass on my nightstand. I used it to wash down another painkiller. As I headed to the bathroom, I heard the electric kettle rumbling in the kitchen. To my absolute horror, I thought of the pile of dirty dishes that had been accumulating in the sink all day, and of our battered old kitchen where Maks was making tea.

I took another quick shower and changed my pad. With every period, I would think that I had never had cramps this bad and had never lost this much blood, but in reality, it was equally painful and grueling every single time. When I returned to the room a few minutes later, wearing my new pajamas and Christmas slippers, Maks was already sitting in Urška's chair. A mug of tea sat on the nightstand, and the scent of chamomile filled the room. He glanced up from the book he was holding, Chris Shilling's *The Body and Social Theory*.

"Is this for the Anthropology of Gender and Sexuality class?" When I nodded, he remarked: "It's not a bad book, just a bit rudimentary."

"Probably," I said weakly, sitting on the bed. My abdomen was still tearing with pain. "Can we turn off the overhead light? It's bothering me." I reached over to the nightstand and switched on the Himalayan salt lamp. Maks nodded, got up, and turned off the main light. Then he looked at me: "Does it always hurt so much?"

I nodded, then told him through gritted teeth that it always catches me off guard.

"My periods aren't very regular," I said in a ragged voice. "Well, my gynecologist tells me it's perfectly fine since I get it almost every month, but I have very long cycles, thirty-eight, sometimes even forty days. She suspects it's because I'm too skinny." I took a sip of tea, it was still hot, and it burned my tongue slightly.

"I see." Maks watched me, chewing on his lip. Facing me sitting on the bed in that cluttered little room, he seemed larger than usual.

"Lie down," he instructed, and I obediently slipped under the covers. I felt warmth flooding my body, and the pain in my stomach slowly began to subside. Maks sat on the edge of the bed and stared at me. I got the feeling he wanted to say something.

"What is it?" I smiled.

"When I was at the border, there was a girl in the exact same state you're in now," he said quietly. "A refugee. Maybe a little older than you." He paused for a moment. "Of all the things there, that was the hardest for me. She really was in terrible pain. She was throwing up and almost fainting. We had no idea what was wrong with her at first, we wondered if she had gotten sick or something. Well, when the doctor examined her, he told us it was just a very heavy period, though something didn't seem quite right to him, but a gynecologist would have to check. He said she also had a bladder infection. She must have been in excruciating agony, but she just suffered in silence until it became too much to bear. It was just awful. I can't imagine what it's like for all those women on the road going through that. And of course, some are even pregnant, giving birth along the way. This entire refugee crisis is totally dehumanizing," he concluded in a passionate tone, his eyes trailing over Urška's posters—horses, dandelion clocks, and sunsets—that had been taped to the wall above her bed since elementary school. I told him I agreed and that I wouldn't want to be in their shoes.

"Anyway, when that happened, they asked me to go to the store for pads, and I went and bought so many that they won't run out for a while." A tiny smile played on his lips, betraying his pride. Then he said that he thought the tax on pads should be abolished, and that women should be granted the right to one day off a month, called a 'day of rest'. I moaned that this would be entirely appropriate, as a sharp pain ripped through me. He tore his gaze away from Urška's wall and looked at me. His eyes shimmered in the pink light cast by the salt lamp.

"I'm sorry you're hurting so much."

With that, he placed his palm flat against my stomach, made a slow circular motion, and let his hand rest there. The blanket separated his hand from my aching abdomen, but I could still feel the warmth flowing from it into my body, and for one long, blissful moment, the pain vanished. But just as quickly, he pulled his hand away, placed it on his own thigh, and unexpectedly chuckled, as though nothing had happened. I asked him what was so funny.

"The fact," he hesitated, "that I texted Gaja today to ask if she wanted to meet up."

I lowered my eyes. I had no idea what was funny about that. For a moment, I felt a terrifying revulsion toward him, that he was even here, sitting on my bed with a bad case of blue balls. A shudder ran through me as I realized that the very same hand that had just been resting on my sore stomach was the one he used to caress Gaja's naked body, touch her breasts, and grab her ass. I felt myself growing hot.

"And she wasn't down for it?" I asked in a frail voice, trying hard to hide its trembling. Maks shook his head.

"No. She texted back that she couldn't because she's on her period."

He laughed, but it was a rather lonely laugh, as I didn't find it the least bit amusing. When he saw that I wasn't laughing, his smile dropped as well: "It just seemed funny to me. Because she's on her period, she wasn't up for it, get it?"

Of course I understood, but out of sheer stubbornness, I shook my head with pursed lips, and his sigh only infuriated me more. In a weary voice, as if trying to extricate himself from an awkward situation, he mumbled that it was just ironic that he then met up with me, only to find out I was on my period too.

The expression on my face must have made it abundantly clear I didn't find this funny at all. I maintained a stubborn silence, and he explained: "She wouldn't meet up with me because of her period, but you did *despite* yours."

I scoffed in annoyance and rolled my eyes.

"Well, it's simply not relevant for us," I snapped, and Maks's eyes widened in surprise. To lighten the mood, I added with a laugh: "Because we aren't sleeping together." Maks grinned, but then we both fell silent, and he looked away.

"I read the other day that in Islam, a husband isn't allowed to divorce his wife while she is menstruating." He said that after that incident at the border, he had read everything he could on menstruation in Islam. He began telling me what they call it, what the Quran says about it, about the prohibition of prayer and sexual intercourse while bleeding, and the mandatory ritual washing afterward. He was saying he might write an article about it someday when I cut him off: "Would you ever have sex with a girl on her period?"

He stared at me in surprise.

"Just because, well, I read somewhere that having sex during menstruation can ease the cramps," I hastily added.

Maks nodded, then said: "I don't know why not. I mean, if she was cool with it. I have no problem with that."

"You mean you don't find it repulsive?"

He shook his head with conviction: "Of course not. And I'm genuinely repulsed by what it says in the *Quran*. Like, for example, the fact that a menstruating woman isn't allowed to touch the *Quran*. She can't even enter a mosque. Honestly, I try to think about Islam with as little prejudice as possible, but certain aspects are highly problematic, to put it mildly. Then again, you can find similar commandments in the Old Testament." I thought of the copy of the *Holy Bible* in his nightstand drawer, and of the photograph of the two of us that he kept tucked inside a white envelope. My stomach clenched.

I said that I agreed.

"What about you?" he asked me.

"What about me?"

"Would you have sex on your period?"

I took some time to formulate an answer. A dull ache was still pricking at my lower abdomen.

"No," I finally determined.

"Why not? You're so conservative," he joked. I sighed.

"I wouldn't like someone pushing inside me while I was on my period. And I'm not conservative," I rolled my eyes. "You're doing it again."

"Doing what?"

"Projecting theories onto how I feel. You think I'm conservative because I don't want to have sex while menstruating, when it just doesn't suit me. It has nothing to do with how society perceives a menstruating woman. So, if you ever want to have sex with a girl on her period, make sure to check if she is genuinely okay with it first."

"Absolutely," he mumbled. I took a deep breath and rubbed my stomach.

"The pill has finally kicked in."

"I'm glad."

A brief silence settled between us, then I rubbed my stomach again and sighed: "I have to say, this has left me pretty exhausted." Perhaps he took it as a hint. He said he should get going so I could rest.

"I'll walk you to the door."

When I stood up from the bed, I felt the blood flow out of me. My knees buckled and I grew dizzy, and I had to lean against the wall for support. Maks's eyes traveled down my pajamas and he gave a faint smile, but said nothing. He followed me out into the hallway.

"Oh, yeah, I'm heading to Serbia in two weeks," he suddenly said as he was putting his shoes on, while I leaned against the wall watching him.

"Weren't you just there? For New Year's, I mean."

He nodded, tying his shoelaces with a deadpan expression. We hadn't talked about how we had celebrated the New Year, even though I was immensely curious as to why he was still awake at half past five in the morning.

"I'm not going to Belgrade this time, but to Dimitrovgrad. To the border." He pulled on his winter coat and studied himself in the wall mirror. I stood in the background, and our eyes met in the reflection.

"Great," I said, bitter. I was struck by the same wistful sadness that had seized me the first time he told me he was leaving. I envied him the experience. I would have gone too if I could, but I had to remain faithful to my commitments in Ljubljana, to the choir foremost. Besides, standing next to him in my pajamas, I felt physically too frail for such a task, whereas he seemed to brim with the energy that would allow him to brave the exhaustion and cold at the border.

"You could send me another email," I said, still bitter, and he nodded. I opened the front door, and he stepped out into the hallway.

"See you," I said one last time, then closed the door behind him. I leaned against it and listened to the sound of his footsteps retreating down the hall. I could hear that he had opted for the stairs.

I moved from the door and made my way back to my room, where the salt lamp was still on. The apartment fell silent after his departure. I crawled into bed, picked my laptop up off the floor, and opened it. The track *Firestone*, which I had been listening to on YouTube before Maks texted me, was still on pause. I hit play, and the soft beat filled the room. Then I opened Facebook, where Blaž's message—which I had no intention of answering—had been waiting for me all day.

Hey
How are you?

I stared at those few words, then typed back:

Hey
Fine, you?

3

Before I knocked, I heard Agata singing on the other side of the padded door. I listened closely. She possessed an exceptional soprano, thin and piercing, yet she could sing softly and her voice would remain just as penetrating. She was plucking chords on the piano, now minor, then major, and singing along to them, a song without a clear melody, a sort of impromptu.

I knocked and grabbed the gold doorknob, worn smooth from use. The door creaked. I stepped inside. Agata sat at the piano, still playing chords, and went on singing without looking my way. I walked over to the coat rack and took off my coat with slow, deliberate movements, then rummaged through my backpack as if searching for something. When I positioned myself by the piano, she stopped singing.

"What do you think happened after Tuesday's practice?" Her thin eyebrows arched high. I shrugged, though I had a pretty good idea of what it might be.

She narrowed her mascaraed eyes, then began in an agitated voice: "Emails! One after the other!" She went on, mocking them: "*Twice a week is too much for me, I'm in another choir besides this one,*' and '*unfortunately I won't be able to make it, I already have something else on Thursdays—dance practice, yoga, Pilates, scouts,*' who knows what else! But on Tuesday, they stayed quiet. Quiet!"

We looked at each other without breaking eye contact, but neither of us said a word. Then Agata added in a calmer tone: "Anyway, Barbara also decided she won't be able to do it. Because of the baby. That, I can understand." She cleared her throat and added: "The mere fact that she came back after giving birth exceeded my expectations."

She gazed wistfully at the white keys in front of her. "You know what this means, don't you?"

I was watching myself in the mirror as I nodded. My arms hung awkwardly at my sides. Agata turned to the stack of sheet music on the music stand and picked it up.

"Your backup will be Klara. Well, since the solo is yours now, the two of us will do things differently. We're all going to do things differently. You'll have less support from the choir than Barbara had, because there will be fewer of us in the new lineup. Take your sheet music." Her voice was no longer ragged, it was resolute. I pulled the music from my folder, and she instructed me to read the lyrics to my solo. I began reading it in rhythm, but she stopped me, telling me to read it as if I were reading poetry. I cleared my throat and read: "*When the thorny branches sprout, I press you to my heart. And only when you wound me to the blood, will I truly know who you are.*"

She asked me how I interpreted the lyrics. When I stared at her in surprise and asked what she meant, she sighed and explained wearily that whenever she works on a solo with a singer, they first explore the text, so the soloist actually knows what she's singing. I nodded, raised the sheet, and read the lines again.

"I think it means," I began slowly, "that we only truly get to know another person once they hurt us."

Agata asked me seriously: "Has anyone ever hurt you like that?"

The question was unexpected. I looked at the words again. *And only when you wound me to the blood, will I truly know who you are.* I thought of my botched infatuations. At the end of elementary school, I was madly in love with a boy from the parish. That summer before high school, the two of us met up several times, and I thought he was in love with me too, but when he went to the seaside, he stopped replying to my messages. But it was such a fleeting crush I would have been embarrassed to tell Agata about it. And in high school, I dated a classmate for a month, but I was the one who dumped him—that hadn't meant anything. Then I remembered something.

"A friend of mine hurt me once."

I stayed silent until Agata motioned for me to continue.

"It was two years ago. I went to Metelkova with a friend and we bumped into him hanging out with his buddies. Even though the two of us had gone for a walk together just a week before, there, in front of his high school friends, he was completely cold to me, as if we were merely acquaintances."

I didn't tell her that when we saw him, I had told the girl I was with that he was my best friend. But when we approached Maks and he acted as if he only knew me vaguely from college, doubt was written all over my friend's face.

Agata scrutinized me with an indifferent gaze, then stared at the keys and said coldly: "Friendships are complicated, especially between men and women."

I waited for her to say something else. Judging by the expression on her face, my story hadn't convinced her. This time, no sound of instruments seeped into the classroom, all was quiet in the Academy's hallways. The window overlooking the empty Upper Square, flurrying with tiny snowflakes, was shut tight. The only sound was the gurgling of water in the radiator. Then Agata looked at me and asked: "I know the song is about a man, but what about a woman? Could you say one has ever hurt you like that?"

Her question caught me off guard. I associated sorrow with romantic love, and the song in my hands made me think of no one but boys. What Agata was asking about was something entirely different.

I could have instantly rattled off the names of several female friends who had gossiped behind my back, but I couldn't, because I had gossiped about them too. I had a best friend in high school, we shared a desk for four years, but after we passed the matura exam, she grew distant. I figured she resented the fact that, even though I had been copying off her for four years, my matura scores were higher; when we got our report cards, she remarked that it was no surprise, since I had picked the easiest subjects. We only met up a few times over the summer, and each time, she showed signs of being fed up. When we ran into each other at college in October, she only greeted me in passing, and soon after, I saw on Facebook that she had found a new group of friends. I thought the void she left would be filled by a new classmate at college, but that wasn't the case; many of the female anthropology students struck me as competitive and hypocritical. In general, I feared female friendships, they seemed unpredictable.

But I couldn't bring myself to say this in front of Agata. I stared at her for a few long moments. I was just beginning to wonder what the point of this exercise was when she looked at me and asked: "What about Urška, for instance?"

I sighed. I hadn't even thought of my sister, but now memories rushed through my mind like a film reel. There had been plenty of pointless arguments, screaming, and grudges between us, but we always managed to make up somehow, perhaps just so we could live with each other more easily.

"Urška..." I began slowly, and Agata pivoted her entire body toward me. I thought of Barbara, standing in this exact spot at the end of September, interpreting the solo that had been hers at the time. What had Agata dragged out of her?

"You know how she is. She always has such a moralistic attitude."

I paused, gathering my thoughts. "Every time our parents teamed up on me over some stupid thing I'd done, she took their side. And I always defended her in front of them." I felt my face flush hot. I remembered Mom screaming at me in my sophomore year when I got a reprimand in Slovenian class. Urška joined her, saying I never did any chores around the house, and ratted me out for watching anime on my computer at night. I was grounded, and until I brought my grades up, my computer was kept in our parents' bedroom. I told this story, which still angered me, to Agata.

"Whereas I always kept her secrets. Once, instead of going to the Stična Youth Festival, she met up with some guy she'd met at the seaside, and I fed Mom a bunch of lies on her behalf. And another time, our parents punished her by changing the Wi-Fi password and strictly forbidding me from telling her what it was. But I told her anyway." I fell silent, my heart thumping a few times harder in my chest.

Agata was quiet for a few moments, then let out a very faint sigh. A glimmer of mild displeasure flashed in her eyes.

"Interesting," she said. Judging by her expression, this still wasn't what she was looking for. Then her face twisted slightly.

"Urška..." she shook her head a little. "She disappointed me very deeply once, too. Did you know I tried to help her when she wanted to try again for the Academy entrance exams?"

I shook my head; I hadn't even known she was planning this. Agata gave a curt nod: "When she joined the choir and started coming to me for vocal technique, she told me she hadn't passed the entrance exams. I told her she should try again and that I would help her, that we would prepare together. At first, she was all for it. But then... Then she met Andrej. Suddenly, she was perfectly content studying primary education, and she told me she just wanted to finish her degree as soon as possible, and that studying music would be... a waste of time. That's what she said. It crushed me."

She sighed deeply and straightened up in her chair; I realized that was the first time I had ever seen her slouch. Her face was ashen gray and weary. Sorrow rested in her eyes. I was bothered by her words—she spoke about my sister as if Urška had done something truly horrendous to her, whereas earlier, she had met my story with complete indifference.

At first, I didn't know what to say, then I replied: "I didn't know that. But I have to say... Urška really was deeply disappointed for a very long time. And when she met Andrej..." I trailed off. I wished I didn't have to admit to Agata just how happy Andrej made Urška. How transformed she was when she came home, how intensely she fell in love with him, and he with her. I was happy for her, yet at the same time—though I would never admit it—I was eaten up with jealousy. I didn't envy her the relationship she had with Andrej, but rather her unwavering certainty that "this is it." And how they put each other first without a second thought, while I was distrustful of boys and relationships. In the couples and marriages around me, despite their apparent happiness and stability, I sensed many cracks, restrictions on freedom, as well as a certain boredom, resignation, and disappointment. I was a freshman in high school at the time, and my skepticism set me apart from most of my friends. I looked down on their crushes, and sometimes ruthlessly doomed a newly formed relationship to failure right from the start.

"When she met Andrej, she became happier," I finally concluded.

Agata briefly nodded, but said nothing, and I got the feeling I hadn't convinced her. She pressed her index finger onto a piano key, which rang out deadened and muted; I caught a glimpse of her foot resting on the middle of the three pedals.

"My sister," she began to relate in a fragile voice, as she lifted her finger and the note faded, "started ignoring me at one point. Not really ignoring, but... She never asks how I am, for example. She has no interest in my life. You won't believe this, but she has never once paid us a visit. Because of her, I stopped going home. Every time I went to Zagorje, I'd ask her if I could drop by for a visit, and she always found an excuse: that she was on call, that she was having lunch at her mother-in-law's, that one of the kids was sick. Eventually, I got tired of it."

I didn't know what to say. Her gray eyes looked downcast with melancholy. Then I asked her if she knew why that was.

She smiled bitterly: "Of course I do. It started when I was at the conservatory in Ljubljana, and she applied too, but didn't pass the entrance exams. Nor in Maribor. She ended up going to the secondary nursing school in Celje. She could never get over it. But that's not my fault, you know?" She looked at me, and I nodded vigorously.

"If you're very good at something, you sometimes get the feeling like you're guilty in front of others. Because they are so average," she added more quietly, before continuing louder: "Anyway, the purpose of this... exercise was for you to truly feel the pain and convey those emotions through your voice. The world we live in today is full of kitsch. Of forced happiness. I want us to perform this song as the exact opposite. Not like just another women's choir singing pop songs, folk tunes, and liturgical hymns. But as women who dare to look truth in the eye. To admit that life is sometimes utterly miserable. So that the audience will also feel a certain... Discomfort. So they'll think: Wow, this piece really brought me down. It's so real."

I swallowed hard and nodded.

"Alright, let's warm up," she instructed me, and played the first chord. I assumed my singing posture and followed her directions. The intimacy that had formed between us made my voice much stronger.

After vocal technique, I ran into Sara outside the Academy. I was surprised to see her, as I knew her vocal technique was on Thursdays. She told me she came because Agata had asked her to help with something, but couldn't tell me more because she had no idea what it was about.

"I'd love to hang out with you," she said, and then asked if I wanted to come over to her place on Saturday evening. She accompanied the invitation with a mysterious smile, saying that we could bake a pizza. I said I would come, and she disappeared behind the Academy doors.

4

Sara lived with her mother in one of the apartment blocks in the Savsko naselje neighborhood, where I arrived with the bike despite the cold. The apartment wasn't large, I didn't even see her mother's bedroom, and I assumed that she made her bed every night on the living room couch, below an icon of Mary with her arms outspread and an image of Jesus on her chest. There were no other paintings in the living room, it was modestly and coldly furnished, with dark-spined books tightly packed together on the shelves, and an overall impression of perfect order. There was no television, just a large desk with a computer sitting against the wall. The room reminded me of the bleak reception parlor in the convent where my mother had once taken me on a visit to her Ursuline friend, and such an uncomfortable feeling of alienation overwhelmed me that I wondered how Sara could live here. I hoped she would show me her room, but she led me straight to the kitchen.

The kitchen, where we set about baking the pizza, was battered and outdated, much like ours. There was a postcard pinned with a magnet to the fridge, the kind of postcard you buy in museum gift shops, depicting a painting of two men on a walk. One of them was in a white robe, with a black hat on his head and holding a walking stick, while the other wore a black suit.

"What's this?" I asked, nodding at the postcard while Sara pulled the ingredients from the fridge, setting two cans of beer on the counter.

"This? It's a painting called *The Philosophers*, a portrait of Sergei Bulgakov and Pavel Florensky. It was painted by Mikhail Nesterov, my mom's favorite painter."

She closed the fridge door, and I went closer to the image for a better look. It really was beautiful, the man in the black suit stared straight ahead with a vexed expression, while the taller but seemingly younger man, evidently a seminarian, cast his eyes downward, pressing his left hand to his chest.

As I stared at the replica of the painting, I was struck by the plainness of the environment I grew up in. Neither of my parents had a favorite painter, and they would never have pinned a museum postcard to the fridge. Despite the discomfort I had experienced in the living room, I sensed a certain intellectual atmosphere pervading Sara's apartment, and I could just picture the two of them sitting at the dining table deep into the night, discussing Sara's studies and the books her mother was translating. I remembered Maks once mentioning that his father had bought his grandfather a painting by Arjan Pregl for his birthday, and how I had to pretend to know who that was. I thought of Blaž's home, and realized I was closer to him than I was to Sara or Maks.

"You know what I've been meaning to ask you?" I began, grabbing the can of beer. "Maks told me that Blaž had apparently been talking to one of our professors about becoming a doctoral student with her. Do you know anything about that? Is Blaž really that good of a student?"

I struggled to conceal the doubt in my voice and took a relaxed sip of beer. I had tried talking to Blaž on Facebook a week ago, but the conversation was incredibly boring and led nowhere. I kept asking him what he thought of certain subjects and professors, but his answers were very sparse.

Sara nodded without looking up from the large stainless steel bowl in which she was preparing the pizza dough.

"He has a talent for academic writing. He gets tens on all his term papers, and shines at presentations. The professors always hold him up as an example. As far as I know, he breezes through anthropology with his eyes closed. He really is good."

I took another sip of beer and stared silently at Sara's hands, kneading the mixture in the bowl.

"Why do you ask?"

I shrugged. Then I set down my can, picked up the knife Sara had laid out for me, and set about dicing the onion.

"Actually, I wanted to ask you something related to that," Sara finally said, clearing her throat. I motioned for her to go on. "What happened on New Year's Eve? Why did you disappear?"

I blushed and saw she was scrutinizing me.

"I mean, I'm really, really sorry, I overdid it with the weed and didn't notice you were gone for a long time, but when I realized you'd vanished, I got genuinely scared. But you then just texted me that you were already home. I had no clue how you made it from there."

The onion made my eyes water. I put the knife down, covered my eyes with my hands, and groaned from the stinging. Blinking through my tears, I met Sara's doe eyes watching me with concern, and I realized she was feeling guilty. I quickly explained that I had hitched a ride to Maribor with her friends, and caught a ride-share from there to Ljubljana.

"And then I got sick, so I forgot to call you back. Don't worry about it."

Sara raised her eyebrows.

"But why? I still don't get it. Why did you just go home in the middle of the night instead of waiting for us to go together in the morning?"

Her hands froze in the bowl, and she stared at me with wide eyes.

"Did something awful happen?" she asked very slowly. I realized she was genuinely worried, and that I would have to tell her the truth, otherwise she would suspect everyone at the party of sexual assault.

"Blaž and I kissed," I said. My eyes were still burning from the onion, and a tear slid down my cheek. I wiped it away with my sleeve. "I'm crying because of the onion. Nothing else happened, I swear."

Sara moved the dough onto a floured surface and began to knead it. It seemed I hadn't entirely convinced her. To reassure her, I told her everything from start to finish: how he invited me upstairs, what we talked about on the balcony, and how the kiss was essentially how he wished me a Happy New Year.

"And what happened *next*?"

I took a long sip of beer and breezily explained that we moved to his room, where we made out a little more.

"But then it started feeling off, and I left. I sobered up a bit and realized I wasn't into it. That's all, I went downstairs, he didn't do anything, and the whole thing was over very quickly." I set the beer down on the table. Sara stayed silent for a few moments, frowning.

"I don't know. You just ran away. Why didn't you wait until morning and leave with us, like we agreed? Oh, come on, Maša, something must have happened."

I rolled my eyes.

"First of all, the driver didn't strike me as someone who would be in any condition to drive in the morning. And I 'ran away'"—I made air quotes with my hands, still holding the knife—"because... I panicked." Sara waved her hands, sticky with strands of dough, as if to point out that this was exactly what she was talking about, so I quickly added: "Not because I was afraid he'd do something to me. I got worried that I would decide to sleep with him."

I sighed deeply. By admitting this to her, I was also admitting it to myself for the first time. Sara raised her eyebrows in astonishment, then silently went back to kneading the dough.

"And not because I like him or anything," I went on, pressing the knife against the firm skin of a tomato. "But because... Because right before New Year's I had watched *Fifty Shades of Grey* and... and I was totally... under the influence."

Sara stared at me in disbelief, then rolled her eyes and snorted with contempt: "A film that literally glorifies the idea of the patriarchy and depicts male nostalgia for lost power in the most disgusting way possible, brimming with massive amounts of misogyny, sexism, and cliché..."

"Yes, yes, yes, yes. All of that, I know. But... I was bored. And my life just isn't as, I don't know, *exciting* as yours. So, I watched the movie. Go ahead, judge me." I pretended to be angrier than I really was. I sliced the tomato very aggressively and didn't even look at her.

"I'm not judging you at all," she said in a calmer voice. "And my life isn't any more exciting than yours," she added softly. "Anyway, sorry for interrupting you. Go on, tell me what happened."

I sighed and brushed the hair out of my eyes with the back of my hand.

"I don't know, to be honest, I did go to the party with a quiet desire for something to happen. Not necessarily with Blaž, really. At first, I thought the guy who was driving was cuter." Sara nodded. "But when we arrived, I saw the way Blaž looked at me. We locked eyes a few times, and eventually he came over and quite directly invited me to join him upstairs." I could see that Sara's concern had now been replaced by curiosity. "And I don't know... I wanted to go. As we were walking upstairs, I wasn't thinking that maybe this wasn't a smart idea. Then we had a pretty cool conversation on the balcony. And out of nowhere, he kissed me."

Sara watched me, slowly shaking her head. Then she let out a broad chuckle, but didn't say anything.

"But then, when we were in his room, I suddenly sobered up and..." thought of Maks, I should have said. Who, at that very moment perhaps, was kissing Gaja somewhere in Belgrade. "And realized I'd rather not continue," I said quietly, watching Sara shape the dough into a ball. I was done with the vegetables, they lay chopped on a plate.

"It's good that it ended there. I really was worried," Sara said, placing the ball into the bowl and covering it with a cloth. She set an alarm on her phone to let us know when the dough will have risen.

"You know," I hesitated over telling her, then went on anyway, "it's very hard for me to be with someone... with someone who isn't Maks."

Our eyes met. Hers were much more serious this time, while my cheeks were radiating heat. I pulled off my sweater and draped it over a chair.

"Don't think I haven't tried," I added grimly, "but... This has been dragging on since the university information day, when I saw him for the first time in ages. So... Three years."

Sara grabbed her beer can from the counter and sat down at the table, where the ceiling lamp cast a rather dim light.

"He came over to my place a week ago, and he was very sweet at first. But then he said something about Gaja, and it really pissed me off."

I told Sara the whole story, and when I finished, to my surprise, she said he probably hadn't meant to anger me at all.

"I think he just wanted to tell you he's grateful you're not pretending in front of him."

"Of course I'm not, but I did tell him that my period is completely irrelevant in our case," I objected.

"I know, but... I'm just saying what I think he was getting at.

It's just that he isn't mature enough to know how to express it, so he dragged out the stupid story with Gaja," she prudently concluded with a chuckle.

"It felt like he wanted to brag about having sex, while I have nobody to do it with."

Sara was contrite: "That's also possible, I agree. Maybe he was subconsciously trying to make you jealous."

I waved my hand and shook my head: "I doubt it. He's never been interested in me. Not in that way."

Sara took a long sip of beer, slowly set the can down, and stared at it for a while. Then she looked at me and asked how I could be so sure. She asked me what I sometimes asked myself: "Then why does he hang out with you?"

"Well, because we're friends and we've known each other our whole lives. Sometimes he texts me to go for a walk. That's all. We never go out together."

"I feel like the walks are more intimate than just sitting around over drinks," she remarked somberly, "plus, he sent you that email."

I sighed and shrugged.

"I don't know. I mean, I agree with you. Sometimes I get the feeling he finds something about me interesting." I had never said this out loud to anyone. I took another sip of beer and was about to put the can down, but then I drained it completely.

Sara pointed her finger at me.

"Exactly," she said, satisfied. She got up, opened the fridge, pulled out a fresh can, and gave it to me. She sat back down in her chair with an air of confidence: "I was thinking about this the other day after the freshman party. He's not nearly as indifferent to you as you think he is."

She gazed dreamily at the hands of the wall clock above the table, to the point that I had to nudge her and ask her to go on.

"I know Maks. Or rather, I don't know him super well, but we were in the same class for four years and we hung out sometimes. I know the people he was closest friends with, the girls he was with"—I reached for the can and popped it open—"and you are very different from all those people. And he is different when he's with you. It occurred to me that he finds you interesting because you live a life he never will. He tries so desperately hard to understand the world, but he knows surprisingly little about actual people. No matter how many books by Žižek and Chomsky he reads."

I laughed, she merely smiled, then continued: "Look, for instance, you have the experience of a religious upbringing, whereas he only ever had endless freedom and opportunities, which left him in a state of total confusion throughout high school. You understand how normal people live, while he's a privileged, spoiled brat who's had everything handed to him since he was a kid. You're the one who dedicates yourself to singing, even if it isn't the coolest possible hobby, while he'd rather die than embarrass himself in front of his buddies. If you ask me, he likes you more than he dares to admit."

I raised my eyebrows and pressed my palms to my cheeks, which were still radiating heat.

"You don't think so?"

I decided to ignore her question.

"What did you mean when you said he's different when he's with me?"

Sara frowned, thinking.

"With you, he's... more natural. He's not constantly trying to seem cool. Honestly, I was surprised when you told me you were friends.

I didn't know how you put up with him. Back in the day, we had to listen to him brag all the time, about how he was the best, all the stuff he had, what he was doing, the things he knew, and where he and his family were traveling next. I was meaning to ask you how you endure all his strutting, but then at the freshman party, he was actually really cool. He was very protective of you, and he spent fifteen minutes explaining to Blaž that you're one of the rare few who actually know why they're studying anthropology."

I blinked at Sara in surprise. When had Maks talked to Blaž about that? What else had I missed in my stupor?

"And then he turned up to our concert. I invited him more as a joke, the Maks from high school would have never showed his face. But he did. And he didn't even come to say hi to us. He spent the entire evening with you."

I leaned back in my chair and crossed my arms over my chest. I held Sara to be a wise person, and the facts she laid out before me seemed true, yet I was still plagued by doubt. She had a very idiosyncratic way of interpreting things, and sometimes she could be absolutely convinced she was right, only to completely miss the mark. I sighed deeply.

"Run that by me again: what exactly did he say to Blaž?" Now I was the one frowning, staring at the wall and trying in vain to patch the holes in my memory.

"He told him you're curious, that you ask the right questions, that you're an excellent observer, and that you read a ton. Honestly, it sounded a bit patronizing, and it felt like he was taking some credit for your... intellectual awakening." She shuddered. "But I figured you'd still like what he said. Even if it was a bit, well, you know." She cut herself off and laughed out loud, and I joined in.

"*Intellectual awakening.* Yeah, that sounds like Maks," I giggled, my heart resounding in my chest. I felt it radiate with a warm glow—from the beer and from what Sara was telling me. I found myself wishing I were alone so I could mull over what she had said. I would go for a run. Despite the cold, I would run from Savsko naselje to the city center, and then along the Ljubljanica river to Trnovo. I would run through Mirje, Krakovo, and Prule. Maybe I'd run up to the castle. Only then would I head back to Šiška. And the whole way, I'd be listening to *Lucky Ones.* "*Every now and then, the stars align. Boy and girl meet by the great design. Could it be that you and me are the lucky ones?*"

Sara snapped her fingers in front of my eyes and grinned when she saw how startled I was. I smiled. A soft silence settled over us. It was hot in the kitchen, the heat was wafting from the radiator beneath the window.

"Hey, so what did Agata want with you?"

Sara had just stood up from the table, walked over to the oven, and turned it on.

"She wanted to show me her score," she said quietly. "She wanted to know what I thought of it. She's composing a piece right now." I nodded to imply I already knew that. "And she wanted to show it to me because she knows we write our own music in my band. I guess she figured that meant I know a thing or two about it."

"And? What was the verdict?"

Sara was crouching by the oven. She shifted her gaze, and her green eyes met mine—something mighty flashed within them.

"Šavli can't hold a candle to her."

I laughed. The alarm on her phone went off: the pizza dough was ready.

5.

Maks Hafner, February 11, 2016, 23:07
Field Report 2

Hey. I've been in Dimitrovgrad, on the Serbian-Bulgarian border, for a few days now. The days are incredibly exhausting, and by evening I'm usually so drained that I can't bring myself to write, but I decided to drop you a quick line today. I'm sharing a room with three Polish guys who are very friendly, and we've organized our schedules to take turns, which allows us to get some rest and spend some time doing other things. If you're constantly there with the refugees, you start to think you'll lose your mind. And they, the refugees, are stuck in this chaos all the time and have no idea when (or how) it will end.

The conditions here are even worse than on the Slovenian borders, but not because of the organization. The atmosphere is more stressful because the refugees are already completely on edge. These are mostly the people who were turned back at the Slovenian or Croatian borders. There are about 300 of them, and they are housed in a former hospital. There are a lot of children among them. We brought them a car full of toys, crayons, and coloring books, and each child was allowed to take one toy.

The refugees have more freedom here than on the Slovenian borders, the kids can play outside on old, battered playground equipment, and the men organize themselves to play volleyball and football. But in a psychological sense, because they were rejected, they are definitely much more messed up than the ones I worked with in Slovenia.

There is no military or police presence here. As volunteers, we are very free, we can work however we want. The rooms where the refugees are staying are in better condition than back home, they have showers, and there are about ten to fifteen people per room, which is great because they have some privacy. They can feel like human beings here.

The first thing I noticed when we arrived was the relationship between them and the staff. The cleaning ladies chat with the refugees, I have no idea how, since they don't speak the same language, and the few police officers around mostly just drop by to "have a look," drink coffee, and smoke a cigarette. It seemed hard to believe, compared to Slovenia. It even made me feel a little ashamed of how we act, how poorly we tolerate foreigners, we are always so skeptical, cowardly, and distrustful. I asked them how they could be so relaxed with the refugees, and they said they remember the war all too well and that being a refugee is horrible. That they still remember the people from Kosovo and Bosnia. "We are all human," they say. Everybody's helping, handing out food, preparing formula for the babies. If you work too hard, they start teasing you to slow down, that you don't have to do so much.

But it's not all so great. In the evenings, for instance, after dinner, when they are supposed to calm down and relax, and we have workshops to keep the kids busy, a child sometimes has a meltdown, a panic attack, there's screaming and crying. One evening, a kid, not even three years old, crawled under a bed, screaming, and refused to come out. I don't know what they saw or what they remember. But when they're drawing, they often draw explosions, police officers, and guns, it looks horrific. The child psychologists would have their hands full here, but I can't say anyone is doing much about it.

Sometimes I get the urge to just pack my things and go home. I'm worried about my thesis, when I'll even find the time to write it, and whether I can finish it by summer. On the other hand, the things "outside" sometimes seem distant, unreal. Ljubljana, college, Martin, Darja, Mitja, my friends, Gaja, you, everything feels like it belongs to some other world.

There's another thing that really got me thinking, and I need to share it with someone. With the volunteers we somehow got into the habit of saying a few words when we sit down at the table before we start eating. It started spontaneously, a Polish guy kicked it off by wanting to say something before a meal. He gave thanks for the food on the table, for the fact that we were eating in a peaceful environment, that we were healthy and safe, and that we were able to do this work. It caught on, and we started taking turns. Sometimes someone will ask that blessings be returned to those who prepared the food for us. The short, spontaneous ritual really made me think. Anywhere else, this type of behavior would strike me as kind of cringe. But then it made me wonder why it's so normal for us to just pounce on our food, eat it by ourselves, in front of the TV, separated from one another...?

I noticed something else, too. I often see the refugees, the men, praying here. They move away from the group, though not so far you'd lose sight of them, and they lay out their prayer rugs. They don't care at all if anyone is watching them or anything. I thought that they might even like to be seen doing it. It's hard to say. But when they pray, that is the only time they truly seem at peace.

I'm going to sleep.

Best, Maks

Zayn's *Pillowtalk*, which I had been playing on repeat ever since it came out, was echoing in my earphones. Sitting propped up in bed in the dim light, my hair still wet from washing, I read Maks's email for the fourth time that evening. *On the other hand, the things "outside" sometimes seem distant, unreal. Ljubljana, college, Martin, Darja, Mitja, my friends, Gaja, you, everything feels like it belongs to some other world.* He sent it a week ago, but I still haven't replied, because everything I wrote felt empty. I just sent him a brief text saying I received the email and would write back soon. I bit my lip and wearily closed the email tab.

I opened YouTube and dragged the slider back to the beginning of the music video. I had watched it so many times over the past few days that I knew it by heart, but I simply couldn't tear myself away from it. I found it beautifully mesmerizing how, when the Black woman spread her legs, an oriental lily blossomed between her thighs. *We'll go slow in high tempo. Hold me hard and mellow.* It struck me that Gigi Hadid looked a bit like Gaja. When she ran her hand through Zayn's hair, I imagined Gaja doing the same to Maks as they start making out and undressing in his room. Even though the thought weighed heavily on me, it was also arousing. *I'm seeing the pain, seeing the pleasure.* I had caught myself inventing their love story several times by now: how he finally admits that he has fallen in love with her. The next morning, they walk to college together, order a croissant and a cappuccino at the Domača Peka bakery before class, but then they change their minds and head back to his place, where they make love again and spend the entire morning in bed. I was torturing myself on purpose, there was something masochistic about it. A minute and a half into the video, there was a shot of a woman screaming, and that was exactly how I felt thinking about them.

I love to hold you close, tonight and always, I love to wake up next to you. Zayn moved closer to Gigi, and I thought of *haram*, of the fact that in the strictest form of Islam, listening to music is forbidden, and it was clear to me why: it distracts you from Allah, inflames you, awakens your senses. Agata always claimed that music nurtured us. When we sang sacred music, we became solemn and serene, when we sang gospel, we became fiery and full of life, when we sang folk music, we became simple and natural. This music I was listening to now was also transforming me: it filled me with a hot Californian summer, with frothy white waves licking a sandy shore and a dry wind rustling through palm trees, that could turn livid in an instant and spark a wildfire. *So we'll piss off the neighbors in the place that feels the tears, the place to lose your fear, yeah, reckless behavior. Things from before sometimes seem distant, unreal… you… everything feels like it belongs to some other world. A place that is so pure*—I slipped my hand down the pants of my pajamas—*so dirty and raw*—and touched my vagina, which felt dry to the touch. I knew what would happen if I kept touching myself. It would grow wet, and I would be consumed by a powerful, unbearable craving for a man's body. *In the bed all day*—I didn't stop, my index finger began to slide against my still-dry skin with a practiced motion—*bed all day, bed all day.*

I closed my eyes and began to picture my favorite scene. That weekend house in the Karst. I thought that I could remember the cold stone walls and the faint light filtering through the small windows, casting a white glow over the dusty rooms. Wasn't there a fire crackling in the fireplace, filling the space with melancholy? I couldn't remember if it had really rained when we were there, but in my daydream, it was raining. Rain lashed against the windowpanes, and a gloomy, muted light filled the house while Maks was undressing me on a mahogany-colored double bed with white sheets, working me over with his tongue, kissing my navel, wantonly going through his favorite positions. *Fucking and fighting on.* I pushed my middle finger deep inside myself, as far as it would go, until it stung. *It's our paradise and it's our war zone.* I kept my hand moving intuitively, until I opened my eyes and saw Gigi's face staring back at me. Red tears were streaming down her cheeks like blood. In a flash, I pulled my hand out of my pants, placed it on my mouse, and clicked on it with a damp finger to open a new email. My heart was pounding in my chest, and I was out of breath.

Maša Pavlin, February 20, 2016, 23:36
Re: Field Report 2

Hey. I really enjoy reading what you write, I've read your email several times now. Write more when you find the time. Nothing new on my end, same old. But something has been bothering me for a while, and I've been meaning to ask you. Why do you keep the photo of the two of us in your drawer?

6.

Every year before the Ljubljana Choir Revue, Agata would give us a speech about the importance of this performance, pointing out that other choirs and their choirmasters would hear us sing. Philomela, she stressed, could hold its own against all those academic choirs and chamber ensembles; we just had to prove ourselves. This year, her speech was even stricter, warning us to treat the concert, where we would perform our competition program in full for the first time, almost like a dress rehearsal.

The singers who remained in the choir—there were nineteen of us—had been on pins and needles for a good month before the revue. *Ave Maria* didn't sound the way it was supposed to, we were constantly losing our pitch and singing out of tune. It was a similar story with the other two pieces. But we fared worst with Šavli's score, which simply refused to come together. The thought that the composer would be at the revue made us uneasy, and Agata couldn't hide her bad mood either, restlessly brushing her stiff curls from her face while we practiced.

On the day of the revue, Ivana and Sara picked Urška and me up in front of our apartment building, as usual. Ivana informed us that we'd have to go pick up Agata too, as she apparently had no other ride. I was already highly on edge because of the solo, and the thought of sitting next to Agata made me even more nervous. What if I messed up on stage? How would the two of us ride home together afterward?

When Agata, equipped with a garment bag and a large purse, got into the seat to my right, making me scoot to the middle, her sickly-sweet perfume instantly filled the car. It was obvious she was high-strung.

"Did you see who's up before us?" The question was directed at Ivana, who gave a weak shake of her head and apologized, saying she hadn't managed to read the program. "The mixed choir led by Peter Mušič." When Agata said his name, I noticed her voice tremble ever so slightly.

Ivana's face in the rearview mirror remained expressionless, though her cheeks flushed just a little. Urška asked who that was, and Agata explained: "Peter was a colleague of mine at college, we studied at the same time. Now he works at a high school as a music teacher and choirmaster. On top of that, he runs this mixed choir." After a brief pause, she added in a frailer voice: "They're not bad. Do you know who he reminds me of?" This question was also directed at Ivana, who shook her head. "Of your brother. Primož."

Primož was Ivana's oldest brother, a successful lawyer who had been often appearing on news programs as a political commentator recently. I had just seen him on television not long ago, offering commentary on the replacement of the barbed-wire fence on the border with a paneled one, which was supposed to be more animal-friendly—the barbed wire had already claimed a few victims among the wildlife. I gathered he was a staunch supporter of the border fence, which made me think of Maks, who was sharing outraged reactions from abroad on his Facebook profile regarding Slovenia's decision to erect a barbed-wire fence on the Croatian border.

To my right, Urška whistled in appreciation, while Ivana rolled her eyes with a smile on her face. "Primož is *very* handsome," my sister explained to puzzled Agata, "and his delivery is always excellent. He really is a top-notch rhetorician." I swallowed hard. "So, if the two of them really look alike..." She laughed, not finishing her sentence, and Ivana shook her head. "I'm telling Andrej," she said with a smile.

"The choir is good, then?" I asked Agata, trying to drown out Urška's giggling.

Agata nodded. "Very. But Peter is a bit arrogant, as you'll see. He thinks he's the best at everything, even though he puts on an act of false modesty. Anyway, he and Ciril can't stand each other. Word is, Peter refuses to perform his compositions."

"Why?" Ivana was curious.

"I don't know. He had ambitions to compose already back in college. Now he's been working at that school for a few years, producing nothing, he has two kids... If you ask me, Ciril's success rubs him the wrong way."

None of us said anything; we had just pulled up in front of the building where the revue was taking place.

The performance by the mixed choir under Peter Mušič's direction, which we listened to from backstage while waiting for our turn, was excellent. True, they weren't perfectly in tune, but despite the slip-ups, they were good. We walked onto the stage after them, and I couldn't help but think that the most observant people in the hall must have noticed the singers' faces contorted with stage fright, and our choirmaster's trembling hands.

Just then, I saw him: Ciril Šavli was nonchalantly leaning against one of the pillars, his arms, dark with thick hair, crossed over his chest. He was wearing a white shirt that practically glowed in the darkened hall. I thought I smelled patchouli, though that was impossible, he was too far. Seeing him standing there, I knew I was going to screw up. He reminded me too much of Shia LaBeouf for me to be able to sing with confidence.

When it came time for my solo, I sang it feebly, without recalling a single vocal technique exercise or a single piece of direction from Agata. What were the lyrics about? I didn't know, not in that moment. When the first sopranos took over the main melody, partially saving the piece with their flawless voices, my shoulders slumped.

As I changed my clothes in silence, I got the feeling the girls were ignoring me. I didn't care, I might have even preferred it. Only Sara squeezed my shoulder and told me I'd sung "okay." I wished Urška would come over and offer some praise. But she was giggling with Ana and didn't even notice me. Ivana, like me, was changing in silence and didn't look my way.

At the reception, I helped myself to a canapé, keeping an eye on Agata and making sure I didn't come too close. In her black attire, she practically blended into the crowd. She was leaning against the wall, holding a glass filled to the brim with red wine. I couldn't see who she was talking to, the crowd blocked my line of sight. She was laughing nervously and loudly, taking large gulps one after another.

Sara, Ivana, and Urška gathered beside me, each with her own glass.

"Well, that was uncomfortable," Urška said without looking at me, and Ivana nodded. "I overheard Agata and Peter talking…" Frowning, she looked toward Agata, who was chatting wildly. The people blocking my view dispersed, and we saw the handsome, tall man she was talking to with a forced smile. Evidently, despite his resemblance to Ivana's brother, Peter Mušič had not charmed Urška, as she stared at him without enthusiasm.

"He told her that he doesn't think Šavli's score is bad per se, but that it's rather pretentious."

Though she said it with aversion, it struck me that I had been searching for that exact word for the last few months of practice. *Pretentious.* Šavli's score really was exactly that. It was as though he tried to cram it with everything that was possible in choral music: folk singing was periodically interrupted by modernist dissonances, at one point we whispered and the whisper developed into a scream, there was a part when we had to laugh grotesquely, and then there was my solo, along with changes of rhythm, leaps, resonant chords, and painfully beautiful but overly long sections in G-sharp minor. It occurred to me that if Svetlana Makarovič heard what some young composer had done with her poem, she would ban the performance of the piece outright.

"Well, maybe it really is a little pretentious," I gathered the courage to say. To my surprise, Ivana nodded and, as if reading my mind, said: "I agree. There's too much of everything."

Urška's eyes darted between the two of us. "Do you really think so?"

We nodded. Sara didn't say anything.

"Well, maybe you're right. What bothers me most about this piece is that he set to music a poem by a person *like that...*"

"Ahoy, Agata's singers!" At the booming greeting, we all startled.

Ciril appeared behind our backs, and observed our faces with a full glass in his hand. It had been a while since I had seen him up close; he was even more handsome than Peter Mušič, and I immediately noticed that the smell of patchouli was real.

"Ciril!" Ivana exclaimed, blushing visibly. The expression on her face betrayed her worry that he had overheard Urška. She awkwardly nudged him in the shoulder and asked: "So, what did you think?"

"You were good, bravo. Maybe just a little lacking in confidence and decisiveness. I'm going to tell Agata to stop harping on you so much. If you ask me, you'd sing twice as well if she wasn't constantly criticizing you." He grinned, while I prayed he wouldn't recognize me as the soloist.

"And what did you think of *The Bush*?" Urška bravely asked him, voicing what we all wanted to know.

He gave a thumbs-up, then stated confidently: "You're on the right track. You're performing it differently than I envisioned, of course, you're very... solemn. I imagined..." He paused, then clenched his free hand into a fist and spoke with passion: "A sort of feminine energy, wildness, intensity. But right now, you're all still too timid. It's not such a... serious score. It flirts with folklore, primal instincts, dark elements too, naturally, but also with carnival-esque elements... You're supposed to sound more... untamed," he explained and took a sip of wine, then glanced across our faces. "Couldn't you feel that?"

"We did," Ivana answered curtly. "You can definitely feel that duality, yes."

"But the lyrics are quite direct, aren't they? I don't see much playfulness in them, but... rather a certain ruthlessness," Sara, who had been observing Ciril skeptically, spoke up for the first time. I got the feeling there was something about him that was bothering her, too. He didn't say anything, but merely pointed at her as if to say he agreed. Then his face disappeared behind his glass again.

"Did you choose the poem?" I suddenly asked. Ciril lowered his glass, looked at me, and shook his head.

"No, that was Agata's suggestion. But I think it's a great choice."

I noticed how my sister pursed her lips and looked down at the glass in her hands.

"It's a good choice, definitely," I agreed, leaning toward the table next to us and grabbing a glass of orange juice. Turning back, I met my sister's hard stare.

"Well, girls, I wish you the best of luck at the competition. I believe you can win," Ciril said, placing his empty wine glass on the table. Then he patronizingly put an arm around Ivana's shoulder and told her more quietly, yet still loud enough for all of us to hear: "Agata smells divine. Bravo." He winked at her and disappeared into the crowd.

Urška blinked in surprise at Ivana, whose face had turned to stone: "What was that all about?" Ivana sighed wearily and rolled her eyes.

"Back in December I had no idea what to get Agata for Christmas, and then I ran into him at the Müller store[6] and he helped me pick out a gift."

"Now that's a man with taste," I remarked dreamily as I stared after his white shirt dissolving into the crowd. I heard Sara snort, but I ignored it. I was evidently the only one in our little group who still felt some affection for the young composer.

"I find him very haughty," Sara said, displeased, and Ivana, arms crossed over her chest, nodded fiercely. "And the fact that it was Agata who picked the lyrics? When you asked him about that, it felt like he doesn't even know why he wrote the piece."

"He doesn't. But he would do anything for Agata," Ivana said, her cheeks looking like strawberries in early June. "I really wish he would leave her and Gregor alone once and for all." I didn't know who Gregor was, I assumed he was Agata's husband. "Just because his marriage fell apart doesn't mean everyone else's has to."

"Oh, no," I suddenly heard my sister yelp. Agata was coming towards us.

Her steps were unsteady, and as she drew closer, I saw her gray eyes were glassy and distant.

"Girls, we're going home," she ordered, then let out a very slight burp. I realized I had never seen her not completely in control of herself. A few strands of hair had escaped her bun, and a layer of red

---

6 TN: Popular European retail and drugstore chain.

nail polish on her index finger had chipped off.

"And you and me are going to have a little tête-à-tête," she wagged her finger and gave me a chilling wink. I said nothing; I felt as if I would never be able to open my mouth again.

7

At the first vocal technique lesson after our performance at the revue, Agata gave no indication that she was angry with me. If anything, she was suspiciously nice. I figured her finger-wagging at the reception was caused by the wine, and that she was slightly embarrassed about it. She offered no comment on my solo or the performance. She also spared us any criticism during rehearsal, which made me think that Ciril really had told her she was too hard on us. But she did announce that in the fourth week of March we would have our first separate rehearsal for Urška's wedding. The singers weren't exactly thrilled by the news, but seeing how ecstatic Urška was, none of them dared to object.

Given that the wedding was barely three months away, my sister asked me to keep the first Saturday in March free for wedding dress fittings. Because our tastes in wedding dresses differed quite a bit (she liked princess styles, while I preferred minimalist ones), I suggested that we bring Ivana along to help her make the final decision, and Sara to keep us company. On that Saturday morning, the four of us drove to a bridal boutique in downtown Ljubljana.

When we walked into the store, it was like finding ourselves in a highly feminine heaven. The white dresses surrounding us were gorgeous: there were countless models on the racks, fitted, wide, short, with a train, with a corset. Sara and I initially watched with skepticism as Urška and Ivana fawned over the lace, fabrics, pearls, and buttons, but were soon captivated by the intricately crafted details as well. We sat in plush armchairs as the sales assistant brought wedding dresses to the bride-to-be, and eagerly waited for Urška to emerge in the first one. Ivana was rooting for a dress with a wide crinoline, and I tried to convince my sister to go for a fitted dress that would accentuate her breasts, but she refused to even put it on. She fell in love with a beautiful dress by an Italian designer that was both simple and opulent, but the price was staggering, so she practically begged the sales assistant, in tears, to take it away. In the end, she settled on a dress from a previous season that could be rented for a fairly low price, but it was quite average compared to the other one, and her disappointment was palpable.

"Isn't it gorgeous?" Urška kept asking us later, when we sat down at a table in a downtown restaurant for lunch, insistently showing us a photo of the wedding dress she had chosen. All three of us repeatedly assured her she looked wonderful in it.

"That is exactly the kind of dress I envisioned for myself," she professed after we had placed our orders, still staring at the photo. "The other one was also very beautiful, but this one is more me, don't you think? And Andrej will like it better, too. Don't you agree?" She looked at me from behind her phone screen, and seeing the insecurity in her eyes, I nodded firmly.

"It suits you beautifully," I said with conviction, and the girls agreed.

"I can't believe the wedding is in less than three months," she said, her face glowing, and took a sip of water. She told us that she would be watching her figure until the wedding, so she ordered water and a chicken salad. I thought about ordering the same out of solidarity with my sister, but then opted for a pizza anyway. Urška was curvier than I was and often outspokenly envied my slender figure, vowing that she intended to lose weight. To console her, I would praise her full breasts; next to hers, mine were like two apricots.

"The other day, Agata and I were talking about wedding dresses," Urška said when the waiter brought our food, and we all perked up our ears. "Did you know she got married in a red dress? She showed me a photo, and I had to pretend I liked it." Seeing us puzzled, she explained: "I mean, red just looks kind of weird at a wedding. It looked like they were at their high school prom." After a brief pause, she added: "I think it's most beautiful when the wedding dress is white."

"Frida Kahlo got married in a green dress. And she had a red shawl draped over her shoulders. But alright, if her dress was to blame for her unhappy marriage, then of course it makes more sense to get married in white," Sara chimed in with a chuckle. I detected a hint of mockery in her voice and wondered if our conversation was boring her.

Urška frowned. "That really has nothing to do with it. Even though... Isn't it true that she and that husband of hers, whatever his name is, have a rather difficult relationship?" She looked up from the salad she had speared on her fork and glanced at Ivana. Ivana was slowly chewing a piece of pizza, saying after she swallowed: "Gregor. I wouldn't say they have a *difficult relationship*, just... They had some issues in the past."

"What happened?" I asked, curious. Ivana scrutinized me for a few moments, deciding whether to tell me or not. Finally, she shared that she had heard the two of them had lived apart for a while.

"After the wedding," Urška eagerly contributed, clearly knowing part of the story that she never told me. Ivana confirmed and said: "But as far as I know, they're okay now. Though it's true they are both musicians and have a very complicated relationship."

Urška snorted: "What do you mean they're both musicians? Andrej and I both sing in a choir too, yet our relationship is stable and healthy. Maybe Agata is just, you know how she is, selfish and does everything her own way, plus she's completely focused on her own success."

None of us said what we were all probably thinking: just because Urška and Andrej sang in a choir didn't make them musicians.

"What does their complicated relationship look like?" I asked Ivana, who was chewing her pizza bites very slowly and ignoring Urška. She was evasive: "He works a great deal." After a short pause, without looking any of us in the eye, she added: "And sometimes I even get the impression that Agata is competing with him and even envies him, because he is a rather well-known organist. But don't tell anyone," she looked at us so fearfully that we had to reassure her.

Urška sighed and shook her head, and when we looked at her, she said: "I don't understand how someone can compete with their *husband*. She should be his support, not his competition."

"Maybe I expressed myself poorly," Ivana said, blushing, then added in a lower voice: "It probably doesn't help that they don't have children."

Urška nodded solemnly.

"Maša, didn't you tell me they had some kind of problem?" Ivana looked at me from across the table with wide eyes, as if she had been waiting with bated breath to broach this topic. I froze with my knife and fork suspended in the air above my plate and stared into her inquiring eyes. Had I really ever told her about that? What had I told her, exactly?

"I don't know, really. She did tell me that she was having some issues, yeah. I don't remember exactly what they were."

Ivana frowned: "You told me they were having trouble conceiving."

Saying nothing, I lowered my gaze and resumed cutting my pizza. I only vaguely remembered my conversation with Ivana and no longer knew what I had or hadn't told her. I had also forgotten what Agata actually said, but Urška and Ivana were dying to know the exact details of my conversation with her. I wished I kept a diary so I could simply flip to the page where it clearly stated who had said what to whom. Like probably every girl, I had tried keeping a diary in the past, but it had only ever lasted three days at most.

"Didn't you say she was having some kind of surgery? She told me about going in for surgery in December, too. That's why we ended our rehearsals early."

"That explains a lot," Urška said without looking at us, saving me from Ivana. We stared at her, and she went on: "Poor Agata, I really feel sorry for her. I can't imagine something like that happening to me. But..." She frowned, as if weighing whether to continue. "We can't really say that Agata... That she makes space for that. If you know what I mean." She looked up at our faces. When we shook our heads, she explained that she felt Agata was too focused on her work and that, with our competition looming, she couldn't plan on having children anyway.

"Maybe she doesn't want children," Sara suddenly spoke up, surprising us all; she had been so quiet for the past few minutes that we had almost forgotten she was there.

"Maybe, but... I doubt it, really," Urška countered, gesturing at me: "Especially given what she told Maša."

I swallowed hard and nodded.

"Or maybe her relationship with her husband doesn't make for a safe space to start a family," she added with a teacher-like undertone. "What?!" she then snapped at Ivana, who was staring at her in shock. Sara was also glaring at her fiercely, but didn't say anything.

"What do you mean?" I asked my sister, hoping to break the tension.

"Well, take her relationship with Ciril, for instance... Didn't you say he would do anything for her?"

Ivana nodded and said with disdain: "But that's just how he is. He relishes women liking him and adoring him. I know he's hit on her before, but she's professional enough not to play those games."

"But she still collaborates with him? I don't know if that's smart. In marriage, those kinds of friendships can be very dangerous," Urška said, making air quotes for *friendships*. I figured this was something they discussed at her marriage prep classes.

This time Sara nodded and said in a softer voice than before: "You're right about that."

Ivana shot her cousin an uncomfortable glance, then lowered her gaze.

"My parents got divorced because of that. Well, *also* because of that," Sara said casually, as if talking about the weather. Urška and I looked at her, and she explained that her father had had a few close female friends and that her mother could never shake the feeling that he was having affairs with them.

"I think they just expected different things from the relationship," she added calmly. She leaned back in her chair so the waiter could clear the plates from the table, and ordered an espresso. I ordered a cappuccino, Urška a white coffee, while Ivana shook her head to say she didn't want anything.

"Anyway, I invited both of them, Agata and her husband, to the wedding," Urška said when the waiter placed a cup in front of her. She emptied two packets of sugar in the coffee, as if she had forgotten all about her weight-loss plan. It seemed Sara's story had made her uncomfortable and she wanted to change the subject. "Do you think he'll come?" she asked Ivana. She shrugged and said she didn't see why not.

"Gregor is a wonderful person, you'll see," she said knowingly and smiled.

"Are you going to bring Maks to the wedding?" Sara asked me unprompted, at which I nearly choked on my coffee. I looked at her in surprise, searching her green eyes for a trace of mischief. She was looking at me completely seriously.

Maks had never replied to the email I sent him asking about the mysterious photograph. I had already come to terms with the fact that this time our friendship was truly over.

"Maks? To our wedding?" Urška's eyes widened as she stared at me. I waved my hand. "Of course not. I don't know what *she's* talking about," I said, gesturing toward Sara.

"Sorry, I just thought that —"

"I mean, you can invite him if you want to," Urška told me earnestly. "I know you're friends. It's just... I don't know... You know."

"I know."

"Who are you talking about?" Ivana asked in confusion, looking from one to the other.

"Maša's friend."

"We're just friends," I said to Ivana for absolutely no reason, "buddies from college. Urška knows him because our parents used to hang out with his."

"Yeah, and since they had a falling out, I don't know if it's the smartest idea..." Urška began quietly, blushing out of nowhere.

"Why did they have a falling out?"

How did we end up on my favorite topic? Urška's sigh showed she was uncomfortable as well.

"Because of their differences," Sara explained for us.

"What kind?"

If I didn't say anything, maybe they would forget what we were talking about and switch to a different topic. But Urška said: "They used to be quite close, but our dad and his dad argued a lot. It was mostly for fun, but not always. They disagreed on politics, and from there, soon every subject became delicate."

I noticed how intently Sara and Ivana were listening to her. Ivana was nodding empathetically.

"Anyway, one day things came to a head. I don't know what the reason was, but they got into a heated argument, debating all those exhausting topics, you know... The secret police, independence, Janša... and it went too far. My mom and Maks's mom were really good friends, but after that, they grew apart too."

I brought my hand to my mouth and started chewing on my thumbnail. I didn't remember the argument; it must have happened when we kids weren't around. Urška was four years older than me and perhaps understood what was going on better than I did. Sara shot me a cautious glance.

"And what about the two of you? Do you never talk about it?" My sister observed me intently, as if she had wanted to ask me this before but never found the right moment.

"No, the two of us aren't interested in those topics —"

"I don't mean that. I mean what happened between them."

I shook my head. Maks and I persistently ignored that fact. Only once he joked about what his father had said about us, but when he saw I didn't find it funny, he dropped it.

"Do you remember their weekend house?" I thought of what I had wanted to ask her many times. Urška's face lit up.

"Of course I do. We went there often during the summers. I remember our visit to a nearby cave. And sometimes we'd go swimming near Trieste, remember?"

I nodded wholeheartedly, but Urška's face darkened: "I once

heard Dad say that before independence, Maks's grandfather kissed up to the authorities, grabbing enough money so the Hafners could buy a house in Ljubljana, and they also got that house in the Karst."

All four of us fell silent. Urška's words sent a sharp pang beneath my sternum, and I stared into the empty coffee cup in front of me, where brown spots were forming at the bottom, as if I were gazing at an antique map. I could imagine our father saying something like that. I knew Maks's family was well off, but it didn't seem fair to hold that against Maks. After all, it wasn't his fault he was privileged. Was he supposed to voluntarily renounce the capital others had secured for him?

"What does that even mean?" Sara spoke up, looking around at our faces. "The part about grabbing money? I mean, this isn't the first time I've heard something about people getting rich by collaborating with the authorities, but what does it actually mean?"

We were silent until I said: "I don't know, you're the one who should tell us, you're studying sociology," and laughed. They laughed as well, but still, no one offered an answer; it was obvious we didn't know.

"Come to think of it," Urška said, "it would be nice if he came to the wedding. It's time to let those things go."

I gazed into my sister's eyes, so similar to our mother's. She was often extremely exhausting and highly judgmental, but she could also be very tender. The thought of bringing Maks to her wedding thrilled me, but also repelled me. It was a family event where he would meet my entire extended family. Though it was true Urška was dreaming of a huge wedding, so we could easily blend in among the guests, and I wouldn't have to deal with our relatives or their friends. I grimaced insecurely, while Urška motioned to the waiter for the bill.

"What if you invited Maks to your birthday party, so you can make up, whatever it was that happened between you?" Sara asked me quietly on our walk back to the car, with Ivana and Urška walking ahead of us in excited conversation. I had told her discreetly that I had said something stupid to him and felt he was angry with me, which was why I couldn't invite him to the wedding. I was planning to celebrate my birthday in two weeks, and I had already told Sara, Ivana, and Urška to come. I originally had no plans to celebrate at all, but Urška convinced me I had to.

I shook my head: "I can't. It'll just be me, you, Urška, Andrej, and Ivana. He'd be bored."

"Then invite Blaž too, just for fun. So he won't be alone. We'll set Blaž up with Ivana," she added so seriously that I couldn't tell whether she was joking or not.

"I can't invite Blaž after what happened on New Year's."

"Invite him, it was nothing."

"But why Blaž, of all people?"

"Who else are you going to invite to keep him company? Gaja?" she teased me, sending blood rushing to my cheeks.

"Why is everyone nagging me about inviting Maks to things?" I groaned in mock anger, and she smiled: "I don't know, we can just see that he means a lot to you."

I sighed. "Well, alright."

8.

I didn't make any special preparations for my twenty-second birthday party; Maks hadn't replied to my invitation, so I concluded he wouldn't come. I figured the get-together would consist of grabbing something to eat, watching a movie, and then everyone would go home. I made a selection of three of my favorite films that I thought the others might enjoy: *American Beauty*, *Lost in Translation*, and *Little Miss Sunshine.* I had already watched the latter with my sister, who wasn't thrilled with it, saying it "was about a dysfunctional family and had no positive message." I had a hard time explaining that the portrayal of a dysfunctional family was exactly the film's charm. I had even printed out a screenshot of the scene where Paul Dano tells Steve Carell, "*Fuck beauty contests. Life is one fucking beauty contest after another,*" and taped it above my desk.

On the very day of my birthday, Saturday, March 19th, Andrej and Urška were already lounging on the living room couch when Ivana brought Sara and Blaž over. Blaž and I sometimes ran into each other in the college hallways and exchanged dry greetings. I had invited him to my birthday via Facebook, and as far as I could tell, he had stayed in Ljubljana just for my mediocre little party. He brought along a canteen of homemade white wine, bragging that it was produced by his uncle somewhere in the Goričko region. They gave me a fifty-euro Müller gift card, which I thought was quite generous.

I ordered pizzas over the phone, and while I was in the kitchen fixing drinks, the doorbell rang. It seemed a bit early for the delivery guy, and when I went to answer the intercom, I heard Maks's voice.

Leaning against the doorframe, I waited for him to step out of the elevator. We had last seen each other over two months ago, and we hadn't spoken since—apart from that email. He looked the same as usual, but his greeting was somewhat cold, he wished me a happy birthday without touching me, holding out a gift bag. I tried in vain to read his face for a clue on what was going on and why he was acting so enigmatically. We exchanged a few empty pleasantries on the way to the living room, as if we barely knew each other. When we joined the others, Urška enthusiastically asked me to show them what I had gotten for a present.

Gift bag in hand, I sat down on the couch while the others watched me open it. I pulled a small box out of the bag, and when I read *Olympus* on it, I looked up at Maks in shock.

"Are you out of your mind?" I asked him, stunned, and a triumphant smile flitted across his previously somber face. Andrej asked what it was, and Blaž told him it was a handheld audio recorder used for field research.

"This little gadget wasn't cheap," Blaž commented, shooting Maks a cold look. There was no need for him to say that, as I was well aware. I had been looking at this exact model, and it cost over fifty euros—an amount that, in my case, required careful consideration.

I met Sara's eyes as she sat relaxed in my father's armchair, clutching a can of beer. She winked at me.

"Thank you," I said to Maks quietly, and when our eyes met, I felt the tension between us ease. He smiled and said it was something every anthropologist needed. I nodded and, with a trembling hand, slipped the box back into the gift bag. So he really isn't that angry, the thought crossed my mind.

The doorbell rang again, it was the pizza delivery guy. I brought the pizza boxes into the living room and set them on the coffee table.

Everyone but Maks hungrily pounced on them. Urška handed him a plate and asked him which one he wanted, but he warily approached the open boxes and looked at me: "Are any of them vegetarian?"

I covered my mouth with my hand and whimpered. Of course, Maks was a vegetarian, but since I wasn't expecting him, I didn't order any pizzas without meat.

"You don't eat meat?" Andrej asked him with his mouth full. Maks shook his head.

"Didn't you eat it back in high school?" Sara frowned. She hadn't started on her slice of pizza yet. He nodded.

"Yeah, I only stopped about a year and a half ago," he said, taking a sip of wine and nodding at Blaž to say it was good. Andrej grinned, and I looked at him in surprise. He nudged Maks in the shoulder, saying: "Now I get why you're so scrawny." I looked at Maks with concern, but he merely gave a dry chuckle.

"That has nothing to do with meat. It's just my genetics," he said placidly. "But even if I was scrawny because I didn't eat it, I honestly couldn't care less."

I wished our eyes would meet so my gaze could tell him that I didn't think that about his body. I had seen him tagged in friends' vacation photos on Facebook, and I knew Maks had a firm torso under his shirt. And he wore short-sleeved shirts most of the year, which gently hugged the taut skin of his upper arms. In fact, I suspected Andrej's comment stemmed from his own insecurity; he was quite a bit taller than Maks, but also chubby.

"No, it's fine," Andrej mumbled with his mouth full, "I obviously don't care if you don't eat meat. But for me, the old wisdom holds: until I have a taste of lion, the king of animals remains the pig." We all laughed, some more sincerely than others.

"I don't have anything against vegetarians either," Urška chipped in, "but I don't like it when someone moralizes to me about animal cruelty."

"Why not?" I recognized the distinct cranky undertone in Maks's voice, one I had often heard in our conversations. I knew him well enough to know it only came from an eagerness to debate, not a tendency to be argumentative. But I didn't know if the others knew that.

In a slightly more academic tone, he continued: "Many people compare mankind's treatment of animals to the Holocaust. Speciesism is highly problematic in general, and in many ways, it closely resembles racism and the exploitation of the weaker parties, women, for instance." When he said that, I remembered we had already talked about this once.

"Women?" Andrej spoke up. "What do women have to do with you not eating meat?"

Maks watched him in silence for a few moments. It seemed to me he was searching for the words to explain this to a person who knew absolutely nothing about it.

"Ecofeminism," he said very slowly and with a tone like Istenič's, "is an idea that recognizes the way men manage and exploit women in their dominion over nature. It contains a very interesting premise, namely that it opposes liberal feminism, which fights for women to achieve equal positions in society as men, since the men in those positions ruthlessly exploit natural and human resources."

Everyone present listened to him very intently, even though I detected disapproval or at least a lack of comprehension on Andrej's face. Maks paid no attention to this and continued confidently: "In opposition to an anthropocentric feminism, which advocates for women to have the exact same status in society as men, ecofeminism points out that a society ruled by men is inherently bad and exploitative.

I might have veered off course a bit," he cleared his throat and took a sip of wine, "but in short, ecofeminism is based on an idea that opposes dominance over nature and dominance over women."

"Does that mean," Sara said in a perfectly calm voice, and I looked at her gratefully—it seemed to me that she alone would know how to steer this debate forward without it deteriorating into a fight—"that women who, for instance, get involved in politics, work at universities... And who simply fight for equal treatment as men, that these women are making a mistake because they are forcing their way into a world based on male principles?"

Maks shook his head vigorously: "I'm not saying that, just as I'm not saying I'm an ecofeminist. I merely wanted to explain what —"

"No, I'm not saying there's anything wrong with it. I should read up on it more," Sara said thoughtfully. "But it does feel like the premise that women are the ones closer to nature could be problematic, because it's a classic patriarchal stance that was always used to portray women as inferior, ascribing them with a certain neuroticism."

Maks took a breath and, with the voice of an intellectual, continued: "I absolutely understand what you mean, and I agree that this aspect can be problematic, but ecofeminism is interesting because it claims that it is precisely for this reason, because they were expected to cooperate with nature and mediate it for society for so long, women will actually have an advantage in the future, as they possess skills that can be used to protect natural resources. Ecofeminism argues that women, just like farmers for instance, in fact have a greater capacity for managing natural processes."

Blaž, sitting on the opposite end of the couch from Maks, now snorted loudly: "Oh, give it a rest, man. I find it funny it's you talking about farmers, when I'm not sure you've ever even seen one up close."

The coarseness in Blaž's voice surprised me, but Ivana and Urška laughed lightheartedly. Maks shot Blaž a disdainful glance, but offered no objection.

"And I just think," Blaž continued, "okay, maybe not so much vegetarianism, but veganism, that it's, how should I say, a habit of the wealthier classes of society. Or rather, a bad habit. Vegan substitutes are obscenely expensive, vegans must take a bunch of dietary supplements, and it's patently clear they don't know hunger at all." Andrej gave him a thumbs-up to say he agreed, his mouth full of pizza.

Hadn't Sara told me to invite Blaž so Maks wouldn't *stand out*? And now it was precisely Blaž making him stand out.

"You're partially right," Maks said, and I prayed Blaž was aware of his passion for debating, "but veganism also has very strong arguments, in reality far stronger than vegetarianism. The dairy industry is in no way better than the meat industry. Animals are exploited there, too. And this is where feminism and ecology strongly overlap: just think about how, for example, calves are taken away from their mothers immediately after birth."

"Listen, I wasn't finished," Blaž went on. "I also wanted to say that all this moralizing about meat, and now dairy products too, bothers me because I happen to have people in my immediate family who make their living from the meat industry. And they are not wealthy people. They couldn't just go out and buy a little gadget like this"—he nodded at the gift bag holding my new voice recorder—"to hand it out to a friend for their birthday. They'd have to think twice."

I blushed vividly at his words. What did my new voice recorder have to do with what we were talking about?

"Well, your gift is wonderful too," I chirped, winking at him as I raised my glass, filled to the brim with wine, to him. "You remembered that I prefer white wine," I smiled. It was his turn to blush. We hadn't spoken this directly since that unfortunate New Year's kiss.

I glanced over at Maks, who was watching me with his eyebrows drawn together. Then he turned to Blaž: "Of course I'm aware of that, and I'm sorry it's that way. Yes, vegan substitutes aren't cheap, and many people depend on the meat industry. But personally, I won't eat meat anymore. And there's one more thing I'd like to say that I've been thinking about a lot lately. When I was at the border, I realized that in both Islam and Judaism, there are dietary rules that also tie into animal cruelty. And I asked myself: why does Christianity have absolutely no dietary restrictions?"

None of us said anything and he added: "It's no wonder our society is viewed by others, by Muslims for instance, as completely shambolic."

Urška got up from the couch, placed her empty plate on the coffee table, and went to open the window; she opened it wide, letting a cool March breeze sweep into the stuffy room. I could already see my future brother-in-law preparing to plunge into a new debate with Maks—about religion, Islam, and Christianity. I knew Maks—he wouldn't give in easily—and I knew Andrej couldn't win this debate, nor would he handle defeat gracefully.

"Maks, let me go see what I can make for you," I said as I stood up hastily to avoid having to listen to the conversation and headed to the kitchen. In the cupboard, I found an unopened pack of toast bread, and some cheese and tomatoes in the fridge. I busied myself with preparing the food when Sara appeared in the kitchen doorway and asked if I was okay. Lips pursed, I shook my head.

"I didn't expect Maks to come. I wasn't prepared for this," I mumbled about the thing that bothered me the least. Sara comforted me, telling me not to beat myself up over it, since, as she could see, I had already found food for him.

"I don't know what's going on. First, he didn't reply to my email, then he ignored my birthday invitation, and suddenly he shows up here, and with an expensive gift, no less," I was bewildered. Sara nodded with sympathy.

"I don't understand him either. I just came to tell you not to stress over the debates out there," she said, as if reading my mind. "I see this every Wednesday at band practice. My three bandmates have a verbal war before, during, and after practice nearly every time we get together; they think they have to express themselves about everything and have an opinion on everything. They are... men. But they get along well despite it."

I looked at her, exasperated: "That's just it. Your bandmates get along well. But Andrej and Maks are very different. You have no idea how much."

Sara, leaning against the doorframe, shrugged with the certainty of someone who knew what she was talking about and said: "I don't know. I don't think the two of them are all that different."

"Maks and Andrej?"

She nodded.

"They might have different backgrounds, but they are both stubborn in their principles. I might be wrong though, who knows." She shrugged again, less convincingly now.

I put the sandwiches into the toaster and turned it on.

"What happened after I left?"

"Maks went to the bathroom. When he left, Blaž and Andrej started talking about wine. Everything will be fine," she said with a wink. I looked at her joylessly, and she turned and disappeared out the door.

I waited until the sandwiches were fully toasted, then stepped into the hallway with a plate in hand. Just then, I saw Maks coming out of my room.

"Hey, what were you doing in there?" I asked him.

He approached me, looked so deeply into my eyes that I broke a sweat, and said: "I took some time to look in your nightstand. Now we're even, right? Nice underwear collection, by the way."

He grabbed a toasted sandwich from the plate I was holding out, took a bite, then pranced away to the living room.

9

I followed him into the living room without a word, where the atmosphere was different than before: someone had turned on the TV, which was playing a music video featuring Selena Gomez writhing on a bed in black lingerie, and Maks, who had sat down in my father's armchair, was staring at the screen with a strange look. Blaž's canteen was emptying, and a bottle of the teran liqueur that my mother made for Christmas every year had appeared on the table. Sara, sitting at Blaž's feet, was eagerly explaining something to Andrej and Blaž, while Urška and Ivana were sitting on the couch with their legs tucked under them, quietly talking to each other with glasses in their hands.

I put the plate of toast down on the coffee table and sat on the couch next to Blaž, took a glass of wine, and tried to follow their conversation, but my thoughts kept wandering back to the incident in the hallway. There was no Bible or condoms in the drawer of my nightstand, like in Maks's, just the underwear I had no room for in the closet. I pictured him opening the drawer and staring at its messy contents. His hands, with their bulging blue-green veins, had sifted through pairs of panties smelling of fabric softener, and he might have caught the scent of the lavender moth-repellent pouch. Perhaps his fingers had touched the white pair with the pink bow, which, despite repeated washing, still bore a faint bloodstain, or the floral cotton panties my mother had bought me in a multi-pack, or perhaps he had found the black lace thongs stuffed in the corner. He might have pushed aside the padded H&M bras and found the photograph of the two of us underneath them.

"Want to go for a smoke?"

Maks, ignoring me, nudged Sara, who was right in the middle of a sentence. She raised her index finger, finished her statement, then stood up and motioned for him to come. My stomach churned with envy: neither of them had thought to invite me along, probably because I didn't smoke. I found myself wishing I did. Actually, I didn't know why I didn't smoke, I had tried it once, wasn't convinced, and then never did it again. If I smoked, I could have joined them without it looking weird.

Like a pile of misery, I sat there on the couch next to Andrej and Blaž, who kept on talking, and I couldn't shake my anger at myself for not smoking until, after a few minutes, I couldn't take it anymore. I went to the kitchen without knowing what I was looking for, rummaged around a bit in the drawers, and opened the fridge. Then I went into my room, closed the door behind me, and opened my underwear drawer. It hadn't been neatly organized before, so it was impossible to tell if someone had been rooting through it. I sighed and closed it. Then I gave in: I went to check what Sara and Maks were up to on the balcony.

They were leaning against the railing of our enclosed balcony. Looking at their backs, I felt entirely superfluous. Maks had just handed Sara a rolled cigarette, and she took a drag, creating a certain special intimacy between them. Only then did I catch the scent. The stink of a swamp on a hot day after the rain. I turned to leave when Sara noticed me and pulled me in between them.

"Want some?" she asked, offering me the joint. I sighed, accepted it, and took a drag. The tip of the joint was slightly wet from their saliva.

"Just don't tell Urška about this," I grumbled.

"Relax, it's your birthday," she said dreamily. I made a face and said that I wouldn't be smoking if the party wasn't so bad. I passed the joint to Maks, who immediately protested that he was having a great time, and Sara backed him up.

"Of course you are, acting like a smart-ass with my future brother-in-law and dragging him into tedious debates," I scolded him, looking away.

"We were just talking," he said very calmly, took a drag from the joint, and offered it to Sara. A brief silence followed, before Maks said wistfully: "You guys have a really beautiful view. All these apartment blocks, the illuminated windows... And behind them, people who will always be unknown to us."

I raised my eyebrows, and Sara giggled. She offered me the joint, I took another drag. The view from our balcony didn't particularly move me: there were apartment blocks all around us, a human silhouette appearing here and there in the yellow windows, while the loud Celovška Street roared below.

"I love Ljubljana," Maks went on, "these socialist blocks, the gloomy staircases, the dirty elevators. Šiška is truly beautiful, it has a sort of Warsaw-esque melancho—"

"What is wrong with you?" I interrupted him with a laugh. "You might find it beautiful, when you're living in a renovated terraced house in Bežigrad, with a white facade and brand-new windows. Dirty elevators? I ride that elevator every single day." Maks shot me an offended look. He had put on a hoodie that gave off the fresh scent of fabric softener over the T-shirt he was wearing in the living room.

"Now you're starting too," he said bitterly. "First Blaž tried to paint me as someone who can't see past Ljubljana's beltway, and now you're accusing me I don't know what it's like to live in an apartment block. It's unfair."

I swallowed my spit, tasting of weed, and quietly apologized. Maks said nothing, he took the joint from Sara and inhaled. I looked out over the balcony. In his own way, he was right: the view of the Ljubljana apartment blocks was beautiful, and the scent of late March hung in the air; it smelled of warmer days, and the birds were chirping with sorrow.

"Would you ever live anywhere else?" Sara asked. I took the roll from Maks and took a slow drag, thinking he would answer. But he remained silent.

"I would," I finally spoke up, passing the cigarette on to Sara. "I'd live in a bigger city in a heartbeat. I'd even settle for Zagreb," I laughed weakly. "Ljubljana is too small for me. I really had a blast in Barcelona."

"Seriously?" Maks looked at me in surprise. "I wouldn't have thought that. You seem so..."

"Slovenian?"

Sara chuckled, blowing out smoke. She had to cough. But Maks shook his head.

"Not Slovenian, whatever that means. You seem... You know."

"No, I don't know."

"Well," he grimaced, "you don't strike me as a person who needs external impulses. You're somehow content in your own world." He took the joint from Sara and brought it to his lips.

"Are you saying I'm boring?"

Maks shook his head firmly and stared at me. "Not boring. On the contrary."

His lips were slightly wet, perhaps from the saliva we had left on the joint. I blinked at him slowly; between the teran liqueur I was sipping while deciding whether to join them on the balcony, and the marijuana, my eyelids were growing heavy.

"Much more special than the rest." His words reached me very slowly, like an echo. Behind us, the balcony door clicked shut, and we both flinched. Sara had left without either of us noticing.

"Why were you snooping through my drawers?" he suddenly asked me, handing me the joint. There was only curiosity in his voice now, no trace of anger.

"I guess I was curious. Nightstands are interesting."

He smiled and nodded.

"What did you think you were going to find?"

"What did you think you were going to find in mine?"

"I don't know, a dildo," he grinned, and immediately turned serious, as if realizing his attempt at a joke was pathetic. I rolled my eyes and took another drag of the joint, even though I was feeling slightly nauseous. It was nearing the end, so I stubbed it out in the flower box attached to the balcony railing.

"No, I'm just kidding, I don't know. Anyway, you asked me why I keep that photo of us there. It's there because it's the only one left." He had grown serious. He wasn't looking at me, but was scanning the street below. A young man was walking a small black dog on a leash. The dog stopped at a lamppost and lifted its leg.

"The only one left?"

He nodded.

"Darja was clearing the photos. She left a small pile of them on the table before she threw them in the trash, and that one was among them." He looked at me with a sad smile.

"That's a sad story," I said very slowly. He stayed silent for a moment, then said in a muffled voice: "That's their problem."

I didn't ask him who "they" were; I knew. I asked him about the other three photographs.

"They were duplicates," he explained. "Darja said I should take them as a keepsake."

It was my turn to nod sadly. I thought of our shared photographs and saw them, creased in half, lying on crumpled receipts and torn envelopes. In a way, I wished he hadn't told me.

"Hey," I suddenly remembered, nudging him gently on the shoulder. "I wanted to ask you something. Would you go with me to Andrej and Urška's wedding?" I hoped he couldn't hear my heartbeat. Maks's face lit up.

"Yeah, cool, when is it?" I told him the date, and he nodded.

"Is it going to be a church wedding?" I nodded and smiled, and he did too. He mumbled that he thought that was awesome because he had never been to a church wedding. I, on the other hand, had never been to a civil one, I told him. A silence fell over us, and Maks stared solemnly into the distance again.

I watched him with concern. It seemed to me that the weed had awakened a certain melancholy in him that I had never known him to have. His eyes seemed more sunken than usual.

"What were you and Sara talking about?"

He let out a short sigh.

"I told her something very personal," he admitted, smiling weakly. I raised my eyebrows and asked him what.

"Sara and I..." I waited tensely for him to finish. It seemed to me that he was speaking slower than usual and that I was processing things slower, too.

"Before the freshman party, we last saw each other at a funeral. Last April. Our high school classmate killed himself." He swallowed hard. "We were talking about how we processed it. She said she wrote a couple of lyrics for her band and, on her mom's recommendation, started reading Dostoevsky." He chuckled, then turned serious again and cleared his throat.

"What about you?" He looked up and stared at me. The color of his eyes was darker. He hesitated before answering.

"Shortly after the funeral, I went out with my high school buddies, and I ran into Gaja. We went home together and... That was the first time we hooked up."

I blinked slowly, my eyelids felt increasingly heavy. I asked him what he told Sara.

"Well," he waved his hand, "what I just told you. That was how I processed it."

Between the pizza, the alcohol, and the weed, I felt slightly nauseous. I knew that Urška had baked me twenty-two muffins and decorated them with candles, but I couldn't imagine how I was going to stuff one into myself.

"I understand," I said coldly, and Maks stayed silent.

"Want to go inside?" I finally asked him, as I was starting to get cold. Maks nodded.

"Are there going to be any activities?"

I nodded: "Yeah, we're going to watch *Little Miss Sunshine*." I had decided on it at that very moment.

"Great," he grinned, as if it were all just one big joke. "I've never watched it stoned."

10

"I invited Maks to our concert in Trieste."

Sara wasn't looking at me. After she said this, she absentmindedly watched Agata, who was standing by the piano in a somber dark purple dress, writing something down in a tiny notebook.

"Why? When?" I blinked at her, a painful tightness gripping my chest; the concert was in four days, and after every one of my solos, Agata's face clearly showed that she still wasn't completely satisfied with it.

"Yesterday. I ran into him at Foerster's. Well, actually," she tore her gaze away from Agata and looked at me, "we got together with some former classmates for drinks. To commemorate something." She gave a weak smile. "You're okay with that, right?" she asked me cautiously, as I was staring at her with a furrowed brow.

"I don't know." I brought my hand to my mouth and pulled on a bit of cuticle with my teeth until it stung.

Sara was pleased with herself, smiling mysteriously: "We agreed to go on a trip. Me, you, and him. He'll drive, we'll head out in the morning, and while we're at the dress rehearsal, he'll go for a walk around Trieste. It'll be great, you'll see."

I sighed deeply. It seemed Sara had thought everything through, so there was no point in resisting. Just the thought of my solo made me shift uncomfortably in my chair.

"There was something else I wanted to tell you. Just not here. Want to step outside for a bit?" She cast a glance at the frowning Agata, who had just bitten into an apple.

I nodded and followed her out into the hallway. A few girls were standing outside the hall doors, chatting quietly. We moved slightly away from them, and Sara sighed.

"The rehearsal last week was exhausting." I raised my eyebrows and tried to remember what had happened a week ago, but Sara shook her head: "Not the regular rehearsal, but on Wednesday, the one for Urška's wedding." She grimaced, illustrating her thoughts on the extra burden.

"Oh, that," I whispered. Agata kept telling me about those rehearsals, too, and a week ago she had even sent me a message in the middle of the day asking if I was going to come. I made up an excuse that I had lectures: I had been feeling weary, which I attributed to my impending period, which I then got the next day. I stayed in the university library's reading room until seven in the evening, afraid I would run into Urška at home and Agata would somehow find out I had lied to her.

Sara folded her arms across her chest and began to talk restlessly; her usually calm demeanor was turbulent, her eyes darkened, and her eyebrows knitted together in anger. She told me the atmosphere at rehearsal was tense because the girls were tired of the extra practices, and on top of that, Agata had changed her mind about the mass piece and, instead of the one they had been practicing for a while, brought in a new one.

"She acts like it's a concert, not a wedding. She keeps saying that music is an essential component of the ceremony, whenever she notices our motivation waning. She thinks it will encourage us. She even says: make an effort for Urška's sake, even though it doesn't look like she's thinking about Urška at all."

After this brief outburst, she fell silent and stared angrily at the painting hanging on the wall behind me. I noticed that the other girls were watching us. Sara looked over at them and gestured with her head: "Let Klara tell you how it was."

Klara approached us, with Ana and Zala at her heels.

"On Wednesday?" Klara asked, and when Sara nodded, Klara looked at me and sighed. "Maša, I know Urška is your sister, but Agata is taking it too far. She's changed the repertoire for the mass for the second time already, and she also wants to prepare some special surprise for her after the ceremony... I know they agreed that Urška's going to pay us, but—"

"She might really be overdoing it a little," Ana chimed in with a thin voice. Even though she was otherwise cut from the same cloth as Ivana and genuinely idolized Agata—she had even confided in us that she only auditioned because of her—she now continued warily: "We had already pretty much mastered the mass, but then Agata found another, considerably harder one. Did Urška ask her to do that?"

I assured them that I knew nothing about it, but that I thought my sister had left the choice of wedding songs entirely up to Agata. "And to Ivana," I added.

"Ivana," Klara rolled her eyes, glancing carefully at Sara as she did so. "On Wednesday after rehearsal, I told her she had to make Agata understand she needs to be a little less demanding, or she's going to lose another singer, but—"

"Why should Ivana have to be the one to make her understand that?" Sara pushed back, glaring at Klara, who blushed and lowered her gaze. "I think we should tell her ourselves, to her face. Ivana isn't some messenger between us and her," she added in a combative tone.

"We can be calm about it, when we tell her," Zala spoke up, a tall girl who stood next to Sara in the choir. "Agata isn't so crazy that she wouldn't understand if we told her we're tired and that we'd like to slow down a bit after Trieste until we leave for Tallinn. The tempo really is unbearable."

"Be my guest," Klara remarked sarcastically, but Sara shook her head: "Zala is right, we have to tell her what we think." She stared resolutely toward the doors. The singers were slowly streaming in the hall.

"But if you do this in front of Urška, it's going to be weird," I finally said. "I understand there are too many rehearsals, but Urška's going to feel responsible." My pleading gaze met Sara's.

She swallowed and nodded: "Fine. We won't speak with her. What if I write her an email?"

"Good idea," Klara clapped her hands in satisfaction and pointed at her. "Agata likes emails when it comes to something important. And she won't feel attacked."

Zala and Ana nodded, too. There were only the five of us left in the hallway when Ivana appeared at the doors and called out to us that rehearsal was about to resume.

11

Maks was supposed to go to Savsko naselje to pick up Sara first and then come for me, but when I saw him outside my apartment building in his father's white Volvo, he was alone.

"Where is Sara?" I asked him, hanging the garment bag with my concert dress inside the car door.

"She's not coming. Something came up," he said, and our eyes met in the rearview mirror. I closed the back door and sat down next to him in the passenger seat.

"What do you mean?" I opened the backpack in my lap, pulled out my phone, and was about to send Sara a message when Maks explained: "I went to pick her up, but she came down and told me she couldn't come. Apparently, her dad was coming for a visit. They didn't expect it."

"Hm. And what, she's going to miss the concert?"

"I think so."

"Agata won't be happy."

"Yeah, but it's her dad. You know he lives abroad. They practically never see each other."

I didn't say anything as I put my phone back into my backpack and settled into the leather seat. There was no point in explaining to Maks that Agata wouldn't care who was coming for a visit; it could be the Queen of England, and she would still expect to see Sara at the concert.

"Fine," I said in resignation, and Maks turned on the left turn signal, before we took off.

"Can I put on some music?" I asked him after a few minutes of silence.

He nodded and handed me his iPhone, saying it was connected to the radio. I asked him if he had a musical request, but he shook his head. I realized the importance of this moment: I had his phone in my hands, I could choose anything to create a unique atmosphere. We had already merged onto the highway from Celovška Street, and the car was picking up speed, swiftly gliding past the others. I thought I could catch the faint scent of the shower gel Maks had showered with before leaving home. My fingers, wrapped around his iPhone, were becoming damp, leaving light smudges on the cold metal. The seconds ticked by.

Lana Del Rey, Sia, Selena Gomez, Ariana Grande, Beyoncé, Lorde. Which of them would tell him how I felt?

I made up my mind. *Wildest Dreams* by Taylor Swift. Even if I rarely listened to her, maybe Gaja liked her, and that would impress him. I pressed play, and the first beats rang out from the radio, followed by the singer's voice: "*He said: 'Let's get out of this town, drive out of the city, away from the crowds.'*" When the chorus began, I sang along with Taylor with the best voice I could muster. I closed my eyes, happier than I had been in a long time.

We got lucky and found a parking spot not far from the center of Trieste. When we left the car, the air smelled of coffee and salt. The wind kept the streets clear of people. Seagulls were calling out above the Austro-Hungarian façades, and as we crossed Oberdan Square, Maks looked at the white buildings with disgust, labeling them "an example of repulsive fascist architecture."

We walked toward the Piazza Unità d'Italia.

"When I was little, we came to Trieste a lot," he explained when I asked how he knew the city so well to guide me down the narrow streets with such assurance. "My grandfather," he continued guardedly, "used to visit the city and the surrounding villages often; he was very interested in the cultural heritage of this area. He even bought a house nearby."

"Where?"

We stepped out of the narrow street onto the square. A strong wind was blowing in from the sea.

"On the Slovenian side of the border, not far, in Kreplje. You know it; you've been there."

"Oh, that house. I didn't know it was so close to Trieste."

I could picture the outline of the old Karst house in my mind; from what I could remember, it was set a bit apart from the other houses in the village. I thought of the dim light of gas lamps and white sheets.

"Is your family there often?" I asked, hoping he wouldn't notice that I blushed.

"Martin is there almost every weekend, Darja rarely. I almost never go," he said tersely.

We found ourselves sheltered from the wind again. Maks pointed at a coffee shop that had "Illy" written in white letters on the door. He went in, and I followed.

"How's your thesis coming along?" I asked as we sat down at one of the small tables. His answer was forestalled by the waiter who had come to take our orders. Then he ran his hand across his freshly shaven chin and sighed.

"It's going fine. I went to Istenič for consultations a while back, and the conversation turned to his plans of opening a Young Researcher position in the next couple of years. He asked me if I would be interested."

The waiter placed two cups of coffee in front of us. I stared at the white foam on my cappuccino. It had been years since there was a Young Researcher at the Department of Ethnology and Cultural Anthropology. I thought of what Blaž had told me on the balcony on New Year's: his professor said she couldn't guarantee him a job at the department. But apparently, different rules applied to Maks.

"But first you have to get your Master's. And then... There will be a lot of competition, certainly, but as a Hafner, I think your odds are good," I teased him, and he winced.

"I don't even want it," he objected. "I don't want to stay at the university. I have other plans."

"Then you could maybe recommend Gaja." My tone was bitter, and our eyes met. I couldn't stop myself: "Even if most of her intelligence comes from the privileges she's enjoyed. If she hadn't been born into a family like that, she'd be as dense as this cup."

Maks's eyebrows shot up in surprise. Panic washed over me; I might have finally betrayed just how much I was bothered by their relationship. I was expecting him to come to her aid, but he just asked: "Is that what you think of her?"

"That's what I think about the majority of your friends."

"Why?"

I prayed he couldn't tell I was being guided by emotion. I tried to make light of the situation and I snickered. "When you guys get together, you come off as a bit unapproachable."

I didn't know what else to say.

"Well, we're friends. We get along well."

"But if you get along so well, why were you sending those emails to me when you were at the border? Why not to one of them?"

I looked up from my cup and turned toward the street, where a couple our age was passing by. Arms around each other's waists, they walked past us, laughing as they looked at the shop windows. They were wearing similar blue quilted jackets and matching jeans. Despite the simplicity of their clothes, they looked very put-together.

"And how would you know what I was or wasn't sending to the others when I was at the border?" Maks said, irritated, and I blushed.

"You're right, I don't know," I said very quietly, tearing my gaze away from the couple receding from view, and drummed my fingers on the table. I wanted this conversation to end, so I changed the subject. "What are your plans, then?"

"Here's what I was thinking," he was quick to answer, as if he also wanted to clear the tension. "After my Master's, I want to join an expedition, maybe somewhere in the Middle East. The American Association for Middle East Anthropology organizes first-rate expeditions. And before that, it might make sense for me to go to the USA to get inducted into their way of work."

I had drunk all the foam off my cappuccino; only a pale brown liquid remained in the cup, and I stared at it. What he said surprised me. On our walks, Maks was always disparaging American society, calling it ultra-capitalist and exploitative, militant and corrupt, a source of unrest in the world, while laying the blame for practically every global problem on capitalism. But now he was telling me he wanted to go there and "get inducted into their way of work." Obviously, he was harboring dreams of living in big American cities, breathing in the exciting air of a metropolis.

I could already picture him walking across campus, debating Islamophobia, Marxism, and Black America with colleagues over coffee, attending guest lectures by Deepa Kumar and Fawaz Gerges. It struck me: he would go and find himself a girlfriend in America.

"If you can afford it," I sighed, stirring my coffee with a spoon. "After I finish college, I'm going to find a job."

He asked if I didn't think that, as an anthropologist, I should also do fieldwork somewhere.

"This is my field," I pushed back, waving my hand toward the window overlooking the street. "The world around me. You can be a good anthropologist anywhere."

Maks smiled, as if this was what he wanted to hear.

"You already have the recorder." He winked at me, and the wink felt like a caress.

I gave him a faint smile. Then I turned serious. "The expedition sounds great, but… I'm still paying back my parents the money they lent me for the exchange program. And do you have any idea how much Urška's wedding is going to cost? Her dress, the photographer, the invitations, the reception, all of it? And Urška getting married is important to them. They're not so enthusiastic about my plans."

Maks was biting his lip and said nothing. He reached into his jeans pocket, pulled out a pack of cigarettes, and laid it, still unopened, on the table. The street outside the window was now illuminated by the hazy April sun breaking through the clouds, and it seemed the wind had died down. A man and a woman with a stroller entered the café and sat at the table next to us.

The broad-shouldered man had a thick, dark beard, and the woman's hair was covered by a light brown headscarf. For a moment, I admired her perfectly groomed eyebrows with envy. She wore a light blue dress that covered her entire body, from her neck to her wrists and feet. She parked the stroller by the table; there was a year-old boy with big brown eyes and black curls inside, chewing on a rubber giraffe. The woman sat down next to the man, smiled at the child, and said something to him in a foreign language.

"Shall we get going? Leave it, I'll pay." Maks took the pack of cigarettes from the table, put it back in his pocket, stood up, and headed to the bar to pay.

We stepped out onto the street and headed toward the sea. There were more people in the square now, and the cars on the road along the waterfront were honking in agitation. We walked in silence to the Audace Pier and sat on the edge. Weak sunlight shone onto the pier through tattered clouds, and the ground was warmer than I expected.

"Do you remember when I wrote to you that I saw refugees praying in Dimitrovgrad?"

I nodded, embarrassed at remembering how I had replied to that email.

"One evening, one of the refugees opened the Quran and began to sing. Have you ever heard how Muslims read from the Quran?"

I shook my head, and he pulled his iPhone out of his jacket pocket, offered me one earbud, and put the other in his ear. Then he showed me a YouTube video of a young man in his room, sitting before an open book, reading, or rather singing, surahs from the Quran.

His voice was both deep and gentle. The melody wasn't predictable; it seemed like he was improvising it on the spot. I closed my eyes, and for a long moment, I experienced the Middle East. I wished I were with Maks in Beirut or Tripoli, walking hand in hand along the coast while a muezzin sang, and seagulls called out just as they were doing now in Trieste.

It struck me how silly Taylor Swift had sounded in the car earlier compared to what we were listening to now. I felt Maks's fingers on my cheek and flinched. He took the earbud out of my ear, and I opened my eyes.

"Isn't it good?" he asked, putting the phone away. I nodded.

"That was what that boy sounded like. You know, it was a tough time for me. The work we were doing, the whole situation, I was constantly stressed out. But hearing him pray, I felt an instant calm. I just sat there, listening."

Maks stared at the ships, not far from the pier, gliding across the surface of the sea.

"Are you thinking about becoming a Muslim?" I asked in jest, with a hint of earnestness. He laughed and shook his head.

"Not really. I'm still an atheist... And I always will be." He fell silent, then said very slowly: "Only, something hit me. You know that couple in the café earlier?"

I nodded.

"Sometimes, when I see a scene like that, I become aware that I will never have that for myself.."

I searched his face in vain for signs that he was joking. It had never occurred to me that Maks might be thinking about getting married and having a family.

"What do you mean?"

He frowned, searching for a way to express his thoughts.

"Hearing that prayer in Dimitrovgrad, something strange dawned on me. I realized that I envied these people. Even though they were on the run, they remained so steadfast in their traditions, their heritage, their... truth. Even though they were leaving their homelands behind and heading to the 'quasi-developed' West, they were still so reverentially unfurling their rugs, opening the Quran, praying."

He paused and cleared his throat. "I began to take stock of myself almost in a state of panic, telling myself who I was and what I believed in. My heritage is the education my parents made possible for me, a trust in science, theory, culture, the humanities," he was listing the concepts with fervor, staring at the sea, "these were the values I could hold on to. And I believed they would also benefit these people coming to the West. But then it hit me: how could I think that our way of life is the better choice for them? Won't it change them? Won't the way we live here soon teach them that the rug, the Quran, the prayer, the fasting... that these things have no real value in this world?"

He looked up, and our eyes met.

"And then I realized something else." His voice dropped a little, dying in his throat, before he cast a resolute gaze back at the ink-black sea and went on: "I realized that I don't have any real way to prove to them that our culture, mine, at least, was worth fleeing to. Okay, there's no war, no conflict, there's less violence and poverty, more equality and social security, but they are used to living in a world that has much more meaning than our own. And it made me think that they had things, which the war took from them, that I will never have."

"Like what?" I asked.

He looked away from the sea, stared at me, and winced.

"What they have. Their relationships, families."

It was my turn to scowl. "You mean having multiple wives? Are you trying to tell me you'd like a harem?"

I smiled, but my smile soon faded. The expression on his face was chilling. I added quickly, with some anger: "You mean relationships where women have no rights, inherit nothing, and are stoned if they're caught cheating?"

Maks sighed and shook his head.

"Listen to me, okay?" He sounded desperate and I nodded. He went on: "Look, I wouldn't be saying this... I wouldn't be saying this if it wasn't for the thing we had with Gaja."

I shifted nervously and looked away from his face, but he continued, as if he hadn't noticed my distaste.

"The stuff we did. That she sometimes played the submissive role during sex."

I fixed my stare at a seagull flying and screaming above us, as if it was the most interesting thing in the world, while Maks kept talking, oblivious to how I felt: "And when I heard that boy read from the Quran, the whole thing began to feel like the most perverse game, because we were just acting out something that never really existed between us. Not because we weren't a couple. Because we *played* at being one; because during sex, we *pretended* there was something between us that wasn't really there. I avoided her when I got back home from the border, and it was over. We were done."

The screaming seagull flew off toward the open sea and soon turned into nothing but a tiny dot. I stared at it so hard my forehead began to ache.

"I still don't understand what this has to do with Muslims," I finally said, my voice coming out very high. I thought about the fact that I had to perform a solo in a few hours, and I felt a sharp pecking pain in my chest.

Maks sighed and then contritely admitted: "Nothing. It's just that seeing all those people at the border, I was at times really tormented by the question of why we were so sure ours is the right way to live. They made me realize that I might never be in a relationship like... like that man and woman in the café had, for example... because... because I would always be gnawed by a feeling of guilt. Just this... this male guilt. Which exists, believe it or not."

He cast a mischievous smile in my direction, then quickly looked away.

"The guilt over the fact that the world is dangerous and unfair to women. And that despite being aware of this and feeling guilty because of it, I still feel a desire for... For not having to burden myself with it. That I wouldn't have to care about all the things I mentioned before, science, theory, culture, the humanities... that I simply wouldn't have to care, that I could abandon myself to my instincts and desires and not stress over it at all. After your birthday party... Fuck," he shook his head, as if he couldn't believe the words he was about to say, "after the party, I found myself thinking how I envied Andrej for having such stupid, narrow-minded, bigoted convictions. You don't understand why, do you?"

I shook my head in disbelief.

"Because he isn't some humanist who needs to watch over every word he says, you know? People like that, with convictions like that, they simply plow through life without being tormented by a sense of guilt. They just blurt out whatever, and it's okay; they'll probably never realize how wrong they sound. And it hit me that sometimes I wished I was like him. I wished to be *normal*, I don't know, a normal human, a normal man. A man who would, without feeling he was doing something wrong, go and circle 'Against' at the Family Law referendum, tell the refugees to fuck off back home and fight for their sick militant country, and tell his girlfriend to," his voice trembled, "to do what she's told."

He was staring straight out at the sea. An empty plastic bag with a green "DESPAR" logo floated by. His cheeks were slightly flushed, but that could have been from the wind. The skin on his neck bristled, but his jaw was clenched, as if he didn't want to show he was cold.

"Do you understand?" he finally asked me.

I nodded slowly and stared back at the water.

"I think so," I said.

He looked at me for a few moments, and then, as if we had been talking about the weather the whole time, asked, "Are you hungry too?"

The question was so unexpected I had to laugh.

"Actually, I am. A slice of pizza would really hit the spot right now."

Maks nodded, got on his feet, and held out his hand to help me up. We walked at a slow pace back toward the center of Trieste, and my hand rested in his for a few long moments before he let go.

12.

By the time Maks dropped me off in front of the Cathedral of Saint Just, the sun was already setting over the sea. I arrived at the rectory, where the singers were changing, my mind racing with thoughts of how I would perform. I looked for Sara among the girls in vain; Ivana gingerly told me that she wouldn't be coming, without giving a reason. I changed and checked my phone, opened the Facebook Messenger app and sent her a brief message: Hey, where are you? I put my phone back in my backpack and reviewed the sheet music one more time. The musical staves with their black dots danced before my eyes. I felt slightly nauseous; the pizza sat heavy in my stomach.

When we arranged ourselves in a semicircle so Agata could give us her final instructions before we headed into the church, Ivana approached her and whispered something in her ear. I saw Agata raise her eyebrows and ask her something, and Ivana shook her head. They looked at each other for a few moments without exchanging a word.

The church was full, and the people applauded as we made our way in our black skirts to stand next to each other on the worn marble steps. The purple mosaic glistened in the light of the church fixtures. Breathing shallowly, I stared at the rose window above Agata's head. Agata raised her hands and we began to sing; the first piece on the program was Čopi's *Ave Maria*.

After a few measures, her hands stopped shaking because we were singing well. The months of hard work on the score showed; our voices faithfully followed her hand, and the stern expression on her face grew softer. We sang the first three competition pieces almost flawlessly. The fourth in line, and the last of the competition pieces, was Šavli's *The Bush*.

The second altos began, entering with a dark tone. They sang more weakly than usual; you could tell that something was missing, and it soon dawned on me the missing element was Sara. Agata's face darkened, and her hands trembled. But then the first altos came in, livelier than at rehearsal, and the sopranos' voices intertwined with theirs: "*Do not go courting to the mountains, you won't be my husband nor my brother,*" when the altos cut through the folk harmonies with an achingly beautiful melody: "*Nobody knows anybody anywhere in this world.*"

With this piece, too, it was evident that we had finally mastered it. The disharmonies filled the church with a mournful yet stunning beauty. But even though our voices complemented each other boldly, I couldn't shake the feeling that there was simply too much of everything in the composition. I thought of Peter Mušič's words at the revue about Šavli's piece being pretentious, and it struck me that the composer used it to show off everything he knew. The composition was practically overflowing with harmonies, dissonances, and bright and dark chords. But I couldn't let my thoughts wander, the first sopranos were already singing with piercing voices: "*Do not go courting to the mountains and do not call across the abyss; the voice you hear is not my voice, it is an echo, it isn't me.*"

Then the altos sang woefully: "*If you get closer, I will end you and I will make you new in the image of a thorny bush in the sturdy rains of May.*"

I stepped in front of the singers, as the choir sang one of its most beautiful chords, filling me with awe at Šavli's talent despite the piece's excess. I opened my mouth and calmly, tone by tone, sang my dirge: "*When the thorny branches sprout…*"

My voice echoed softly yet sharply through the church. As I sang the first few measures of the solo, I felt a pleasant relaxation wash over my body, as if singing came entirely natural to me.

"*I press you to my heart...*"

I closed my eyes. The other singers sang along with a barely audible melancholic chord. My heart beat with a dull thud in my chest, anticipating the moment when I would have to hit the highest note.

"*If you wounded me to the blood...*"

The melody of my solo was truly beautiful. It was as if it had been created specifically for my voice. Resolutely, with desolation in my voice, I sang the final words: "*...then I would know who you are.*"

I opened my eyes; the sky behind the rose window was a dark blue, and an orange light persevered inside the church. I went back to my place and sang the next chord with the other singers. The singing then restlessly filled the whole church with rhythmic repetition: "*If you woun-ded me to the blood, on-ly then would I know who you are, if you woun-ded me to the blood, on-ly then would I know who you are, if you woun-ded me to the blood, on-ly then would I know who you are,*" and then louder and louder, "*if you woun-ded me, if you woun-ded me, if you woun-ded me, if you woun-ded me...*" Until we ended abruptly with a loud cry: "*On-ly then would I know who you are!*"

A total silence reigned, so quiet you could hear the wind battering against the rose window from outside—there wasn't a cough or a creak of a pew to be heard—and then a loud applause resounded through the space. Agata, her face glowing, motioned for me to step in front of the choir, where I bowed in a trance as the audience kept on clapping.

"I heard you had a nice voice earlier in the car, but I didn't know you could sing so well," Maks said when we found each other by the cookie platters after the concert. The other singers were stopping by with quick compliments. I noticed some of them eyeing Maks with curiosity.

"Thank you. You enjoyed the concert?" I asked him as casually as possible, so he wouldn't notice I was utterly exhilarated; the competition program had been a success, and we had performed the other eight songs well, too. My cheeks were pleasantly warm, and I unfastened a button on my blouse to cool down a bit, even though I was at the same time shivering slightly.

"Yeah, it was great. Only that last competition piece, the one with your solo, felt a bit unpolished."

I gave a curt nod and tried to hide the discomfort his words caused me.

"There's too much of everything, right?" I asked him, draining my glass of water and choking on it. Maks patted me on the back and nodded while I coughed.

"But I liked this one the best," he said, unrolling the program he had been holding in his hand like a tube, "*Death in the Hills*. I never heard it before, but it's really beautiful."

My coughing finally subsided, and I nodded: "Yes, that's also my favorite song on the program. It's simple, but it's lyrics are beautiful."

"Not to glorify war, but Partisan songs have a certain grandeur to them. While you were singing, I was reminded again of the importance of the national liberation struggle and how much it bothers me that some people in Slovenia try to degrade the very thing that brought us freedom."

Andrej and Urška appeared beside us, catching what Maks was saying. For a split second, I held my breath and followed Andrej's gaze as it swept across Maks's face, thinking: surely they aren't going to get into a fight right here at our concert over the Partisans and the

Home Guard.

"Good solo, Maša," Andrej said calmly, patting me on the shoulder. "We just came to tell you that we're going to head home soon. Urška's feeling sick."

My sister looked a bit green in the face, her eyes were somewhat sunken. I asked her if she was alright, and she nodded with pursed lips.

"If Agata asks, tell her we had to go," she rattled off, patting me on the shoulder as well, and they vanished into the crowd.

"Want to grab another drink?" Maks asked while I was watching them leave. I suddenly stopped caring about anything: Urška and Andrej, Šavli's score, my solo, the national liberation struggle, and the Partisans. I was thinking only about how Maks and I would head down into the city and stroll through the evening streets of Trieste.

At the first rehearsal after the concert, you could tell the singers had arrived full of drive, as they fervently reminisced about the parts of the performance that had gone best. Many didn't even notice Agata, leaning against the piano with her hands clasped, staring motionlessly at an indeterminate point on the parquet floor. Her face, covered with a thin layer of light powder, was like stone. Only one chair was still empty when we sat down: Sara's.

Agata finally looked up and softly instructed Ivana: "Ivana, please take that chair away." Despite her soft voice, her words sounded very harsh. Ivana silently obeyed. Agata cleared her throat and said that we were excellent on Saturday and that we were ready for the competition.

Agata didn't explain what had happened with Sara, and it seemed to me that the girls didn't care; intoxicated by her praise, they started clapping and whistling—as if Sara had never been a singer in this choir. Agata smiled, though her gray eyes remained as sunken as before.

I felt a flash of anger toward my fellow singers, unbothered with the question of Sara. Very carefully, I pulled my phone out of my backpack and covered it with my sheet music so Agata wouldn't see. I looked at the screen. It was blank, no messages. I opened the messaging app and checked when Sara was last active. Thirteen minutes ago. But the message I had sent her on Saturday remained unread.

During the break, I walked over to Ivana to inquire about her cousin, but I got only a meager explanation. She said that Sara had been thinking about quitting for a while, which I hadn't known. She kept averting her gaze as she spoke, so I wasn't sure if she was telling the truth. At the end of rehearsal, I told her and Urška to wait for me in the car, and I stayed behind to catch Agata alone.

"Forget about her as soon as possible," Agata said without looking at me, packing away her sheet music with swift movements. "Really, I can assure you this is better for us," she said, looking up from her bag and fixing me with a stare. "Please, Maša, don't put so much effort into her. She isn't worth it," she added with contempt.

Raising my eyebrows, I observed her for a few long moments. Why was she being so ruthless toward Sara, what had she done to her? I asked her what had happened. She hesitated, then said that Sara had different priorities and that this sometimes happens. I frowned.

"She didn't reply to my message. She didn't even read it," I admitted, crushed. Agata snorted and rolled her eyes. "Didn't I tell you? She showed what she thinks of us."

"What about Ivana? Did she say anything?"

Agata was putting on her neat trench coat. She buttoned it up, then tied the belt into an elegant bow. "Ivana has nothing to do with this. Just because Sara is her cousin doesn't mean she has to answer for her actions. I've already told her, but you should tell her too, to make her feel better."

With decisive steps, she headed for the door and placed her hand on the light switch. I followed her, and she turned off the lights before I had even stepped out of the hall.

"Go," she told me as she slid the key into the lock.

"Let me tell you this," she spoke suddenly, when I was already a few steps away, and I turned around. "You should remember: it is very rare for two people to mean the exact same thing to one another. Maybe Sara meant a lot to you, but you meant nothing to her. It was probably like that. That's simply how it is in life."

13

After Ivana dropped us off in front of our apartment building, I told Urška about my conversation with Agata. But I soon noticed she wasn't listening to me at all, she was merely nodding vacantly, and when I asked her for her opinion, she didn't even know what I was talking about. When we were changing in our room, I concluded that something was wrong. Just as I decided not to pry, she lay down on the bed half-undressed and stared at the ceiling. Then she covered her face with her palms, and barely audibly said: "Agata is going to kill me."

Concerned, I asked her what was going on. Urška moved her hands from her face and sat up abruptly. Her look was almost crazed: it seemed as if she was going to cry, but at the same time, as if she couldn't hold back her laughter. I noticed that greenish-pale complexion on her cheeks again.

"I'm pregnant," she suddenly squeaked, covering her mouth. Then she really did start to cry, but I was right—she was also shaking with laughter.

"Oh my god!" I exclaimed, and Urška instantly stopped sobbing, waving toward the door as if to say keep it down, our parents will hear us. I got up from my bed, sat next to her, and put my arm around her shoulders. I kept repeating in a whisper, "Oh my god, oh my god, oh my god."

"Alright, it's not that big of a deal, come on," she reproached me, though the restlessness in her voice suggested otherwise, and she wiped her damp eyes with a swift motion. "Just please, don't tell our parents. Actually, don't tell anyone, alright? Nobody!"

I solemnly promised her that I wouldn't, then bombarded her with questions: when did she find out, and how did Andrej react.

"Oh, Andrej is thrilled," she began. "I mean, a little in shock, but... I think more so than me. I mean, not that I'm not, I was just surprised," she said, her otherwise pale cheeks reddening. She told me she had found out two weeks ago; she had taken the test because her period was a few days late.

"What does Agata have to do with any of this?" I remembered what brought us here. Urška's face grew dark, as if someone had turned off a light inside her. She covered her face with her hands again, and her engagement ring flashed in the glow of the nightlight. I nudged her to tell me what was going on. Almost a little angrily, she asked me: "How don't you get it? I won't be able to go to Tallinn."

I blinked at her in surprise and remained speechless for a few moments. Then I asked her what this had to do with Tallinn. She was astonished and said with indignation: "I'll be more than three months pregnant. I don't want to get on a plane pregnant, and I especially don't want to be away from Andrej when my belly starts growing. And anyway, I don't know how much I'll even be able to go to rehearsals; I might still be feeling sick!"

I frowned. "You're exaggerating. It's no big deal. You're not the first singer to get pregnant, Barbara sang almost until the very end. Besides, we'll only be in Tallinn for a few days, you'll survive that long without Andrej."

Urška glared at me. "Barbara is different. She treated her pregnancy like a minor nuisance," she said with scorn. "She decided that her child meant more to her only when Agata wanted to have rehearsals twice a week."

I tried to ignore Urška's judgmental undertone. I was overcome by the feeling that there was something she didn't dare admit, probably not even to herself; namely, that she simply didn't want to sing in the choir anymore and was just waiting for the first sufficient excuse to leave it.

"So, you've decided to stop singing?" I asked her with a lump in my throat. I couldn't imagine the choir without Urška; I could barely picture myself in the choir without her. She massaged her forehead with her fingers.

"Agata will go ballistic," she said quietly. "There are not enough of us in the choir as it is. Almost half left in January, then Sara, now me... There will only be... seventeen of you left." She shook her head in despair. "That isn't even a choir anymore, it's a vocal group."

There had been whispers among the singers since January that Philomela was no longer a choir, but no one dared say it out loud. When we applied for the competition in Tallinn, there were more than thirty of us.

"Did you tell Ivana?"

Urška shook her head with a grimace.

"She won't take this well either," I judged, without thinking about how this would upset Urška, who was indignant.

"I'm so happy," she groaned. "I mean, I'm feeling sick, and I'm worried about the wedding and the wedding dress"—her eyes widened in fear with the thought—"but I can't even really enjoy it. Whenever I think about the pregnancy—and that's all the time!—I also think about Agata."

I silently bit my lip for a few moments, then confronted my sister with the truth: "If you're not going to sing anymore, you need to tell Agata as soon as possible."

She looked at me with eyes that said she knew this, but that she couldn't do it. With pursed lips, she shook her head, as if I had told her to do something incredibly mean.

"I don't even know how I'm going to tell Mom and Dad," she wailed, waving toward the door again, blushing deeply as she did so. "Because I'll have to. If I had gotten pregnant right after the wedding, I would have given birth in February, but this way I'm going to give birth in December, Maša, *December*!" Her gaze was desperate, and I rolled my eyes.

"Well, come on, they know the two of you have been having sex, you're at his place every weekend."

I pretended not to notice how Urška flinched at the phrase "having sex." It was the first time we talked about intimacy. To my surprise, she shook her head wildly: "First of all, I don't think they know, and besides, this is a *pregnancy*. We were *supposed* to wait until the wedding."

My incredulous look let her know that I didn't understand the difference between waiting until marriage for sex and waiting until marriage for a pregnancy. Urška didn't bother explaining, and stared anxiously at the wall above my bed.

"I can't believe I'm getting married *pregnant*." She said this with such disgust, as if it were something she truly hadn't planned for, that I almost felt sorry for her.

I realized how little I knew about my sister. I had no idea how the pregnancy had even happened, because I knew nothing about what kind of contraception she and Andrej used. I would never admit this to anyone, but a part of my brain was also surprised by the news of her pregnancy, perhaps because I had somehow assumed that they were doing it with their hands, patiently waiting for their wedding night. But my misconception surely wasn't entirely unfathomable: Urška and Andrej did, after all, present themselves as a model Christian couple.

"Everything will be fine," I gave my sister the worst possible advice and patted her on the back, then stood up and began to undress.

14.

Urška and Andrej would probably have kept the news they were having a baby a secret for much longer, had Urška not wanted a bachelorette party so badly and felt her invited friends deserved to know. But before her friends found out, she insisted she had to tell our parents. She was stressing out over this, even though Andrej kept saying that "it's no big deal," while taking no initiative himself. Eventually, they decided they would share the news after her first gynecologist appointment. Urška kept me, as the sole keeper of their secret, informed about every little detail of the appointment, where the gynecologist confirmed that my sister was eight weeks pregnant.

They showed the ultrasound photo to our parents at Sunday lunch. Looking at their flushed faces, I realized that this news would have landed in a completely different way just two months later, had they shared it as newlyweds. Mom and Dad reacted with exaggerated enthusiasm, and looking at their beet-red faces, I thought that perhaps they had truly lived in the belief that Urška was still a virgin. The situation amused me in its own way, and I mocked their narrow-mindedness in my head, until Andrej tried to break the tension by stating that "it doesn't matter what the gender is, as long as the boy is healthy." I finished eating in silence and left the table as soon as we were done with the main course, without waiting for coffee.

As the maid of honour, organizing the bachelorette party fell on me. One evening, Urška told me that Andrej's friends were taking him on a trip to the Soča Valley, where they would spend the night, go rafting, and visit an adrenaline park. I sensed a shadow of envy in her recounting; when I asked her what she wanted for her bachelorette party, she stated with feigned certainty that she couldn't afford "anything wild" at the start of her pregnancy and that she'd also rather not go out, because then everyone would be offering her alcohol. I promised her we would stay home, even though I knew full well how thrilled Urška had been thinking about other bachelorette parties when the bride-to-be is paraded through the city dressed in a makeshift wedding gown. As for me, I was just relieved that we wouldn't have to go through that.

The closer we approached the dates of the bachelorette party and the wedding, the more my sister got on my nerves. Purely as "something interesting," she showed me photos from some other bachelorette parties, which had everything from matching t-shirts worn by the girls in the photo, to balloons, glasses, and a lavish cake in coordinated pastel colors. When I checked the price of such decorations online, I realized that if I invested money into the decor, I could kiss the idea of getting a new dress for Urška's wedding goodbye. My sister was in general acting like we had all been saving up for months just so we could give her an unforgettable bachelorette party and a wonderful wedding.

I confided all this to Agata during one of my vocal technique lessons, as she had clearly read the bad mood on my face. She shook her head and sighed.

"Boundaries, Maša," she said seriously. "You have to start setting clear boundaries, otherwise everyone will walk all over you, and Urška with her personality even more so." I nodded, and she continued: "I've already seen that women can act quite arrogantly when it comes to their weddings, husbands, and marriages. Just wait until she gets pregnant"—I flinched, hoping Agata didn't notice—"she'll become downright greedy, she'll think she's entitled to everything. God forbid you tell her you don't have time or that you're busy. She'll instantly find a way to let you know she is a mother and that you just don't understand how time-consuming motherhood is."

My sister was already talking about either the pregnancy or the wedding all the time. Outside, the streets smelled more like flowers with each passing day, and in the evenings I would open the window to let the scent of freshly cut grass from the meadow by the nearby school into the room, but that was all I took from spring. Accompanied by the sound of bouncing basketballs, I was writing field trip reports late into the night, while she complained that the light bothered her, the sounds bothered her, that she couldn't get enough sleep, that the baby wouldn't develop properly because of it, and that I should go do my work in the living room.

With the preparations for the bachelorette party, the wedding, and the competition in Tallinn, the days slipped by quickly, and on May 14th the day of the bachelorette party arrived. I hadn't been looking forward to the moment Urška's friends took over our living room, because they had been pestering me all week in our Facebook group chat with their program suggestions. However, it seemed the bride-to-be was immensely enjoying the activities we had prepared: wearing a pink t-shirt with "Future Mrs. Klinar" written on it, she had to apply makeup without looking in a mirror, paint her nails blindfolded, change a baby doll's diaper, and bake bread without a recipe. All afternoon, watching Urška's ecstatic friends made me feel like an alien, since I wasn't particularly entertained by Urška's tasks. Seeing the gift we gave her—a cookbook with an attached wooden spoon and an apron that read "Caution! I'm a Beginner!"—I thought about pitching a seminar paper to my Anthropology of Gender and Sexuality professor on the symbolic meaning of bachelorette party gifts. It was then that I truly grasped what Maks had meant by what he told me in Trieste: how much easier it would be for him if he didn't constantly ruminate and try to interpret the hidden meanings of everything happening around him. I, too, wished I couldn't see the covert sexism in Urška's gift and could just enjoy the female company, but it felt like I was incapable of doing so.

When the girls got tired of the games, I sat down next to Ivana, who, after being very loud and taking part in the activities all evening, was now sitting in silence on the couch. It occurred to me that her good mood had merely been a mask to cover up her anxiety over her friend's party and her pregnancy, and that the mask had now slipped off. I tried to strike up a conversation, but she answered my questions with clipped replies, as if I made her uncomfortable. She probably knew what I wanted to ask her.

"Have you talked to Sara at all?"

With pursed lips and without looking at me, she shook her head. I thought she would remain silent, but she looked at me and said: "I think she's angry because Agata kicked her out of the choir."

I looked at her in surprise and echoed her words. Ivana blushed, then nodded.

"It was Agata who told me that, not Sara. I haven't seen her since the last rehearsal before Trieste. And we haven't talked, either. I mean, she's my cousin, but it's not like we're super close," she said, and the coldness in her voice surprised me. "We're too different," she added.

"And what did you find out from Agata?"

She told me that the day after the concert in Trieste, Agata had emailed Sara, telling her not to come to rehearsals anymore.

"But why?"

Ivana picked up the diaper-clad plastic baby doll that had been left lying among the glasses and bowls of chips from the coffee table, placed it on her thighs, and fixed its strangely protruding little arms. Then she wiped a few potato chip crumbs off its plastic forehead with her finger. The baby doll was hers—she had offered to bring it a few days prior.

"Because she didn't show up for the concert."

That should have explained everything. There was nothing Agata resented more than someone missing a concert. I asked Ivana if she knew why Sara hadn't been there. Without tearing her gaze away from the doll, she nodded: "Her dad came for an unannounced visit. As far as I know, he was on his way from Berlin to Sarajevo and stopped by. They have had minimal contact for a few years now."

"And did Sara tell that to Agata?"

"I think so."

"But Agata would understand."

"I don't know. She probably would. Or maybe not." She sighed, then gave the baby doll in her lap a little shake so that its blue eyeballs rolled in its plastic head and its eyelids with their black eyelashes fluttered.

So many questions had been swirling in my mind for a month now. Why hadn't Sara replied to my message? Why hadn't she even read it? Judging by the Facebook app, she was active online.

"Sara..." I began uncertainly, then fell silent. The baby doll resting on Ivana's knees looked grotesque, while she blankly stroked its little hand. Emboldened, I said: "Sara and I hit it off. I find it weird that she didn't say anything to me." I could have said more: it had seemed to me that we confided in each other a lot, but the more I thought about it now, the more it felt like I was the one who confided in her, while learning very little about her in return. I swallowed the thick slime that had built up from the Coca-Cola.

Ivana said nothing, then gave a brief sigh: "Sara can be very secretive. Why don't you call her if you're so curious?"

Only Urška knew that I had a phobia of phone calls. She handled all my phone conversations, even official ones, like when I had to make a doctor's appointment. Mom and Dad knew I didn't like talking on the phone, but they didn't realize how much anxiety it caused me. I wasn't about to explain this to Ivana, so I just shrugged, leaned forward, grabbed my glass, and took a few sips of Coke.

"I think Agata didn't like Sara very much. As a person. Their personalities clashed. Did she ever mention anything to you?" Ivana asked me.

"You mean Sara?" I placed the glass back on the coffee table; the glasses were leaving round rings on the glass top. Ivana nodded. Frowning, I shook my head: "No, she never said they didn't get along. On the contrary. Agata even showed her a composition she's been writing."

Ivana looked up from the baby doll and stared at me with wide eyes. Her pale cheeks were flushed, and I noticed her lip quiver, but she said nothing. She lowered her gaze back towards the doll in her lap.

"Is that right..." she whispered, and after a short pause, continued: "Well, what I heard from Agata was that she was mainly bothered by how Sara was acting, her meddling in the organization of rehearsals, the preparations for the competition, and apparently even the program. There was also the issue of an email she sent her, where she claimed the girls were complaining about the extra rehearsals for Urška's wedding." She said this last part in a hushed tone so that my sister, who was showing her wedding planner to her friends, wouldn't hear her.

I realized I had been forgetting an important piece of the puzzle. It was right before the concert when Sara decided to write an email to Agata. Had that perhaps been the catalyst for the whole situation?

"But if Agata reacted so negatively to this thing with Sara, what on earth is she going to do when she finds out Urška isn't going to Tallinn?" I asked Ivana, shaking my head with worry. She looked up from the baby doll in her lap and stared at me in disbelief.

"And why wouldn't Urška go to Tallinn?!" she whispered so sharply that a few drops of her spit landed on my cheeks. She bowed her head and began shaking it despondently. She obviously knew about Urška's pregnancy, but not that Urška had decided not to go with us.

"She says it would just be too exhausting…" I tried to soothe her, but she cut me off:

"The whole thing is going to fall apart."

I didn't know what to do. She was genuinely upset. I patted her bony shoulder and said that everything would be okay. But hearing her say it out loud, an anxious knot twisted in my stomach, and I was overwhelmed by the feeling that something bad was going to happen.

15

I told Maks he didn't have to come to the gate crashing,[7] fearing he would think the tradition was silly, but as soon as I stepped out of the apartment building, I spotted him among the wedding guests milling around out front under their umbrellas as if waiting for a funeral. When he saw me, he raised his hand in greeting, and I waved back. I opened my umbrella and headed his way when I was surrounded by my cousins who began to praise my dress. I had ordered a raspberry-colored satin dress from ASOS, which had put my sister in a bad mood when she saw it, as she felt it was "appropriate for a prom, not a wedding." Out of the corner of my eye, while talking to my cousins, I examined Maks's outfit: he wore a coal-black men's suit, a stark white shirt and a thin black tie. I could just picture him at home, tying it in front of the mirror with the help of YouTube.

The wedding guests were already growing impatient, especially the groom, who had just arrived and was now talking to his best man with his arms crossed over his chest, while the best man held a black umbrella over him. We were running a bit late, as the irritable bride had decided to wait with those at the gate crashing for the rain to stop, looking at the weather forecast. Andrej's eyes met mine, his look saying: What are we waiting for?

The best man handed him the umbrella and walked over to me.

"Can we start? It's barely raining anymore."

I moved my umbrella aside: the rain really had almost stopped,

---

7 TN: An ancient custom called *śranga* where the boys from the bride's village would set up a barrier for the groom and demand payment before letting him take her to the wedding, updated for contemporary times with traditional wedding games.

so I closed it. I noticed several people following my lead. I nodded.

Nejc, Andrej's best man, pulled a doubly folded piece of paper from his pocket, and three of Andrej's friends and both of his brothers immediately walked up to him. I was grateful to them; they had organized the thing by themselves.

I did notice that Nejc wasn't completely relaxed either, as his hand was shaking when he addressed the guests. He announced that if Andrej wanted to get his bride, he would have to pass a few tests. Andrej's brothers and two of the guys jumped over to a car parked nearby and brought a large log and a handsaw out of the trunk—eliciting laughter from the guests—as well as a small silver milk jug, the contents of which I had no clue about. One of the guys strapped on an accordion.

"Dear groom, it is our estimation that your bride is worth somewhere around... three thousand euros." The guests laughed again, and I sighed. I couldn't relax. I was thinking about Maks, standing among people he was seeing for the first time in his life, observing the proceedings.

"But we can lower this price... If you correctly answer a few questions. Here we go, first question: How many stairs lead up to the bride's apartment?"

I knew the answer; I had to count them a few days ago, even though I always used the elevator.

Andrej laughed, then pretended to count in his head. "A hundred and fifty?"

The guys were satisfied, he was only off by ten. They lowered the price to two thousand seven hundred euros.

"When are your future father-in-law and mother-in-law's birthdays?"

Indignant shouts were heard from the guests, that the question was too hard, while my dad, standing by the folding table with the aperitifs, laughed. Andrej went completely red in the face and, with a wide, awkward smile, began: "Um... My mother-in-law's is... Oh man, you've got me now." His gaze met mine. I mouthed: *In January. The eleventh of January.*

"In January?" Andrej wavered, guessing, "and my father-in-law's is, I think, in April."

I nodded.

"Alright, fine, we'll let this one slide," Nejc said with a chuckle. "And thank you, Maša, for the help," he added, nodding toward me.

The wedding guests laughed, and I gave a clumsy smile. "We're already down to two thousand five hundred euros, you're doing well. Now, a question for five hundred euros: Who is the best singer in the Pavlin family?"

We had agreed with Nejc that after the third question, I would call Mom and tell her that my aunt, playing the role of the fake bride, should start getting ready. Before the doors to the apartment building closed behind me, I caught Andrej's answer. The best singer in the Pavlin family was, of course, his future wife.

When I came back, Andrej was singing a serenade to Urška. This was less an actual test than an opportunity for him to show off. The curious faces of our neighbors began peering out the windows. The guys were pleased with the singing and lowered the bride's price to one thousand seven hundred euros. Then, one of the guys blindfolded him, and another poured a white liquid from the silver jug into a glass and gave it to him to drink. Andrej had to guess what he was drinking. He took a sip and grimaced in disgust.

"Goat milk?!" he cried out in horror, wiping his mouth with his sleeve.

The guys started clapping, and the guests joined in amid the laughter. The bride's price dropped to one thousand five hundred euros.

"Now, we were thinking..." continued Nejc, who had relaxed somewhat in the meantime. "We're going to lower the bride's price on our own accord—by a whole five hundred euros—because we heard she isn't entering the marriage alone."

A murmur rippled through the guests. I noticed some people exchanging surprised glances, while others, as if only half-following the proceedings, missed the implication entirely. A few of Urška's friends who had been at the bachelorette party laughed, while my dad busied himself intensely with pouring liquor into shot glasses. I realized I was biting my lip, knowing that Urška would not be pleased with what had just happened.

"So, for one thousand euros, we hand over the bride!" Nejc called out, pointing toward the doors of the building. My aunt walked out, dressed in an old white slip with a white crocheted shawl draped over it, her face covered by a white silk scarf. The guy with the accordion started playing, and my aunt walked up to Andrej. Nejc asked Andrej if he thought this was his bride. Laughing, he shook his head.

"Let our beautiful young bride remove her veil!" Nejc proclaimed, and my aunt revealed her dramatically made-up face: her red lipstick was smeared past the edges of her lips, and her cheeks were heavily rouged. The guests burst out laughing, along with Andrej.

I looked around at the guests and spotted Maks. He was holding his phone in his hands, taking a picture. The expression on his face was surprisingly serious. I noticed him zooming in with his other hand, his eyebrows drawn together in thought. He looked as if he were out in the field somewhere, meticulously documenting the event.

"You're right, this isn't the real one, but unfortunately, Andrej, we're still not entirely sure you've earned your bride just yet. First, you'll have to dance with the fake bride, and then you're going to need to attend to this log." He gestured toward the log, which Andrej's brothers had set down in front of the building entrance, just as our neighbor was coming out with her dog. She had to help her Italian Greyhound jump over the obstacle.

Andrej invited my aunt to dance, and they twirled around the courtyard in front of the building to the rhythm of the accordion. The rain had completely stopped, though it was still cloudy. After the dance, which the guests backed with cheers and applause, Andrej grabbed the handsaw his younger brother handed him and began to saw the log. After just a few strokes he grew hot; he stood up, took off his suit jacket, and handed it to me. He went on sawing, while the guests cheered him on. I noticed damp circles beginning to form under the armpits of his white shirt, and his forehead glisten with sweat.

"Alright, alright, I think you've proven yourself," Nejc stopped him. "You get the bride for three hundred euros!" The guests applauded, and Andrej, exhausted from the sawing, motioned for me to hand him his jacket, pulled an envelope from the pocket, and handed it to Nejc. The guests clapped even louder.

"Bride, come on out!" Nejc called. My mom held open the building doors, and out came Urška, wearing the dress she had first tried on in the bridal boutique a few months ago. There was no trace of the bad mood the rain had caused on her face. She looked nervous, to be sure, but a wide smile skillfully concealed it. The wedding dress and her pinned-up hair made her look very beautiful, though her makeup aged her slightly, with fine lines I had never noticed before visible under the grainy powder. She held a simple bouquet of blue hydrangeas.

The guests greeted her arrival with enchanted gasps. Mom, who had stayed by the door, dabbed her eyes with a tissue, while Andrej walked up to Urška and they embraced. The guys clapped and began clearing the scene, while the guests made their way to the table with the aperitifs and pastries. I scanned the guests and saw Maks approach.

"Hey," I greeted him, agitated. A few of my female relatives turned towards us, and one of my aunts asked Mom—who was still standing by the doors, watching the two of us—a question, to which Mom shook her head. Despite the black suit, Maks looked younger than he was. He was freshly shaven and he had just gotten a haircut. My heels made us the same height. His suit looked to be made of high-quality material, but on his feet, unlike most of the men there, he wore black Vans sneakers. I was immediately overwhelmed by the feeling that his suit alone was worth more than my entire outfit. I was getting hotter and hotter in the unbreathable synthetic material, acutely aware of the cheapness of the Chinese-made dress I had bought online.

"Did you know that the motif of the fake bride appears in the Bible?" he asked me after returning my greeting. I shook my head. I noticed my dad walking over to us with two shot glasses in his hands.

"Yeah, I don't remember the guy's name, but Jacob wants to marry Rachel, and this guy tricks him with his eldest daughter, Leah," Maks explained.

Before I could reply, Dad appeared beside us. He patted Maks on the back and offered him a shot glass. I thought the second shot glass was for me, but he actually brought it for himself: they clinked glasses and emptied them.

"Wow, homemade, huh?" Maks asked. Dad nodded and told him what they were drinking. I frowned. Everyone seemed more relaxed than I was. I waited for my dad to say something to Maks, to ask him something, but someone else butted in with a question for Dad, and Maks turned back to me.

"This was interesting. A gate crashing in the city. When people refuse to stray from their traditions, so they adapt them to the circumstances. Interesting, really. Also a bit funny."

I nodded and said I agreed. There was a strange burning sensation in my stomach, I was as restless as if I were the one getting married. I glanced over at my sister, who was holding a glass of apple juice. The expression on her face revealed her unrest. Our eyes met, she gave me a faint smile, then mouthed: Let's go.

"We have to go. See you in church," I told Maks, who nodded. The crowd was thinning out: it was time for the church ceremony.

16.

Sitting down in the restaurant, I slipped off my white high-heeled sandal and began to massage my foot. I had ordered the shoes online as well, opting for a cheap pair since I was running low on money. I already got blisters from the low-quality straps, and since it was colder outside than I thought it would be, my feet were freezing.

"What are you drinking?" Maks sat down in the chair next to mine, his spot was marked by a name card on the table. All through the church and civil ceremonies, the receiving line for congratulations and gifts, and the photo sessions, I only watched him from afar. I hadn't expected to find my sister's wedding so stressful; my duties were mostly to help the bride. I held an umbrella over her during the occasional showers and brought her water and salty snacks after she quietly told me she had heartburn. I kept waiting for Maks to approach me on his own, but he had deftly avoided me, so I wondered why he had even accepted the wedding invitation in the first place.

He poured white wine into my glass and filled his own with apple juice mixed with sparkling mineral water.

"You're not drinking?"

He shook his head, took a sip, and without looking at me, replied: "No, I'm trying to cut back on alcohol."

"Why?"

The bride and groom entered through the main doors of the hall packed full with wedding guests. Everyone welcomed their arrival with clapping and cheering and they made their way to the head of the table where we were seated, with Nejc and Andrej's brothers not far from us. Once Andrej and Urška sat down, I asked Maks again why he wasn't drinking.

"I'm leaving for Oman in ten days. For three months."

"You're going where?" My eyes widened in surprise while he calmly explained that he had applied for fieldwork in Oman not long ago.

"Istenič put me in touch with an acquaintance from that American Middle East Anthropology Association I told you about in Trieste, and they offered me the opportunity," he explained. "I'll be living with a Muslim family while working on one of the Association's projects. And I'll be learning Arabic."

While Maks was telling me about this, he was casually scanning our surroundings. He had already taken off his suit jacket and loosened his tie a bit. I got the feeling he was trying hard to seem relaxed, as if he were just talking about the weather, but his eyes gleamed with delight.

"Wow, that sounds really amazing. But what about your thesis?" I didn't mean to sound like a nagging teacher, but it was the first thing that came to mind at the news he would be spending his summer abroad.

"I've already written most of it, and I'll finish the rest over there. That's why I'm coming back in August, and I'll defend it in September."

I took a sip of wine. I was also feeling a slight burn in my stomach, as I had eaten nothing but pastries since the gate crashing, which was now joined by a tightness in my chest. I was growing hot. Three months in Oman, while I'd be left wandering the streets of Ljubljana. I looked around at the guests: most had already taken their seats, and a sense of anticipation filled the air.

"Isn't it a bit too hot there in the summer?"

Maks replied in the affirmative then said he was going to the city of Salalah, where the rain makes temperatures much more bearable.

"Nice," I murmured, taking a piece of bread from the basket.

Waiters carrying silver soup bowls entered the dining room. When a bowl of beef soup was placed in front of us, Maks asked if there was a vegetarian option. The waiter nodded, saying they had mushroom soup and that he would bring it right away. An unfamiliar man stood up at one of the tables; his collar gave him away as a priest. He addressed the crowd and invited them to join him in prayer. Judging by the response, most of the wedding guests were accustomed to praying before a meal, while Maks simply rested his hands beside his plate and silently observed.

"This wedding is like participant observation for you," I joked as I ladled soup into my plate. Maks smiled.

"You know how it is. For me, religion is primarily a source of conflict, and besides, the Church is corrupt and rotten. We'd all be better off if it didn't exist, or if it at least didn't meddle in politics. But then you have priests telling people who to vote for, which is exactly why we never get anywhere."

"That may be, but politics is corrupt and rotten, too," I shrugged, dipping my spoon in the soup.

"I think that no woman who considers herself even slightly a feminist should have anything to do with the Church. Despite operating in the 21st century, it still indulges in extreme sexism," Maks said, ignoring my comment entirely. "That's why I'm really glad my mother, even though she came from a Christian family, cut ties with the Church," he said.

I asked him what that looked like. He paused before explaining: "She stopped going to church and didn't even put up a front for her parents. She used to, sometimes, just to keep them from carping. And she decided I can skip the confirmation. I only went to Sunday school for the first couple of years."

"You went to Sunday school?"

Maks reiterated that it was only during the first few years of elementary.

"As far as I can tell, Sunday school is just a waste of time; no one takes it seriously, and the topics are strictly limited to Catholic indoctrination. Which is a shame. We could have learned about other religions, for instance. Or about Christian art."

I burst out laughing. He looked up from his plate, eyeing me in surprise.

"Christian art?" I asked through my laughter. "At Sunday school?"

"It's not as silly as you might think, since it is Christianity's only notable contribution to modern society," he stated in a serious tone, unfazed by my giggling. "Besides, I always get the feeling that Catholics don't actually know the Bible," he added more calmly, casting a thoughtful gaze around the room. His remark sobered me up, as there was a grain of truth to it.

"Take Protestants, for example—not that I hold them in particularly high regard, but they actually study the Bible. I'm not saying it's a smart thing to do, but then Catholics in elementary school focus only on those silly sacraments, whose only purpose is really so kids can get cash and presents."

His incisive take on Catholic upbringing caught me off guard; it seemed he had a fully formed opinion on the matter, so he must have thought about it a lot. I didn't know what to say.

"How come you know the Bible so well?" I asked, hoping he wouldn't recall my snooping in his nightstand, where I found a copy of the Bible in the drawer. I qualified the question: "Given what you brought up earlier at the gate crashing." I would never admit it to him, but I barely remembered the story of Leah and Rachel. Maks hesitated, then murmured quietly: "My grandfather told me about it once."

I had read everything available on the internet about Maks's grandfather. Florijan Hafner, born in Ljubljana in 1944, had pursued further studies in Prague and Paris, and dedicated his life primarily to folkloristics. Apart from these scant details, I knew almost nothing, because Maks rarely ever spoke of him.

"Well, sometimes I found Sunday school more interesting than regular school," I admitted. Maks looked at me in surprise, and my confidence grew. "Especially toward the end of elementary school, when we covered sexuality. And abortion," I added after a short pause.

"But in a completely indoctrinated way, surely."

"Sex education in regular schools is indoctrinated too, just in a different way," I countered coldly, then quickly said, "I get your point, though, because sure, we talked about it so they could brainwash us more easily"—I used air quotes for brainwash—"but at least we talked about it. We simply didn't discuss abortion as openly anywhere else. I'm not saying it's still like that today... That was, what, back in 2009. Things have probably changed in schools by now."

I had finished my soup and leaned back in my chair, while Maks ate much slower, having done most of the talking.

"You surprise me," he said coldly after a brief silence, "defending all this."

I rolled my eyes: "I'm not defending anything. I'm just saying it's not exactly how you imagine it to be. And that there is indoctrination elsewhere too." I said this as calmly as possible. I really didn't want to get into a shouting match with Maks at my sister's wedding, like it sometimes happened on our walks.

"Absolutely, school is an ideological apparatus of the state," he quoted Althusser in a conciliatory tone, as if agreeing this wasn't the right time for a verbal war. I nodded, and he brought the final spoonful of mushroom soup to his mouth. I frowned: "Hey, then why did you drink that schnapps earlier at the gate crashing if you aren't drinking alcohol?"

Maks looked at me, grinning, and said, "I didn't dare say no to your dad."

The wedding dinner dragged on for hours, and we passed the time between courses by chatting and toasting the newlyweds, whom the guests kept urging to kiss by clinking their glasses. On my way to the restroom, I had to assure my aunt and her two daughters that Maks was not my boyfriend, just a friend. In the restroom, I ran into Agata. Despite her usually exquisite taste in clothes, the tight, large-floral brocade dress she wore today did not suit her at all; she looked as if she had draped herself in old curtains.

"You all sang beautifully," I told her while we washed our hands. It was the absolute truth; the music at the church ceremony had been perfect, and Urška's tears had ruined her bridal makeup. Agata smiled modestly.

"Thank you. We have another little surprise prepared for her. We arranged with the band to announce us shortly after dinner. Is that your boyfriend over there?" she then asked me as I dried my hands.

I shook my head. "A friend from college."

I waited for her to respond, but she stayed quiet. She dried her hands as well, brought her pale face closer to the mirror, and began examining her lips. Then, pulling a lipstick from her purse that matched the flowers on her dress, she applied it with precise movements.

"Beautiful dress. Where did you get it?" she asked, meeting my eyes in the mirror.

I stood by the trash can, watching her. One of Urška's friends emerged from a stall behind us, silently washed her hands, and left.

"I ordered it from ASOS. Where is yours from?"

She straightened up over the sink, put her lipstick away, and smoothed her hands over the rough fabric.

"This? I've had it for a few years. I had it custom-made. But it gets harder to squeeze into it every year," she said with a bitter smile.

"It suits you perfectly."

Her smile grew genuine, the lilac tint on her lips softened her features. She continued to stare at herself in the mirror. I got the feeling she wanted to say something else. Finally, she asked, "You won't be in such a rush to get married like your sister, will you?" It sounded like a mild joke, yet serious at the same time. She maintained a calm smile, but her brows knit together in a probing gaze. I chuckled and shook my head.

"You know how Urška is," I said as casually as I could. "She wants a family and... She always says you should have kids while you're young." I knew no one had told Agata about Urška's pregnancy yet. I hadn't seen her at the gate crashing, so she might have missed Nejc's heavy handed hints. It was probably time someone prepared her for the reality that one of her best singers was expecting and would soon be stepping away from the choir.

Agata drew a sharp breath through her nose, a faint pink flush spreading across her face. After a long pause, she smiled and shook her head.

"My sister says the same. And she got married *really* young. Now, working as a nurse at the local clinic, she lectures teenagers about it. She's supposed to be teaching them about contraception, but she uses the opportunity to warn them against waiting too long."

She gave a strange little laugh at her own words. Without giving me a chance to respond, she pushed on: "And when she got married, I suddenly felt the urge to do the same, since I'm older than her. Looking back now, I don't know if it was a smart move. Or rather, I feel like I was too young, even though I was," she paused briefly in thought, "four years older than Urška. Yes, twenty-nine. For a woman," she continued, never breaking eye contact with her reflection in the mirror, "thirty is treated like some golden threshold, the absolute deadline to get married and get pregnant." Only then did she turn to look at me, her eyes appearing icy cold. She waited for me to say something, but I kept quiet.

"While we're on the subject, I wanted to ask you something," she finally said, her voice sharp as her eyes settled heavily on my face. It felt like she wasn't even blinking. I raised my eyebrows.

"Did you really tell Ivana that Gregor and I can't have kids?"

I swallowed hard, my brow furrowing. I began frantically racking my brain to figure out when this supposedly happened. Agata noticed my confusion and stated coldly: "You told Ivana I was getting a laparoscopy because they suspect I have endometriosis, which is why I can't get pregnant. Didn't you?" She spoke so sharply that I understood the question wasn't a question at all. She was already convinced her words were the absolute truth, while I couldn't for the life of me remember if I had actually said it or not.

It took me a long time to admit: "I don't know, I don't remember exactly. I might have said it, I just can't remember," I repeated feebly. "But... When we met up in December, you mentioned something about not having kids, and I don't know, maybe I misunderstood you," I tried to backtrack, recalling events from several months ago.

Agata stared at me unblinking, then let out a dissatisfied sigh and leaned back against the sink.

"Ivana tried to drag it out of me. She can be extremely annoying," she rolled her eyes and crossed her arms over her chest. Her voice softened a bit, losing some of its biting edge.

"The past few months have been incredibly tough for me," she went on. "I tried so hard to make sure you girls wouldn't notice a thing, so you wouldn't worry. But it was so hard... Because they did confirm the endometriosis, and the surgery didn't help, so I've often been in terrible pain." Her eyes dropped, and although the confrontation made me tense, I felt a pang of sympathy for her.

"I tried not to show it, so we could keep up our good work. My gynecologist told me it would be a good idea to get pregnant, because apparently pregnancy helps with endometriosis. But in the end, I just couldn't take it anymore. We had to keep practicing, and there was no way I was going to skip Tallinn, so I went back on the pill just to endure the pain," the words poured out of her in a rush, her eyes drifting over the water-spotted tiles. She nudged a soggy piece of paper towel that someone had dropped on the floor with the toe of her shoe.

"But Ivana realized something was wrong and tried every trick in the book to get it out of me. She told me you had confided in her that I couldn't get pregnant. Seriously, if there's one thing I didn't need, it's Ivana snooping around." She looked at me, anger flaring in her eyes, as if this were entirely my fault. My mind flashed to Ivana's pale face, remembering how, over coffee a few months ago, Sara had told me about her messy involvement with that personal trainer. Ivana idolized Agata and always defended her whenever the rest of us complained; yet here Agata was, speaking of her with remarkable harshness.

"Maybe she is just worried about you," I offered softly. "And... things like this, the bonds between us, they keep the whole group going," I said, anxiously watching her sour expression. She pressed her lips together and fixed a hard stare on the stall door in front of her. I swallowed and waited for her to speak, when the restroom door swung open, and my sister barged in. She looked flustered, several strands of hair having escaped the elegant bun her stylist had crafted hours earlier.

"Bravo, Maša," she let out a nervous laugh, her voice dripping with irony. "You're doing a brilliant job watching my bouquet, just brilliant! I only just noticed it's been stolen."

I sighed. I knew this was all part of the wedding games she had prepped me for, but I lacked the courage to tell her this might not be the best time.

We followed the bride back to the main hall, where the atmosphere had shifted considerably. Dinner had ended, a few people had moved to the dance floor, some guests were ordering coffee, and the blasting music made the room incredibly loud. I headed toward my table, only to spot Maks, arms crossed over his chest, deep in conversation with my father. The sight of them made my stomach churn. I approached tentatively; when he saw me, my dad gave a small wave.

"Urška's bouquet got stolen," I informed them after my father said I looked distracted. In truth, all I wanted was to find out what they were talking about.

"Yeah, we heard," Maks replied, flashing a pleased grin. I raised an eyebrow as my father stood up from my chair so I could sit down, then headed back to his own seat.

"Hey, relax. Why have you been so tense all evening?" Maks's question made me want to punch him right in the face. I rolled my eyes.

"Agata, our choirmaster, just really upset me in the restroom," I explained grumpily, "and the bouquet vanished while I was gone. What were *you two* talking about?"

"Nothing much, just chatting. I didn't know your uncle was a hunter."

I nodded, scanning the room. Nejc was dancing with one of Urška's friends, and a few of Andrej's buddies were sitting around a table talking. Urška had already dragged Andrej onto the dance floor, which made it clear that the bouquet hunt was entirely up to me.

"He was telling me he goes hunting with him on occasion. And with your cousins."

I nodded, explaining that the four of them were members of the hunting club down in the Pivka region, where my dad is from, though he rarely joins them. Maks already knew this.

"Your cousin was here too, telling me what it's like sleeping overnight in a hunting blind."

"Matjaž?"

Maks nodded.

"Did you lecture them about slaughtering animals?" I asked, suddenly worried, but he just chuckled and shook his head.

"I didn't. Matjaž was telling me about a run-in he had with a bear. He told me I could tag along sometime."

I swallowed hard, then drained my glass. The waiters had already cleared away the dirty plates; an empty toothpick wrapper lay next to my glass, most likely left by my dad.

"And? Would you go?" I asked, though I figured the chances were slim to none. Maks just shrugged, then said, as if it were the most ordinary thing in the world: "He gave me his number."

The fact that Maks now had the phone number of my cousin who hunts in his spare time almost made me laugh. He caught my reaction and demanded to know what was so funny.

"I just don't understand what you would find so fascinating about hunting."

"Is that so surprising?"

"Maks, you're a vegetarian and you've spent your entire life in Bežigrad. Knowing Matjaž, he's not kidding around; he *actually* encounters bears and shoots wild boars all the time."

"I'd simply sit that part out, although he did explain that it's necessary because humans are shrinking the boars' natural habitat. I really would love to spend a night in a blind and see a bear in its natural habitat, though." From the deadly serious tone in his voice, I knew he wasn't joking.

"Alright, we'll call him up sometime and go together."

My words must have disappointed him, because he averted his gaze ever so slightly. I asked him what was wrong.

"I don't know. I kind of want to do it alone." He was being honest.

I laughed, feeling a bit awkward: "Fine. Just keep your anarcho-liberal convictions to yourself when you do, so Matjaž doesn't blow your head off in the middle of the woods."

"And what exactly are these anarcho-whatever convictions of mine?"

I chuckled, though the blood rushed to my cheeks, making me uncomfortably warm. "That's what my mom calls all leftists," I explained by way of apology, "she says they're anarcho-liberals. But I honestly have no idea what it means," I confessed, clearing my throat. Maks just observed me in silence. Finally, he spoke up: "Well, I'll contact him after I get back from Oman."

With everything going on, I had almost forgotten about Oman. I let out a short sigh and rubbed my eyes delicately, trying not to ruin my makeup.

"What if Matjaž is the one who stole the bouquet?" the thought suddenly occurred. "Did you happen to see him?"

Maks shook his head, saying he hadn't seen when the bouquet disappeared.

"Want to go look for it?" I asked, and he nodded, when the music died down. The crowd on the dance floor settled and turned their attention to the frontman, who announced that he was about to be joined by the singers from the bride's choir.

"We're not going anywhere," I stopped him. The guests cleared the floor for the girls, while the bride and groom returned to their seats. The frontman handed the microphone over to Agata, who took it and introduced herself.

"Dear Urška," she said softly, "you've been one of our most loyal and talented singers all these years, and with this song, we'd like to send you off into a marriage we know will be wonderful." Her words struck a very different tone from the one in the restroom. The singers arranged themselves in a crescent, and the room grew silent; only the faint clatter of cutlery echoed from the kitchen.

The girls began to sing in perfect harmony. "*Bride, say your farewells,*" their sharp, pointed female voices rang out, "*to your maiden life. You will be wed, leave your girlhood behind, and enter the marital state.*" I glanced over at Urška. She was wiping a wet cheek with the back of her hand, right before Andrej pressed a tender kiss to it.

"*You will be wed, leave your girlhood behind, and enter the marital state.*" It suddenly hit me that my sister was a married woman, and that we had just spent the last night together in our shared childhood bedroom in which she was an unmarried girl. She had already moved her things out and emptied her wardrobe, but above her desk, hanging like mute witnesses to a childhood gone by, she had left her posters of horses and dandelions, alongside the photographs: her with her friends in Barcelona, with Andrej in Piran, with me on the island of Pag, and with our mom and dad at the high school prom.

"*The sun is already shining so bright, as I bid my home goodbye.*"

I realized we would never again go to the Kolosej cinema to watch Harry Potter, and that we'd never again brew hot chocolate with cinnamon in the wintertime. I felt a tiny tear form in the corner of my eye and trace down my cheek. I wiped it away frantically, praying Maks hadn't seen it. But he probably had; the moment I rested my hand back on the table, he gently brushed it with his pinky finger.

17

"Hey, and where is Sara?"

The wedding guests awarded the singers with raucous applause. Urška stood up, ran over to Agata, and jumped into her embrace. The singers surrounded them, while the photographer excitedly jumped around, trying to capture the emotional moment.

"She doesn't sing anymore," I answered Maks. I hoped this would be enough, but he wanted to know why.

"To tell you the truth, I don't really know. After her no-show in Trieste, she never came to sing again." I paused, then added: "Rumor has it Agata was so mad with her that she kicked her out."

Maks frowned. "She didn't tell you anything about what happened?"

I shook my head, then admitted: "No. I wrote her a message, but she never replied." I picked up a toothpick, unwrapped it, and snapped it in half.

"Maybe she didn't see it," Maks offered an explanation I had also considered myself. "Although," he continued slowly, "it wouldn't be the first time Sara just vanished overnight."

"Yeah?"

He shook his head. "After high school, she cut ties with everyone from our class. She didn't hang out with anyone anymore, didn't answer calls, and ignored messages. It was only last year, when one of our high school classmates died while climbing in the mountains, that she started talking to us again after the funeral."

"Why did she do that?"

"That's just how she is."

"What do you mean?"

"She's a perfectionist."

I frowned. To me, at least on the surface, Sara didn't seem like a perfectionist.

"In what way?"

"Somebody does something she doesn't like, blurts something out, makes a mistake, and she punishes them with silence."

I realized I was unconsciously mangling my cuticles with the sharp tip of the toothpick.

"So, I did something wrong?" I sighed, placing the broken half of the toothpick on the tablecloth. Maks waved his hand.

"You didn't do anything wrong. She's just a bit maladjusted. She demands too much of people."

I observed the crowd of bodies in their Sunday best, swaying to the rhythm on the dance floor, flashing every so often with the whiteness of Urška's wedding dress.

"Her mother is a bit of a weirdo too," Maks said.

I remained silent, still trying to figure out what I could have done to make Sara resent me. Nothing came to mind.

"Should we go look for the bouquet?" I suddenly remembered. We stood up and began looking around the room.

"You check all the chairs and underneath the tables," Maks suggested, "and I'll check the restrooms."

After I had spent a few minutes searching for the bouquet as intently as I could in the main hall—dodging relatives trying to catch me for a quick chat and guests jostling on the dance floor—Maks came back and shook his head. "Nothing. It's not in the restrooms, nor in the foyer. I asked the waiters if they'd seen it, and they said no."

"It's not here either."

"Did you look behind the curtains?"

I nodded.

"Do you think they took it outside?"

I groaned with fatigue, and Maks frowned.

"Maša, come on, relax. It's just a game. You've been tense all day."

I sighed and motioned toward the exit. Inside, I could barely hear what he was saying, and the air was stuffy from the smell of food and bodies. The moment we stepped out of the restaurant, we were embraced by the freshness of the spring night. Maks asked a group of men lounging in front of the entrance smoking if they had seen the bouquet anywhere, but they said that they hadn't.

"Can I bum a smoke?" he asked one of them, Andrej's cousin. I barely stopped myself from rolling my eyes, but the guy was already offering Maks the pack, and he helped himself to a cigarette. I crossed my arms over my chest; it was a bit chilly.

"Maks," I nudged him, "can I borrow your jacket? I'm cold."

He took off his suit jacket and draped it over my shoulders. It smelled of his cologne, which made me think of the sea, salt, and summer. I thought I caught a hint of bergamot.

"In Switzerland, they held a referendum on a ban of the construction of minarets," the man standing next to Andrej's cousin resumed their conversation. Instantly, Maks's jacket felt like too much, as a wave of heat washed over me. Out of the corner of my eye, I watched Maks take a drag from his cigarette, as though it were his first in a long time.

"Switzerland is twenty years ahead of us. Democracy actually counts for something there, while here our media is completely beholden to liberalism, and they keep forcing it on us as the only option. They don't really represent pluralism," Andrej's cousin said.

"Could I get a smoke too?" My little voice sounded weak and high-pitched compared to theirs. Andrej's cousin, looking slightly annoyed, pulled the pack of cigarettes from his jacket pocket and held it out to me. I took a cigarette, put it in my mouth, and leaned in so he could light it. I leaned back and took a drag. The taste of ash filled my mouth, and a nasty tickle scratched at my lungs, but I struggled and managed to hold back a cough. I could feel Maks's eyes on me.

"The money for the construction came from Qatar," a third man chimed in. "We're talking amounts we can hardly even imagine, and what the mayor Janković loves above all is the smell of money." I took another drag from the cigarette smoldering between my fingers, this time with a bit more elegance.

"The problem is the young men coming in. Europe has almost zero natural population growth, young people aren't choosing to have families, so there are going to be more and more Muslim children," Andrej's cousin spoke up again, also taking a drag from his cigarette.

"And veiled women," added a younger man who had been quiet until now, laughing as if he wasn't completely serious. "Meanwhile in France, where multiculturalism spiraled out of control, they banned burqas to try and curb the madness," he then added more earnestly.

"The fact that they banned burqas in France is more of a sign of the extreme secularization that is characteristic of France, and I don't know if that's something we should strive for in Slovenia," I spoke up, and went on with a slight tremble in my voice: "As it's not clear how good that is in the long run: a secularized state loses control over education, which is why marginalized groups attend their own schools, leaving them vulnerable to radicalization. To me, that's far more dangerous than a society that allows women to wear a headscarf out of habit." I took a quick breath, then hastened to add before any of the men could interrupt: "Besides, they banned the burqa and the niqab, but not the hijab."

"But the headscarf oppresses women," the younger man objected. "And you women should be the first ones to oppose it," he added with a barb.

"Removing or, even worse, banning the headscarf doesn't solve the problem of patriarchy," I countered. I noticed the guy swallow.

"Maša, have you found the bouquet yet?" The bride appeared behind my back with flushed cheeks and stared at me inquisitively. I detected a hint of annoyance in her furrowed brows. Her eyes locked onto the cigarette held between my fingers and widened in surprise. I clumsily lowered my hand to my thigh.

"Not yet, it wasn't inside and now the two of us are looking for it out here." I dropped the cigarette to the ground and discreetly crushed it under my foot, while Urška snorted and rolled her eyes: "Yeah, I can clearly see you're looking hard."

"Let's go check over there," Maks was quick to say, gesturing with his cigarette hand toward the pond shimmering not far from the restaurant. There was a bench with someone sitting there by the pond. I nodded and, without looking at my sister, headed that way with Maks at my heels. As we walked in silence, I waited for Maks to comment on my performance in front of the men, but he said nothing. When we got close enough, I recognized the silhouette on the bench as Agata.

"Are you looking for the bouquet?" she asked us in a soft voice. "It's right here." She nodded at the blue hydrangeas lying next to her. "It was under the bench. Whoever put it there doesn't have much respect for bouquets," she added in a bitter tone.

"Thank you, Agata." I felt a wave of relief as I got my hands on the missing bouquet. Even though I should have taken it back to the restaurant immediately, I slumped down next to her and wrapped myself tighter in Maks's jacket against the cold breeze.

Agata extended her hand to Maks and introduced herself, and he shook it.

"You were at the concert in Trieste, right?" she asked him, and he nodded. "What did you think?"

"You girls are good," he answered. "I don't know much about music, but that much I can see."

Agata smiled and asked him if he thought we had a chance of winning in Tallinn.

Maks chuckled. "I don't know what the competition will be like, but I think so, yes. Although," my chest tightened, "I already told Maša that the last song, the one with her solo, feels a bit forced."

"Forced?" Agata's eyes widened. "In what way?"

"I mean, like I said, I don't know much about music," he tried to backtrack, then doubled down: "But it's just a bit too experimental."

"Experimental," Agata repeated, shifting her gaze to the moonlit pond, before conceding: "You're probably right. Ciril simply wanted to show off with it, I've been guessing for a while now. But it has some truly excellent parts." She tore her gaze away from the pond and looked at Maks, her eyes filled with melancholy. He nodded.

"What are you doing out here?" I asked her to steer the conversation elsewhere. She said that she craved a bit of solitude: "But I'll be heading back. Do you want me to take the bouquet to Urška?"

I murmured "please," and she stood up, then headed towards the restaurant with the bouquet in hand. After a few steps, she turned back and said to Maks: "Thank you for your opinion. I really appreciate the honesty." Maks gave her an awkward smile and took a long drag from his cigarette. She left and he sat down on the bench.

"Interesting woman," he said to himself. I raised my eyebrows, waiting for an explanation.

"She's completely immersed in music, you can tell she truly lives for it." I nodded and was just about to say something when he said: "There's something fatal about her." He gazed at the water lilies floating gently on the surface of the pond.

A painful knot formed in my stomach. Was it possible that Maks found the cold, distant Agata attractive? Did a thirty-five-year-old woman possess something inside her that he couldn't see in me?

Overcome by a wave of heat, I slipped off Maks's jacket and placed it in my lap. I asked him something that had been on my mind all day: "Do your parents know we're friends?" I deliberately avoided the word "colleagues," which wouldn't have meant anything in this context.

Maks chuckled and blew out a puff of smoke. "Not really," he admitted. "I don't talk to them about these things," he clarified, quickly adding: "Like, who I hang out with and what we do. To tell you the truth," he appended after a pause, "we aren't very close."

I nodded and, trying to sound as natural as possible, said, "Well, we also aren't exactly—"

"It's not the same," he objected with surprising coldness, his stony gaze still sweeping across the pond. "From what I've seen, you guys get along perfectly fine. I don't know if you know this," he swallowed hard, keeping his eyes on the water, "but my old man is a very difficult person."

"I know," I admitted soberly. "My mom says the same."

He finally looked at me and asked what she had told me about him. It felt like it would be better not to explain, but I was already in too deep.

"That he is... argumentative and... combative," I added a word that was completely redundant. I could have said that my mother also claimed he was a "secret police informant," but I bit my tongue.

In general, my parents avoided talking about Maks's father. I heard my mom say once that "Darja is a wonderful woman who married the wrong man."

"He's unhappy," Maks said, his voice unchanged as he stared back at the pond, "and he's quick to stick his nose into things. They are constantly at each other's throats with my grandpa, and one day grandpa will have enough and cut him off."

The passion in his voice took me by surprise. I had never heard him use the word "grandpa" before. I was also puzzled by the idea that it would be the grandfather breaking off contact with his son, rather than the other way around.

He tossed his cigarette onto the gravel and stomped on it.

"We had a huge fight two years ago, and it made me decide I wanted nothing more to do with him," he said quietly, looking down at the extinguished cigarette. He swallowed hard, while I waited patiently for him to continue with shallow breath. He shot me a wild look.

"You know what he said to me? He said that anthropology is for dumb, lazy cunts. How can a supposedly educated man say something so sexist?"

I kept quiet. I was overwhelmed with gratitude that, despite everything, I had never heard anything like that from my parents.

"And he didn't stop," he continued, angrier now. "He said I should stick to an academic career because it's the only thing left for me, even though educated people no longer hold any power since, according to him, expertise doesn't matter anymore—which is true in a way, but he presented it as an argument for why he thinks I screwed up my life. But it's not like that's even the real issue, this could all be resolved with a discussion, it's everything else he does that's much worse. He berates Darja, starts fights out of pure boredom, you never know what will set him off and what he'll say next. He humiliates Mitja because he hasn't graduated yet, mocks my interests and my opinions on things, and"—he swallowed hard again, almost painfully—"he is constantly plugged in to the internet, leaving disgraceful anonymous comments on various media sites."

He finally fell silent, his chest heaving with agitation. Music from the restaurant drifted to us across the distance. I thought I recognized the melody of *If these were only lies*. The clouds had broken up during the day, and the night was clear, with a star here and there twinkling in the sky.

"That's not okay," I said quietly.

Maks just shook his head in response, then rested his elbows on his knees, buried his head in his hands, and stared brokenly at the gravel between his feet. Instinctively, I reached out and stroked his back.

"It's hard hearing that someone acts like that. Especially since you are genuinely... exceptional," I said softly. I wasn't just saying anything that came to mind; in truth, I was choosing my words very carefully. My hand slid up his back all the way to his neck. Maks lifted his face from his hands but didn't look at me. I reached with my finger toward his freshly shaven jawline and stroked it ever so lightly. My heart was throbbing in my chest, and I felt a faint tingling in my panties. The band was still echoing in the background.

"I'm not exceptional," I heard him say.

I leaned closer to his face and whispered: "Of course you are."

Our eyes met. My thumb was now gently stroking his cheek, which I could feel glowing with warmth. The sadness vanished from his eyes, replaced by a restless, excited shimmer. I drew even closer to his face and pressed my lips against his. I placed my free hand on the nape of his neck as his lips gently parted and our tongues finally met. The jacket in my lap slid off my knees and fell to the ground, but I didn't care. I tasted the sweet tobacco, then forgot about all of my feelings when he finally wrapped his arms around me and pulled me into his embrace.

18.

While Maks was taking off his black jacket to place it over the backrest of the desk chair, I was thinking of Urška, who would be leaving her wedding any minute now, then slipping out of her wedding dress in Andrej's loft, before falling asleep with her husband, too tired from the party, and Max and I would be the ones getting laid for the first time on their wedding night.

I stood barefoot in the middle of Maks's room, holding the shoes I had taken off before climbing the stairs behind him so as not to wake Darja and Martin. When we entered the room, we didn't turn on the lights, but his face was visible in the muffled yellow light cast into the room by the streetlamp, as he approached me and kissed me again.

Savoring the kiss, I was surprised by the memory of his thirteenth birthday, which we had celebrated in this house: I had always liked Maks, but at that party, I fell head over heels in love with him, and for weeks afterward, I would spend my evenings daydreaming that he would ask me to be his girlfriend. I couldn't wait for us to get together with the Hafners again, but something went wrong between the adults at the party; we never saw each other again.

Still kissing, we moved to the bed where I had slept over a few months ago and where, as he had told me himself, he had sex with Gaja and probably other girls too. His hands glided restlessly over my body, as if he were in a hurry to reach everything as fast as he could: his right hand reached under my skirt, while his left hand stroked my breasts.

My youthful infatuation had almost faded, when I saw him again the summer before starting high school. Walking down Celovška he rode past me on his bike; I only caught his face for a split second before he was gone, so I couldn't be sure if it was really him. Despite the briefness of the encounter, I spent weeks hoping I would see him again.

Maks's hand reached my panties. I felt his palm waver, as if entering dangerous territory where it needed to be more careful. With his other hand, he kept gliding over my breasts. I was wearing a padded bra, and I thought of how disappointed he would be after he unclasped it and saw the small, barely noticeable breasts underneath.

In high school, I tried to think about him as little as possible. We didn't mention the Hafners at home, although I had a hunch that mom and Darja maintained polite contact. Or perhaps it wasn't just a matter of politeness, and they truly wanted to preserve their friendship, but it just no longer seemed possible. I would convince one of my friends to go to Metelkova on a Friday, or to the Trnovo beach in the warmer months, hoping to see Maks there. And I did see him, once: he was kissing a girl in front of the club Gromka, so I never went to Metelkova again.

I started unbuttoning his shirt, one button after another, and brought my lips closer to his neck, which gave off the scent of bergamot mixed with tobacco, leaving a bitter aftertaste on my lips after I kissed it. Maks took off his shirt, and I sensed that he didn't just smell of perfume, but also of the several hours spent at the wedding, as I caught a whiff of the sweetish scent of sweat. Looking at the sparse hair on his chest, I remembered how he had taken off his shirt in the moonlight a few months ago after the freshman party, and how I had watched him do it in secret.

I had finally forgotten about him by the time of the university information days, but after that encounter, the feelings returned. I persisted in my infatuation month after month, knowing that nothing would ever happen between us because I was from a world that Max wasn't interested in. But now here he was, struggling with the zipper on my dress, and when he finally unzipped it, I took it off and pushed it off the bed to fall on the floor like shed scaly skin. He didn't wait: he brought his face close to my tiny breasts, still hidden in the bra, then slid his tongue down my stomach, leaving a wet trail behind.

"You have a condom, right?" I knew perfectly well that he did and where he kept it. But Maks lifted his gaze from my navel and said in a serious tone: "Wait a moment, we're not there yet."

The words disarmed me. I had the feeling I was playing at something I simply didn't know much about, which he would soon realize and dejectedly send me away. Shame washed over me, and I froze. He did not seem to notice, however, and reached for his belt. He took off his pants, dropped them on the floor next to my dress, and brought his hands to the clasp on my bra. I was relieved to see the restlessness of his movements: he was in a hurry too.

I helped him unclasp the bra and found myself in front of him in nothing but my panties. My breasts had never felt so small, but it didn't look like this turned him off; on the contrary, he poured over them with gentle kisses, and I closed my eyes. With each moment my body was becoming more and more supple under his hands, and when he reached into my panties, I forgot that there was a world where we were just friends outside this room. As I grew ever softer and wetter, his grips became firmer and faster.

He rose to his knees and took off my panties. In the half-light, he couldn't see the red dots from shaving, which I thought about now that I was naked in front of him for the first time. Then it dawned on me that it wasn't the first time; the photograph in his drawer testified that long ago we had bathed without swimsuits in a kiddie pool, back in the nineties, when the differences between us weren't yet so destructive. Our bodies were completely changed after all these years—something I grew starkly aware of when Maks also took off his underwear, leaned toward the nightstand, opened the top drawer, and pulled out an unopened box of condoms.

"Why didn't I open this earlier," he muttered, frantically searching for the part of the wrapper he could tear in the half-light. Eventually, he succeeded and pulled the condom packet out of the box, opened it, took out the condom, and rolled it on with practiced ease, at which I felt a trace of petty jealousy, knowing that he had gained this confidence with other girls. But the very next moment, when his hand returned between my thighs, this all slipped out of my mind.

At first, he didn't look me in the eyes, but let his gaze glide over my body. Then our eyes met, and for a second everything we were doing stopped. It was strange, because we knew what was coming, and because it was us—we who had entrusted our thoughts and doubts to each other under the faint constellations of stars in the black sky above Ljubljana, in illuminated stadiums, on obscure streets in Šiška, on worn-out sidewalks, on the gloomy staircases of Bežigrad apartment blocks, on dark paths and in hidden parks, rarely staying silent in each other's company; but now we didn't know what to say.

He looked away, then pushed inside me, and my eyes filled with tears from the pain. I couldn't hold back and softly groaned from the burning in my vagina, which he might have taken as a sign of pleasure. He pressed his lips to my neck and kissed it while thrusting gently.

"You're—very—tight," I then heard him say between individual gasps. His words cleared my head, and I asked him, with worry, if that was a problem.

"No," he could barely answer.

In the half-light, I saw him close his eyes. His face wrenched.

"I can't hold back," he said. Suddenly, he opened his eyes and looked at me. I caught a trace of panic in his brown eyes. It seemed as if there was a question stuck on the tip of his tongue: was it possible that I was—

I thought he was going to continue, but as if someone had yelled "Cut!", he stopped. Unexpectedly, he pulled away from me and lay on the bed, looking away. Nothing of his body was touching anything of mine. The room filled with the sound of his shallow breathing.

Finally, he turned on the nightlight. He took off the condom and it was covered in blood. He didn't say anything, so I asked him: "Is everything okay?" My voice sounded distant, as if it weren't mine. He nodded in silence. I got out of bed, put on my bra, panties, and dress, and then tiptoed to the bathroom.

What happened? Why did he stop before he came? What made him scared? Asking all these questions, I observed myself in the mirror. The harsh light made my face look greenish and sleep-deprived, I had a few flakes of mascara under my eyes. I sat on the toilet and tried to pee, but couldn't, for several minutes nothing came out, and I just sat there waiting. Finally, a few drops slipped out of me. The toilet paper blotted up the blood. I threw it into the bowl and flushed, watching it until it disappeared down the drain.

Again, I opened the drawer where Darja kept her cosmetics: creams, makeup remover milks, makeup. I found a brush and, with slow strokes, brushed my hair, which grew static with the brushing. I opened a drawer with men's razors and shaving foam. This probably belonged to Maks's father. I remembered what Maks had told me about him a few hours ago, and closed the drawer in disgust.

I returned to the room, where I found Maks sitting on the edge of the bed in his underwear and a T-shirt, staring and swiping at his phone screen. The condom was nowhere to be seen, but the bed was still unmade, and I noticed a pale red stain on the snow-white sheet.

I asked him if he would drive me home. When he looked up from his phone screen, I thought I caught a hint of relief in his eyes.

"Absolutely," he replied, stood up, and pulled on a pair of jeans he grabbed from the closet.

We didn't talk on the way. A yellow light was blinking at most of the intersections, and we made it to my building in no time. The clock on the radio showed thirteen minutes to three.

"Here we are," Maks said jarringly loud, and it sounded so banal that I almost laughed.

I unbuckled my seatbelt and, without looking at him, said: "Thanks for the ride. And if we don't see each other before you leave, have a great time in Oman."

Maks said thanks and replied, "you too," which sounded funny, but neither of us laughed. I opened the car door and stepped out into the cold spring night. The yellow moon looked down on me as if it had caught me at something.

"Bye," I said before closing the door behind me, and I climbed the stairs to the building's entrance without looking back. I did turn around when I opened the entrance door, just to see the white Volvo drive away.

19.

I told Agata I was pregnant and that I wasn't going to Tallinn. She didn't take it too well. Just a heads up.

I read Urška's message standing at the entrance of the classroom at the Academy where Agata was waiting for me. I put the phone into my backpack with a sweaty palm and took a deep breath. Then I knocked and went in.

Agata was sitting at the piano as usual, but she wasn't playing any melody, just randomly pressing one key after another. She gave me an offhand greeting, and straightened up a bit in her chair as I approached. Her voice was despondent: "Did you know Urška isn't planning to go to Tallinn?"

I hesitated for a moment, then nodded. She shook her head and looked toward the window. Her gray eyes were as sorrowful as the eyes of a neglected stray dog.

"You should have told me."

I didn't agree, as I felt this was Urška's responsibility, but I just couldn't bring myself to say it; it was as if the words had gotten stuck in my throat.

She sighed, but said nothing. The window overlooking Upper Square was slightly open, and lively voices drifted in from the street, while the classroom was oppressively quiet.

"I'm sorry."

Perhaps I said it because I didn't know what else to say. I wished we could just start with the vocal warm-ups, as if nothing had happened.

"Yesterday, I cancelled our plane tickets."

I didn't understand at first, and then I gaped at her in surprise. As I said nothing, Agata rattled off, sounding very bitter: "Luckily, I insured them against cancellation when I bought them. I couldn't even explain why to myself. Maybe I had a feeling it wasn't going to work out." She cleared her throat and coldly added: "So, luckily, we'll get a partial refund. Only partial, of course." She swallowed hard and waited for me to say something, but I remained silent.

"But why?" I suddenly heard my own weak voice say.

Agata shook her head and, forcing a smile, asked: "You still don't get it? We can't go to Tallinn in this state. There aren't enough of us, but that isn't the problem. The problem is your commitment to this. Which is nonexistent. We can't perform with that kind of energy, the whole thing would fall apart, we'd make fools of ourselves. Well, you all made your choices, and these are now the consequences."

So many questions were swarming in my head. Did the other singers already know? How did Ivana react?

"And... Urška is to blame for this?" I stared at Agata in disbelief. She snorted and shook her head.

"You are all to blame for this."

She challenged me with her gaze, as if expecting me to react explosively, but even though I felt a restless bubbling under my skin, outwardly I remained completely indifferent.

"What do you mean, all of us? What does, I don't know... Ivana have to do with this? Klara? Zala? Ana? And... me?"

It seemed that mentioning the singers softened the expression on Agata's face, but the very next moment it turned to stone again, and she said in a sharp voice: "All of you wanted fewer rehearsals. All of you felt that the pace was too brutal, that I was demanding too much, while I was the only one who truly believed in you. I was convinced, and I still am, that we could have won first place in Tallinn. We have that potential. But you yourselves didn't want it. And you are Urška's sister. You had the power to convince her to come to her senses, but clearly, you don't find this important enough."

It was my turn for a deep sigh. But that was all I did. I let my eyes drift over the white wall behind Agata, before my gaze rested on my sleep-deprived and pale face in the mirror.

"I understand," I murmured and looked at her.

Agata raised her eyebrows. She was expecting something different, but instead of telling me what, she pressed her lips tightly together. I shrugged and smiled faintly: "So, that's it then. The tickets are canceled. Can I go now?"

Her angry gaze turned into an indignant one, while I still gave no signs of agitation.

"You can."

That was all she said. I grabbed my backpack from the chair by the wall and slung it over my shoulder. In a natural voice, as if nothing had happened, I asked her if there was a rehearsal tomorrow. Agata observed me for a moment.

"We won't be having a rehearsal. We will meet up, do a reflection, and then disband," she finally said coldly. I said "okay," and opened the door. I walked out of the classroom with a "bye."

Stepping out of the Academy onto the street, I could feel the relaxed atmosphere in the air, so typical of the last days of May, when students realized the academic year would soon end, but exams were still far enough away to let them relax. The café to the left of the Academy was full, bicycles rattled over the cobblestones, and I almost collided with a pair of women pushing baby strollers who were so engrossed in their conversation they didn't see me. I apologized, then turned onto Stiška Street with brisk steps.

I felt like nothing could truly hurt me. Agata could have called me on the phone right then, blamed everything on me and my solo, and it wouldn't have bothered me. I was almost afraid of my own lack of response. I wished that her decision would crush me, but it didn't. I was completely indifferent, as if I had been silently expecting such an outcome all along.

I slowed my steps as I headed towards the Faculty of Arts, replaying the dialogue that had just taken place in the classroom in my mind. Was it right for me to storm off like that? What did Agata expect from me? Could I have convinced her that we should go anyway? But why would I even do that, after she had accused me of acting wrongly by not convincing Urška to change her mind?

The world outside seemed so carefree. Ljubljanica flowed calmly down its riverbed, people sat along its banks, clusters of young people gathered in front of the Faculty of Architecture; everything was bubbling with life, while I alone drifted down Zoisova like a fog. When I stopped at the traffic light at the intersection by Križanke, I reflexively reached into my backpack and took out my phone.

I kept glancing at my phone screen the entire time. I opened the Facebook Messenger app, clicked on Maks's name, and checked when he was last active. I waited for the three little dots to appear, indicating he was typing a message. But it never happened; the phone never changed.

I made my way to the Foerster Garden, where I wanted to buy a cheaper copy of *Tristes Tropiques* at the book fair. A new translation had recently been published and I wanted to have it on my shelf. The *Studia Humanitatis* publisher's stand was located next to the mighty ginkgo tree in the middle of the park, and I soon found the book I was looking for.

"Hey."

Blaž had appeared beside me. At first, I didn't notice him, but when I did, I gave him a faint greeting. We exchanged a few pleasantries, then he looked at the book I was holding in my hand and asked if I was going to buy it.

"I don't think so. It feels like one of those books you really need to have on your shelf, but despite the discount, I still think it's a bit too expensive," I admitted and dejectedly put the book back on the pile. "Maybe I'll just check it out from the library."

Blaž said he agreed just as I spotted Maks by the entrance to the park, not far from us. From where I stood, I could see he was wearing the exact same Vans sneakers he had worn at the wedding. I felt such a sharp pain in my stomach that I unwittingly placed my hand over it. Maks was standing near the fence, with his bike next to him, talking to someone. I didn't see the other person at first because some students were blocking the view, but when they moved aside, I saw it was Sara.

"Do you have time for a drink?"

Blaž was looking at me, not noticing the pallor on my face. Our eyes met. His seemed unusually large behind the lenses of his glasses.

"Um... I'm sorry, but I don't have time right now. I have to go home."

Disappointed, he said he understood. I needlessly told him that we could arrange to meet up some other time, even though I knew that wasn't going to happen. I backed away from him so I could keep my eyes fixed on Maks and Sara, who were talking intently, before I turned around and practically sprinted toward the college building.

I wanted to get out of the park and away from the college as quickly as I could. I unlocked my bike, chained to the rack in front of the Faculty of Arts, hopped on it, and rode frantically down Aškerčeva, with my heart thrashing in my chest.

Did they bump into each other by chance, or had they arranged to meet? Were they talking about me? Probably not, and even if Sara asked Maks if he had seen me around, he wouldn't tell her what had happened between us. And he would never bring me up on his own. Evening was falling, and the birds were chirping with sorrow, while I pushed the pedals so hard that my thighs and calves burned, as if I didn't know how to slow down.

It should have been me standing there next to Sara instead of Maks. I would have told my friend what had happened after the wedding, and she would have helped me figure out why it ended the way it did. We would have turned the difficult conversation into a joke, until we would tire of talking about him, and I would update her on what was going on in the choir.

I made a turn by the Orthodox church and descended the ramp into Tivoli. Usually, when riding down, I gently squeezed the brakes to keep from going too fast, but this time I just hurtled down the decline. A man on a bike coming from the opposite direction barely managed to dodge me, and I heard him yell after me, but I didn't care.

Maks and Sara kept flashing before my eyes. Not Sara—I should have been the one standing next to Maks. He would be showing me books he found interesting; when I would dither over buying *Tristes Tropiques*, he would offer to buy it for me, and then he would take my hand so that Gaja and the rest of his crowd could see us and ask themselves: What *the fuck* is Maks doing with Maša Pavlin from the third year? Are those two together? How on earth did that happen? So that Blaž would see us, smile sourly, turn around, and go find himself another girl. That was how it was supposed to be in a world where the first night we slept together hadn't failed, in a life where I would know what I needed to do to not disappoint him, in a universe where it wouldn't matter at all who his parents were and who my parents were. But instead, it hit me, no one will ever know that only a few days ago, Maks Hafner pulled down my underwear, kissed my breasts, and pushed himself inside me. Neither of us will ever tell anyone.

When I reached the park, I stepped off the bike and took a deep breath. My throat was burning from the crazed cycling, my chest felt tight, and my legs throbbed painfully, but I was relieved to be far enough away from college, where I couldn't run into either Sara or Maks anymore. I took my phone out of my backpack to put on some music when I noticed an email notification on the screen. I opened it at once.

Agata Trinko, May 24, 2016, 18:12
After consideration
Greetings,

After careful consideration, I have come to the conclusion that our choir cannot perform at the competition in Tallinn. It might seem crazy to some of you that I am cancelling our participation just two weeks before the competition, but I have already spoken to the organizers and they were understanding.

The reason for my decision is as follows: I would only want to enter the competition with singers who are 100% committed to singing in the choir. I know there are some among you who are, but sadly, too few.

From this decision follows another, one for which I have been gathering courage for quite some time. Namely, that I will no longer be your choirmaster. When Klara, Barbara, and I came up with the idea for the choir in 2010 and founded it, I probably wasn't fully aware of the responsibility such a decision brings. Our idea was an amateur women's choir that would provide an opportunity for singers to sing who, while not classically trained, are still excellent. Many among you are like that. Perhaps this will give you the will to find a choir with some other choirmaster. Sadly, I can no longer fulfill this role.

Thank you for your understanding, and I hope you realize that this means we are also finished with rehearsals and vocal techniques. I have sadly run out of the energy necessary to run this choir.

Have a nice summer,
Agata

I read Agata's words twice, three times, and then my eyes just kept gliding over the text. Even though it seemed like it was truly over, I had the feeling that Agata was really waiting for us to ambush her with tears in our eyes on her way out of the Academy and beg her on our knees to change her mind. One of the singers wrote in the Facebook group chat: *Oh my god, what just happened?* A flood of comments poured in, which I didn't read. I suddenly felt a strong aversion toward the girls, which they perhaps hadn't deserved, but I knew I wanted nothing more to do with the choir, and I impulsively left the chat.

I put my earphones in and mounted my bike. I searched for a specific track on the music app. *Old Money* by Lana Del Rey. Two years ago, when her album *Ultraviolence* came out at the start of the summer, I sat in the dim light of my room for days on end, listening to it from start to finish on repeat while scrolling through the endless pages of Tumblr—looking at the photos of my American peers, fans of Arctic Monkeys, skating down the wide streets of Sacramento. I often wandered onto Tumblr profiles full of erotic black-and-white photographs and pictures of couples my age, happily in love. I had my own Tumblr as well. I named it *Blue hydrangea*, after a verse from Lana's song. Maks, do you know which flower that is? It's the flower from Urška's wedding bouquet, which we had looked for together, and which brought us to the bench where it all began. Or where it ended?

20.

The ground floor of the Academy of Music was empty when I entered. When I opened the door, the June sun shone into the vestibule so brightly that I could see dust particles in the air, gently flickering, looking like stardust. When the door closed, the room grew dark.

I knocked on the door bearing a brass plaque with the number two nailed to it, and waited until I heard a resonant male voice from behind it say: "Come in." I entered. A younger man sat on the piano bench, his face framed by somewhat greasy blond hair, looking too warm in his jeans. I greeted him.

"Maša Pavlin?" Peter Mušič read from the list, looked at me, and smiled. I nodded. He asked me to sing something.

"*In the summer glow on the rocky cliffs,*" I began to sing, "*with lead in his breast a partisan lies.*" *Death in the Hills.* My lips curled into an involuntary smile as I remembered what Maks had said about the song at the concert in Trieste. That evening in the car, he had confessed to me that sometimes, before falling asleep, he fantasizes about being a Partisan through the Second World War. I couldn't stop laughing at that, and seeing me laugh, he turned red in the face, then joined my laughter. Later, before falling asleep, I too fantasized that he was a Partisan and I was a village girl hiding him in my house.

"*In the Gorizia hills, I am dying alone,*" I finished forlornly, but I could tell that the smile had helped brighten the tone of my voice.

Peter grimaced with some uncertainty and stroked his beard.

"Can you sing something else? Something for the second soprano?"

I sighed. I thought about what to sing, and decided on my solo from Šavli's piece, adapted to be sung without the background voices.

I sang: "*When the thorny branches sprout, I press you to my heart.*"

My voice unexpectedly died in my throat. The lyrics of the second half of my solo flashed through my mind.

And when you wound me to the blood, only then will I know who you are.

A few months ago in Agata's classroom, I didn't know how to answer her question: "Has anyone ever wounded you like that?" If she asked me now, I would know what to say.

"Sorry," I apologized to Peter. "I got a bit confused. Can I start from the top?" He nodded, and I began to sing.

"Wow," he said when I finished. I had never sung so well—not even in vocal technique with Agata, at rehearsals, or at the concert in Trieste. I understood what Agata meant when she told us that we had to truly embody the lyrics.

"I've heard this before," he said. I nodded:

"It's from the piece *The Bush*, which Ciril Šavli wrote for Philomela, based on a poem by Svetlana Makarovič."

"So, you sang with Agata?" I nodded. "Second soprano?" I nodded again.

Peter picked up the list, where he had checked something off earlier, and stared at it.

"You have a very beautiful color. And your hard work with Agata shows. I heard you didn't make it to Tallinn in the end." He looked at me, curious. His eyes were sea blue. I knew Peter enjoyed a lot of admiration among women, but from what Urška told me, he paid it no mind. I noticed a wedding ring on his finger.

"Yeah, we cancelled at the last minute."

"Why?"

I searched for words and finally shrugged.

"We hadn't been making any real progress for a while."

"And you won't be singing with her anymore?"

"Agata's choir fell apart," I said indifferently. Peter didn't seem surprised, as if he had already heard about it somewhere and just wanted to be sure.

He frowned and said: "But I heard that she's starting a new one."

I raised my eyebrows, since I hadn't known this, but then I said with a sharp edge to my voice: "Let her."

Peter chuckled at my tone, as if recognizing the grudge.

"Ah, Agata. A top-tier musician. She was brilliant at the academy, we all knew she was the best. She knew it too, and she enjoyed it. Justifiably so." A content smile settled on his face, as if he had made his peace with it a long time ago.

"But?" It seemed to me he wanted to say something else, but changed his mind. He pressed a random key on the piano.

"Nothing. She's good. That's all I wanted to say." It didn't seem like this was entirely true, but I sensed I wasn't going to get anything more out of him. I simply nodded, agreeing.

"Anyway," he finally said, "welcome to our choir. The girls in the second soprano will be happy to have you," he winked at me. I nodded without a smile. "Will that be alright?" he asked, noticing my lukewarm response.

"I always wanted to sing first soprano," I admitted.

Peter looked at me, then placed his hands on the keys and told me to repeat what he played. He spent a lot of time testing my voice, we went into the high notes, and then he focused on the low ones. Finally, he sighed.

"If you really want to sing first soprano, I can put you in the first soprano. You aren't very strong on the high notes, but that can be trained to an extent. But I have to be honest," he paused, "there is a lot of potential for you hidden in the lower registers. When we were singing just now, by the end, I thought you were almost a first alto."

My smile was bitter, which he might have noticed, and he said more quietly: "You're a good second soprano, you know?" He smiled at me gently, as one would smile at a small child.

I swallowed hard and said nothing. Peter reached for a sheet of paper, pressed it against the piano with one hand, and grabbed a pen with the other.

"But the main thing is that you're happy, so—"

"No," I interrupted, "you're right. In truth, I'd rather sing second soprano."

The hand with the pen hovered a few inches above the paper. Then he nodded and wrote something down.

"Accepting ourselves is always the priority, even when it comes to singing," he was somewhat patronizing. I had already heard this about him: that he liked to throw in some life wisdom with his advice. I said I agreed and leaned towards my backpack to put it on.

"In any case,"—he placed the paper on a folder on the piano and turned to me—"you're not an opera singer, but, interestingly enough, the typical roles for second sopranos in opera are witches, wise women, like for example Azucena, the gypsy from Verdi's *Il Trovatore*, and other kinds of"—he stretched out his arm, clenched his fist, and spoke passionately—"kinds of villainesses and seductresses, like Amneris from *Aida*." He fell silent for a moment, then said with a proud smile on his face: "My wife is a mezzo-soprano, too."

"I didn't know that," I said. Peter nodded and then slapped his thighs with his hands.

"Well then, see you in the first week of September. Have a great summer."

I replied, "you too," and walked out of the classroom into the hallway, which had been empty before, but now there was someone sitting on the bench outside the classroom, in the exact spot I had sat almost a year ago waiting for my audition with Agata.

"Hey."

I didn't recognize her at first—her hair was dyed gray-green and looked like an intruder in the conservative environment of the Academy. It took me a moment. The girl on the bench was Sara, and she was waiting for me to greet her back.

First Readers

Ellie Walton (UK)

Helen Stanton (UK)

Stephen Ramsek (USA)

Lian Sing (1) Philippines

Nurus van Vliet (1) New Zealand

Eric Dorman (1) USA

Chris Roughead (1) Scotland

Randal Greene (1) USA

Kristina Ledl (1) Slovenia

Makana Eyre (1) USA

McKenna Knych (1) USA